GIRL ON THE HLL

D1564189

CJ CROSS

LIQUID MIND PUBLISHING

Copyright © 2021 by C.J. Cross.

All rights reserved. No part of this publication may be copied, reproduced in any format, by any means, electronic or otherwise, without prior consent from the copyright owner and publisher of this book.

Liquid Mind Publishing

This is a work of fiction. All characters, names, places and events are the product of the author's imagination or used fictitiously.

ALSO BY CJ CROSS

Stay up to date with C.J. Cross's new releases and download her **free** Dana Gray Prequel, *Girl Awakened* by heading to the link:

Find more C.J. Cross books and follow her on Amazon today!

PROLOGUE

This is going to work. It has to work. I trust him. He loves me. Everything's going to be okay.

That was easier to believe when she wasn't alone in the dark. But she promised him she'd wait. She hadn't expected it would take quite this long. She knew he was busy. Important men were always busy, but still, he'd always made time for her.

He made her feel special. That's why she was here. But how long could she wait? People were going to start to miss her.

She reminded herself of the promise she'd made. She stayed put. Not that she had a choice. She didn't want to go back to her old life. He'd promised to take her away from all of that.

The door creaked open, flooding the cramped space with light. The brightness momentarily blinded her. Holding up an arm to block the light she spoke, her voice hoarse thanks to her parched throat. "I thought you forgot about me."

"I never forget a pretty face. Speaking of, you look just like her."

She shivered, fear slipping beneath her skin. It wasn't him. Did he send someone for her? "Who-who are you?"

"That's not important." His hand shot out grabbing a fistful of her blonde hair. He yanked her to her feet, and she screamed. It was a mistake. He wanted her to scream. With her mouth open the rag slipped in easily, gagging her until the only sounds that escaped were weak gurgles.

"Good girl," he crooned, stroking her hair. "Play along and this will go much easier."

He slipped something over her head, and the world went dark.

1

"WHY ARE YOU STARING AT ME LIKE I'M ONE OF THOSE CRUSTY OLD BOOKS you're trying to decode?" Jake asked.

Dana tilted her head. "Because you look different."

He couldn't help himself. He'd missed her more than he should have and now that they were finally back together, he couldn't seem to rein in his flirtation. "Good, different?"

"Tan, different."

He laughed. "Well, Florida tends to do that to a person."

"So you enjoyed Key West?"

"Everyone enjoys Key West. Palm trees, sunshine, piña coladas. It's paradise. I'd move there in a heartbeat."

"Why don't you move there now?"

"'Cause I still have work to do here. Like teaching you how to shoot. Come on, you have to hit the target at least once before we call it a day."

Jake sent the untouched paper target back down the lane and reloaded his Sig Sauer 9mm. "Square up."

Dana pulled her ear protection back in place and did as instructed. Her long brown hair was pulled into a ponytail. It swayed down her back as she moved into her shooting stance. Even with her safety glasses on, she still somehow managed to be the best thing Jake had laid eyes on in months.

A few weeks of vacation had turned into a few months. Key West had no shortage of gorgeous women, and Jake had enjoyed himself with a few, but none were Dr. Dana Gray.

That was the problem, and partly why Jake had extended his vacation. He'd been trying to get the sexy librarian out of his head. They weren't partners anymore, no matter how much he might want her to be. He couldn't blame her. Their last case had even made Jake reassess his commitment to the FBI.

Ultimately, he still felt he had unfinished business to atone for. But it was different for Dana. She wasn't an agent. She'd only been consulting on the case, and it had almost gotten her killed. He understood why she wouldn't be eager to go down that road again.

He told himself it was for the best. Dana was a distraction. In his line of work distractions could be deadly. Yet here he was, appreciating her ass when he was supposed to be correcting her form.

Jake had only been back in D.C. for two weeks before he caved and called Dana, using these promised shooting lessons as an excuse to see her. But then again, if her aim hadn't been so bad, they could've ended their last case before things got out of hand.

Refocusing, Jake nudged Dana's stance wider, tapping his shoe against her boots. He moved his hands to her hips and shifted her balance back into her seat. "Now bend your knees a little. That's it."

Feeling her warm body against his was testing his willpower, but he fought through his desire, determined not to be one more person to take advantage of Dana.

She deserved better.

Certainly better than him.

Reminding himself of that, Jake brought his hands up, correcting Dana's grip and lowering her arms a bit more. "Okay. Now pull in a breath and squeeze the trigger on your exhale. Three round bursts in one breath, like I taught you."

Dana gave a slight nod and Jake stepped back, giving her the lane. He watched her shoulders rise on the inhale and relax momentarily before she discharged the weapon. Three shots in succession, just like he'd instructed. And this time, she nicked the target. Dana whirled around glowing with delight. "I did it!"

Jake reflexively neutralized the gun. Pointing it down-range until the safety was on, he holstered it and grinned. "Nicely done. A few more lessons and you might be able to hit the broad side of a barn."

She cut her eyes at him, before striking out with a playful right hook meant for his shoulder. He dodged it and pulled her into his arms instead. For a moment they were both caught by surprise. Dana glanced up at him, her brown eyes full of questions. He could feel her heart beating against his chest.

How many nights had he'd ached to have her in his arms like this? Had she thought about him, too? He had to know. His whole body was vibrating with anticipation as he gathered his nerves to just man up and ask her already.

"Jake?"

Dana's voice brought him back to reality. "Yeah?"

"Your phone's ringing."

"Oh. Right." He cleared his throat and straightened, backing away until he had enough space to think coherently. He wasn't vibrating, his phone was. *Moron.* Swallowing his embarrassment he answered the call. "Agent Shepard."

He listened intently as his new supervisor filled him in on a missing person case. "I know you're still settling in, but we could really use your help on this one. It's high profile, and I don't want to see it get out of hand. We need to get ahead of the Press."

Jake agreed. "Text me the address. I'll head there now."

"Report back here ASAP."

"Roger that."

Jake hung up and turned to Dana. She was already putting her jacket on. "Sounds like shooting lessons are over for today."

"Yeah. Missing person case just came in."

"I'm sorry."

"Yeah, these are never easy."

"I know."

Their eyes met. Of course, she did. Dana had been through more than her fair share of heartache. "It'll be strange not having you in the field with me. You're good at it. Ever think about a career change?"

She shook her head. "I'm done with that, Jake."

"You sure? We've proved we work well together."

"I'm sure. I'll stick to my area of expertise."

Jake nodded, but he couldn't fight his disappointment. He knew it was probably for the best that Dana wouldn't be involved in another high stakes FBI case. He cared about her too much already. A little distance would be safer for them both. "Need a lift back to the Smithsonian?"

"No, the weather's nice for a change. I'd rather walk."

"All right." They moved toward the exit together. "This case is probably going to keep me wrapped up for a while. But I'll touch base when I resurface."

Dana caught his hand and gave it a squeeze. "Take care of yourself."

He grinned faintly. "Always do."

2

"DR. FREDRICK?" DANA COULDN'T HIDE THE SHOCK IN HER VOICE AT seeing her boss in her office when she returned to the Smithsonian. The occult studies library didn't get many visitors. "Is there something I can do for you?"

"I'm not sure there's anything anyone can do."

Dana shrugged off her coat and hung it on the antique Alcott in her office. She gestured for her boss to have a seat, while she took the worn leather one behind her ornate fourth century desk. "What's this about?"

"The Kincaids."

The name needed no further explanation. Everyone in D.C. knew the Kincaids and their wealth. Archer and Elizabeth Kincaid were the Smithsonian's largest donors. It was no wonder Dana's boss looked so distraught. He was probably preparing for their visit, or maybe the Kincaids wanted to host another gala at the museum. Dana knew how stressful it could be trying to impress such a prestigious family. They were intimidating, but to Dana they didn't seem so bad. Mostly because she'd befriended their eldest daughter, Meredith, during her summer internship at the Smithsonian a few years back.

Dana briefly wondered how her old friend was. It had been ages since they'd spoken. Last she'd heard, Meredith was following in her father's footsteps, working her way up the political ladder as a junior aid.

"Do you need help preparing something for the Kincaids?" she asked, hopeful they were planning something extravagant that Meredith would have to make time for.

"No, the opposite actually. I'm afraid I have some bad news."

Dana frowned. "I don't understand."

Dr. Fredrick sighed, pinching the bridge of his nose. "I don't know how to tell you this. I know you're close to the family, so I wanted you to hear this from me first. Their daughter's been abducted."

Dana's stomach dropped. "Meredith?"

"Yes."

"When?"

"I don't have all the details. Just that the FBI has officially taken over the case. Are you still in touch with Agent Shepard? He might know more than I do."

Dana nodded. "I'll check with him."

"Please do. And keep me informed." Dr. Fredrick stood. "My heart just breaks for that family. Meredith was such a sweet girl."

"Is," Dana corrected. "Meredith *is* a sweet girl." She reached across the desk and squeezed her boss's hand. "We'll get her back."

Dana would make sure of it. And not just because Meredith was some rich donor's daughter. Dana wanted to find her because they were friends. Or at least the closest she'd come to having a friend until Jake Shepard walked into her life.

With Dr. Fredrick's footsteps fading further and further away, Dana's mind filled with memories of her missing friend.

Meredith Kincaid had interned at the Smithsonian during one of her summer breaks from college. Dana had gladly taken the bright young girl under her wing. They were only a few years apart and had gotten along instantly. She remembered late night movies, philosophizing about politics over wine and popcorn and sneaking into the museum after hours to play tourist.

Of course, they hadn't actually been doing anything illegal.

Dana had a key to the Smithsonian, but it made Meredith so excited to think she was getting away with something. The girl had a rebellious streak. Had she taken it too far?

Shepard's offer itched beneath Dana's skin. What was she waiting for? She knew there was no way she could sit this one out. Picking up her phone she dialed his number.

"Dana? Everything okay?"

"Not really."

"What's wrong?"

"Is your missing person Meredith Kincaid?"

"How did you know that?"

"Does your offer to help still stand?"

"Yes."

"Good. Because I've changed my mind."

"Dana. What aren't you telling me?"

"I'll explain when I see you."

Dana opened the desk drawer. The temporary badge was right where she'd left it. She'd kept it as a souvenir. But apparently her work with the FBI wasn't done yet.

3

JAKE HANDED THE SOBBING WOMAN A BOX OF TISSUES. "I NEED YOU TO answer the question, Mrs. Kincaid."

Dana gave him a warning glance, then moved closer to the woman on the sofa, taking her hand. "Elizabeth, I know this isn't easy, but we're here to help."

"I just can't believe this is happening. Meredith is a good girl. She knows better than to get mixed up in anything like Agent Shepard is suggesting."

Jake fought the urge to laugh. If he had a dollar for every time a parent *thought* they knew what their children were up to. He'd worked more than enough missing person cases to know nothing could be taken at face value, least of all the alibis of kids who still lived with their parents.

Granted, Meredith Kincaid wasn't really a child. But the twenty-eight-year-old still lived at home. Not that Jake blamed her. The Kincaid Estate was hardly the average home.

The house Jake stood in was just one of the many dwellings on the massive property. He'd seen stables, a carriage house and even a private heli-pad on the manicured grounds once he'd been allowed past the manned iron gates.

It was easy to see why Meredith wasn't eager to leave such a lavish nest.

A staff of three women whisked away discarded tissues, refilled teacups and offered Mrs. Kincaid her anxiety medication. Jake glanced around at the art-lined walls and the rich leather upholstery of the sitting room. The place smelled of old money; a mix of leather, mahogany and aloofness that just couldn't be duplicated.

Elizabeth Kincaid, formerly Elizabeth Blair, wouldn't know that. Her family had helped found the Nation's Capital and carve out its political system. She'd never known anything but this level of lavishness.

Jake had done his research.

The Blair family was more than just old money. They were political royalty. Their bloodline was host to the founders of the College of William and Mary, Privy Councilmen, US Constitution signers and Supreme Court members.

The only deviation in prestigious stock came when Elizabeth married a nobody banker from New York. But it seemed she, like her forefathers, had an eye for success because Archer Kincaid quickly climbed his way up the political ladder. He was now Chairmen of the Council of Economic Advisers. That meant he was a cabinet member and the President's chief economist.

It seemed everyone in this part of town had an office at 1600 Pennsylvania Ave, which would only make this case more difficult.

The Kincaid home was on the same block as the Defense Secretary and National Security Advisor. Jake needed special top-secret clearance just to get in the front door. Clearance he wouldn't be able to get Dana. Lucky for him, she didn't need it.

The moment Elizabeth had seen Dana, she'd opened her arms, overcome with gratitude that her daughter's friend was there to help. And she was helping.

Jake wasn't good at dealing with the sickeningly affluent. Dana didn't seem to have the same affliction, as she stroked Elizabeth's stylish blonde bob. "I just want to know she's okay."

"She will be. Agent Shepard is very good at his job."

Jake took his cue and started asking questions again. “Can you tell me what Meredith was wearing the last time you saw her?”

“This season’s white Alexander McQueen. I remember because I complimented her on it.”

“When was this?”

“Two nights ago. We had dinner at The Inn. We left around seven.”

“When did you suspect something was amiss?”

“When Senator Scott called me after she didn’t show up for work the next day,” Elizabeth snapped. “I already told the police and the other FBI agents all of this. Why are we wasting time going over it again?”

“It may seem redundant, but I assure you it’s important, ma’am. These questions might jog your memory and help you remember something new.”

Dana nodded her encouragement and the older woman conceded. “Fine. What else do you want to know?”

Jake went back to his original question. The one that made Mrs. Kincaid dissolve into tears earlier. “Is there any reason to believe that someone might want to harm your daughter?”

“No. Like I told you. Meredith is a good girl. She goes to work and comes home. That’s it.”

Yeah, as far as you know, Jake thought. “And where does she work?”

“She works for Senator Warren Scott in the Capitol Building. She’s his legislative assistant.”

Jake knew the answers to these questions already, but sometimes asking them repeatedly helped him read between the lines. He went over the details he’d scribbled in his notebook again.

Age. 28.

Height. 5’9.

Build. Athletic.

Hair. Blonde.

Eyes. Blue.

Scars. None.

Tattoos. None. *That her mother knew about.*

Vehicle. Silver Mercedes E-class.

Besides the age, it sounded like Elizabeth Kincaid was describing herself, right down to the matching Mercedes in the driveway.

Jake had already seen photographs of the missing girl, and the Kincaid home was full of portraits of the entire family: mother, father, Meredith and younger sister, Abigail. The resemblance of all three Kincaid women was unmistakable.

Despite his cool demeanor, Jake felt for Elizabeth. No parent deserved the stress of worrying about their child's safety. Guilt coiled inside him, knowing he'd caused his own mother this same distress each time he'd signed on for another tour.

His Army days were behind him, but the danger wasn't over. He was fighting a different kind of war now. This one was stateside, but he didn't know if working for the FBI was better or worse. He just knew he had to do his part to make a difference.

It was the price he paid for being alive.

He had a lot more cases to solve before the life debt he owed was repaid. Even then he knew he'd never escape the survivor's guilt of returning home without his teammates. But one thing Jake had learned in his recovery was mountains were summited one step at a time.

Returning his focus to the task at hand, he continued with the monotonous questioning. The fact that Meredith Kincaid was from such a high-profile family was making his job more difficult.

The Kincaids might have all the resources in the world, but loose lips weren't one of them. And that was precisely what he needed if he was going to find their daughter.

Jake did his best to squash his rising irritation. He didn't have patience for those who believed they deserved special treatment because of their bank balance. Death didn't discriminate. And right now, the clock on Meredith's safe return was ticking.

Someone needed to start talking.

4

"HAVE YOU CALLED HER PHONE?" JAKE ASKED.

Elizabeth erupted. "Of course I've called her phone!" She glared at Dana. "Is this really the best the FBI has to offer?"

Deflecting, Dana changed the subject. "What about her computer? Do you have access to her social media accounts for any clues to her last whereabouts?"

"Meredith's not very active on social media. It's not in our family's best interest. Anyway, her laptop's not here. Even if it was, I don't know her password."

"What about Abby? Would she know?"

Elizabeth frowned. "I don't want Abigail involved in this. She's just a child."

Jake looked up from his notes. "Says here she's twenty-two. That's hardly a child."

Dana spoke before Elizabeth's seething glare could set Jake on fire. "I just remember how close Mere and Abby are, that's all."

Elizabeth's bottom lip began to tremble. "They are close. If something's happened to Meredith," she paused to sniffle, "it will kill Abigail."

Just then, Abby burst into the room, streaking toward them like a blonde comet. "Mom! Mom! Is it true? Is Mere missing?"

She stopped in her tracks when she saw Dana sitting on the couch next to her mother. Abby surveyed Jake. Dana could only imagine how much scarier their presence was making this. But Jake was right. Abby wasn't a child anymore.

Gone was the little girl Dana remembered. Abigail Kincaid was a young woman now. Almost the spitting image of her older sister Meredith.

The Georgetown T-shirt Abby wore tugged at Dana's heartstrings. Meredith had worn one just like it the summer she'd interned at the Smithsonian.

Dana had always appreciated that Meredith never flaunted her family's wealth. She briefly wondered if Meredith was still that same girl. Hearing about her expensive suit and luxury car made her think not.

Another concern spiked through her mind. How much help would she actually be if Meredith wasn't the same girl she used to know?

"Will someone please tell me what's going on?" Abby demanded.

"You're Abigail Kincaid?" Jake asked.

"Yes. Where's my sister?"

Before Jake could respond Elizabeth was on her feet rushing to her youngest daughter. "Darling, you should be at school. You have exams this week."

"Like I can concentrate on exams with Mere's face plastered all over the news."

Jake pulled his phone from his pocket and shook his head, his shoulders tight with frustration. Dana stood and walked over to him, shocked by the headlines scrolling across his phone. *Kincaid Kidnapping – Political Princess Imprisoned.*

"Everyone's saying Mere's been abducted." Abby's blue eyes filled with tears. "Is it true?"

Jake spoke up. "I'm Agent Shepard. I've been assigned to your sister's case. She's officially a missing person. Anything you can tell us about the last time you spoke to her would be helpful."

"I spoke to her on Wednesday night." Abby sat down and so did Jake.

Dana took her spot on the upholstered sofa again, but Elizabeth went to stand behind the wing-backed leather chair her daughter occupied.

"Are you certain it was Wednesday?" Jake asked.

Abby nodded. "We talk every Wednesday."

Dana's heart squeezed. That used to be their thing. "Mere still does Wednesday Wine-a-thons?"

"We never miss them." Abby glanced up at her mother. "Since I turned twenty-one, I mean."

"Darling, your drinking habits are the least of my worries right now."

Dana couldn't help the wave of nostalgia that washed over her as she thought about the many Wednesdays she and Meredith had spent drinking wine and talking about boys. Meredith did most of the talking, since Dana and relationships didn't really mix, but she loved listening to her friend's exploits.

Thanks to the notoriety surrounding her parents' death, Dana hadn't made many friends in school and she didn't have time for them in college. Working in the dungeon of the Smithsonian hadn't helped her connect with her colleagues either, but then Meredith had come into her life. She became the little sister Dana had never known she wanted.

Jake's voice broke through Dana's memories. "Do you remember what time?"

"We chatted until around midnight." Abby pulled her phone from the thigh pocket of her black yoga pants. "The last timestamp was 12:03 AM." Abby held up the phone. "Does that help?"

"Yes. May I?" Abby handed her phone over, and Dana watched Jake scroll through the chain of messages. "Do you mind if I keep this?"

Abby's eyes bulged. "My phone?"

"Abigail!"

Abby's shoulders slumped at her mother's harsh tone. "As long as I get it back."

"You will." Jake slipped it into his jacket pocket, then handed Abby his notebook. "Can you write down the password for me?"

She did as she was asked and handed the notebook back.

"Thanks. I'll have my analysts scrape this and get it back to you as soon as possible. Your text messages with your sister will be a big help. Without her laptop or social media, we don't have a lot to go on."

Abby perked up. "Would access to her social profiles help?"

Jake snapped his notebook shut. "I thought Meredith didn't have social media?"

"She doesn't," Elizabeth insisted.

"Mom, she does. She just doesn't want you to know about it."

"Can you get us access, Abby?" Dana asked.

"Yes."

Jake stood up. "Lead the way."

5

Dana sat on the edge of Abby's bed. Jake stood next to the desk, his phone to his ear. He nodded to Abby. She began typing the password to a Facebook account for Charli Maine.

"You're sure this is your sister's account?" her mother asked.

"Yes, Mom."

"But why would she use that name?"

Abby shrugged. "Besides to keep it secret from you, I don't know. Mere said it was some inside joke from work or something."

Dana fought her urge to chew her nails as the screen loaded. Readjusting her glasses, she watched the profile load. There she was; Meredith, in vivid color, her bright smile lighting up the screen.

"Are you getting this?" Jake asked into the phone.

He was speaking to a software analyst at FBI headquarters. They would be worming their way into Meredith's private life now. It's not that Dana was against it—if Meredith was in danger, she'd do whatever it took to find her friend—but this was precisely why Dana didn't have social media.

She didn't like the idea of people being able to browse through her personal life like it was a tabloid magazine. The media was already having a field day with Meredith's disappearance. Dana could only imagine what they'd do with access to the photos Abby was scrolling through.

Meredith in a skimpy bikini on a yacht.

Meredith laughing with men over martinis.

Meredith looking cozy with the Senator.

Dana knew exactly how the public would perceive these photos. They wouldn't see a happy, vibrant young woman, with career aspirations. They'd see a D.C. debutant turned party girl, wasting her potential by sleeping her way to the top.

It'd been so long since Dana had an actual conversation with Meredith, she didn't know which version was closer to the truth, but she knew it wouldn't matter. Once the public judged her, there would be no changing their minds.

Photo after photo of Meredith and Senator Warren Scott filled the screen. It shouldn't be strange considering he was her boss. But their closeness seemed too close; bordering on inappropriate.

Jake came to the same conclusion. "Was Meredith involved with the Senator?"

Elizabeth snapped. "What an absurd question! Of course not. They worked together."

"Ma'am, I'm not judging anyone here, but if they were more than co-workers, that would make the Senator a person of interest."

Elizabeth harrumphed. "My daughter is Senator Scott's legislative assistant. Nothing more."

Dana's attention moved to Abby. The girl was still sitting at her desk watching whomever was on the other end of Jake's phone take over her laptop. The screen moved on its own, scrolling through photos of Meredith's life like a ghostly slideshow.

Abby watched, chewing her lip and cracking her knuckles.

She knew something.

Dana cleared her throat and stood from her perch on the plush white comforter. "I need some water. Abby, do you mind showing me to the kitchen while Agent Shepard has a conversation with your mother?"

Abby rose, wordlessly following Dana out of the bedroom. In the hall, she turned right taking the lead as she led Dana through a maze of creaking floorboards until they reached the first floor of the historic home.

Once in the kitchen, Dana placed her hands on the white granite countertops, letting the coolness of the stone seep into her bones. She craved the numbing effect it had on her, wishing it would carry all the way to her heart.

She had a sinking feeling Abby was keeping dangerous secrets. Dana needed to find a way to get her to spill them. Befriending people didn't come naturally to her, but for Meredith, she'd try. "Mere moved out of the main house, right?"

Abby handed Dana a bottle of sparkling water. "She moved out to the carriage house after college."

"When was the last time you were out there with her?"

Abby shrugged. "I'm not home much. I have an apartment on campus."

"You're at Georgetown?"

"Yeah."

"Just like Mere."

Abby nodded.

"You said you and Mere still talk every Wednesday?"

"Yep."

"She and I used to do that, too." Dana's lips curved at the fond memories. "It started the summer she worked at the Smithsonian. We would go to my place and drink wine and eat popcorn and talk about guys. Well, Mere did most of the talking. I didn't really have a lot of guys to dish about."

Abby smiled. "That's Mere. You can always count on her for the boy drama."

"I guess some things don't change."

Abby sipped nervously from her own bottle of sparkling water.

"You don't think some of her guy trouble turned into actual trouble, do you?"

Abby's big blue eyes met Dana's. Confliction flashed across them like lightning bolts.

"Abby, if you know something, you need to tell me. Mere's life might be in danger."

"No. He wouldn't hurt her."

"Who?"

"I'm not supposed to say."

"She's my friend, Abby. I want to help her just like you do. I promise I'll keep what I can confidential."

"What about that FBI guy? Are you going to tell him?"

"Not if I don't have to."

Abby bit her lip, weighing her options. Coming to a hasty decision, she grabbed Dana's hand. "Come on. There's something you need to see."

6

Afternoon sunlight filtered through the antique Georgian windows in Meredith's bedroom. It warmed the pale linen chaise Dana perched on as she waited for Abby to stop stalling. She knew the girl was reluctant to say too much because of her family's notoriety. She was smart enough to know whatever she was about to share about Meredith and the Senator could have catastrophic implications in the powerful political world they were involved in, but Dana was growing impatient. Abby needed to understand the reality of the situation.

The FBI didn't get called in to investigate idle threats. If they thought Meredith's missing person case was important, then Dana had every reason to believe her friend was in trouble.

"Abby, you said you brought me out here to show me something."

"I know. It's just, Mere will kill me."

Not if she's already dead. Dana shook the morbid thought away. "She'll understand you're concerned for her safety."

"I still don't think he'd do anything to hurt her."

"Who?"

"The Senator."

"What makes you think she's with Senator Scott?"

Abby shrugged. "He's all she talks about."

"Well, they work together."

"It's more than that." Abby stood up and crossed the room to a mirrored dresser. Pulling open the top drawer, she reached in and fiddled around with the lining. Dana stood up and craned her neck, catching a glimpse of silk and lace as Abby pushed the velvet lining back in place. She held a slim white envelope to her chest. "These photos can't get out. Mere will kill me."

Dana held out her hand. "We have to find her first."

Abby conceded, handing the envelope over before sinking dramatically onto Meredith's bed.

Dana opened the envelope and slipped the photos out onto her lap, briefly wondering if she should be wearing gloves as she examined them. Unlike Jake, she didn't make a habit of carrying latex gloves with her everywhere she went.

The FBI had already been here and thoroughly examined the home, but based on where these photos were hidden, this was new evidence. If the FBI had seen them, Senator Scott would be in custody right now.

While sleeping with your legislative assistant wasn't a crime, it was certainly suspicious. In Dana's experience, there was only one reason to keep a relationship secret during an investigation of this magnitude, and it didn't bode well for Meredith.

Innocent people didn't hide innocent relationships.

Innocent people didn't belong to secret societies either.

Ignoring the explicit nudity in the photos, Dana zeroed in on the Senator's hands. She hated the way he was gripping Meredith's neck. But even more frightening, was the ancient symbol adorning the gold ring he wore.

A chill rippled through Dana at the implications of what Meredith might have stumbled upon. If the ring was what Dana thought it was, she might be more suited to this missing person case than she first thought. And Senator Warren Scott might not be who he seemed.

She slipped the photos back into the envelope. "I have to show these to Agent Shepard."

"No! You promised!"

"The only thing I promised, was to help find your sister. And that's what I intend to do. You shouldn't have helped her keep this secret. She could be in a lot of trouble."

"No, you don't understand. They weren't just sleeping together. They're in love. She told me he was going to propose."

Dana whirled around. "And you don't see how that's dangerous? What if he changed his mind and Mere was threatening to go public with these?" She waved the envelope.

Abby's eyes welled with tears. "She wouldn't do that."

"How do you know?"

"Because, the way she talked about him ... she sounded so ... infatuated."

Dana could only imagine. Powerful men loved captivating naïve women. And if Senator Scott was who she thought he was, they had a bigger problem on their hands than a political scandal.

7

"THIS WILL KILL YOUR FATHER," ELIZABETH SOBBED.

Speaking of... Jake spoke up. "Where is Mr. Kincaid?"

Elizabeth erupted. "Archer has nothing to do with this!"

"I didn't say he did." Jake was losing patience with the woman's sensitivity. Ever since Dana returned to the main house with the photos, ranting about conspiracy, Mrs. Kincaid had been stonewalling him. "I still need to know his whereabouts."

"You'll have to ask his secretary."

"I will."

Jake had hoped with her daughter in a potential life or death situation, Elizabeth Kincaid would've been more cooperative. He'd also hoped that Mr. Kincaid would've made himself available. However, Jake knew better than to say that out loud.

He was pretty sure if his toe moved one more inch over the imaginary line the high-strung woman had drawn, she would have him riding a desk for the foreseeable future. It didn't help that Dana was filling her head with cloak and dagger nonsense pertaining to some symbol she'd identified on the Senator's ring.

Juggling emotional women was not his forte and right now, he had three on his hands. But he couldn't afford to screw this up. It was his first case after coming back from leave.

Jake didn't need any more friction with his new boss. He already worried he hadn't made a great first impression since he'd extended his mental health leave while in the Keys. He'd been told to take as much time as he needed, but that was before Assistant Director, Victor Holt, took over. He wasn't known for leniency.

Jake rubbed his brow. Everything about this case was making him second guess his decision to come back to the FBI.

Despite hating these high-profile cases, he found this one intriguing. It potentially gave him the opportunity to stick it to two things he despised. Corrupt politicians and violence against women. Plus Dana was involved.

Selfishly he wanted more time with her. And knowing how important finding Meredith was to Dana, made it even more important that he succeed.

He'd thought his days of playing hero were over, but the damn woman just brought it out in him. Not that Dana would ever be okay with being rescued. She was more than capable of saving herself, but that didn't stop him from wanting to be the guy she leaned on from time to time. *Sucker.*

Jake took the photos Dana found in Meredith's room back from Elizabeth. Mrs. Kincaid claimed she didn't know anything about them. If she did, she wasn't going to admit it. There was too much at stake for her precious reputation. Jake figured that out right off the bat, but he still had a job to do.

"You're not taking those photos out of this house!" Elizabeth yelled, trying to snatch them back.

"They're part of the investigation now, ma'am."

"You don't understand. If the media gets a hold of them, we're ruined."

"Do you want us to find Meredith, or not?" Dana snapped. "She could be out there in the hands of a very dangerous man right now, and these photos are the only leverage we have to get her back. That should be your only concern!"

Her outburst stunned Jake, and apparently Mrs. Kincaid because for the first time all day the woman didn't have a comment. Personally, he was pleased Dana told her off. He'd been wanting to do the same thing from almost the moment he arrived. Unfortunately, he had to adhere to the unbiased professionalism of the FBI. Dana didn't have the same requirements. But, since she was here under his invitation, her mouthing off to a victim's family would be his responsibility.

"Dana." Jake stepped forward, putting a hand on her shoulder hoping to calm her. She shrugged it off. "Take a breath," he ordered.

"No! Not until I know if Meredith still has that same privilege! We need to stop wasting time and go after Senator Scott. He's involved in this somehow. The photos prove it."

He moved closer. "This isn't the time or place to make speculations."

"It's not a speculation. If you knew what that ring represented, you'd understand."

Jake grabbed Dana's arm, not letting go when she tried to shake him off. "We have what we need for now," he said, addressing the Kincaid women. "If either of you think of anything else pertinent to the case, please give me a call." His gaze landed on Elizabeth. "I'd like to speak to Mr. Kincaid. Please let me know when he gets back into town. I'll be in touch."

Then he headed for the door, hauling Dana along with him.

"LET GO OF ME!" Dana yelled as Jake shoved her toward his SUV.

"Not until you calm down."

"I'd be a lot calmer if you'd stop manhandling me."

"Get in the car, Dana."

"I have my own car."

"Yeah, well it's staying here."

"Um, no it's not."

"Yes. It is."

She dug her heels in. "I think you're mistaking me for someone who has to follow your orders."

Jake squeezed her arm, pulling her close enough to kiss. But that was the last thing on his mind at the moment. "The only one making a mistake here is you."

Dana sucked in a breath, but before she could bite his head off again, he cut her off. "If you care at all about finding your friend, you'll stop making a scene, get in my car and talk to me rationally about your theory, because that's what it is right now. A theory. And you can't arrest US Senators on a theory."

"I know that."

"Good. Then get in the car and help me find some proof that he's involved. Because if he is, it'll be my pleasure to help you nail the bastard."

Finally, he'd said something right, because Dana conceded. She stopped fighting and got into his SUV. Relief swept through Jake as he jogged around to the driver's side. It calmed him to have Dana where he could watch her. He didn't trust her not to go after the Senator on her own, which was why he hadn't wanted to let her get into her own car.

He'd learned previously just how much trouble her stubborn streak could cause when she was left to her own devices. Jake wasn't taking that risk again. Especially not when politics of this level were involved. Being a Fed only went so far. If Dana pissed off the wrong people, he wouldn't be able to protect her.

He knew how that felt and wasn't anxious to revisit it.

Pulling out of the drive, he turned onto a street lined with scarlet oaks and cherry trees. Jake accelerated, hoping some distance between Dana and the Kincaids would help. At the very least, driving gave the illusion they were doing something. He understood Dana's frustration. Sometimes investigating these types of cases was a whole lot of hurry up and wait.

Still, outbursts weren't really Dana's thing. He glanced at her while navigating traffic. "Wanna tell me what that was about?"

"Excuse me?"

"Your outburst back there with Elizabeth Kincaid."

"Her daughter is missing. Do I really need an explanation?"

"I think it's more than that."

"Of course it's more than that. I told you, we're friends. At least, we used to be."

She said that last part so quietly Jake wasn't sure he was meant to hear it. But he did. Following his gut, he made a left on Maryland Avenue and changed direction.

"Where are we going?"

"To get something to eat."

"I'm not hungry."

"Fine, I don't have much food at my place anyway."

Dana's dark eyebrows shot up. "Are you serious? My friend is missing, and you feel like taking me back to your place?"

The back of Jake's neck prickled with heat. "That's not what I had in mind." Though now he couldn't deny he was thinking about it. As appealing as the thought was, he was currently more interested in getting into her mind than her pants. *How was that for irony?*

Dana crossed her arms. "What *did* you have in mind?"

"Getting to the bottom of what's eating you."

"I told you. Meredith is my friend."

From the way Dana had been staring at the photos, he had a feeling it was more than that. He knew that look—guilt, riddled with regret. He'd seen it in his own reflection enough times to recognize it and knew how destructive it was.

Jake wasn't one to talk when it came to facing demons, but if Dana didn't face hers, she'd be useless to Meredith. If he was going to get her to open up, he was going to have to be the one to do it first. And that would require a stiff drink and privacy, hence the U-turn toward his place.

He wished he'd reached out to Dana when he was in the Keys. Maybe if he'd gotten her to join him, she would be in a better headspace. But he'd needed the escape to get his own head right after being blindsided and backstabbed by his old boss. He'd also needed time away from Dana.

Jake spent half his time in the Keys trying to convince himself that they were better off apart. But it seemed fate had other ideas. Now that they'd been thrown back together there wasn't much he could do but lock away his desires and help Dana get her head on straight so they could solve this case before she self-destructed.

"We're still going to my place."

"Why?"

"Because digging up dirt on a US Senator isn't something we can do just anywhere."

In D.C., everyone knew everyone. They couldn't exactly discuss things like dirty politicians over a meal in public. Besides, Jake was still confident a stiff drink would help calm Dana's nerves, if not get to the root of her incessant nail biting.

"I really don't think it's necessary. We could go to my office."

Jake shook his head. "I have a secure network. And more importantly, whiskey."

8

DARK, STIFF, STERILE. IT WAS EXACTLY WHAT DANA EXPECTED AN FBI agent's home to look like. Or maybe it was just what she'd expected Jake Shepard's home to look like.

It's not that she thought he lacked character, but his home certainly did.

Just like Jake, it gave nothing away on the surface.

It probably looked the same as it did the day he moved in. Actually, she couldn't tell the difference. For all she knew, he might've just moved in.

The walls were bare, painted stark white, no artwork, no personal photos, no hint of who he was beyond face value. The only thing someone might learn from visiting his home was his taste for whiskey.

The vast collection of whiskey was hard to miss considering the wet bar was his first stop. Jake pulled two rocks glasses off the spotless glass shelves above the liquor and placed them on the black granite countertop before selecting a bottle. He poured the deep amber liquid with a heavy hand before recorking the bottle.

Jake handed her a glass and carried his own over to the kitchen island. He set it down and shrugged out of his suit jacket, draping it over the back of the black leather and steel barstool. She watched him loosen his dark tie and undo the top button of his crisp white shirt before she turned away.

Though his home wasn't very revealing, there was something intimate about being there. He'd made it perfectly clear why he'd invited her. There was no place for her lust. Taking a sip of the whiskey, she let the alcohol burn away her embarrassing reaction.

"Make yourself comfortable," Jake said. "I need to grab my laptop."

Dana nodded and moved from the kitchen to the living room. It only took a few steps thanks to the apartment's open floorplan. She took a seat on the black leather sofa facing the floor-to-ceiling windows. The view was the most spectacular thing about the place.

Jake probably paid a pretty penny for his eagle eye view of the National Mall, but in Dana's opinion it was worth it. She watched the busy city below. She bet it looked gorgeous at night. An image of her spending the evening here with Jake blazed through her mind, heating her to her very core.

She took another large gulp of whiskey trying to drive away the tempting idea.

What the hell was wrong with her? She could admit she'd missed Jake while he was gone, but was it more than that? Being in his apartment was reminding her just how much she liked having him in her life.

Dana took another sip of whiskey. She was starting to enjoy the warm feel of it.

Without Jake in the room, she let her gaze roam the rest of the apartment. She took in the tidy living space with the keen eyes of a researcher, picking out things she found interesting.

No television. Maybe he had one in the bedroom.

No plants or pets. He probably wasn't home enough to care for living things.

No trace of his time in the military. That was unexpected. She'd seen a photo of his team in his office at the J. Edgar Hoover Building once, but other than that, it seemed like a subject he preferred not to revisit.

She knew it haunted him and with good reason. The small bit he'd shared with her about the friend he'd lost on his last tour had stuck with her.

Her attention snagged on the glass bookcase in the corner. It was the only item in the apartment that made the place look lived in. There was a collection of *Time* magazines, a mantle clock made of dark wood and brass, and a folded American flag in a glass case. It rested on the highest tier of the shelving, representing its importance.

The flag was folded neatly into a triangle, the way often done after a soldier's funeral.

Dana wondered if it belonged to Ramirez, the friend Jake had told her about, or perhaps it belonged to one of the other soldiers whose dog tags he wore around his neck.

Her mind flashed back to their time in Las Vegas. Jake, bare chested and scarred. Three dog tags dangling around his broad neck.

Jake walked back into the room, pulling Dana from her memories.

She watched him cautiously, wishing she could ask him about the flag. But she knew it was none of her business. Even if they had the kind of relationship where personal questions weren't off limits, she wasn't in the right frame of mind to bring it up.

From its prominent display, it was obviously very important to him. Probably a friend or family member's, and that wasn't a subject she was well versed in.

She was lacking in the friends and family department. Reality came crashing down on Dana. She took another sip of her whiskey, relishing the burn.

If she'd been a better friend to Meredith maybe this wouldn't have happened. Having a secret affair with a senator who also happened to be her boss? That didn't sound like the Meredith she remembered. But that was the problem. Dana had been so absorbed in researching her parents' mysterious deaths that she was too busy to check in on her friend.

Dana lost her parents through no fault of her own, but she couldn't say the same things about her friends. Or more accurately, friend.

Meredith was it.

Dana was close to her intern, Claire, and sometimes Jake, but both relationships were professional. Could she even count them as friends?

Friends aren't usually people you consider sleeping with, her subconscious chided.

Dana drained the rest of her whiskey.

"Whoa, slow down there, killer. That's the good stuff. You're supposed to enjoy it."

"Who says I'm not enjoying it?"

Jake shook his head, a good-humored grin on his face as he joined her on the couch. He placed the laptop on the glass coffee table and opened it, logging on to his secure network with his FBI credentials. She watched him type Senator Warren Scott into the search bar.

"So you believe me?"

Jake's blue eyes sparkled. "I never said I didn't."

"It didn't seem that way at the Kincaids."

He turned to face her. "Because you were ranting about going after him, guns blazing. I'm trying to find a way to trap him without losing my job."

Relief swept through Dana. She didn't know if it was because Jake hadn't completely dismissed her or maybe the whiskey was taking effect, but emotion tightened her throat. It felt good to have him in her corner again.

She was stupid for driving him away after everything he'd done to help her find the truth about her parents' murders. He'd helped her through her recovery and even gotten her a copy of their case file. Not to mention, he'd probably saved her life.

Her eyes misted. *Shit.*

Maybe she wasn't as past it as she thought. She should've gone to more therapy sessions, but she'd felt foolish and quit after the first one. Opening up about her feelings wasn't something she was fond of. But if she didn't find a way to, she knew they'd eventually swallow her whole. Especially if she didn't find Meredith and get a chance to make up for being such an absent friend.

9

JAKE GRUNTED HIS APPROVAL TO HIS IT TEAM ON THE OTHER END OF THE call. He could feel Dana staring at him, her anxiety almost palpable. By the time he'd hung up, she'd inched so close that her thigh was pressed against his, vibrating with worry.

The friction of her warmth rubbing against him while her knee bounced like a jackhammer was so distracting, he'd had to ask the senior analyst to repeat himself twice. Jake told himself the double confirmations just made him appear diligent, but he didn't like the lack of control he had over his body when Dana was around.

Putting the phone down, he reached for his glass. It was empty. Considering he was working, he didn't need more, but it was a good excuse to get up and put some distance between them.

Dana had other ideas.

She followed him to the wet bar badgering him with questions. "So? What'd they say?"

"They're still going through the Facebook account Abby shared with us, but so far, nothing."

"Nothing? What do you mean, nothing?"

"Meredith has thousands of contacts under her alias. And each of those contacts has thousands of contacts, and so on. My team is combing through every one of them, looking for patterns, specific phrases, anything suspicious, but it takes time. Especially when every single person on social media overestimates their self-importance by oversharing selfies and pictures of every meal they've ever eaten."

"So, we're back to square one?"

"Not exactly. Because Meredith went through the trouble of creating an alias, she might be hiding something. We just need more time to figure it out."

"We don't have more time. Meredith is in danger. We need to go after Senator Scott before he can cover his tracks."

"We've been over this. We can't go after him without a smoking gun. We can't even let him know we're sniffing around. I've dealt with politicians before. In a case like this, we need their cooperation and that means they can't be afraid we're going to point fingers without concrete proof."

"You want proof?" Dana marched over to the coffee table. "Here's your proof!"

She rushed back over, waving the photo of Senator Scott and Meredith in the midst of some very kinky sex. Meredith was wearing a blindfold. Her wrists bound behind her back by the same dark satin material. Jake had to admit, it was off-putting seeing a beautiful, young woman straddling a fat old man, but it wasn't exactly unusual in the political world.

Sex was traded for power almost exclusively behind closed doors on Capitol Hill. As long as it was consensual, it was none of Jake's business. Still, knowing Dana's connection to the victim, he tried to be sensitive. "Look, I know she's your friend and this kind of thing might seem disturbing, but—"

"I'm not talking about the sex," Dana interrupted. "The ring is what's disturbing. This is your smoking gun," she said, pointing to it. "It's all the proof you need that Senator Scott is behind Mere's disappearance. He belongs to the Bonesmen."

Not this again. Jake turned his back on Dana, pouring another two fingers of whiskey. "We tried looking up the symbol on the ring. We didn't find anything. It's a dead end."

More like dead wrong. He'd actually heard more convincing arguments from the rantings of the homeless guy living in the cardboard UFO on 14th and P. But Jake wasn't going to risk starting World War III by telling Dana her life's research sounded more like a bad conspiracy documentary.

Since she'd been right the last time they'd worked together, Jake had humored her, searching the fabled secret society Dana was trying to pin everything on. But nothing came up. He was ready to drop it. Dana wasn't.

She wanted him to ask the analysts to add it to their search query. There was no way he was doing that. He wasn't looking to deep six his career.

Busting his former boss for satanic worship was bad enough. If he landed back-to-back cases tied up in occult rituals, he'd end up with a label that would get him laughed out of every department in the Bureau.

"Jake, please. We didn't find anything because we're not looking in the right place. We need to go to the Smithsonian. I can prove it." Her hand wrapped around his bicep, desperate and clawing. "The Priory of Bones is real."

Jake tensed. Her touch nearly snapped his resolve. He hated the Jekyll and Hyde reaction she evoked. Having her this close was driving him crazy. So was her refusal to let this go.

She was like a damn dog with a bone about her occult beliefs. Not that he could blame her. Strange deaths seemed to follow her.

He'd only had a few months to wrap his head around the sinister outcome of their last case, but Dana had been dealing with the fallout ever since her parents had been murdered by the same organization. Twenty years of trying to unravel something like that had to take its toll.

He felt for her, he really did. But not enough to throw his career away on her hunch.

"Jake ..." she whispered his name, her impossibly dark lashes blinking up at him. "Please, I know I'm right. I just need your help to prove it."

This was why he didn't bring women to his home. Especially not women he'd been fantasizing about bedding. Getting involved with Dana Gray was a bad idea for so many reasons, but right now, staring into her pleading brown eyes, he couldn't think of any.

Thankfully, his training kicked in when he needed it most. Jake was always a soldier first. His mission: find Meredith Kincaid. His twisted feelings for Dana would have to wait.

It was time for her to face the facts. If they were going to have a chance at rescuing Meredith, Jake was going to take point on this investigation. That meant doing things his way.

"Dana, we don't have time for a field trip into your underground world of conspiracy and legends right now. This is a missing person investigation. I have protocol to follow and not a lot of time."

"Then stop wasting it."

"I'm not. We've been looking into Senator Scott all day. The man is squeaky clean. I can't arrest him for liking kinky sex with co-workers. Or for being an alleged Bonesmen."

"It's not alleged. He went to Yale. All we have to do is find his name on the Skull and Bones registry to prove he was in the Order."

"Also not a crime."

"The Priory of Bones is different than Skull and Bones. They're the real deal. And one of the most powerful and violent fraternal orders in the world. Did you know, they're credited with starting human trafficking? They're rumored to have a network so infiltrating and far reaching, nothing is off limits."

"Do you hear yourself? I can't arrest someone based on a rumor."

Ignoring him, she continued. "What about talking to Scott in public? His agenda shows him at the IWP Gala tomorrow. We could go and question him and see—"

"We're not crashing a black tie event at the National Gallery."

"We have to!" Dana slammed her empty rocks glass down on his granite countertop to punctuate her frustration.

The sound surprised her. Shock turned her rosy cheeks paper white. That's when he saw it. The crimson spiderweb spreading across the palm of her left hand.

She let go of the glass and it splintered to pieces.

Shit! He knew how queasy she got around blood. As her eyes widened with horror, he was reminded of their first crime scene.

Jake moved fast. He caught Dana around the waist before her knees gave out, easing her onto the cool concrete floor. "Breathe," he commanded, pushing her head between her knees.

He knelt next to her, one hand propping her up while the other fumbled under the kitchen sink for the first aid kit he kept stashed there. He found it, making short work of locating the gauze. A cold sweat broke out across his brow as he took Dana's blood-soaked hand in his. A flashback ripped through him—Ramirez's hand in his, blood coating them both like rain.

Pull it together, Jake.

Dana was not Ramirez. Her injury was a papercut compared to the IED that had torn his best friend apart. She was going to be fine.

Jake took his own advice to breathe. He pulled in one steadying breath after another, assessing Dana's injury. His training told him something so insignificant didn't even warrant a second look. In the field he would've rubbed some dirt on it and moved on, but he reminded himself that Dana was a renowned research scientist, not a soldier. She'd probably appreciate her hand healing without inflection or big, ugly scars.

Defying his instincts, Jake gently treated the wound. Dana sucked in a breath when he cleaned her palm with the sterile wipe. "Damn. There's a piece of glass in there."

She looked down at the bright red laceration, her face paling further. "I think I'm going to be sick."

"No, you're not."

"I am. I drank too much and the blood ..." She squeezed her eyes shut.

"Mind over matter," Jake ordered as he pulled the trash can toward them just in case her mind wasn't stronger than her stomach.

He shook his head. Dana wasn't built like a ballerina. A glass of whiskey shouldn't make her pass out. Either the woman never drank, or her phobia of blood was worse than he'd expected.

When she began trembling, he reached out with his free hand, sternly grabbing her chin. "Hey, keep your eyes right here." He maintained eye contact. "I mean it. I have to dig the piece of glass out, unless you want to go to the hospital."

He wouldn't blame her. But he'd have to call a cab to be safe. He didn't need to add DWI to his already spotty record. Dana shook her head. "No. I trust you."

The conviction in her voice made something in his chest ache. He pushed it down and concentrated on her hand.

10

Jake sat back, resting his head against the sturdy wood of his kitchen cabinets. The coolness of the concrete floor seeped through his pants, calming him as his adrenaline began to ebb. Even though Dana's wound hadn't been life-threatening, the injury had still gotten his blood pumping. He hadn't been forced into crisis mode since he'd returned to work. Leave it to Dana to be the first. Trouble seemed to follow the woman.

Eyes closed, she pulled in a shaky breath. He could feel the emotion radiating from her—pain, fear, worry. He regretted involving her in this case. She wasn't ready for it.

To her credit she'd held it together while he dug out the tiny glass shard and patched up her hand. But her pain tolerance wasn't what concerned him. She hadn't coped with what happened on their last case. And that meant she probably couldn't handle being thrown into another one so soon. Especially one that, yet again, held personal interest.

Jake ran a hand through his short hair. He should've just left her alone. He'd meant to keep his distance, to keep her safe ... but here they were, sitting on his floor in what looked like a crime scene thanks to all the bloody gauze still littering the kitchen.

What on earth had possessed him to contact Dana when he got back to D.C.?

She rested her head on his shoulder with a sigh, making his cock twitch.

There was his answer. *Asshole.*

He should've stayed away. She didn't need him bringing more dark shit into her life. But walking away now would hurt her, and she'd been hurt enough.

Jake exhaled deeply, letting his cheek rest on Dana's head. Her shiny brown hair felt like satin against his skin. She smelled like heaven; light floral perfume and fresh shampoo invaded his nostrils. He let himself soak it up for a moment before asking the inevitable. "Are you okay?"

She shifted, lifting her head so she could look at him. "Yeah." She held up her bandaged hand. "It looks worse than it is. I'm sure it'll heal pretty quickly."

"I'm not talking about your hand."

She looked down at her lap, understanding registering in the softness of her voice. "Oh."

"Have you spoken to anyone about what went down with Cramer?"

She shrugged. "Once."

He didn't want to nag her. Baring his soul to a shrink wasn't his cup of tea either. He'd done his FBI mandated counseling and then got the hell out of Dodge. He'd never found anything that worked better than salt therapy. As far as he was concerned a few days on the open ocean could cure anything. But that wasn't the point. "I don't know if working on this case is going to be the best thing for you."

"Jake, I have to! Mere—"

He held up his hands. "Hear me out. I'm not saying I'm cutting you out of this, but I don't think I should officially bring you on board."

"You think I'm a train wreck?" She let her head fall back against the cabinets with a thud. "I can't really blame you after today."

"That's not it."

"Then what?"

"Well for one thing, I have a new boss, and he's not as liberal as, well, you know."

"As your serial murdering ex-supervisor? Yeah, I'm familiar."

Jake frowned. "After what Cramer did, the Bureau's been in major crisis mode. He shook a lot of branches, including the ones high up. Holt is in charge now, and he's been running a tight ship while the dust settles, cracking down on clearances, not outsourcing to anyone outside the agency. I doubt he would even consider letting you come on board. Especially given you know the missing person."

"But that's why you need me. No one's going to be as invested in finding Meredith as I am."

"You're wrong, Dana. This is what I do. I find people. And I bring them home."

The majority of his time with Special Forces was spent locating high level operatives and bringing them to safety. Or eliminating them if rescue wasn't the objective.

At least he knew he wouldn't have to go that route on this case.

It wasn't likely that Meredith Kincaid was a liability to national security. She was just a poor little rich girl who pushed her luck too far. Maybe it was with the Senator, maybe not. But Jake was confident of one thing, he'd get to the bottom of it. "I'm going to do everything in my power to find her and bring her home safely."

"And what am I supposed to do? Just sit back and pretend everything's okay?"

"I know it won't be easy, but sometimes taking a step back is the best thing you can do in this kind of situation."

"You don't understand." Emotion swam in Dana's eyes. "I let her down. She was my best friend, and I didn't have time for her. If I hadn't been so self-absorbed, I would've seen this coming. I could've stopped it." She pulled in a strangled breath. "If something happened to her, it's on me."

That wasn't true, but Jake knew it was impossible to erase that kind of guilt, no matter how irrational it was. He teetered on the edge of it daily as he fought with his guilt returning from war, when so many others hadn't. It was a losing battle. But still, he hated seeing Dana so torn up. It made him want to pull her into his arms.

He resisted, tucking a loose strand of her hair behind her ear instead. "Meredith Kincaid is her own person, Dana. Her choices belong to her."

"I can't lose her," she whispered, her eyes dark pools of sorrow. "She's all I have left."

Jake took her good hand in both of his and squeezed. "Not true."

Her lower lip began to tremble, and he couldn't stop himself this time. He pulled her into his arms and crushed her to him while she continued to hold back her tears.

11

Dana didn't know how long she spent on Jake's kitchen floor, wrapped in his embrace.

Long enough for his warmth to seep into her.

Long enough for her legs to fall asleep.

Long enough to memorize his heartbeat.

Its steady rhythm reassured her, as did the deep tenor of his voice rumbling though his chest as he spoke. The more he explained the process of a missing person investigation, the more comfortable she felt. He obviously had a lot of experience. And just as much success. He elaborated on a few of his military missions, but she stopped asking questions when most of his answers were "it's classified."

Switching gears, he was back to talking about Meredith's case. "This is going to be a jurisdictional nightmare once the Press gets involved, and with a high-profile case like this, they're sure to. I need you not to read too much into what you see on the news."

Easier said than done, but she nodded.

"And one more thing." Jake's blue eyes were tranquil pools of concern. "No running off on your own to play hero. If you think you have something solid, come to me with it first."

"I thought you said I was off the case."

He grinned. "I know you. You're not going to let it go."

Jake was right. Just because she wasn't going to be working the case in an official capacity didn't mean she had to sit by and do nothing. Her gut told her the Senator was involved and she wouldn't be able to let go of her Priory of Bones theory until she ruled it out. But agreeing with Jake for now was better than working against him. "Fine, but only if you promise to do the same."

Jake grinned at her defiance. "Two things I don't do. Promises or apologies. But I'll do my best to keep you in the loop."

Knowing it was as much as she could hope for, Dana shook his extended hand.

12

Jake pulled Dana to her feet. "Come on, let's get you cleaned up. You look like an extra for the *Walking Dead*."

Her stomach rumbled as he led her to the couch, prompting Claire's voice to pop into his head. Dana's intern was always reminding her to take a break from her research to eat.

The girl was a master at ordering Thai food. It was her menu wizardry that had won Jake over. Now, thanks to Claire, he couldn't go a week without visiting Thaiphoon.

It hadn't only been Dana who'd frequented his dreams while in the Keys. Jake had been fantasizing about the dumplings Claire got him hooked on. He looked at his watch, frowning when he realized it was too late to call in an order. He glanced at Dana, guessing that she hadn't bothered to eat today. It would justify her earlier wooziness. He'd blamed it on the whiskey and blood loss, but added to an empty stomach, it explained a lot.

Dana had spent her lunch break at the shooting range with him. Then the rest of the afternoon had been chewed up investigating Meredith's disappearance. He'd bet money she'd missed at least two meals. "You eat anything today?"

She seemed to ponder the question before giving a shrug. "I

meant to."

He knew the feeling. It was easy to get sucked into work and forget about simple things like refueling your body. That's why he started every day with a hearty breakfast and a protein shake. Today, he'd found time to scarf down one of the emergency protein bars he kept in his SUV. But that was hours ago. "Why don't I see what I can scrounge up for dinner."

Once Dana was settled on the couch, Jake returned to the kitchen to clean up the crime scene-worthy mess he'd made with the first aid kit. Thankfully, cleaning supplies were plentiful. His cleaning service left the essentials in the laundry room.

Jake opened the black cabinets above his never-used washer and dryer set. As far as he was concerned, the massive chrome beasts were a waste of space since he sent his clothes out to the building's laundry service. If only he used the grocery service as well.

After cleaning up the kitchen, Jake stared glumly into his barren pantry. The only things inside were a large box of salt and the unused spice rack that had come with the apartment. He peered deeper inside, moving the spices aside. A flash of yellow near the back caught his eye.

He pulled out the box of Bisquick. There was a bottle of maple syrup tied to it with a red ribbon. Neither had been opened.

Jake briefly remembered the date who'd been so bold as to bring over breakfast assuming she'd be spending the night. He smirked. What was that saying about assumptions?

Either way, he grinned at the synchronicity of it all as an idea sparked to life. The woman he'd sent packing had given him a gift after all. He'd just be sharing it with Dana instead.

Jake read the ingredients. Eggs and water? Yeah, he could handle that.

Once he found the last item he needed buried among his seldom used pots and pans, the meal came together quickly.

Wishing he had some OJ, Jake opened the fridge one more time. He knew he wouldn't find anything but eggs and his protein shakes inside, but it was hard to break the habit of looking for things that weren't there.

He heard his uncle's voice in his head as he stared into the mostly empty refrigerator. *The answers aren't in the icebox. You want something, get off your ass and get it.*

Jake's gaze drifted back to Dana. He could just see the top of her head over the black leather of his sofa. He looked back at the two plates in front of him. He was being stupid. And he didn't do stupid. But the homemade waffles said otherwise.

Shit. This was a bad idea. But it was too late now. The foreign smell of fresh baked goods filled his apartment making his mouth water and his insides squirm. Feeling ridiculous, he straightened his shoulders, grabbed the plates and headed toward the couch, telling himself he hadn't made the waffles because he knew they meant something to her.

That would make him soft. And he wasn't soft.

No. He'd only made them because he happened to have the ingredients, not because of the sappy story she'd told him about how her parents used to make them.

It was one of the few personal details she'd let slip. It stuck with him.

Jake shook his head. He couldn't help it. The girl got to him, even when she wasn't trying.

Walking over to the couch, he huffed a laugh when he found Dana asleep. All his anxiety had been for nothing. He set the plates down on the coffee table as quietly as he could and returned to the kitchen for the syrup and utensils. While he was at it, he refilled his rocks glass.

Whiskey and waffles. It had a nice ring to it, and it was too late to be picky. At this point it didn't really matter to him what he put in his stomach. It was just fuel to get him through the endless pages of data the analysts had compiled from Meredith's Facebook account.

Jake settled on the couch, Dana on one side, his laptop on the other as he shoveled the warm pastry into his mouth.

It wasn't half bad.

Dana shifted, stretching out her bare feet until they hit his leg. He paused, a forkful of waffle halfway to his mouth. The feeling of Dana tucking her toes under his thigh ... that wasn't half bad either.

13

DANA WOKE, THE FEELING OF LEATHER AND WARMTH SURROUNDING HER.

It took her a moment to remember where she was. In the dim lamp light, she saw Jake, his head slumped back on the couch. *His* couch.

That's when it all came flooding back. The whiskey, her embarrassing behavior, the cut on her hand, the way he'd bandaged it.

She sat up. A soft gray blanket slipped from her chest to her waist with the movement. Jake must've draped it over her. He was making this difficult. But her conflicting emotions over the brooding FBI agent would have to wait. Meredith was missing. Finding her was all that mattered.

Frustrated that they'd both fallen asleep on the job, she angrily rubbed the grogginess from her eyes. Untangling her glasses from her hair she put them back in place. The room came into sharp focus. Her eyes landed on two plates on the coffee table; one empty, the other clearly meant for her. The dull ache that lived inside her chest intensified.

He made me waffles?

Her eyes stung with emotion as she looked from the plates to the dozing FBI agent. She was grateful he was asleep or else she might've thrown her arms around his neck.

Why did he have to be so impossible?

One minute he was kicking her off the case, the next he made her waffles. She'd shared what they meant to her and he'd remembered. A lump formed in her throat. Was this his way of apologizing, or something more? She wished she had time to unpack all the questions racing through her mind. But they would have to wait. Meredith took priority.

Dana reached for the plate of waffles. She'd think clearer with a full stomach.

The meal was clearly made hours ago, but even cold it warmed her heart. She doused the waffles with maple syrup and dug in. The first bite was so sweet and delicious she moaned like she was slipping into diabetic ecstasy. Jake's head snapped up, his blue eyes open and alert.

"Sorry," Dana mumbled around a mouthful. "These were for me, right?"

He rubbed the sleep from his face. "Yeah. They're probably cold."

"They're perfect." She took another large bite then looked around for something to wash it down. Jake caught her eyeing his half empty glass of whiskey.

He passed it to her. "Whiskey and waffles might be my new favorite thing."

She took a tentative sip. The sticky-sweetness of the maple syrup and sugary dough cradled the tingling burn of the alcohol. It was the perfect combination. "Mine too."

Jake warned, "maybe go easy on the whiskey though."

Her pounding headache agreed. "Do you have any water?"

Standing from the couch, Jake stretched, popping his neck from side-to-side, before padding barefoot to the kitchen. Again, Dana was struck by how intimate it felt to be in his home. They'd tracked down a serial killer together, but somehow this was more uncomfortable. Mostly because she didn't like the feelings that kept distracting her from what was important.

She'd made her decision about Jake. They were better off as friends, and apparently occasional partners. And once Dana made up her mind, it wasn't easily changed.

The notion comforted her. She was good at making decisions. She trusted herself. She just needed to remember that. And right now, her mind was made up about Senator Scott. If they wanted to find Meredith, he needed to be their focus. She just had to convince Jake.

He returned with two glasses of water, sat down on the couch and passed her one. After drinking deeply, she set the glass down next to her empty plate on the coffee table. "I know we've been over this, but if I can prove that the Priory of Bones is real and that the Senator is involved, will you agree to question him?"

A flash of impatience crackled across Jake's face, but he rubbed it away with the last of the sleep still clinging to his shadowed eyes. "Dana, I'm not ruling the Senator out as a suspect."

"But you said—"

He held up his hands, cutting her off. "I said I wasn't going in guns blazing accusing a US Senator of kidnapping. The man is Meredith's boss. He works closely with her; I'll definitely be speaking with him to go over his statement."

"Isn't that a waste of time?"

"We go over the questions again in different ways at different times. It's a technique we use to try to confirm accuracy and consistency. If someone's lying it's an easy way to trip them up. I meant what I said. I'm good at this. I need you to trust that I'm going to do everything I can to find Meredith Kincaid."

"And the Senator?"

"I have eyes on him. And now that we know he and Meredith had a secret relationship, I have ammunition if we need it."

"Are you going to confront him about it?"

"Showing my cards isn't my style."

"But it might rattle him enough to confess."

"We have to authenticate the photos before we can use them as leverage. Without Meredith's computer, or access to the Senator's, that's not possible."

Dana exhaled, her temples throbbing with frustration.

"Trust me, I know how to handle this. With someone like Senator Scott, you only get one shot. I'm gonna make it count."

"So you've said."

"Look, it's been a long night. There's not much we can do at the moment. Why don't you try to get some rest?"

Rest was the last thing Dana wanted. She wanted to beat down every door in the city until she found her friend. Jake assured her that the D.C. police had practically done that as soon as the report was filed. She appreciated they were taking the high-profile missing person case seriously. But she still felt useless sitting around in Jake's glass tower of an apartment while Meredith was out there, potentially hurt and afraid, or worse.

Shuddering, she shoved the thought from her mind. Negative thinking bred toxicity, bogging down the mind with unproductive worries and depleting the body of precious energy. She needed to reserve hers to get to the bottom of this.

Standing, she collected her glass and the empty plates from the coffee table and carried them to the kitchen. She put everything in the dishwasher and started toward the door before she remembered Jake had driven. Swearing under her breath she pulled her phone out of her pocket scrolling for a ride share app.

"What are you doing?"

She turned back to see Jake staring at her from the couch, laptop back in front of him. "Going home to get some rest, like you said."

"It's nearly three in the morning. Just stay here."

"It's fine. I'll just order a ride."

"No. I don't need to worry about you getting into a car with a stranger at this hour. Just use my room. The sheets are clean. I haven't spent a night here all week."

She didn't want to think about the implications. It was none of her business where he spent his nights. "Don't you need to sleep?"

"There's a lot of things I need. I don't always get them." He turned back to the laptop. "Besides, I have pages of data to read through."

"Can I help?"

He turned back toward her. "I thought I made myself clear about involving you in this investigation."

"Right."

"Bedroom's down the hall. Make yourself at home," Jake called, returning to his work.

Sighing, Dana set her things down on the sideboard near the door.

Jake was right. It was late. Staying here made sense. Her place was all the way across town. Not that there'd be traffic at this hour, but still. She could catch some quick shuteye here and then be on her way to her office at first light. Plus, she liked the idea of staying close by. It meant Jake would be forced to keep her in the loop.

Dana made her way down the dark hallway. The first door she passed was open, revealing a half bath. With only one other door remaining, she grabbed the doorknob with confidence. Her poise slipped the moment she entered the master bedroom and stared at the huge king size mattress. The linens were dark gray, the headboard black and modern, just like the rest of the furniture in the well-appointed space. This room was just as devoid of personal effects as the rest of the apartment but somehow, she could feel Jake all around her.

Her eyes raked over the bed again, skin tingling at the thought of slipping beneath Jake's sheets. *Get your mind out of the gutter, Dana!*

Maybe this wasn't such a good idea after all. She didn't know how much rest she'd actually get in the massive bed that was clearly meant to be shared.

14

"JAKE!"

He startled awake at the sound of her voice. Dana stood in his living room wearing his dress shirt and a look of fear that made him sit up on the couch. "What's wrong?"

"I can't sleep." She took a tentative step toward him, and he couldn't help but let his gaze wander the length of her bare thighs. "I'm worried."

He held out a hand coaxing her forward. She moved like a doe, her legs graceful and lean, footsteps measured, timid. "It's okay."

"No, Jake. I don't think it is." She moved closer until she was standing right in front of him. She leaned in, her hands gripping his shoulders as she straddled him, settling her knees on either side of his hips. "You need to find her."

He nodded, unable to keep his hands from moving up Dana's thighs. Her skin was warm and silken, like a rose petal in a greenhouse. He wanted to caress every inch of her. His grip moved from her hips to her waist. She leaned into his touch, and he throbbed for her.

"Promise me," she begged, her hands moving to tangle in his hair. "Promise you'll find her."

"I will," he breathed, gripping her tighter as his lips ached to meet hers.

She fisted his hair and tugged hard, forcing him to look into her dark eyes. "Promise me."

"I promise."

She smiled, throwing her head back as he pulled her closer. His lips grazed her throat, and she arched her back gasping with pleasure.

Hell yes. He wanted this. He needed this. How many times had he imagined this very moment?

"Jake." Dana moaned his name in a way that made him want to come apart. She grabbed his hands and pulled them from her waist, moving them up her body to where she wanted them.

He gripped the warm column of her neck, letting his hands close around her slim throat. Her pulse pounded furiously beneath his grip. He felt his fingers tighten around the delicate skin. She gasped, and he squeezed tighter. She opened her mouth to scream, but no sound came out. But not because of his grip.

Dana's mouth was full of dirt!

She tipped her head back further, and a spider crawled out of the earth-packed cavern. Suddenly there was a blindfold blocking the fear from her eyes, and her wrists were bound.

Throwing the nightmare off of him, Jake felt the floor rise up to meet his head. His fitful tumble off the couch brought reality racing back.

He rubbed the back of his head where it had hit the floor. "It was just a dream." He needed to say it out loud to chase the last of the lingering vision away.

Christ! He needed to get a grip.

Rubbing his eyes, Jake righted himself where he'd landed on the floor. Heart still pounding, his head ached, and his face itched from the growth of stubble waging its daily war. It was the lesser of the uncomfortable itches he'd like to scratch at the moment. He should've known better than to invite Dana to stay. Knowing she was sleeping in his bed was wreaking havoc on his sexual appetite.

Jake had imagined her here so many times, but in his dreams, he hadn't been sleeping on the couch. She also hadn't turned into a creepy missing person nightmare. His attention shifted toward the dark hallway. The one that led to his bedroom. He briefly wondered if she'd locked the door.

He checked the time. There was no sense trying to go back to sleep. The watery dawn light would be reflecting off the National Mall any minute.

Jake stood up and grabbed his keys. It was going to be a shower at the gym kind of day. He kept spare clothes there for such occasions. Though he'd admit this was a first. He wasn't usually sneaking out of his own place after not sleeping with a woman. It was usually her house, and he always left satisfied.

Ignoring his hard-on, he scribbled a note to Dana and left it on the counter, then he grabbed his gym bag on the way out the door. If the early bird got the worm, then he'd be fat and happy by the time he got back home. Too bad it rarely worked out that way.

He'd yet to work a case on the Hill that hadn't gotten tied up in endless bureaucratic red tape. Involving the Kincaids wouldn't make it any easier. But then again, Jake wasn't the kind of guy to back down from a challenge.

15

Dana felt like a criminal sneaking down Jake's dark hallway. But all her stealth had been for nothing. She stood in the kitchen, reading the scribble of a note he'd left for her.

Doc, heading in early.

Lots of ground to cover.

Keep you in the loop. — Jake

She checked her watch, comparing it to the military timestamp he'd left on his note, a remnant of the soldier that still lived within him.

She'd just missed him. Sniffing the air, she found herself disappointed that he hadn't brewed any coffee. The lingering scent of baked dough still clung to the kitchen. Her stomach growled as she thought again of the waffles. It was a sweet gesture. Whether he'd meant it to or not, it meant something that he'd made them for her. No one had ever made her waffles except for her parents.

She ordered them out whenever she found them on a menu, but that wasn't the same as having someone make them specifically for her. She firmly believed that homemade food held a specific quality that couldn't be replicated on a commercial level. Homemade meals, if done right, could capture nostalgia and bring memories back to life, if only for a moment.

The perfect waffles could transport Dana back to cherished moments with her parents.

With one bite she'd been right back inside their cozy West Virginia home, the distinct smell of maple syrup in the air as they tugged on their jackets and mittens, boasting about who would have the fastest run on the toboggan. It was always her, but only because her parents let her win, their laughter the only sound as she raced through the falling snow.

She bit the inside of her cheek to chase away the memory. At this hour, even the leftover smell of waffles was too bitter a reminder. She needed to get to work. Meredith needed her.

Dana wasn't able to save her family, but maybe she could save the Kincaids. If she could apply her knowledge of death to save the living, then maybe it wouldn't have all been for nothing. The Kincaids had given her the keys to her library in the Smithsonian. It was time she repaid them.

Collecting her things, she headed out Jake's door bound for sublevel three with the belief that she could apply her field of study in a practical way. Many objected to occult studies having a place in the science-based institute, but Dana had proven time and again that her life's work was more than just a soft science. With the understanding of death, came the knowledge of life.

If she could figure out why someone would want Meredith dead, she might be able to stop it from happening.

16

Carefully brushing the dust off of the ancient leather cover with her soft bristle brush, Dana prepared to open the book. First, she secured it in the rare book cradle to protect the brittle binding from damage, then she lowered the protective lens over her lamp so as not to damage the pages with the harsh light. The book seemed to sigh when she opened it, as though it didn't want to give up the secrets held in its pages to someone who hadn't earned the right to call themselves one of the Bonesmen.

But Dana didn't need to drink blood out of a skull or wear a long, dramatic black robe. She could discern fact from fable about the elite Yale secret society just fine from the safety of her office.

There was something fitting about being buried deep below the Smithsonian while she researched the history of a hidden subculture. The Skull and Bones fraternity was one of the most widely known secret societies on the planet. Being a famous secret society was a bit of an oxymoron, but when it came to Skull and Bones, it was unavoidable.

The rumors and accusations that plagued them only served to sensationalize their exclusive status. The fact that they churned out presidents, senators and an alarmingly staggering proportion of the world's most powerful CEOs was always cannon fodder for conspiracy theories. But it was their belief about the concept of eternity that had always interested Dana.

Most of what went on inside the walls of The Tomb was known only to its members. Over their nearly two-hundred-year reign, some secrets slipped through the cracks of the Egypto-Doric style hall in New Haven, Connecticut. Put together, they pointed toward the Bonesmen's preparation to rule in this world by putting together a group of insiders nearing Illuminati proportions. Their goal: to lift members into positions of power, ensuring the preservation and success of the one percent.

The little-known Priory of Bones took it one step further. They wanted to rule not only in this life but in the next. And from what Dana had been able to discern from researching the whisperings of the secret extremists, they'd tried some pretty experimental rituals to ensure their success in the afterlife.

From human sacrifice to being reborn in a coffin washed by the blood of those who'd passed on before them, the Priory of Bones had a reputation for taking things too far. The problem was with all the power and wealth behind them, they were nearly flawless at flying under the radar. *Until now.*

If any harm came to Meredith and they were involved, Dana wouldn't stop until she brought the whole organization to its knees. The trouble was, she didn't have much to go on. The naked photos of a senator wearing a ring with a signet that may or may not be related to the murderous cult weren't a lot to go on. Especially since the phrase Memento Mori that was rumored to be etched onto the rings of members was missing, or undetectable in the photograph.

Still, even if the words were there, they wouldn't prove anything. *Remember that you have to die.* Though ominous, the Latin phrase wasn't obscure enough to imply guilt. Its use had become oversaturated thanks to pop culture's goth era and its fascination with the macabre. Dana would be just as likely to find the saying adorning the fingers of dozens of patrons in D.C.'s underground club scene.

Even knowing all of that, she couldn't shake the feeling that the ring meant something.

It was out of place on someone like the Senator. Furthermore, he was a missing woman's boss and secret lover. It was too much to ignore.

Dana let her mind wander back to the photos of Meredith and the Senator. She wished she'd grabbed them. She knew chances of getting her hands on them again were slim thanks to Jake kicking her off the case. If only she had Claire's eidetic memory.

Dana closed her eyes and let her mind fill in the details more clearly. She blocked out the way the Senator's large hands had been wrapped around Meredith's neck and focused on the ring. It was gold, a red stone set in the middle; perhaps ruby or garnet. It was a trillion cut, with a compass and square surrounding it similar to the Freemason symbol, except the masonic instruments were made up of bones. Two side emblems adorned the thick band. A snake coiled around a challis and a skull.

Her researcher's mind wrapped around the symbology and ran away with her. There were almost endless possibilities for interpreting the meaning. But the one her mind kept returning to was the compass of bones. To her, that meant mapping death. *But whose death?*

Letting her eyes slowly open, Dana prayed she'd find a way to decode the ring before it was too late.

17

THE KNOCK ON HIS DOOR WAS A WELCOME DISTRACTION FROM THE elevator music on the other end of the line reminding him how tired he was. Jake cradled the phone to his ear with his shoulder and waved his secretary in.

Margot approached his desk cheerfully, carrying a coffee and bag of pastries from his favorite coffee shop down the block.

"You are a godsend."

She grinned, her cheeks glowing at his praise. "You know, I can do that," she said, nodding to the phone pinned to his shoulder. "That's why they pay me the big bucks," she teased.

"They should." God knew she earned every penny putting up with him for the past few years.

Jake was glad when he heard that she stayed after what went down with Cramer. He wouldn't have blamed her if she'd been rattled enough to quit. A few of the other aids and secretaries in his department weren't as resilient as Margot. The wisp of a woman just kept showing up with a smile and breakfast in hand.

She set her mouthwatering gifts down on his desk. "Two sugars, just how you like it," she said, taking the lid off the coffee.

Jake stared down into the steam swirling up from the revitalizing black elixir. He preferred no sugar, but he didn't have the heart to tell Margot that. It was his own fault for saying "just the way I like it" on her first day. She'd been bringing him his coffee with two sugars ever since.

Today, he'd drink hot tar if it made him feel human again. He was running on fumes when it came to sleep and sustenance. In the moment, he truly meant it when he thanked Margot, taking a large gulp of coffee before digging into the bag. He waited until she returned to her post outside his door before he pulled out the large chocolate almond croissant and tore off a hunk. He washed the sweet, buttery goodness down with another gulp of scalding coffee.

It managed to renew his resolve enough that he stayed on hold for another six minutes before hanging up.

Jake had been on the phone all morning trying to arrange appointments with Meredith's coworkers. The problem was, they all worked in the Senate Building. Gaining access wasn't a problem thanks to his FBI clearance, it was their calendars that proved challenging. Apparently, no one on the Hill had time in their busy schedules to talk to him face-to-face.

He'd had about all he could take. Even Dana's idea of showing up at the gala was starting to appeal to him. He did his best to shake off the dead ends he was facing, but the roadblocks were starting to feel familiar.

This was nothing like the last case he worked, and yet he couldn't help the sense of déjà vu that stippled his freshly shaven features. For once, he hoped Dana was wrong. Jake had enough darkness in his life without being dragged back down into her world of demonic death and conspiracy theories.

Finding Meredith was already a needle in a haystack scenario. He could do without setting the proverbial haystack on fire. And that's what adding Dana to the mix would do. Finding a missing person in D.C. was challenging enough. Setting the town ablaze with outlandish accusations about senators involved in secret societies would only make it worse.

He knew she meant well. She couldn't help it. Her mind just worked that way. The same way his was still battle ready even though he hadn't worn a uniform in years. In Jake's case, his instincts and abilities suited him for this case. Dana's didn't. She was too close to the victim. It made her desperate to see things that weren't there.

She wasn't wrong thinking the Senator was a suspect. But not because he wore some gaudy ring or attended an Ivy League university with an infamous frat. Senator Scott was on Jake's radar because the politician was sleeping with Meredith Kincaid, and he didn't want anyone to know.

Statistically speaking, those having sexual relations with vics were more likely to be involved regarding foul play. Whether that foul play went too far ... that was what Jake needed to prove. He honestly didn't give a rat's ass if the boogie man told the Senator to do it. Murder was murder. All he needed was motive. But he had nothing.

The Senator's alibi was solid. According to his initial statement, his whereabouts could be accounted for thanks to his meticulous calendar and multiple sites retweeting his public speaking engagements. He'd also been the one to first suggest contacting the authorities after Meredith had gone MIA. Jake hadn't been the one to take the statement, but right now it was all he had to go on considering getting an audience with the Senator was impossible.

He leaned back in his chair, lacing his fingers behind his head. So far, Dana had agreed to stand down, but he knew if he didn't find a lead quickly, he wouldn't be able to keep the tenacious woman at bay for long.

He stared at the timeline he'd constructed of Meredith's last moments. They didn't add up. The Senator was the easy suspect. But he was accounted for. Perhaps it was one of the men Meredith met at the bar the last night she'd been spotted. She snapped a photo with them, shared it on Facebook, then vanished.

Had a few drinks gone too far? Sometimes the simplest explanations were the most accurate. Jake's gut resisted the idea. It didn't feel right. Meredith wasn't some nameless good-time girl no one would miss. In his experience, simple was seldom the case when dealing with people with too much power and money. Their influence complicated things.

That meant Jake had to go back to the basics. He studied the timeline again, ready to work it backwards just like he had in his Special Forces missions.

According to the details they'd gotten from her Facebook account, Meredith's last known location was a bar in Deadwood. That in itself was a mystery. Deanwood wasn't exactly the type of place girls from the Hill frequented.

The local PD had sent officers there to get statements from the staff. Jake had the report, but he preferred a more hands-on approach. Especially since the bar didn't have any security footage.

He checked the time. The bar wouldn't be open yet, but maybe he could throw the Bureau's weight around a bit and get someone down there to open the place up and let him have a look around. It wouldn't hurt to get his own statements from whomever he could wrangle in at this hour.

His energy spooled at the idea of doing something other than hitting Capitol Hill roadblocks. He could turn over his list of Meredith's co-workers to Margot. She was exceptionally skilled at getting him in front of people he wanted to question. Plus, she would do it with more patience and finesse.

Jake was just picking up the phone to ask for her assistance when Margot poked her head into his office after a quick knock.

"Just the face I wanted to see," he greeted.

Her pink lips pursed together with worry. The expression looked so foreign on her heart-shaped face that Jake stood up. "What's wrong?"

"Holt wants to see you."

Jake's fleeting energy waned. He grabbed his jacket anyway. "Tell him I'm out."

Margot slipped all the way into his office and closed the door, her large green eyes full of worry. Jake's shoulders sagged. He knew that look. It was one the new assistant director instilled in everyone he stood in front of. "He's standing out there, isn't he?"

She nodded and swallowed thickly.

Today just keeps getting better.

"I'm sorry. He ambushed me. I told him you'd been on the phone all morning pertaining to the case, and I wasn't sure what your schedule was like, but ..."

But he didn't care. She didn't have to finish her sentence. Holt had a reputation for impatience. "It's fine, Margot. I'm going to forward you a list of contacts. Can you get me on their schedules?"

"Right away."

Sitting back down, it only took a few strokes of his keys to send Margot everything she'd need. Jake slipped his jacket over his broad shoulders as he made his way around his desk. He wished it was his flak vest or any kind of body armor that might deflect Holt's brand of aggressive leadership.

Jake was not in the mood for the assistant director's trial by fire bullshit. He'd earned his stripes. He had the scars to prove it. What he needed was room to do his job. Squaring his shoulders, he remembered who he was. He didn't back down from a fight. And if he had to go toe-to-toe with his new boss to get off the short leash Holt was trying to keep him on, then so be it.

18

It wasn't even noon and Jake was unwrapping his fifth piece of cinnamon gum. Things weren't going as planned. His tête-à-tête with Holt was turning into more of a dressing down than a conversation. It didn't help that once again, Dana was keeping things from him. Yet here he was defending her.

"I don't want her on the case either," Jake argued with the surly assistant director, "but if Archer Kincaid is insisting it sounds like our hands are tied."

"Maybe he wouldn't be if you'd handled this properly. Why hasn't anyone taken Kincaid's statement?"

"I tried. He was out of town. Trying to get cooperation from the high and mighty on the Hill has been a bitch. I'm getting stonewalled left and right."

Holt leaned closer, his coffee breath pungent. "You're a goddamn FBI agent, Shepard. Get the job done or I'll find someone else who will."

"Yes, sir." Jake barely managed to get the words through his clenched jaw.

"And I don't care how rich Kincaid is. He doesn't make the rules here. I do. Your Witch Doctor has no business in this missing person case."

"With all due respect, sir, her insight might be valuable. She's good at thinking outside the box. I wouldn't have been able to bring Cramer down without her."

"Cramer was a serial killer."

"And without Dr. Gray, he'd still be working in this building. Sitting in your new office."

Holt's dark eyes flashed with anger, but Jake knew he'd gotten his point across. "Fine, but she's your responsibility. Don't fuck this up, Shepard. One more strike and your next vacation will be permanent."

Jake watched his boss march away, replaying the unpleasant conversation they'd had in the hallway for everyone to overhear.

Nothing like having his shortcomings publicly broadcast through the building. But that was what happened when an enraged father and cabinet member called the assistant director and requested a Smithsonian librarian be assigned to the case because the FBI wasn't doing its job.

For a heartbeat, Jake wondered if he even cared about keeping his job. But then Meredith's face flashed in his mind along with all the other undeserving victims who crossed his desk during his time with the Bureau.

He couldn't go out like this. Jake didn't leave men in the field, and that's what getting kicked off this case would feel like. Even back in his Special Forces days, he'd always brought his team home. Not all of them had made it of their own volition, but he'd gotten them stateside, one way or another.

He thought of Ramirez making that long flight in a pine box. Jake's jaw flexed with anger. He'd finish this, for Ramirez, for all the fallen. Because he was still here, and that made it his duty.

19

"WHAT HAVE YOU GOTTEN YOURSELF INTO?" CLAIRE ASKED, PEERING OVER Dana's shoulder. "Are we hosting an Illuminati exhibit I don't know about?"

If Dana hadn't grown accustomed to her intern sneaking up on her, she might've been frightened by the sudden appearance of the pale girl dressed in black from head-to-toe. Claire moved like a cat, slinking soundlessly in and out of the occult library when she wasn't busy with classes at Georgetown. After more than two years together, Dana was used to Claire's ways.

"No. I'm working a case with Shepard."

Claire's pale eyes gleamed with interest. "I knew we'd drag him over to the dark side eventually."

"Not quite. It's a missing person case."

Claire blinked in brief confusion, but she was a bright girl, it didn't take her long to put two and two together. She gasped. "You're working on Meredith Kincaid's disappearance?"

Dana nodded.

"It's all over the news."

Panic pounded through Dana's heart as she imagined the worst. If those photos had gotten out ... Before her mind could run away with her, Claire thrust her cell phone into Dana's hand. "They're calling her the Missing Girl on the Hill."

Dana exhaled. They'd be calling her a lot worse if those photos got out.

"Didn't you know her?" Claire asked.

"Yes. She actually had your job once upon a time."

Claire gave a visible shiver. "That's frightening."

"How do you mean?"

"First a serial killer comes after you. Now someone abducts Meredith. It's like this place is cursed or something."

Claire's words were a sledgehammer to Dana's resolve. The darkness she did her best to keep at bay came flooding in from the tortured corners of her mind. She couldn't blame Claire for her honesty. Not when Dana had the same thoughts herself. But in her mind, it wasn't the Smithsonian that was cursed. It was Dana.

Death shadowed her.

She used to think it was just her line of work. But maybe all these years of studying death had taken its toll, rubbed off somehow, provoking the darkness to reciprocate. She knew the notion was a bit narcissistic, but it was hard to ignore that everyone she loved ended up dead.

Meredith is not dead. And she was going to do everything in her power to make sure it stayed that way.

Satisfied there weren't any leaked photos in the headlines, she handed the phone back to Claire and flipped open a notebook where she'd done her best to sketch the Senator's ring from memory. "Does this look familiar to you?"

Claire moved closer and studied the drawing. "Looks like a mashup of Skull and Bones and Freemason symbology."

"Exactly. Have you heard of the Priory of Bones?"

Claire's clear blue eyes widened behind her cat eye lenses. "Only in a fictional sense. Their existence has yet to be proven."

"You know as well as I do that's not a reason to discount their validity." Dana cringed at the bite to her tone. "Sorry. Shepard's skepticism must be getting to me."

"Speaking of. Where is tall, dark and sexy?"

Claire was always coming up with clever new ways to refer to Jake. Dana ignored the inappropriate nickname. "We're working our own angles on this one."

Claire crossed her arms. "You're not officially on the case, are you?"

"Not yet, but if you help me find something Shepard can't ignore, he'll have no choice but to give me access."

"Do you really think that's such a good idea after last time?"

The timid way in which Claire broached the subject made Dana bite her tongue. "This isn't like what happened with Cramer."

"How can you be sure? You're looking into a society so secret that their very existence can't be confirmed."

"Then help me confirm it. It'd be one hell of a discovery for your dissertation."

The twinkle was back in Claire's eyes. "I'd say! The Priory of Bones is the holy grail of secret societies. Proving its existence would be earth shattering."

"So are you in?"

Claire grinned. "You know I am. What have you got so far?"

Dana poured over the notes she'd compiled as she filled Claire in on what she'd found, which wasn't much. After bringing her up to speed on everything she and Jake discovered at the Kincaid's yesterday and during their all-nighter, she started in on the angle she was working today. "I've pulled everything I could find on Skull and Bones to see if anything stood out and—"

Claire caught Dana's bandaged hand as she reached for a ledger. "What happened to your hand?"

"I cut it."

"On what?"

"A whiskey glass."

"Since when do you drink whiskey?"

Dana shrugged. "It's all Jake had at his place."

"Wait. You were at Jake Shepard's home?"

"Yes."

Claire looked like a kettle about to whistle. All at once she erupted, spewing questions faster than Dana could answer. "Holy hell! What's it like? Does it look like the bat cave? Did you see his bedroom? I bet he has kinky stuff in there. Did you see anything kinky?"

"Claire! A woman is missing. I need you to focus."

"Fine, but when we find her, you're going to spill. I need details!"

Dana decided it was best not to tell her there were no details to spill. Intense moments maybe, but nothing had come of them. She knew better than to let anything happen between her and Jake. Not that he even wanted that. He'd probably come to the same conclusion as Claire. Getting too close to Dana proved hazardous to one's health.

She ignored the tightness in her chest and got back to work. "The only connection I've been able to find is that the senator Meredith worked for went to Yale, but I don't know for sure that he was tapped by the Bonesmen."

"Where did Meredith go to school?"

"Georgetown."

"Was she in any sororities or secret fraternal orders?"

"None I know of. She graduated with a political science degree so she could follow in her father's footsteps. He's the President's chief economic advisor."

Claire let a low whistle slip between her teeth. "I wouldn't want that job." She paused. "Has anyone explored the idea that she was taken to leverage her father?"

Dana loved the way Claire's mind worked. It was wired much the way hers was, to see behind the veil of normalcy to the dark beating heart of things. "Jake said the FBI looked into it, but there's been no ransom demand. They're confident this isn't a kidnapping. And I know Meredith. She's too considerate to run off without at least letting her family know."

Claire's gaze turned icy. "Sometimes we don't know people as well as we might think."

Dana shook her head. "Meredith loves her family. They mean everything to her."

Her cool demeanor thawed, and Claire pulled a chair up to Dana's desk. "So that leaves her boss?"

"There are no other leads. Shepard said significant others are prime suspects."

"He thinks it's the Senator, too?"

"Not exactly. But with Meredith and the Senator having a secret affair, coupled with the fact that he's a Priory of Bones member ..."

"Allegedly," Claire interrupted.

"Allegedly." Dana resisted her urge to tell Claire she was starting to sound like Shepard. The girl would probably take it as a compliment. "I just have this feeling it's him. If you'd seen the photos, and the way Mere hid them. He's behind this."

"So how do we prove it?"

"I've been pouring over the Skull and Bones records trying to find Senator Scott. It's not easy since they give all their members nicknames."

"How are you going to find him if he's using a nickname?"

"Being a Bonesmen is a pledge you take for life. If he's in the Order, he'll still be using his nickname, especially if he's up to something he doesn't want his constituents to know about."

Claire grinned. "It's like cracking a code."

"Exactly. Find the code. Find the path."

DANA PUSHED her readers into her thick hair and rubbed her eyes, not sure how long she'd been rereading the same line. Her sleepless night was catching up with her. Claire, on the other hand, looked like she could go for hours. She was sitting cross-legged in her cozy corner chair hunched over another copy of the *Yale Daily News*.

The dusty old newspapers held the only public records of Skull and Bones members. The trouble was, the Bonesmen soon realized they benefited from their anonymity and stopped publicizing new members in 1982. After that, any names published were just speculation.

Senator Scott was in his early fifties. That put him right on the cusp of where the trail would run dry.

"Any luck?" Dana asked.

"No. But I've read enough names of conquerors and kings for an eternity. These guys are pretty full of themselves, huh?"

"It's common practice in fraternal orders to name members after past rulers."

"Well, it's unimaginative. Caesar, Charles, Constantine, Charlemagne . . ."

Something registered in Dana's mind, a memory beyond her reach. "Say that again."

"The Bonesmen are unimaginative."

"No, the names."

"Caesar, Charles, Constantine, Charlemagne."

"Charlemagne!" Dana felt as though she'd grabbed hold of a lightning bolt. "Charli Maine! That's the name Meredith used for her Facebook alias."

"What does it mean?"

Dana didn't know, but she had a feeling whatever it was, wasn't good. The former King of Franks was a known Bonesmen alias, one that had been passed down for generations. Meredith wasn't using it as an alias by accident. Had she found out her boss was in the Priory of Bones? Was she trying to bring him down?

Mere, what did you get yourself into this time?

"What do we do?" Claire asked.

"We need to call Jake."

"And tell him what? Meredith Kincaid was abducted by the Skull and Bones?"

"You think my daughter was abducted by a secret society?"

Both women jumped at the sound of the deep male voice in the room. Claire whirled around first, her mouth falling open. Dana was just as shocked but somehow found her voice. "Mr. Kincaid. What are you doing here?"

"I'm trying to find my daughter. I was under the impression that's what you were doing, but now I'm not so sure."

"Archer, that's exactly what I'm doing."

He stormed closer. "Meredith is missing here." He pointed to the floor. “In the real world. If you’re going to find her you need to pull your head out of your books.”

“You don’t understand. I—”

“No, you don’t understand. I went to bat for you. I just got off the phone with the FBI, insisting you be involved in the case because you know Meredith better than anyone.” He paused to run a hand through his graying temple. “But I guess that was a long time ago.”

Dana’s heart constricted. “I can still help.”

“I’m not sure you can.”

20

"Archer, please let me explain."

Jake did a double take when he walked out of the elevator onto Dana's library floor to see her chasing after Archer Kincaid.

He hadn't been prepared for the scene, but he rolled with it. One bird, two stones. It worked for him. Straightening his tie, he entered the fray.

"Archer Kincaid." Jake blocked the man's path to the elevator. "Just the man I want to see."

Kincaid crossed his arms over his thin chest. "And you are?"

Dana jogged up behind him. "Jake, what are you doing here?"

Jake kept his eyes on Kincaid. "Agent Shepard, FBI." He flashed his badge. "Do you have a minute?"

"I have all the time in the world, but do you know who doesn't? My daughter. She's still missing, and you people aren't doing anything about it."

"Let's see if we can change that." Jake held out his arm, gesturing toward the bank of unoccupied library tables.

Dana looked relieved when Kincaid yielded. But Jake wasn't doing this for her. There was a missing woman out there, and it was his job to find her. He pulled out a chair. The legs screeched against the floor, echoing through the tomb-like space.

It didn't matter how many times Jake came down here, he'd never be comfortable being underground. Ignoring his mental image of the walls closing in on him, he sat down and popped another piece of cinnamon gum in his mouth. His distraction technique barely deluded the crushing feeling of claustrophobia that made his skin break out in a thin sheen of sweat, but he'd dealt with worse.

Once Kincaid was seated, Jake dove into his usual line of questioning. "Where were you when your daughter went missing, Mr. Kincaid?"

"I was in New York at the UN budget meeting. But you already know that since you spoke to my secretary."

Jake ignored the older man's agitation. "When was the last time you saw your daughter?"

Kincaid's eyes began to mist. "I don't know. I travel a lot. I'm not able to be around as much as I should."

Dana, who'd taken the seat next to Kincaid, reached out and took his hand. "Archer, this isn't your fault."

If Dana wanted to play good cop, so be it, but Jake didn't have time to coddle the man. "What about the last time you spoke to her?"

"That was two weeks ago. She called me on my birthday."

Jake pulled out his notebook and jotted down the date to add to his timeline. "Did anything about the conversation seem out of character?"

"No. She wished me a happy birthday. We talked about making plans to have dinner so we could catch up. She got called away before we could pick a date."

"Called away?"

"Warren was asking her something, and she said she had to go."

"Warren Scott? The Senator?"

"Yes."

"How well do you know Senator Scott?"

"Well enough. Meredith's worked for him for a while now."

"Do the two of you have a working relationship?"

"Not really. Our paths rarely cross professionally."

"What about unprofessionally?"

"D.C.'s not that big. We run into each other from time to time. Why? Do you think he's involved in Meredith's disappearance?"

"There's no evidence to support that."

"That's not what Dr. Gray says."

Taking his frustration out on his gum, Jake spoke. "Dr. Gray's theories are speculative at best."

"At least she has a theory. What have you got?"

"We're following the proper procedures."

"Well, your procedures aren't getting you anywhere. Meredith has disappeared. She hasn't touched her phone, her money—"

"Her money? You have access to her financial statements?"

"Of course. Her money is my money. Every asset in her name has come from the Trust my wife and I have created for our heirs. I keep track of it."

Jake scribbled down another note. "I'm going to need a copy of the Trust. And you'll need to do an inventory of assets to make sure nothing is missing."

"Meredith didn't run away, Agent Shepard. She was taken."

"Have you received a ransom request I don't know about?"

"No."

"Then what makes you say she was taken?"

"I know my daughter. She loves her life. She wouldn't run away from it. From us. I need assurance that you're taking this seriously."

"I can assure you, Mr. Kincaid, your daughter's case is being taken seriously. I'm working the proper channels. You'll be notified the moment I have anything for you. In the meantime, get me an inventory of assets and access to your Trust."

"And what about Warren?"

"Senator Scott has already given his statement."

"So that's it? You're not going to follow up?"

"The Senator's a busy man."

"Make him find the time! You're the FBI for Christ's sake. Do something."

Jake had about enough of being spoken to like a disobedient dog for one day. It was one of the things he hated most about being a civilian.

No one ever spoke to him like that with his M4 strapped across his chest. He wished he could step up to Kincaid and give the entitled politician a piece of his mind, but Jake was already in enough hot water.

Even though the guy was probably an arrogant prick on a good day, he decided to cut him some slack on account that his daughter was missing. He understood the very real grip of grief. It made him do things he wasn't proud of. Kincaid got a pass. For now.

But Dana couldn't leave well enough alone. As soon as her mouth opened Jake braced himself. "Do you still want me to assist with the case?"

Kincaid stood, seeming to consider for a moment before answering. "Yes, but not so you can dig into wild theories about secret societies. I want you involved because you and my daughter were close once. Go to the places she was fond of. Look for clues."

Jake held in a laugh. This wasn't a nine-year-old missing from a sleepover. They weren't going to find Meredith hiding out in some treehouse. But if Kincaid's warning put a stop to Dana hounding him about secret societies, he was all for it.

Dana spoke up. "The IWP Gala is tonight. Meredith planned on attending. It might be a good idea to go and speak to the people she would've interacted with."

"I disagree," Jake interrupted. "Adding too many people will dilute our suspect pool. Not to mention anything gathered at a function like that will be hearsay."

"Considering you have no suspects I'll take the risk." Kincaid turned to Dana. "I'd attend myself, but I have a standing appointment with the President. I'll have two tickets sent over and get you and Shepard on the guest list." He glared at Jake. "Report back to me afterward."

Report back to me? Who the hell does this guy think he is?

Jake was in charge of this investigation, not Archer Kincaid. He might own half the town, but if he thought Jake was someone he could push around with the weight of his fortune, he was sorely mistaken.

"The tickets aren't necessary. We have a protocol in place for a reason. Our methods work. They just require time and patience."

"Both of which are running out, Agent Shepard." Kincaid stepped up toe-to-toe with him despite Jake having roughly twelve inches, and sixty pounds on the guy. "Find my daughter."

The threat actually earned Kincaid more respect than fear from Jake's perspective. He understood a father's conviction. But Jake didn't need to be threatened to do his job. He lived by his own moral compass. Helping those who couldn't help themselves was his true north.

Meredith Kincaid didn't seem to fit the bill. But he'd give her the same respect as everyone else. Innocent until proven guilty.

21

As soon as the elevator doors closed on Archer Kincaid, Dana geared herself up for a fight. She knew Jake wouldn't let her mention of the gala slide. Despite what he thought, she wasn't trying to be underhanded. She just wanted to find Meredith. And theories or not, a room full of D.C.'s rich and powerful was a good place to start.

"Jake—"

He held up his hands. "I don't need to hear your excuses. By now I should know you do whatever the hell you want no matter what I say."

"It's not like that."

"Isn't it? You wanted on the case. My boss rips me a new one, and you're on the case, thanks to your pal Kincaid."

"I didn't ask him to call the FBI, Jake!"

"It doesn't matter. You got your wish. And it looks like you're going to the gala too so congrats. But if it's not too much trouble, can you try not to fuck it up badly enough that I lose my job? Because, oh yeah, that's on the line thanks to you."

Dana recoiled like she'd been slapped. She knew he was pissed, but she'd never seen him lash out like this before. "How is that my fault?"

"Because according to my boss, you're my responsibility. If you piss off a US Senator and whoever else tickles your fancy at the gala, it's my ass."

"Then come with me," she pleaded. "Help me figure out what's gossip and what's something we can use to find Meredith."

"I'd love to play dress up, but I have actual work to do."

He started to storm off but stopped short, spun around and marched back. "Here! These have been stabbing me in the leg all day. Don't leave things on my nightstand."

Jake grabbed Dana's hand and dumped a pair of emerald studs into her palm. For a moment he lingered on the bandage on her hand, but it did little to stifle the anger crackling in his fierce blue eyes. Without another word he turned around and headed toward the elevator.

She called after him. "Where are you going?"

"To do my job."

Claire was immediately by Dana's side once Jake was on the elevator. "You slept with Sergeant Sexy?!"

"No! Not that it's any of your business."

"But your earrings. Jake said you left them on his nightstand. As in, you spent the night."

"I did. We were working on the case. I fell asleep. Nothing happened."

"That explains his mood," Claire mumbled.

Dana glared at her. Thankfully her intern had the good sense to back down. Dana was in no mood to talk about what didn't happen between her and Jake last night. She was too pissed about what had just gone down here, and in front of Archer Kincaid, no less! "I can't believe Jake's blaming me for making him look bad."

"He sort of has a point."

"What?"

"You two always do this. You're like oil and water when you disagree. I like it better when you're on the same side."

"We are on the same side."

"Are you sure about that?"

Dana knew Jake was dedicated to finding Meredith. They just had different methods. "Yes, but he's going about it wrong. Like coming down here and basically calling my work irrelevant in front of the man who pays my salary."

"I thought our grant was federally funded?"

"It is, but Archer Kincaid's foundation started this program. And he's in charge of the congressional budget. Telling him all we do here is pedal conspiracy is a giant slap in the face."

Claire's milky white complexion paled to nearly translucent. "Do you think he'll pull the funding?"

"I doubt he's concerned about that right now." Dana wasn't either. All that mattered was finding Meredith. It wouldn't matter what Archer decided. There was no way Dana could keep walking these halls if she couldn't find Mere. They'd made too many memories here, and Dana had enough ghosts in her life already. "Call up to the front desk for me," she instructed. "I want to make sure I'm notified the moment the courier arrives with the gala tickets."

"I thought Jake said not to go."

"I make my own decisions." She grabbed her purse and fished out her wallet, handing a credit card to Claire.

"What's this for?"

"I need a dress."

Claire's eyes lit up. "I get to pick it out?"

"I don't have time to. The event is black tie. I need something conservative. Saks has my sizing."

Claire made a gagging sound.

"Is there something wrong with Saks?"

"What isn't wrong with Saks? Conforming to conservative stereotypes so corporate America can tick the box they're comfortable with? No thanks."

Dana crossed her arms. "I'm not making a fashion statement. I'm trying to find my friend." She looked down at the outfit she'd been wearing since yesterday—a soft blue button down and a pair of practical black trousers she'd purchased at Saks. She decided to leave that part out. "I can't go in this. Just find me something appropriate, please."

"Don't worry. I've got you covered. But your dress is not coming from Saks."

Dana watched Claire leave, mildly concerned the girl would come back with combat boots and a black trench coat. But that was the least of her worries. Dana would show up dressed as Neo if it would help find Meredith. Thankfully she had too much work to do to obsess about her wardrobe.

She was determined to find the Senator's ties to Skull and Bones before the gala. She didn't care what the others thought. He wasn't wearing a ring like that by mistake. He was involved in something sinister; she could feel it in her bones. And this might be her only chance to get near him.

22

THE MOMENT THE STEEL DOORS OPENED, AND THE ELEVATOR DEPOSITED him on ground level, Jake regretted his harsh tone. There was just something about being underground that put him on edge. He was calmer when he could see the sky above him, breathe in fresh air. But that was no excuse for how he'd spoken to Dana.

The woman just had a way of getting under his skin.

He didn't even hate the idea of having her on the case. He'd been the one to ask for her help in the first place. But that was before he knew how close she was to the vic. He didn't want to put her through that again.

It wasn't a good idea. For either of them. There were too many emotions involved to think clearly.

Dana had a deep understanding of the wickedness of the world and her instincts were sharp, but this time she was off base. If Jake could get her to drop her outrageous theories and refocus on the physical evidence, that beautiful mind of hers just might prove useful. But right now, he didn't have any evidence to go on.

He aimed to fix that. Without involving Dana if he could help it.

She could be pissed at him now. He'd make it up to her later. Pissed was better off than dead.

The last case they'd worked had rattled Jake more than he'd been willing to admit. Seeing Dana in the clutches of a serial killer still haunted him. But his nightmare last night ... it was something else. Something worse.

He knew it wasn't real, but it felt like a bad omen. And the best way to keep it from coming true was to keep Dana as far away from this case as possible.

He was probably being paranoid, but in the world of politics, that was the only way to survive. One thing Jake knew about politicians; they always had a scapegoat. If things went south with the Kincaid case, he'd be more comfortable if he was the only one in the crosshairs.

It took him thirty minutes to cover the six miles to Deanwood thanks to the D.C. traffic. He'd shaved off about three minutes by getting off Pennsylvania Ave to cut through Lincoln Park, but he paid for the shortcut by getting stuck on the Whitney, thanks to a detour on the northbound ramp to 295.

By the time he pulled up to Ruby's Slipper, his mood was as foul as the weather.

Spring was fickle in the Nation's Capital. It came in like a lamb, luring citizens into the false hope that winter was gone. But the roaring rain pelting his windshield reminded him that the lion of winter hadn't fully released its icy grip just yet.

Sleet and late frosts struck when least expected, devastating the weak seedlings that had begun to reach up from the earth.

Growing up in Nevada he'd heard all kinds of theories about the unexpected weather. Folklores from the reservations, superstitious soldiers spinning yarns, his uncle's idioms on the Ides of March. All Jake knew for sure was D.C.'s consistently inconsistent weather pattern made him miss Florida.

"I should've stayed in the Keys," he muttered. Sitting in the warmth of his SUV a few minutes longer, he observed the area, but no one was lurking around in the nasty weather. A school bus lumbered by, but otherwise the streets were dead.

Jake ran across the street only to be met with a locked door. He pounded on the red door as rain ran into his collar and down his back, soaking him through.

It hadn't rained once the whole time he was in Key West.

If he closed his eyes, he could still picture it; his favorite hole in the wall on the wharf. The place looked more shipwreck than bar. But it'd stood the test of time, surviving hurricanes, pirates and pandemics.

Perhaps that's why Jake had gravitated there. The place was resilient, like him.

Dollar bills covered every available surface; greetings, wishes and dares written on each one. It wasn't shiny or popular. It didn't attract the tourist crowd. But the beer was cheap and ice cold, and no one knew who he was. He didn't have to be FBI or ex-Army. He didn't have to peer into the dark tunnel of his past or add more shadows by chasing down criminals. He could just be.

He missed the gruff bartender sporting tattoos from ears-to-elbows asking him, "what'll it be?" He missed the sun-faded tank tops, the smell of sunblock and salt air. Hell, he even missed the humidity. But the whole time he'd been there, he'd missed her more.

Who leaves paradise for a pain in the ass Witch Doctor?

"Idiot," Jake chastised himself, banging harder on the locked door. Did he really think finding her friend would change things between them? He let his mind wonder if there was still time to catch a flight to Miami. He could be back in the Keys for sunset if he left now.

The tumble of the lock brought Jake back to reality. The door opened a crack and he peered into the face of a man in his early thirties who looked like he'd gotten even less sleep than Jake.

He flashed his badge. "Agent Shepard, FBI."

The guy opened the door further. "I already spoke to the police."

"And now you're gonna speak to me." Jake muscled his way past the baggy-eyed man into the warmth of the club.

Maybe warmth wasn't the right word. Looking around the place left little to feel cozy about. It reminded Jake of an old movie theater from his youth. It was fine when the lights were off, but when they came on at the end of a film, he saw things he wished he hadn't.

The smell inside didn't help either. It was equal parts dirty dish towel and frat house after a kegger. The scent permeated every surface and invaded his senses. At first glance, it wasn't the kind of place he'd expect to find someone like Meredith Kincaid.

Someone who'd grown up surrounded by so much affluence would feel more comfortable in the downtown D.C. scene, with the rest of the Capitol Hill crowd. A few of the less discreet politicians were known for slumming it on this side of town. But that was only because it was easier to get away with debauchery when there wasn't a paper trail.

Jake hadn't missed the handwritten cash only signs posted around the bar. He wouldn't have known Meredith was ever here if it weren't for her tagging the place in her Facebook post. It wouldn't show up on her financial records thanks to the money laundering that probably went on here. But that wasn't Jake's department.

Deanwood was a rough neighborhood. Gang bangers ran most of the block. That meant people tended to turn a blind eye to less violent things like prostitution. A John ran a far less likely chance of getting caught with his pants down here.

Dana's words itched in the back of Jake's mind. One look at the Senator's ring and she'd connected secret societies to sex trade in a single bound. Jake glanced around the seedy club, taking in the stripper pole and the sign over a red door in the corner. *Private Rooms.* As in plural.

This place was definitely the gateway to some sinister shit. But again, sex crimes weren't his division. He was here to find a missing woman.

So what the hell was Meredith Kincaid doing here?

It was highly unlikely she was mixed up in human trafficking. D.C. debutants weren't the typical target. Jake faced the man who'd opened the door. "You the owner?"

"If I owned this shithole, I wouldn't have to drag my ass outta bed after working a double to open up for another cop."

"I'm FBI," Jake clarified.

"So you said."

"What's your name?"

"Pete."

"Got a last name, Pete?"

"It's Turner."

Jake jotted that down, then pulled a photo up on his phone. "You seen this girl?"

"Like I already told the cops, I've seen her around, but I don't know her or nothing."

"Do you know her name?"

"Everyone does now. She's the Missing Girl on the Hill. Her face is plastered all over the news. She's a Kincaid."

It spoke volumes that even out here in Deanwood, that name held meaning.

"Kinda hard to believe it though." Pete's black, wooly eyebrows arched in disbelief. "I mean, what's a girl like her doing all the way out here?"

"That's what I'm trying to find out. You said you'd seen her around. How often we talking?"

Pete shrugged. "Dunno. She's not a regular or nothing, but she's been in a time or two. A face like hers you remember."

"She looks different than other girls that come into the club?"

"You're joking, right?" Pete snorted a laugh. "Girls don't really come to Ruby's."

"No?"

Pete swallowed, suddenly looking uncomfortable.

"Pete, I'm not here to stir up trouble for you or anyone who works here. I just want to find Meredith Kincaid. Anything you can tell me would help."

"That's what you guys always say," Pete muttered.

Jake could feel the bartender's cooperation slipping. He pulled up the Facebook photo of Meredith at the club and held it up, pointing to the date. "Were you working here that night?"

"I'm here every night."

"And you remember seeing Meredith?"

"Sure."

"Was she here with anyone?"

"Dunno. It was busy."

"But you remember seeing her?"

"That hot pink dress?" Pete's thick black eyebrows knitted together. "Hell yeah, I remember seeing her. Tits half hanging out like that. It ain't easy to forget."

Jake could just make out a hint of pink fabric in the photograph. Meredith's face and martini took up most of the frame. The pink tinged liquid in the clear glass magnified her cleavage. The caption, *worth the wait*, with a lipstick emoji was all he had to go on. And if Pete didn't want to give him more, it wasn't enough. Jake zoomed out, showing Pete the photo again. This time the two men she was with were partially visible.

"What about them? Know who they are?"

Pete shook his head. "Like I said, I was busy."

"You remember anything else about that night?"

"I poured her a cosmo."

Jake jotted that down. "Who else was working? I'd like to speak to them."

"Bobby and Franko. They come in at six."

"Any way you can get them here now?"

"Not 'less you're gonna pay 'em. They both got other jobs. Besides, you're wasting your time. They already gave their statements to the police."

"Yeah. I read the report."

"So whatcha doing here?"

"My job." To Jake, seeing was believing. He didn't like taking others' words for things he could experience himself. He preferred looking through his own lens. "What about the girls?"

"The girls ain't gonna talk to you."

"Why's that?"

"They don't talk to the law if they wanna work here."

"I'm not a cop. I don't care what they're getting paid for or if they're undocumented. I'm not gonna call ICE. I'm just trying to find a missing woman."

"How do you even know she's missing? Maybe she's on a yacht somewhere sipping Dom."

"She's not."

Pete shrugged.

"You ever serve any senators or other political types here?"

Pete's eyebrows danced with laughter. "Sure. All the time. The Queen of England was here just last week."

Jake flipped his notebook shut and slipped it into his pocket. It was obvious he wasn't getting anything else useful from Pete, and he didn't have time to let some overworked bartender bust his balls. His answers were consistent with the statement he gave the police. It was time to move on. Unless ... "Mind if I take a look around?"

Pete crossed his tattooed arms. "You got a warrant?"

"No."

"Then, yeah. I mind."

It was the response Jake had expected, but it was worth a try. Realizing he was at yet another dead end, he pulled a card from his wallet and slipped it across the sticky black bar top. "If you remember anything, give me a call."

"I won't," Pete called as Jake headed back toward the door.

Windshield wipers squeaking furiously, Jake drove back toward the city. He'd forgotten how uncooperative people were when missing person cases weren't about children. A lost kid could bring a neighborhood together. A lost woman shut mouths tighter than Fort Knox. People figured odds were a missing woman would turn up one way or another. And that was the problem. No one wanted to be implicated if she ended up in a body bag.

Jake's mind churned during the bumper-to-bumper drive back into the city. Something about this case was starting to feel off. People like Meredith Kincaid didn't frequent Deanwood without reason. But so far, Jake couldn't find one. Pete hadn't seen any senator types there so unless Meredith had a guy on that side of the tracks too, Jake wasn't sure why a woman of Meredith's means would voluntarily drive to one of the most dangerous areas of D.C.

Holt and Kincaid had little faith Jake could solve this on his own. But he was determined to prove them wrong. He'd made a career of doing the impossible. He just needed a new perspective.

He heard his uncle's voice in his mind. *When the trail runs cold, go back to the source.*

He hated to admit it, but maybe Dana was right about the gala. With no other leads, it seemed foolish to let his pride keep him from gaining some insight.

Laying on the horn, Jake switched lanes and pulled onto the shoulder. He turned on his blue and reds and accelerated. Glancing at the dash clock, he gunned it. This was going to take more than groveling. He needed the traffic gods on his side if he was going to get back in Dana's good graces in time for tonight. Another thought occurred to him as the stand-still traffic rushed by in a blur. He hit the speed dial button programmed on his dash screen.

As soon as the call connected, Jake cut off Margot's cheery greeting. "Any chance you got me any of those meetings I wanted today?"

"No, I'm sorry. I tried, but the best I could do was next week. Everyone's swamped with the special elections coming up."

"Yeah, I got the same spiel."

"I'm sorry to have let you down."

"Make it up to me?"

"How?"

"If you can get me a tux in the next thirty minutes, I might not need those meetings."

"Absolutely. I can have one sent up to your office."

"Actually, I need it delivered to Dr. Gray's office at the Smithsonian. The address is—"

"I have the address," Margot insisted, her voice unusually clipped.

"Thanks. You're a lifesaver, Margot."

"You're the lifesaver, Agent Shepard. I just try not to get in the way." The warmth he was used to returned to her voice. "Is there anything else I can do for you?"

"Actually, yes. Can you send over a dress with the tux?"

"A dress?"

"For Dr. Gray. Black tie appropriate. But something that hides the goods. I don't need her turning heads tonight." If they were going to do this, they needed to fly under the radar.

Margot cleared her throat. “Right away, Agent Shepard.”

“Oh and Margot, make it something pricey. I need to win her over.”

The call disconnected.

Jake ignored Margot’s abrupt departure. He had more important things to worry about, like eating enough humble pie to get Dana to go along with his plan. He hoped sending over a fancy dress would help buy him some cooperation. Dana had been keen on going to the gala from the moment she found out about it. Getting her on board wouldn’t be the issue, it was getting her to do things his way that proved challenging.

23

"You've got to be kidding!"

Dana looked at her reflection in the bathroom mirror. Her emerald studs sparkled in her ears, but everything else about her outfit was a disaster. Claire had gone rogue. Dana should've known better than to put her fashion in the fate of someone who dressed like a goth princess. The dress Claire brought back was black, but otherwise it didn't meet any of Dana's requests. There was no way she was wearing a short, backless lace dress with a neckline that plunged to her navel out in public, let alone to a black tie gala.

"Isn't it perfect?" Claire called from the other side of the door.

"It's something," Dana muttered.

"Come out. I want to see you in it."

Dana didn't want to hurt Claire's feelings. She'd come out of her shell a lot in the past few months. She stepped up after the shooting and helped Dana every step of the way with her recovery. It bonded them in a way their work never could. Telling Claire that she wasn't a fan of her fashion sense would reverse all that progress. "Um, I'm not sure it's going to work."

"What do you mean?"

Thinking on her feet, Dana twisted around and grabbed a fist full of lace, tearing it. The low-cut back was now only inches from the slit in the hem, exposing her plain white underwear for the world to see. Dana unlocked the door and opened it a crack. "There's a slight problem."

She turned to show Claire the tear. Gasping, her intern shoved the door open and rushed into the large bathroom. She gawked at the torn lace. "What happened?"

"It ripped when I was trying it on. It's a bit tight."

"That's the style," Claire whined. "Maybe we can fix it. We just need a needle and thread."

"I'm sure I have something at home I can wear. If I leave now, I'll have enough time to change. Help me with the zipper."

Claire tugged on the zipper under Dana's arm. "It's stuck."

Dana spun toward the mirror and gave it a try. It still didn't budge.

Claire looked horror struck. "What do we do?"

Dana refused to give in to the frustration bubbling inside her. She charged out of the bathroom, fueled by determination. She'd cut the damn thing off if she had to. A dress was not going to keep her from interrogating the one person who might know where Meredith was.

As she marched toward her office to grab her jacket, she pulled up a quick mental catalog of her meticulously organized closet. There were no hidden ball gowns in there.

Looking at her watch, Dana wondered if she could still make it to Saks. She should've gone there in the first place, but she'd been determined to decode the Senator's Bonesmen name. It would help catch him off guard or even give her leverage to get him to spill his secrets about Meredith.

Unfortunately, time was up. After a full day of searching, Dana had found nothing about the Senator's involvement.

Maybe Jake was right. Maybe she was off base.

The elevator doors whooshed open, sweeping away the doubt that had been creeping in. It was replaced with validation as she watched Jake march toward her, dressed in a tuxedo. He wore it like 007, complete with the cocky smirk, which was currently slipping from his chiseled face.

Jake stopped a few feet before her, a garment bag draped over his arm. His lips pressed into a thin line, like he was trying to stop his anger from spilling out. He was unsuccessful. "What the hell do you think you're doing?"

Remembering she was still wearing Claire's disaster of a dress, Dana resisted the urge to cringe. She didn't enjoy feeling exposed in front of people, but her grief would always be more revealing than any dress, and Jake had already witnessed that.

Claire darted into the room, and Dana held her head higher, daring Jake to say something about the way she was dressed.

His gaze roamed over her, darkening by the time he met her eyes. When he finally spoke, his tone was accusatory. "You're dressed for the gala."

"So are you," she shot back, hating how he reduced her to such childishness.

He paused for a full breath trying to collect himself. No easy feat. Dana knew his temper ran as hot as hers. "I can't believe I came here to tell you I was wrong."

"You're admitting you're wrong? That's a first."

"No. I wasn't wrong, because as usual, you can't follow orders."

"I don't work for you. And I told you I was going to the gala."

"And I told you to stand down."

"Archer sent me the tickets. I'm not going to let them go to waste when they could help us find Meredith."

"How do you know I don't have a lead?" he challenged.

"You wouldn't be here, dressed like James Bond if you did."

He huffed an arrogant laugh. "At least one of us looks the part."

"Enough!"

Shocked, Dana stopped her bickering to look at Claire. Jake's attention was on the normally timid intern as well. Claire's shoulders shrunk under the attention, but she didn't back down. "You two always do this. Stop butting heads and use your brains and brawn to work together already. You get more accomplished when you're on the same team."

"We *are* on the same team," Jake insisted.

"Then start acting like it." Claire's next words wiped the traces of triumph from Dana's face. "Both of you. Less fists, more finesse."

A strange mix of pride and embarrassment swelled through Dana. Claire had never called her out before. Swallowing her pride, she approached Jake, this time with her guard down. "Claire's right. The important thing here is finding Meredith. Truce?"

Her words doused the flickering flames in his blue eyes. The shift was subtle but unmistakable. "Truce," Jake agreed, handing her the garment bag rather than shaking her outstretched hand.

"What's this?"

"Call it a backup plan."

Dana unzipped the bag, pulse quickening for just an instant at the sight of the designer label. She made a good living, but she rarely indulged in such fine things. She let her fingers slide over the rich material, before she realized Jake was still watching her. "Is this a bribe?"

"Call it what you want. Just put it on. We're going to be late."

24

"Here are the tickets," Claire said, handing Jake an envelope. "Mr. Kincaid is sending a car. It should be waiting out front for you."

Jake nodded, but his focus was occupied by the way Dana looked in the dress she'd changed into.

Were all the women in his life trying to kill him?

First Claire put Dana in the equivalent of a lace cocktail napkin, then Margot picked out a designer gown that made the librarian look like a million bucks. Which it should considering how much it cost. The shock he'd endured at the price tag was nothing compared to seeing Dana walk toward him looking like an absolute goddess.

Chin up, shoulders back, she looked like Katherine Hepburn from one of those old Hollywood black and whites his mother loved.

Ramirez's voice echoed through Jake's mind as he tracked the beautiful woman walking toward him. *It's your funeral.* How many times had they said that to each other when bailing on wingman duty to chase some girl they couldn't resist?

Jake's chest ached in that hollow way that always accompanied thoughts of Ramirez. Sometimes it stunned him how forgotten memories could resurface out of the blue. He hadn't thought about chasing tail with his best friend in years. It felt like a lifetime ago, but Dana had a way of bringing him back to the guy he used to be before his life was blown apart by war.

If only Ramirez had been driving that day, like he was supposed to. But Jake had won that stupid bet. A bet that saved his ass and shipped three of his Army brothers home in pine boxes.

"You ready?"

Dana's voice sent Jake's haunted memories scurrying away like roaches from daylight.

He extended his arm, not wanting to get used to this. He wasn't a spook. Playing spy didn't come naturally to him like it did his CIA counterparts. They might not flinch at dressing up and slipping into the role of Dr. Gray's date, but Jake did. He didn't take that sort of thing lightly. And this was the second time his job had required him to pretend to be involved with the beautiful librarian. It was starting to feel much too comfortable for his liking.

He didn't date for a reason. He needed to keep his head clear; stay sharp and focused.

Right now, with Dana's gorgeous body gliding next his, he was the opposite of focused.

THE RIDE to the gala was mercifully short. Neither of them spoke for the first part, which was probably a good thing considering the only thing Jake wanted to use his lips for didn't involve speaking.

Dana broke the silence. "I can't believe Claire stood up to us like that," she mused. "I'm proud of her. Aren't you?"

Jake stoically nodded.

His noncommittal response made Dana cross her arms. "Is our truce over already?"

"No."

"Then what's wrong with you? You haven't said a word since we left the Smithsonian."

"Given our track record, the less we speak, the better."

Dana's frigid glare could cure global warming. "Meredith and I were best friends, Jake. I'd expect you, of all people, to understand how difficult it is to think about losing her." When her voice broke, Dana turned to face the window leaving Jake feeling like a complete prick.

He rubbed his palms over his face and sent up a silent prayer. He needed to find a way to make things right; with this case, with Dana, with himself. He knew the best place to start was with the woman by his side. If they had any chance of making tonight a success, he needed to stop taking his anger out on her. His messed-up life was all his own doing.

Against his better judgement, he reached out and took Dana's hand. She continued to stare out the window, but she didn't pull away. "You're right. I know what you're going through." He squeezed her fingers, and she finally looked at him. "That's why I've been running all over town trying to get answers. But I've come up empty. Beating my head against a wall all day tends to put me in a bad mood. I didn't mean to bite your head off."

She shrugged. "I get it. I came up empty today, too."

He hated the defeat in her voice. "Then it's a good thing we're both so stubborn."

A small smile lifted the corners of her lips. "So, what's the plan?"

"I can't get near any of the players I want to talk to. At least not through official channels, but most of them will be here tonight. Our best chance is to split up and cover as much ground as possible. I'm going to hit the people on my list. You make your rounds and try to get some dirt."

"Dirt?"

"Gossip. Just bring up the Missing Girl on the Hill. With all the media coverage this is getting, it'll be easy enough to slip it into conversation. But don't give anything away. I don't want anyone to suspect we're working the case."

"And what about the Senator?"

"He's off limits, Dana."

"But—"

"I need you to trust me on this. If he's involved in any way and we spook him now, he's in the wind. And you better believe he'll make sure all evidence we could use to tie him to Meredith disappears with him."

"I still think it wouldn't hurt if I had a casual conversation with him."

Jake's eyebrows rose. "You're about as casual as a hurricane when you want something." She was about to object, but he cut her off. "I need your word that you'll steer clear of him tonight."

"Fine."

"If he's behind this, we'll get him. I'll even let you watch when I nail his balls to the wall."

"I'm going to hold you to it."

"I'd expect nothing less."

Satisfied he'd gotten through to her, Jake relaxed back into his seat until they pulled up to the National Gallery. The mammoth columns glowed like shadowy giants as movie lights lit the colorful Institute of World Politics banners hanging between them. Red carpet led the way up the long stone staircase, announcing this was no place for mere mortals. The upper echelon of D.C.'s political society was here tonight.

Gritting his teeth, Jake wondered how much these so-called fundraisers would be able to contribute if they didn't waste funds trying to out-do each other with over-the-top events. But that was the name of the game. Money was power and everyone who wanted to be someone flaunted it.

Shoving his disgruntled opinions aside, he waited for the driver to park. They'd arrived late enough that no one was waiting to open their car doors.

Good. Jake hated being ushered into places.

Taking the driver's card, he told him to stay close. Jake wasn't fond of having someone drive him around when he was fully capable of doing it himself. Especially when he knew it was probably taxpayer dollars funding this guy's salary. People like the Kincaids didn't get to where they were without knowing how to work the system. But Jake also knew when to keep his pride out of the equation.

Getting a cab or rideshare in the heart of the city was never easy. Throw in a large event during prime dinner hour, and the odds were about as good as winning the lottery. If they needed a fast getaway, this was their best option.

Prepare for the worst, hope for the best.

He exited the sleek town car and jogged around to Dana's door. She'd already opened it, but he was there to offer his arm. It was showtime.

With Dana's arm hooked through his, they showed their tickets and walked into the lion's den. Just like he'd expected, when they strolled under the glowing string lights of the lively ballroom, Dana made heads turn.

25

"We really know how to make an entrance," Dana whispered, her confidence withering under so many powerful gazes. Jake, on the other hand, seemed to come alive. It was like the soldier who lived beneath his surface had just been nudged from his slumber.

She'd only seen that version of Jake a few times. When he handled his weapon. When he'd aimed one at her. When he'd saved her life—twice.

Though she felt safe, she preferred the FBI agent version over the sanctioned killer.

Letting Jake take the lead, Dana did her best to channel his coolness. Then again, the room full of old men in expensive suits probably didn't intimidate Jake Shepard. War tended to do that to a person. But when Dana thought about it, these were the people who viewed war like a chess match, strategically constructing treaties for their own personal gain.

What was more dangerous than that?

Jake approached the bar and held up two fingers. "Tonic and lime."

The bartender artfully slid the drinks toward them on black cocktail napkins. Jake handed her one. Her disappointment was visible. She'd been counting on some liquid courage to take the edge off.

"We're working," he muttered under his breath.

"You're a mind reader now?"

"Don't have to be. Those big brown eyes telegraph your every thought."

Dana flushed and took a sip of her drink, hoping that wasn't true.

"Sip it slowly, and try to blend in. If you need a break you can finish it and come back to the bar for another. Don't let anyone buy you a drink. You won't know what's in it."

She wanted to roll her eyes at his pre-prom lecture. "I don't see a room full of D.C.'s political elite roofieing each other."

"I'm serious, Dana. Keep a drink in your hands at all times. You fidget when you're nervous."

"I got it," she whispered, her voice betraying her irritation.

"Remember what we talked about."

"Divide and conquer. I know."

"And?"

"No senator."

Jake nodded. "If you get into any trouble, tug on your left earlobe."

She felt her face twitch with annoyance, then did her best to smooth it out. She didn't want to play into his open-book comment. "What if you're not watching?"

"I'm always watching."

His words sent goosebumps down her spine. She swallowed thickly and reminded herself to breathe. She stood tall, gripping her drink tighter as she raised it to Jake's. "For Meredith."

"For Meredith."

MAKING small talk was easier than Dana expected. She was getting good at it. A few fake smiles and nods and she blended right in. Casual laughter when approaching a group gained her instant acceptance. Before long she was inserting little morsels to redirect the conversation. She'd just used her most successful one. "It really is sad . . ."

Right on cue the woman next to her asked, "What is?"

"That story about the missing woman."

"Oh I know. I truly can't believe it." The woman clutched the thin gold chain around her neck. "She was so sweet."

"Did you know her?" Dana asked.

"We worked together."

"Really? You work for Senator Scott?"

The woman looked momentarily flustered. "Well no, not exactly. I'm DCHR. But sometimes I'd see Meredith at lunch."

Dana did her best to hide her disappointment. This woman was just another in the long line of those grabbing hold of the self-importance that came with claiming they were touched by the tragic story. She wasn't the first Dana had run into tonight and probably wouldn't be the last.

Holding up her nearly empty glass, Dana gave it a little shake. "If you'll excuse me."

The woman nodded, and Dana excused herself from the group.

Whenever she hit a dead end, she'd move on and start over. She had faith that sooner or later she'd find someone who wasn't just vying for their fifteen minutes of fame.

Walking toward the bar, Dana assessed the room trying to pinpoint the next group she should infiltrate. She caught sight of Jake. Despite his warning that he'd be watching, she made it a habit to keep her eye on him.

Currently, he was across the gallery ballroom casually conversing with a group of stuffy-looking old men in military dress. Jake didn't add more than a few nods to the conversation, but the blathering windbags he'd surrounded himself with didn't notice. Catching his eye, she sent him a wink, feeling quite pleased with herself when she saw his lips draw up ever so slightly.

Overcoming her initial nerves, she'd gotten the hang of things. Slipping around unnoticed was a specialty she'd perfected in prep school. She was proud she'd outgrown her submissiveness. Back then she'd lacked confidence, but now she was accomplished. But it was more than her collection of doctorates that gave her security. She'd seen and done things that would make most of the people in this room pale. Not all of them had been her choice. The important thing was, she'd survived.

She'd always been a survivor. It took facing a serial killer to realize it. Now she owned her perseverance like a badge of honor. Scars and all.

Dana massaged the phantom pain in her shoulder as she waited her turn at the bar. The bullet wound didn't hurt her often, but there wasn't a day that she didn't think about it; another reminder of her strength, and the second chance she'd gotten to do things right.

Her attention wandered back to Jake. She was lucky he had such good aim. Though she knew luck had nothing to do with it. With a gun in his hand, Jake Shepard was a deadly weapon. She was just lucky it'd been Cramer he was trying to kill.

Once again, Dana found herself wondering exactly what it was that Jake had done for the Army. She knew he didn't like talking about it. The same way she didn't like talking about her parents. Some ghosts were better left undisturbed.

"What can I get you?" the bartender asked.

Dana stepped up the ornate bar that had been moved to the gallery ballroom for tonight's event. "Another tonic and lime, please."

She placed her glass atop the rich mahogany surface, wondering if anyone even appreciated that they were being served on a genuine 19th century Jacobean sideboard. Probably the wrong crowd. It was likely these guests owned multiple homes overflowing with historic pieces they seldom took the time to appreciate.

She knew the beautiful piece of furniture had been made to be used, but she was relieved when the bartender wiped away the watermark her glass left behind. "Did you know many sideboards like the one you're using tonight often had secret compartments?"

The bartender humored her. "Really?"

"Yes. A remnant of survival courtesy of the 18th century. Before banks or safety-deposit boxes. People often held their valuables in pieces just like this. They'd have master-craftsmen fashion false bottoms or hidden panels that were so well executed that some of their treasures still remain hidden today."

"Sounds like something right out of *National Treasure*."

"You'd be surprised how much that film got right."

"Really?" This time, the bartender sounded genuinely intrigued. "Are you a history buff or something?"

"Something like that."

Curator of Occult History and Ritualistic Artifacts didn't exactly roll off the tongue. Besides, she was enjoying the way the attractive bartender was assessing her. Admitting her true profession would put that to an end. Most people promptly headed in the other direction when they found out she'd made a profession out of death.

Since she was playing spy for the evening, Dana let her little omission of truth slide. She slipped some cash in the tip jar and gave the bartender a rare smile. "Thanks for the drink."

"Thanks for the history lesson."

Walking away, she let her successful interaction distract her. A large tuxedo-clad shape stepped in front of her so quickly she didn't have time to stop. Colliding with him, her drink sloshed out of her glass, coating them both. It would've been a much bigger commotion if the man's vice grip on her arm hadn't kept her on her feet. Managing to hold onto her glass and her balance, she brushed the tonic off the front of the broad chested man.

An apology was halfway out of her mouth before she realized who she'd run into.

Senator Scott's dark eyes lacked empathy as he glared down his nose at her. Icy fear spider-walked up her spine waking her fight or flight response. But Dana didn't turn away. She wanted to know what Meredith had seen in this man's cold, calculating gaze.

In his clutches, Dana was more convinced than ever that he was behind Meredith's disappearance. She wanted to accuse him, but her words froze in her throat as his hand tightened around her arm. He pulled her uncomfortably close and plastered on a well-rehearsed smile. "Dr. Gray. Just the woman I was hoping to run into."

26

JAKE HAD ENOUGH OF LISTENING TO ENTITLED ASSHOLES COMPLAINING about first-world problems. He'd eavesdropped on every one of his Tangos. Not one of them piqued his suspicion regarding Meredith. He crossed the last name off his mental list when Ben Riley, Scott's congressional aide, left the cluster of men behind him. Riley'd been discussing hedge funds with some Ivy League yuppies, which was just about as boring as the current conversation Jake was stuck in.

He stood with three retired Army men, all proudly displaying their decorated dress blues like they were still active. They weren't. Even when they were, it was easy to tell they'd been REMF. Fast-tracked to the cushy non-combat officer roles thanks to their pedigree. He had no respect for men who earned chest candy on the backs of grunts.

All three of the white-haired pogues were pushing seventy. In the past ten minutes they'd done nothing but gripe about their golf caddies. *Like that was what kept the lazy bastards from making par.* Jake was more than ready to escape the dull conversation. With no targets left, it was time to rethink his approach.

From what he could tell, Dana had been holding her own. Maybe they'd have better luck if they partnered up. She could try her sad story bit with some of his Tangos to see if they took the bait and spilled anything important.

He let his gaze drift to her at the bar. As promised, he kept her in his sight at all times. Pride and jealousy mixed into a bitter cocktail as he watched her flirt with the bartender like a pro. Either she was more experienced than he'd assumed, or she had no clue the effect she had on men.

In that dress, she was a walking bombshell.

Possessiveness had him draining his tonic and lime, ready to interrupt the bartender's fun when an old friend stepped into his path. "Jake 'the Jackal' Shepard. It's been a minute."

Jake froze, the old nickname throwing him. "Sarge?"

"That's Master Sarge now."

Jake grinned, pulling his old CO into a respectful handshake. "Trent Nelson! What the hell you doing in D.C.? You transfer stateside?"

"Yep. Jeanine wanted to lay down some roots." He pointed to a very pregnant woman standing a few feet away. "We're on number three. Hoping this one's a boy. I'm severely outnumbered when it comes to the estrogen level in my house."

Jake laughed at the irony. "That's what they call karma, *Romeo*," he teased, referencing Nelson's call sign.

"Tell me about it." That good-natured smile he was known for creased Nelson's cheeks. "What about you? Did that stunner you've been clocking all night make an honest man outta ya?"

Jake's thoughts drifted back to Dana for a moment. She was still at the bar. "Nah. We're just working something."

Nelson's brow furrowed.

"I'm FBI now."

"A Feeb!" Nelson gave a dry laugh. "Well, they're lucky to have ya. You're one of the good ones, Shep. Anyone who's ever served with ya can attest to that. Speaking of, why aren't you in your dress uni?"

Jake shook his head. "That's not who I am anymore."

"Shep, what happened with your team ..." Nelson shook his head. "The work you boys did was nothing short of heroic. Don't let what went down tarnish that. It doesn't change anything."

Jake swallowed hard. Nelson was wrong, losing his team changed everything. But he wasn't about to get into that here. He gave his old CO a curt nod, hoping he'd take the hint.

Nelson clamped a big hand on Jake's shoulder. "This is for life, brother. That's how we honor the fallen. Hooah."

Jake's muscle memory had his hand in full salute as he echoed the sentiment. Watching Nelson walk away, that familiar hollow feeling filled Jake's chest. He knew he needed to find a way to deal with his baggage. Letting what went down in his last mission stain the memories of men he considered brothers wasn't right. They deserved better.

Once he was done with this case, he'd make that a priority.

Returning to his mission, Jake zeroed in on Dana. Shock nearly knocked him off his feet. She was still at the bar. But she wasn't alone. And the man pressed up against her wasn't the bartender.

Senator Scott had his hands where they didn't belong. The politician pawed at Dana, his hands moving over her slinky black dress as he made a half-assed attempt to dab a spilled drink.

The moment Jake saw the prick put his hands on Dana, he was in motion. He crossed the ballroom like he was preparing for battle. It was Claire's words that made him slow down. *Less fists, more finesse.*

He wanted his pound of flesh, but he reminded himself why he was here. Even though it would be incredibly satisfying to hammer the self-entitled scumbag to a pulp, it wouldn't help them find Meredith.

27

Dana recoiled, but the Senator didn't give an inch. He made a show of using a white handkerchief he'd pulled from his breast pocket to wipe the spilled drink off of her dress, but it felt more like he was groping her. His hands took their time exploring her curves. Instinct made her want to snap into her self-defense training, but the garnet and gold ring on his finger distracted her. She tried to get a better look, but his hands were moving too freely. She wanted to ask him about it point blank, but she heard Jake in her head telling her to play it cool.

She tried again to shove him off. Grinning, he gripped her waist tighter and pulled her against him. Fury burned her fear away as she imagined him using this same overpowering approach on Meredith.

If the devil wanted to dance, Dana was game. "I'm glad we bumped into each other, Senator Scott."

"So am I. I wanted to meet the woman who's been asking so many questions about me."

"Actually, my questions are about my friend, Meredith Kincaid."

"Ah yes. The Missing Girl on the Hill. What a shame. She was so talented. It's quite shocking, isn't it? The way people can so easily disappear."

"You don't look broken up about it."

"I am. I've known her a long time. But I have a lot of people working under me. I make it a habit not to get too attached."

"Are there others?"

"Excuse me?" His cool demeanor slipped.

Dana caught Jake storming toward them. She knew she only had a moment before he'd break up this little chat. Seizing the opportunity, she pressed the Senator. "Are there others like Meredith? Others you made disappear?"

"I don't think I like your tone."

"And I don't think I like your hand on my ass."

She shoved his hand off her and started to walk away before Jake could turn their mild scene into a spectacle, but apparently the Senator wasn't done yet. His hand coiled around her wrist and he yanked her back against him. He lowered his lips to her ear, sending a storm of goosebumps down her spine. "Careful, Dr. Gray. Like you've implied, I'm good at making problems disappear."

Flinching from his threat, she quickly peeled the Senator's fingers from her wrist just as Jake showed up. His arm slipped securely around her waist, flooding her senses with warmth and security. The juxtaposition was dizzying.

"Is everything okay, sweetheart?"

Dana knew this was just part of their cover, but she was over being a shiny plaything for the men in the room. Though at least this one wasn't trying to kill her. Not presently anyway. The phantom pain in her shoulder gave an involuntary throb, as if remembering the bullet Jake had put there a few months ago.

She pulled away from his controlling grip, slipping her arm through his instead. "Everything's fine." She glared at the Senator. "I got what I came for. I'd like to go home now."

"Of course."

Jake started to lead her away, his rigid posture a dead giveaway of his frustration. He was walking so fast he almost pulled her right out of her uncomfortable heels. Exiting the ballroom, he continued toward the coat check.

Sick of being manhandled, she untangled her arm from his and ducked into the first alcove they passed. Jake followed. She opened her mouth to defend her actions, but he cut her off. "Are you okay?"

Even in the shadows of the unlit recess, Dana could see the concern glowing in his blue eyes like twin flames. "I'm fine."

"Are you sure?"

"Yes. Jake, I'm fine. I didn't—"

"When he put his hands on you ..." Jake trailed off, a quiet storm building beneath the surface.

"Wait. You're not pissed at me for talking to the Senator?"

"No. I saw the whole exchange. He instigated it. You were right. There's something off about him."

Validation swelled through her. "I'm glad you feel that way." She reached into her clutch ready to reveal her trophy. The idea had come to her when she was talking to the bartender. Dana just hoped Jake was equally impressed with her hidden compartment theory. "I think this might help us figure out what he's hiding."

Jake's eyes bulged as she held up the heavy gold and garnet ring. "Tell me that's not what I think it is?"

"I slipped it off his finger when he was groping me."

"Dana! You can't go around lifting evidence."

"It might hold the key to finding Meredith."

"Yeah and it's also a crime." He shook his head, beginning to pace. "This is Vegas all over again."

"I stand by my actions in Vegas."

"I know. That's the problem. I'm not debating this with you." He snatched the ring from her. "We're giving this back."

"No. It might have a secret compartment that holds a micro drive. Secret societies thrive on hiding things in plain sight. The Freemasons were famous for hidden compartments." She recapped her explanation of the antique server and how it sparked her idea that the Senator might be hiding something in the ring. "It makes sense that he would be keeping incriminating evidence close. Like the originals of the photographs of him and Meredith."

"Christ, Dana. I don't have time for more conspiracy theories."

"But you said I'm right about the Senator."

"Yeah, about him being a handsy creep who's having an affair with his assistant and any number of other women from the way he came on to you. That's motive enough right there. We can't keep this." He slipped the ring into his jacket pocket.

"I've been right about everything else. Why can't you at least explore this angle?"

"Because the point of all this sneaking around was not to show our hand. If the Senator finds his ring missing, you might as well have just walked up and accused him tonight. Not to mention that you just put yourself in his crosshairs."

"I don't care!"

Jake was doing that thing with his jaw again. The muscles bunched together as if he could chew up his anger and swallow it whole. "If he's behind Meredith's disappearance—"

"He is," she interrupted. "I can feel it, and if I have to put myself at risk to prove it, so be it."

"Dana, this isn't the way."

"Then tell me what is! We're dealing with the Priory of Bones. I don't think you understand their power. There's no protocol for this."

"Dana, I know your brain is wired to see the occult, but he's just another corrupt politician. D.C. is crawling with them."

She stood her ground. "It doesn't fit. Why threaten me if he's not involved in something more sinister?"

Jake stopped pacing. He turned to face Dana, his expression hardening. "He threatened you?"

"He told me he's good at making problems disappear."

Jake blew out a breath, raking a hand through his hair so heatedly she was surprised he didn't pull out tufts. "I need you to tell me exactly what he said to you."

"Fine, but you need to calm down first."

After he took a few calming breaths, she relayed her conversation with the Senator. When she was finished, Jake scrubbed his large hands over his face. She could see the doubt creeping in. She was winning him over. "Please, Jake. Can we at least look into the ring?"

"You know I can't. It'd be breaking the law."

She admired his integrity. But once upon a time, Meredith had been like family to Dana, and she didn't have any of that left. If it came down to it, she would do anything to help her friend, including circumvent the law.

She was about to argue her point when Jake's phone rang. She felt her own buzz inside her clutch. In the hall, ringtones began to echo simultaneously. An eerie cacophony of whispers started to rise above the offbeat song of chirping cell phones.

Pulling her phone from her clutch, she punched in her code on the lock screen. Ivan Chermayeff's sunburst greeted her. She'd chosen the Smithsonian's logo as her home screen because it represented light, knowledge, enlightenment, strength, resolve; all the things she aspired to embody. But as news notifications began to light up her phone, she'd never felt weaker.

The horrifying words stood out, bleeding together into one unimaginable nightmare. *Body found ... Tidal Basin ... missing woman ... Meredith Kincaid ... murder on the Hill.*

Dana felt her phone start to slip from her hand.

28

WHILE SHE DIDN'T REMEMBER THE RUSHED EXIT FROM THE GALA OR EVEN the drive to the crime scene, Dana was sure she'd never forget the walk to the Tidal Basin. She knew the area well from years of running the scenic two-mile loop. It was a place of beauty, where the cherry blossoms fell like snow and people dotted benches. Families feeding the ducks, government workers soaking up the sparse sunshine while enjoying their lunch, but now its surface would be forever scarred.

Dana would never be able to look at the calm surface of the water the same way after watching the first responders carefully pull a lifeless body from its depths.

She'd fought through the crowd of Press and rubberneckers to follow Jake under the crime scene tape. Despite his best efforts to keep her back, she'd stood her ground. She regretted her choice. His words echoed in her mind. "You don't need to see this."

She'd been too stubborn to listen. Now she couldn't unsee it. Every time she closed her eyes, she saw Meredith's head sag to the side, her blonde hair matted and dirty as water ran from it, her limp fingertips skimming the shoreline as the responders tried to carefully remove her from the netting she was tangled in.

Dana stood on the bank a few feet back from where the detectives, agents and first responders gathered. Jake was with them. A few minutes ago, she had been too. But the sight of her best friend's bludgeoned body had been too much. She'd stumbled back, barely catching her balance on the slick, trampled grass. She needed breathing room.

Her head pounded as the sky around her lit up like the fourth of July. Helicopters hovered above, their propellers thumping in rhythm with the flashing blue and red lights. News crews scurried around setting up light towers and aiming cameras where they didn't belong. The police did their best to control the crowd, but everyone was eager for a glimpse, holding up cellphones like it was a concert.

The lack of respect for the dead made Dana feel ill. A fine mist began to rain down, making the scene even more dismal. She shivered, her limbs feeling stiff and hollow, as though she was the one being zipped inside the body bag. She clung to her last kernel of strength as she watched the still shape being hefted onto a stretcher and then carried up the bank.

This was wrong. It wasn't supposed to end like this. Meredith couldn't just be ... gone.

Panic gripped Dana, driving her forward.

"Wait!" she screamed, running to intercept the men in coroner jumpsuits.

Jake got to her first. She collided with his solid chest. The impact made her want to shatter into a million pieces. "Dana," his voice was guttural, cold. "Stop."

The last of her strength dissolved. Anger was the only thing keeping her on her feet now. She turned it on Jake. "This is your fault! The Senator did this. If you weren't so scared of breaking the rules you could've stopped him."

He said nothing, but his eyes betrayed him. She saw pain there, but she was too hurt to care. "Let me go! I need to say goodbye to her!"

Jake's hands remained firmly planted on her biceps. "You will." His gaze moved to the crowd that was still watching. "Just not here."

The phones angled in their direction took the fight out of her.

"Come on." Moving his grip to her shoulders, he steered her back the way they'd come.

"Where are we going?"

"ME's office."

THE MEDICAL EXAMINER'S office was on E Street, less than two miles from the crime scene. Located in an unmarked corner of the Department of Forensic Sciences, the building shared the parking lot with a luxury hotel.

It felt all kinds of wrong to be parking next to the black coroner's van while oblivious tourists walked to their cars, ready to enjoy a night on the town. Dana wondered how many of them would even care if they knew there was a massive freezer full of dead bodies a stone's throw from where they laid their heads on over-priced Egyptian cotton sheets.

The trip tonight, from the National Gallery, to the Tidal Basin, to the ME's office barely covered four miles. It made Dana's heart wrench wondering how long Meredith had been within reach.

Had she been out there, drowning while Dana was sipping fake cocktails and making meaningless conversations at the IWP gala? She knew dwelling on such questions was counterproductive, but that didn't stop them from ricocheting through her mind.

Doing her best to stay focused, she stripped and hung her ruined dress on the back of the bathroom door. The rain laden fabric sagged listlessly against the green metal. Water dripped off the mud-caked hem. Collecting a handful of paper towels, she attempted to soak up the puddle beginning to take shape. She washed her face and hands, then used the rest of the paper towels to dry her damp skin.

Even after slipping into the borrowed scrubs the ME had provided, she still couldn't shake the chill from her bones. It clung to her; the veil of death that would forever mar the bank of the Tidal Basin where Meredith had been found.

Dana took a moment to collect herself before stepping out into the hallway. Jake was there waiting for her in a pair of matching green scrubs. "You ready?"

She was hanging on by a thread, but she knew she needed to do this. Jake had made a good point on the drive over. If Dana could identify the body, then they could officially notify the Kincaids, sparing them the horror of having to do the task themselves.

Following Jake through a set of double doors, Dana tried not to listen to the way her footsteps echoed down the hall in the oversized shoes she'd been lent. She wondered who'd worn them last. Were they from a body left here, unclaimed?

They moved through another set of heavy double doors. This hallway was dark and cold. Only one fluorescent bulb flickered intermittently overhead; its signal an S.O.S, warning what lay ahead.

The foul scent of disinfecting and embalming fluid drove away any possible confusion about what they would find behind the final set of double doors.

This was the home of death.

They reached the end of the dim hallway much too quickly for Dana's liking. She balked at the doors, grateful that someone had papered over the small windows they were fitted with. She felt Jake beside her, hating that she needed him there.

Dana had made a career out of death but studying it in the pages of history was much easier than seeing it up close like this. And when it was someone she knew and cared about ...

Jake's hand brushed against hers making her jump, but when his fingers intertwined with hers, she looked up. His blue eyes held storms of confliction. "Dana, if you don't think you can do this ..."

"No. I have to. It won't feel final until I know for sure that it's really her."

He nodded, giving Dana a moment to take one last breath before he rapped loudly on the metal door and pushed it open.

29

Dr. Reed 'pound of flesh' Fletcher looked up from the steel table he was leaning over. His sharp green eyes crinkled at the corners as he lowered his mask to reveal his grin. "Agent Shepard. It's been a long time."

"Not long enough, Fletch," Jake replied, dryly.

Fletcher was a good guy, with a lousy job. Had he worked anywhere else, Jake would've enjoyed running into him when their cases crossed, but no one enjoyed spending time in a morgue. The stench of formaldehyde lingered. Jake wasn't superstitious, but he never kept the clothes he wore here. Death was a scent that never washed out. This time, he'd borrowed scrubs, but it didn't really matter since the mud and rain from the crime scene had already ruined his tux.

"Gloves and boots are on the counter," Fletcher directed.

Jake led Dana over to a long steel countertop, where a collection of small white cardboard boxes held medical gloves and blue paper booties in varying sizes. The each put a pair on and approached the table where the veteran ME stood. Thankfully, a large white sheet covered the body laid out on the table in front of him.

Jake knew Dana was tough. She'd dedicated her life to studying the kinds of deaths he couldn't even begin to wrap his head around, but it was different when the victim wasn't a stranger. He knew all too well the indelible pain burying a friend left behind.

She approached the table with determination, and he made introductions. "Dr. Fletcher, this is Dr. Dana Gray. She's here to identify the body."

Fletcher wasn't one for words. Probably because he spent most of his time with dead people. Normally it was something Jake admired about the man. He didn't waste time with small talk. But a little warning would've been nice before he pulled the white sheet back, revealing the mutilated body.

To her credit, Dana didn't flinch. The woman had grit; he'd give her that. She'd stolen a ring while being groped by a philandering senator, stood out in the rain for nearly an hour watching a corpse get pulled from the water and now she was identifying a disfigured body.

Jake had little doubt that it was Meredith Kincaid. He should've spared Dana the heartache and ID'd the missing woman himself.

The victim on the table was a blonde female who fit the build and age of Meredith Kincaid, but the nail in the coffin was the dress. It was the same one the bartender at Ruby's had described. Hot pink, low cut, unforgettable. It's what she'd been wearing the night she went missing. Or at least the night she stopped posting her every move all over Charlie Maine's social media.

With slow, steady breaths, Dana took a few steps forward until she was right up next to the exam table. Jake followed, careful to give her space. Fletcher flipped on the exam lights and the violent injuries came to life.

The body looked much worse than Jake had been able to tell at the crime scene. It'd been dark by the water. The police flood lights had cast shadows over the tangled mess of hair covering her face. Here, there was nothing to hide the horror.

Fletcher had swept away her matted blonde hair, revealing a face that, to Jake's best guess, had been beaten in with a blunt object. All that was left of her mouth was a gaping hole and swollen tongue. Not a single tooth remained in her shattered jaw. There was no way to make a dental ID and very little to go on with what was left of her features.

His attention moved back to Dana. He watched her trembling fists slowly open and close as she dug her fingernails into her palms. This was hard for her. She just didn't want anyone to know. He hated that he had to put her through this.

"Not much left of her," Fletcher interjected.

That was an understatement. If Jake had known Meredith looked this bad, he would've held off trying to make a visual and waited for fingerprint confirmation. All government employees had them on file.

Gently placing a hand on Dana's shoulders, he made the suggestion. "Let's just print her and call it a night."

"That's not gonna work." Fletcher pulled the sheet back further and lifted one of the woman's hands.

Jake's heart skipped a beat, his interest pulling him closer. He took the cold arm in his gloved hand for a closer look. Rigor had already set in, making the fingers stiff, but there was no mistaking what he saw. The tips of each finger were missing, cut off at the first knuckle with perfect precision.

"Other hand's the same," Fletcher said, lifting it so Jake could confirm what he already knew. He'd seen this before. As if the mystery surrounding Meredith Kincaid wasn't complicated enough, he'd just connected it to a cold case he worked when he first joined the Bureau.

"No dentals. No prints. Only identifying mark I could find is this." Fletcher pulled back the sheet to reveal a small heart-shaped tattoo on the vic's hip. The letters MD were inked inside.

Dana rushed forward to examine it closer. Jake moved beside her. "Did Meredith have any tattoos?"

She nodded, a large tear rolling silently down her cheek. "It's her."

"Are you sure?"

Dana nodded again.

Jake hated to press her, but the last thing he needed was a false ID. He moved closer, placing a comforting hand on Dana's shoulder. "You have to be one-hundred percent positive. If you have any doubts—"

The anger that stormed Dana's glare made his words trail off. She stepped back, grabbing the hem of her shirt. She yanked up the oversized green material, then tugged down the waistband of the matching scrub pants. "This should clear up any doubt."

As Jake stared at the identical tattoo on Dana's hip, the bittersweet sensation of solving a case this way settled over him. It was now crystal clear that Meredith Kincaid was the Jane Doe on the table.

He cleared his throat and nodded, pulling out his notepad to jot down his findings. Fletcher would send him a full report, but he liked things done a certain way.

Dana pulled her shirt back down, covering the faded ink. Her expression turned forlorn for a moment, her thoughts most likely filling with regret for the time she'd lost with her friend.

People grew apart. It was nothing she should blame herself for. And considering how Meredith had ended up, Dana should be counting herself lucky the woman wasn't in her life anymore. She'd gotten mixed up with the wrong crowd.

He knew the odds when women went missing, but he'd hoped Meredith could beat them, if only for Dana's sake. She'd already lost enough people she cared about. And from their matching ink, Dana and Meredith had been closer than she'd let on.

30

Unfiltered despair rooted Dana to the spot as she stood over her best friend's ruined body.

She couldn't move. Seeing that tattoo stole the last bit of hope she'd been clinging to. Without it, she was swallowed by an emptiness so vast there was no escaping.

The girl who'd been her best friend, her confidant, the little sister she'd always wanted, was gone. The memories they'd shared faded even more. Sometimes Dana felt like the time she and Meredith spent together was a figment of her imagination. Late nights. Endless laughter. Shared secrets and dreams. Without Mere to keep the other half of those memories alive, it made them feel like they'd never even happened. The only proof was the tiny scroll of ink on Dana's hip. But even that was fading.

She could still remember the night they'd gotten it.

"Hold still," Meredith demanded.

"I can't! It hurts!"

"Oh stop being such a baby. You have to put this on or it's going to get infected."

Dana groaned. Relenting, she lay back on her bed. "I still can't believe I let you talk me into getting a tattoo."

Meredith grinned, pulling the ointment cap from between her teeth. "I can get you to do anything."

Dana laughed, because it was true. Meredith was like a sister to her. She was years younger but, even when she was interning under Dana at the library, Meredith was the one in charge. But that's not why Dana let herself be bossed around. It was mostly because she'd never really had someone care enough about her to want to take charge of her life. Her grandparents had only done it because they had to. It was nice to have someone choose to.

Despite having two PhDs, there was a tiny part of Dana that was still the outcast who'd never quite fit in with the popular crowd. Meredith was the poster child of popularity. She could go anywhere, do anything, be anyone, but for some reason, she chose to spend all her free time with Dana.

The warmth that notion brought into her life was addicting, and Dana would do just about anything to keep it. Including getting a tattoo apparently.

Deep down, she actually liked the idea. It felt final somehow. The tattoo was a bond tying them together that could never be broken.

Meredith finished applying the anti-bacterial cream to Dana's fresh ink and tossed the swab in the trash. "It's perfect."

Dana popped up on her elbows to admire the tiny heart on her hip. "It really is."

Meredith plopped down next to her on the bed, tugging her bikini bottom lower so their tattoos were side-by-side. She bumped her boney hip into Dana's. "Two MDs. I finally have my Master's. It feels like we're almost equals now."

Dana's heart gave a tiny flutter. Did Meredith actually look up to her? Dana would've said it was the other way around. She'd always envied Meredith with her perfect family and her ability to charm anyone. "You're more than my equal," Dana replied. "You're my best friend."

Meredith's eyes welled with emotions. "Do you mean it?"

"Of course."

She linked her pinky with Dana's. "Forever."

"Forever," Dana echoed.

Meredith's face glowed as a devilish grin spread across it. "Now let's go show these sexy tattoos off! I want to go dancing!"

Jake's voice poked through Dana's memories. The morgue came back into focus as she watched him pull his phone from his pocket and open the voice recording app. "I hate to ask, but can you state who you've identified for the record?"

Dana nodded, wiping away another errant tear. Before she started speaking, Fletcher held up a hand. "That might not be necessary."

"What?" Both Dana and Jake said the word in unison.

"When did you get your tattoo, Dr. Gray?"

"Five years ago. Why?"

Fletcher grabbed a magnifying lens from his metal tray of tools. Upon closer examination, he shook his head. "Even with bloating and decomp, you can see substantial epidermal scarring and look, the ink is still bleeding. I'd wager this tattoo is only a few days old."

Hope radiated through Dana. "Then this isn't Mere?"

"We'll have to do DNA testing to rule that out," Jake interjected.

Dana's brows drew together. "How long does that take?"

"About twenty-four hours," Jake answered.

Fletcher laughed. "In case you haven't noticed, I'm the only one here, and I have about a dozen cases in front of your Jane Doe."

"Fletch, this case takes priority. The media is having a field day. They're probably camped out in the Kincaids' front yard right now. Anything you can do to push this up the chain would be appreciated."

"Best I can do is day after tomorrow. But don't get your hopes up. I don't have any pull in the lab."

"Just get started on the autopsy. I'll handle forensics."

Jake seemed anxious to move on. She got it, this wasn't Meredith, which meant she was still out there waiting to be found. Dana wanted to be knocking on doors worse than anyone, but she felt like they were standing in front of a piece of the puzzle, and she wasn't through examining it.

Now that she knew the woman on the table wasn't her former best friend, it made it easier to turn off her emotions and study her objectively. Adjusting her glasses, Dana angled her head back and forth to take in every inch of the mutilated woman while Dr. Fletcher began to photograph the body, speaking clearly into his recorder as he noted the damage.

Dana let her mind wander as she processed all the information. She flipped through mental images of ritualistic killings and gruesome occult crimes she'd cataloged. Nothing fit. Not even the Priory of Bones angle she'd been so certain of.

This woman wasn't Meredith Kincaid, but someone wanted them to think she was. "This makes no sense. I don't believe in coincidence, but this doesn't fit with my theory ..." she trailed off, wondering how much she should say in front of Dr. Fletcher. Jake seemed to trust him, but she didn't know protocol for this sort of thing. She looked to him for direction, but Jake was lost in his own troubling thoughts.

He shook his head. "None of this adds up. Whoever did this went to the trouble of removing anything that would help us identify the vic, but then left her in plain sight in the shallows to be found. Then there's the dress and the tattoo. Both staged. We're clearly meant to think this is Meredith Kincaid."

"Why would someone do that?"

"I don't know. But I'm going to find out."

"Maybe the ring can give us some answers?"

Jake gave her a stern look. "Let's talk outside."

Dana's mouth fell open. She stood in the parking lot between the coroner's office and the posh hotel, sure she must've heard Jake wrong. "What do you mean you gave the ring back?"

"I had to. It was only a matter of time before the Senator figured out it was you who took it. I slipped it into his coat pocket on our way out."

"Without him noticing?"

"You're not the only one who can pull off sleight of hand. He was standing in the lobby on our way out, caught up in the news like everyone else. I doubt he even noticed I bumped into him. With any luck he won't be suspicious."

"Jake, that ring was our only lead!"

"Lower your voice," he demanded.

"No! I don't care who hears. You just threw away the only clue that was going to help us find Meredith!"

"The ring was a long shot, and you know it. Besides, it's not our only lead."

"The body?" Her hands were on her hips now. "So far it's given us more questions than answers. "

"I'm not talking about the body."

"Then what?"

"There's another case."

"What?"

Jake ran a hand over his face, working the stiffness from his jaw, something she noticed he did when he was truly worried. "Jake, what aren't you telling me?"

His stormy blue eyes met hers. "There's a chance I got this all wrong from the start."

31

"It was my first case with the Bureau. Jenni James; missing prostitute. It's not something we'd normally handle, but she was an informant. An agent from the New York field office was working with her to put together a sting on a human trafficking ring, then poof, she disappears."

"Like Meredith?"

Jake nodded, keeping his eyes focused on the road ahead of him. He'd gotten Dana into the SUV by promising to share the details of his old case. It wasn't one he liked to revisit, but his mind drew him back to it often, wondering what he'd missed.

In general, he spent too much time thinking about the dead, but unlike a certain occult librarian, he didn't love dredging up all the gory details over a coffee and casual drive about town. But he knew Dana. She wasn't going to let it go. So after stopping at a twenty-four-hour drive-thru for some much needed caffeine, he gave her the abridged version.

Taking a sip of the scalding coffee, Jake continued. "Remi Jenkins was lead on the case. Jenni James goes missing. Last place she's tracked is to D.C. Jenkins comes to town, I get assigned to the case. I help work the field for a few weeks. Check all the usual hen houses, send undercovers to 12th and Massachusetts, but nobody will talk. Then all of a sudden, we get a call about a floater. She's DOA. We fish her out and think we're in luck because she matches our missing person to a tee. On top of that, she'd got a fresh tattoo branding her property of Terrance 'Ivy League' Vega; the baddest pimp in Deanwood. We're poised to nail the prick, but we can't ID the body. Same MO as the Jane Doe we saw today. No prints, no dentals."

"So what happened?"

"Nothing. Case went cold. Jenkins went back to NYC." Jake pushed back the flood of regret the unsolved crime filled him with. "It was Vega, but I couldn't prove anything without an ID."

"How do you know?"

"I just do." Jake could still see the way the smug sonofabitch had grinned when he'd questioned him. It was like he knew he was going to get away with it. And he did.

In the end, the Jane Doe was just one more unclaimed soul he'd sent to the FBI Body Farm. It still haunted him that his first case ended like that. He'd left the Army to get away from that kind of carnage. He was supposed to be able to make a difference here.

Maybe he still could. "I didn't spot the connection before, but I've never seen another body like the Jenni James case until tonight. They have to be connected."

Dana chewed her thumb.

"What's wrong?"

"You said that case went cold."

"That won't happen with Meredith." He wouldn't let it. Not this time. "It's no coincidence a body shows up hours after I went sniffing around in Deanwood. This has Vega written all over it. I can feel it."

Dana sighed deeply, pushing her glasses into her damp hair so she could press her palms against her closed eyelids. "I don't know how you do this every day."

He reached over and squeezed her knee. "Take it one step at a time. Thanks to you, we know the Jane Doe at the ME's isn't Meredith Kincaid. That's a big step. One that means we're getting close."

"So what's next?"

Dana looked exhausted. He knew the emotional rollercoaster she'd just been on was taking its toll. "Next, I take you home so you can get some sleep."

"No, Jake, don't cut me out of this."

"I'm not. But you're no use to anyone like this. You're practically asleep on your feet."

She jutted her chin out and crossed her arms. "I'll sleep when we bring Meredith home. Tell me the next step?"

He shook his head, hating that he couldn't turn off his physical attraction when it came to the stubborn librarian. She was an itch he couldn't scratch, and at times it was downright maddening. Other times, like now, he just wanted to protect her. It was obvious no one had since her parents died. That's probably what made her so opposed to being looked after, but he tried anyway. "Fine. Next we have to dig up the old Jenni James case file. I want to make sure I'm remembering all the details correctly."

He knew he was. The case was one he couldn't shake. He'd been over it a million times in his mind searching for anything he might've missed. Anything to help them nail Vega.

They'd been so close. The moment they brought him in for questioning he'd lawyered up. But Jake would never forget staring into his cold, dark eyes. They were the eyes of a monster.

The man was a predator, brainwashing desperate women under his control and forcing them into sexual servitude. They were so terrified of him they wouldn't talk. And without an ID they had to cut Vega loose.

Jake kept his eye on him over the years. He'd started out as a small fish, but by now he'd buried most of his criminal competitors. He was pretty much independently running the prostitution ring in D.C. So far he'd been smart, but that was the thing about big fish. Their big appetites eventually got them caught.

"Let's bring Vega in for questioning."

"Not yet. He's slippery. The next time I bring him in, I'm making sure they lock him up."

Dana looked pensive. "What about Jenni James, did she have any senators on her client list?"

"She was the corner type. No high-profile customers."

"Then how is this Vega guy involved in Meredith's disappearance?"

"Not sure yet. We liked him for Jenni James. He's built his sex trade empire in Deanwood over the years. We know Meredith frequented a bar there. She could've gotten herself involved with the wrong crowd."

Dana shook her head. "She knows better than that."

"You'd be surprised. A smooth-talker with fast hands and a camera? Sometimes that's all it takes. Slip something in a girl's drink, take incriminating photos, boom, you own her. That kind of blackmail can be pretty powerful. I'd imagine it's like falling under the spell of a cult. You of all people should understand that."

Dana shot him a withering glare. "I understand the concept. And maybe it'd be plausible for some women, but not Mere. She's smart and has the means to make problems like that go away."

Jake shrugged. "Pride is a tricky thing. Plus, she's already shown a disregard for caution and wise decisions based on her affair with the Senator."

"People can't control who they love."

He barked a laugh. "Actually, that's one thing we can control."

"And I suppose you think you're in control of your fate, too."

"Thinking anyone else is in control of my destiny is even wackier than your secret society angle."

"I'm here to look at all the angles. And considering the Priory of Bones basically invented human trafficking, I'd say it's relevant."

"It has to be more than relevant. We need a motive, probable cause, actual connections."

"Fine. If you can tell me there's absolutely no way a powerful, womanizing, known-to-be-corrupt senator could be connected to your pimp in Deanwood, I'll drop my 'wacky' secret society angle."

Dana added air quotes around the word wacky. It was unnecessary. Jake got her point. "If Senator Scott and Vega were mixed up in something and Meredith found out, it could've put a target on her back.

Working with the Senator and sleeping with him meant she probably had access to his most discrete dealings."

Jake hated admitting when he was wrong. He took his eyes off the road just long enough to hit Dana with a glare. "I'm not saying you're right, but if you are, accusing a US Senator of human trafficking is a bit more serious than saying he's a member of a secret society."

"Maybe he's guilty of both."

32

Jake took another sip of coffee and blared the horn when someone who was probably too busy texting missed the light. Tapping the steering wheel, he waited the grueling three minutes for the next one. "Did you ever consider that maybe all these riddles are just meant to distract us from the real problem?"

Dana arched a brow. "Which is?"

"Another corrupt politician with a taste for young women got caught with his pants down and decided to tie up loose ends."

"So what, the Jane Doe caught Mere and the Senator and threatened blackmail so he took them both out?"

"Why not? The simplest explanation is usually the right one."

Dana gave an aggravated grunt.

Jake tried to contain his grin. He couldn't help it, he was addicted to getting under her skin—probably because he couldn't stop imagining what it would taste like. He pushed that thought back into a box labeled "you know better" and continued with his smug teasing. "Did you just roll your eyes?"

"If I did it's only because you're being ridiculous."

"We'll see about that once you've read the Jenni James file. But first, we need to swing by the Kincaids' and ease their minds about the Jane Doe we pulled out of the Basin."

They drove the rest of the way in silence until the shrill tone of Jake's phone sounded through the Bluetooth. Jake pushed a button on his steering wheel to answer the call. "Shepard."

"Hey Shep, it's Larson. We got a hit on something of interest for Meredith Kincaid."

"From the Trust?"

"No. The father wasn't kidding. She hasn't touched her money. It's her meds that are surprising."

"I'm listening."

"Meredith has a prescription on auto refill. It generated an automatic message and sent it to her phone."

"Did she respond?"

"No. But we traced it back to the pharmacy. The order was for folate and Ondansetron."

Dana gasped. "Meredith's pregnant!"

Jake glanced at her. "How do you know that?"

"Ondansetron is a serotonin blocker. It prevents vomiting and is prescribed for severe morning sickness. Folate is the main ingredient in prenatal vitamins."

"That's the logical assessment we came to as well," Larson replied. "Not sure if it helps your investigation, but I figured you'd want to know."

"Thanks, Larson. It actually helps a lot." Jake disconnected the call, his pulse racing from the news and mainlining his coffee. There was no doubt in Jake's mind that the cases were connected.

"Why does this help a lot?" Dana pressed.

"Jenni James was pregnant. That's why she decided to turn informant for the FBI."

"Oh god." Dana's face paled, her hand flying to her mouth.

She was thinking exactly what Jake was. Someone found out about Meredith's pregnancy and took care of it the same way they took care of Jenni James.

It happened more than it should. In the political world, unwanted pregnancies were the billboards of infidelity. Murder was the quickest way to silence the rumors. Jake thought of Dana's conversation with the Senator. He'd told her he knew how to make problems disappear. Was that a confession?

Jake turned onto Massachusetts Avenue, and Dana's eyes bulged. "Are you going to tell the Kincaids about the pregnancy?"

He shook his head. "Right now, there's nothing to tell. All we have is a few prescriptions and a lot of speculation."

Dana gave a sigh of relief. "I can't imagine what they're going through. If there's a baby involved, too ..." she trailed off.

Jake reached over to squeeze her knee again. "Hey. One thing at a time, remember? We're here to tell them the good news. The body we pulled from the Basin wasn't Meredith's. And we have another lead to track down. The clock is still ticking on this case, and we're making every minute count."

She nodded.

"Let's not mention the Jenni James case to the Kincaids. I want to make sure it lines up first." The last thing he wanted to do was shine a spotlight on that shitshow. He could still hear Vega's arrogant laughter as he uncuffed him the day they kicked him loose.

"Jake, let me talk to the Kincaids."

"Alone?"

"You said every minute counts. Let me talk to them while you follow up on all this new information."

"I don't know if that's a good idea."

"Remember what Claire said?"

He raised his eyebrows. "Claire says a lot of stuff."

"You're the fist. I'm the finesse."

"She also said we work best together."

"Right now, I think we'll be at our best if we focus on our strengths."

She was right. He could get a lot more done without Dana's questions and cult conspiracies slowing him down. He also loved the idea of not having to waste time watching Mrs. Kincaid looking down her nose at him. “Okay. I’ll fill Holt in on what we found at the ME’s, get a warrant for Meredith’s medical records so we can confirm the pregnancy, then hunt down the Jenni James file.”

“Hunt it down?”

“It’s a cold case from a different field office. I don’t have access to it anymore. I’ll have to make a call.”

“To who?”

“Technically, Holt needs to sign off on it, but I have a feeling things will go smoother if I call Jenkins personally.”

“The agent who brought you the Jenni James case?”

He nodded.

“You think Jenkins won’t give you the file?”

“It’s complicated.”

“Well uncomplicate it. We have a mutilated doppelgänger on our hands. I don’t want the real one to turn up.”

“I’ll handle it. You just focus on the Kincaids. Are you sure you don’t need me to come with you?”

“I’ll be fine.”

“All right. It’s probably better you talk to them anyway. The Kincaids aren’t too fond of me.”

“That’s not a surprise.”

“What’s that supposed to mean?”

Dana was quiet for a moment, her fingers knotting and unknotting in her lap. It was making him anxious. Finally, she spoke. “You didn’t know Mere. I know it seems like she had it all, but she was just like the rest of us. Lonely, trying to find the place she belonged in the world. Despite what you think, she’s a good person. She’s loyal and brave and hardworking, and she would never stand by and let something unjust go unchecked.

“She might’ve made some bad decisions lately, but we don’t know all the facts behind them. And until we do, she’s still going to be the loyal friend I remember. She’s that same girl to the Kincaids, too. They can see how much I care when I speak about her. They see the opposite when you talk about her.”

Jake swallowed thickly, too humbled to respond. Dana was right. He could do better. He would do better. Starting with doing the one thing he hated most—asking for help.

33

After wading through the line of Press camped out at the Kincaids' gate, Jake dropped Dana off and headed back the way he'd come. He endured fists pounding his SUV and cameras pointed in his direction as he flipped them off.

Jake hated the Press. He hoped they wasted all the space on their SD cards snapping useless pictures of him. All they'd get was their own reflection bouncing back off the government tint job on his Yukon.

The thought made him grin. Unfortunately, the Press wasn't the only obstacle he'd face on his drive back to HQ. He needed to call in a favor to get access to the Jenni James case. One that would make him eat an even bigger dose of humble pie than the one Dana had just served him.

Agent Jenkins wasn't just lead on the case. Jenkins was Jake's uncle's best friend.

Remi Jenkins and Wade Shepard served together in the Air Force. Jenkins got out and got a job with the FBI while his uncle stayed in to serve until his recent retirement. When Jake ended up at the FBI, it was a proud day for both Airmen.

Remi jumped at the chance to bring Jake on board when the Jenni

James case was brought to D.C. Still a rookie by Fed standards, Jake was thrilled to be working with someone he'd looked up to his whole life.

Proving himself while building his confidence with the Bureau wasn't easy. Having someone like Jenkins by his side had all the makings of a career jump start. But the Jenni James case had done the exact opposite.

Jake hated letting Jenkins down. With nothing but dead ends, the case went cold, and the senior agent was called back to NYC. They hadn't spoken since.

Worse than that, Jenkins would know Jake hadn't spoken to his uncle in even longer.

He'd already gotten his ass chewed out once this week. He wasn't looking for a repeat. But his mind wandered back to Dana and what she'd said about Meredith. He didn't like coming across as aloof about his victims.

He knew he put up a wall, but he had to or all the darkness he saw on a daily basis would drag him under. But it didn't mean he didn't care. He did this job to the best of his ability every single day because he did care. Sometimes too much.

All of us or none of us. His uncle's wisdom came to him as it always did when Jake truly needed it. It was something Wade had said to him over and over growing up. It stuck and eventually became something Jake lived by. When he joined the Special Forces, it became his mantra. Everyone was of equal importance.

Meredith Kincaid and Jenni James couldn't be more different. But they both mattered.

"All of us or none of us." Jake said the words to himself to muster courage as he pulled up the number he was looking for in his phone. He took a deep breath and hit call.

A gruff voice answered after two rings. "Well I'll be damned. He lives and breathes."

"Hey, Jenks. I need a favor."

34

WITHOUT THE SHROUD OF FEAR HANGING OVER THE ROOM, DANA FELT like she could breathe again. Not wanting to add to the family's stress she'd walked into the house announcing the good news. "It's not her. It's not Mere."

There'd been a tearful embrace with the Kincaid family, but now everyone was gathered in the study; Archer, Elizabeth and Abby. Dana wanted everyone together, so she only had to go through the gruesome story once. Hoping to spare them, she skipped the gory details when she could, but that only led to more questions.

"I wish I could tell you everything, but right now, the FBI feels the less they share, the better the chance we'll have to find Mere," Dana explained.

Elizabeth dabbed her eyes with a tissue. "I don't understand. Why can't you tell us who you found? The news is saying it's Meredith. She was wearing that awful pink dress from the Facebook photo."

"Darling, you can't believe the news." Archer put his arm around his wife.

"It's that FBI agent, isn't it?" Elizabeth snapped. "He's keeping the truth from us. I want him off this case, Archer."

"Let's not be rash, darling."

Dana spoke up. "Agent Shepard is good at his job. He's the best chance you have of finding Mere. You need to give him time to put the pieces together."

"Time?" Elizabeth's pale blonde eyebrows drew together. "Is that why he sent you? To avoid wasting his precious time?"

"Mom," Abby warned.

"No. I want to know what this man is doing. From where I sit he's had nothing but time, and my daughter is still missing!"

"It was my idea to come here," Dana said. "Agent Shepard wanted to be the one to tell you what we discovered at the Medical Examiner's office because he feels you deserve that respect, but I told him I would do it because he has other leads to follow up. He agreed because the most important thing to him is finding Meredith."

The room fell silent.

Dana regretted her harsh tone. She knew this was hard, and she didn't want to make things worse for the Kincaids, but they needed to bring their focus back to what was important. It wasn't their pride or prominence; it was Meredith's safe return.

"I promise you, there's no better agent. He won't quit. He'll leave no stone unturned. If Mere is out there, he'll bring her home."

Elizabeth's face was unreadable as she wiped away her tears. Archer put an arm around his wife's thin shoulders and squeezed. "Dana's right, darling. This is why we wanted her to help with the investigation. She's always known what's best for our girl. If she says Shepard's good, he's good."

Elizabeth's blue eyes watered with uncertainty as her attention returned to Dana. "You're asking me to trust him with my daughter's life."

"I know," she replied. "And you can. You can because I do. I trust him with my life, Elizabeth. I couldn't work with him otherwise."

Dana surprised herself with her conviction, but every word was true. They may have their differences, but when it came down to it, she believed in Jake.

"Then it's settled." Archer stood from the leather sofa he and his wife were occupying. "Shepard stays on the case. We stay here and wait for more news."

Abby piped up. "Dana, is there anything else we can do?"

"I wish there was. Agent Shepard is following up on a lead and his team is tracking all Meredith's social media and phone activity. If they find anything new, we'll let you know."

Archer spoke up. "If he needs anything at all; use of the helicopter, help cutting through red tape, I'm at his disposal."

"Thank you. I'll pass that on."

Archer leaned in and whispered something into his wife's ear, then straightened up and offered Dana a warm smile. "If you'll excuse us, we're going to try to get some rest."

When they were out of earshot, Abby rolled her eyes. "That means Mom's going to pop another Xanax and Ambien cocktail, while Dad continues to work like it's any other day."

Dana's heart hurt for Abby. It was a lot for someone her age to handle. At twenty-two she shouldn't be worrying about losing her older sister. But life wasn't fair. She walked over to where Abby was perched on the arm of an overstuffed chair. Reaching out, she put a hand on the girl's shoulder. "We're gonna find her. Don't lose hope."

A sob escaped Abby, and she launched herself into Dana's arms. Caught off guard by the sudden rush of emotion, she held the trembling girl for only a few seconds before realizing Abby was burning up. Dana leaned back, holding Abby at arm's length. "Are you feeling okay?"

"Of course I'm not feeling okay."

"No, I mean, are you ill? You feel like you're running a fever."

Dana reached for Abby's forehead, but she ducked away, crossing her arms and pacing to the other side of the study. "I can't do this," she whispered. "I can't do this without her."

"You can't do what? Abby, what's going on?"

Abby faced Dana, her eyes red-rimmed and puffy. "You said you're tracing her calls, so you probably already know. Or you will soon enough."

Dana lowered her voice. "You need to tell me what you know."

"I can't. I can't tell anyone. If my parents knew ..." She dissolved into tears again.

Did Abby know about Meredith's pregnancy? It wasn't a stretch to think the sisters would've confided in each other. If so, and Abby could confirm Dana's suspicions based on Meredith's prescriptions it would save them from getting a warrant and weeding through medical records.

She heard Jake's voice in her mind. *Every second counts.*

Dana's heart was pounding as she crossed the room and cornered Abby. "If you know something about your sister you need to tell me. Any secrets you're keeping for her right now could mean the difference between finding her before it's too late."

"You don't get it. Mere is the one keeping secrets. My secrets."

Dana's face paled as she watched Abby's hands curl protectively over her stomach. The puzzle pieces finally took shape. "The prescriptions are for you."

Abby nodded, silent tears streaming down her red cheeks.

"Meredith's not pregnant. You are."

Abby nodded again.

"Tell me everything."

35

"You finally remember how to use a phone and your first call is to ask me for a favor? You've got some nerve, Jacob Shepard."

Jake sighed, knowing Jenkins was just getting started. The ex-airman and twenty-plus-year FBI veteran was a legend in her own right. Thanks to her tenacity and swift southern justice, she helped blaze a path everywhere she went. During her career with the FBI she'd worked hard to bury her Louisiana accent, but it still came out when she was truly angry.

Right now, it was in full effect. "Are you daft? Your first call shoulda been to your uncle."

"I know."

"You know? Then why haven't you called him?"

Jake settled in for the ass chewing he deserved.

"I know you weren't dropped on your head as a baby. I was there, wiping your ass right alongside Wade. Do you have any idea what that man's sacrificed for you? You can't even take the time to pick up a phone and tell him you're alive? If I wasn't keeping tabs on you, I don't know what he'd do."

"You've been keeping tabs on me?"

"Somebody's got to. Like I've got the time," she muttered. "Don't distract me. Call your uncle. He's been outta his mind since that nonsense with the Cramer case."

Jake couldn't keep the anger from his voice. "You told him about that?"

"Don't you take that tone with me, Jacob."

"Jenks—"

"That's Agent Jenkins to you."

"Yes ma'am."

She gave a sass-filled *uh-huh* and continued his verbal lashing. "I didn't have to tell him about Cramer. The man owns a television. It was all over the news. He had half a mind to storm on down to the Capital, but you know how he hates to leave your mama."

"Shit."

"Yeah, shit is right. Wade's blood pressure was through the roof till I pulled some strings to get your OS. By the way, how was sick leave? Did you have a good time relaxing in the Keys while your family was worrying about ya?"

Jake's stomach dropped. He never intended to make anyone worry. He ran a hand over his face. He was a selfish prick. "You're right, okay. I messed up. After Cramer, I wasn't in a good place. I haven't been for a while. I thought I was sparing everyone by keeping my distance."

"Well you're not."

He was silent for a moment. Part of him still thought staying away was the best way to protect his family. He didn't want to disappoint them. He wasn't the man they remembered. A part of him had died on that last mission, along with Ramirez and the rest of his team.

"Look, I'm not trying to hurt anyone, but what happened over there ..." His voice broke, forcing him to trail off till he collected himself. "I just needed a fresh start."

"I get it, Jake. You went through hell in Ghazni, but you gotta let it go. If you let what happened take away the people who are still here, who still love you, then what was the point of surviving?"

Jenkins' words sunk in. As usual, her tough love was on point. Even when he was a kid, Jake remembered the way she always played bad cop to Wade's good cop. No matter what angle they took, one thing was always clear, they were both in his corner. It was something he shouldn't have let himself lose sight of.

He'd been punishing himself, not realizing how it punished the people who cared about him. It was time he fixed that. "You're right. I'll call Wade and do more to stay in touch."

"Damn right you will."

Despite her stern words, Jake could hear pride sneaking into her voice. "Can you do something for me?"

"What's that?"

"I need access to a cold case."

"Call your uncle first, then we'll talk."

"It's the Jenni James case."

She paused. "Did your supervisor sign off on it?"

"I figured I'd get your blessing first."

"Smart man. Somebody raised you right."

"Jenkins, it's important."

"It always is."

"Off the record, I've got a Jane Doe, same MO as Jenni James."

"Vega?"

"Yeah. I might be able to get the bastard this time, but I need the old case file to compare notes."

"Submit the transfer request, and I'll have it sent over within the hour."

"Thanks, Jenks."

"Don't thank me till you've nailed Vega's balls to the wall. And Jake, make sure it sticks this time."

"That's the plan."

"Good luck."

Jake hung up, clinging to all the luck he could get. He was going to need it to get charges to stick to Vega, especially if Dana was right and Senator Scott was involved. The clock was ticking, but he had a favor to make good on before going inside to brief Holt about the Jane Doe.

Pulling up his uncle's contact in his phone, Jake weighed his options. He knew he owed Wade a call. Hell, he probably owed the man a whole lot more than that considering the way he'd treated him lately. But right now, he had a killer to catch.

He hit the message icon and began typing. **Sorry I've been MIA. Working a case. Will call ASAP.**

Almost as soon as he sent the text message, the three little dots began populating underneath his word bubble. It made Jake feel even worse. The man who'd given up his bachelordom to raise his sister's bastard son was waiting by the phone.

Wade's message came through. **Roger that. Take care of yourself.**

Jake's chest tightened with emotion at the simple message. It meant more to him than he could put into words. It was a reminder that he had someone a phone call away should he ever need back up. The comfort in that knowledge was overwhelming.

With bolstered confidence, Jake sent a message back. **10-4.** Then slipped his phone back into his pocket and exited his vehicle, ready to face Holt and chase down this new lead.

36

WATERY PREDAWN LIGHT WASHED D.C. IN HUES OF BLUE AND GRAY. IT might've been beautiful if Dana's mind wasn't dredging up the unspeakable things she'd seen at the ME's office. She knew the disfigured body wasn't Meredith, and she was determined to keep it that way.

She turned onto 13th Street and dialed Jake's number. His voice was full of concern when he answered. "You okay?"

Dana held her phone to her ear, clutching the steering wheel with the other. "It's not Mere."

"What? Where are you?"

"In my car. It was still at the Kincaids'. I'm coming to meet you. Meredith's not pregnant. Abby is."

Jake was silent for a moment. "How do you know that?"

"I didn't give her any information. She told me on her own." *More or less.*

"And you believe her?"

"Absolutely. She's terrified, Jake. She thinks her parents are going to disown her. Mere's the only one she confided in. She gave Abby her ID so she could go to a doctor and get what she needed without risking her parents finding out."

"Why would it matter if Abby's pregnant? She's not a minor."

"I said the same thing, but apparently the Kincaids have an inheritance clause. If Mere or Abby have any kids out of wedlock, they forfeit their share."

"Well that's some bullshit."

Dana couldn't have said it better herself. "Abby put her trust in me, Jake. We have to keep it off the record so her parents don't find out."

"I'm not going to go broadcasting this to the Kincaids, but it's gonna be pretty hard to hide when she pops out a baby."

"Not the point. I thought you'd be happy about this. You don't need to waste time getting a warrant for Meredith's medical records now."

"That's one thing in our favor. But if someone saw Meredith's name on the prescriptions, they might've jumped to the same conclusion we did."

"You still think someone might've wanted to hide the pregnancy?"

"That's what we need to find out. I'm on my way to get the cold case I was telling you about. It might help clear some things up."

"Where are you? I'll meet you so we can go over it together."

"There was an issue with the files. I'm on my way to the airport to sort it out."

"What do you mean?"

"I got access to the cold case, but the file's blank. Our analysts looked into it. The entire hard drive's been erased."

"That can't be a coincidence."

"Yeah. That's not lost on me."

"So what do we do?"

"Our only hope is the backup drive. They're housed in a storage facility in Brooklyn. I'm heading there now to meet up with Agent Jenkins to help her track them down."

Her. Dana's mind snagged on the tiny word that shouldn't matter, but somehow it stood out, even among all the other chaos. "I'll come with you."

"No. Stay here. With any luck I'll be back tonight. And Dana?"

"Yeah."

"Stay out of trouble."

37

The elevator doors to Dana's library whooshed open. For the first time she wasn't comforted by the familiar surroundings. Normally, the scent of aged paper and leather bindings was like a warm blanket, blocking her worries from the outside world. Sublevel three was a place where time stood still, and the only mysteries were inside the pages of the ancient texts she devoted her life to.

Today, more than one mind-boggling conundrum had followed her to her safe haven at the Smithsonian. Meredith was still missing, and Jake was meeting someone in New York. A female someone.

Why hadn't he told her Agent Jenkins was a woman? She felt stupid stewing over it. He didn't owe her any explanation. He'd called Jenkins an old friend. Maybe that's all they were. Or maybe not.

It wasn't her business if they'd been more than friends once, or even if they were now. She and Jake were just co-workers. Actually, they weren't even that. They were two people whose paths kept crossing, and not in a good way.

She couldn't deny that the harrowing situations they'd endured together had forged a unique bond, but they'd never promised each other anything. They'd never even explored that territory. Not that they'd had time to between serial killers, gunshot wounds, and missing best friends.

Maybe it was better if she didn't consider the possibilities of being more than whatever they were. As it was, death and destruction seemed to follow when they spent too much time together.

Dana drew in a breath, trying to clear her mind of the absurd jealousy that had suddenly gripped her. She refused to behave childishly. She'd never prescribed to the only child stigmatism of hoarding one's things. But then again, she'd never had anything worth holding on to before.

"Dr. Gray!" Claire's jubilant voice pulled Dana from her worries. "You're here! I want to hear all about it!"

"All about what?"

"The gala! Did you dance with Sergeant McSexy? Did you spend the night at his house again?"

Claire droned on, painting a picture of the inappropriate fairytale she'd dreamed up, while Dana tried to wrap her head around the fact that less than twenty-four hours ago she'd been wearing a designer gown while being groped and threatened by a senator.

A wave of fatigue crashed over her all at once. "Claire, I think I'm going to go lie down for a bit."

She grinned. "Didn't get much sleep last night, huh?"

"Something like that."

Claire winked. "Say no more. I'll hold all your calls, but after your nap, I'm ordering dumplings and you're going to dish!"

Waving her off with a noncommittal grunt, Dana headed toward the solace of her office. Once inside she closed the door and collapsed onto the couch. Before shutting her eyes, she glanced at the photo of her parents on her desk. They smiled back at her.

Instead of the warmth the photo should've filled her with, she felt hollow and lost. She was truly alone. All that was left of her family was ash and bone, Meredith was missing and ... and that was it. There was no one else in her life. All she had was her work. But studying the rituals of death did little to fulfill an empty life.

Suddenly, she wasn't eager to shut her eyes and let the darkness in, but necessity outweighed fear. She was so exhausted she was asleep by the time her head hit the couch cushion. But all too soon she was being roused from her rarely peaceful dreams.

"Dr. Gray." Dana's eyes slid open to find the culprit who'd stolen her from a few more moments of restful sleep. Claire stood over her, leering. Dana had half a mind to close her eyes again, but her impatient assistant shook her shoulder again. "Dr. Gray."

"What is it, Claire?"

"I know you said not to bother you, but someone's here to see you."

Rubbing the sleep from her eyes, Dana sat up and braced herself for impact as reality came rushing back. "Who is it?"

Claire handed Dana an unsealed envelope and stepped back. Dana's eyes widened; all traces of sleep gone as she stared at the image emblazoned on the front of the thick white stationary. It was a coat of arms, with the family name scrawled beneath: Scott.

The symbol she'd been searching for sat in the very center of the design. She'd only seen it once before. On the Senator's ring.

Standing, she carried the card and envelope over to her desk to examine it closer. Claire paled when she saw the symbol. "Is that ..."

"The Priory of Bones." Dana flipped open the card and read the message aloud. "Your presence is requested immediately. My assistant will accompany you." She raised her eyes to Claire. "Where is he?"

"You're not going with him, are you?"

"Mere is missing. I need answers, Claire."

"Okay, but at least get Jake to go with you."

"Jake's in New York. I'll be fine."

"What if you're not?"

"If I'm not back by tonight, call Jake and let him know about this."

Dana grabbed her purse and started to head toward her office door, but Claire caught her hand. The younger woman's grip was as icy as the fear in her clear blue eyes. "There are things more dangerous than what we keep hidden away in these books, Dr. Gray. You need to be careful."

Doing her best to shake off Claire's chilling words, Dana strode out of her office into the library. A well-dressed man waited by the bank of tables. With sandy brown hair, green eyes and perfect bone structure, he was alarmingly good looking. His face lit with a disarming smile when he saw her approaching. "Hello, Dr. Gray. You're a difficult woman to track down."

She gestured to her underground library. "Casualty of the job, I'm afraid."

He chuckled. "Luckily I'm good at my job. Ben Riley, Senator Scott's congressional aide."

"Congressional aide? So you just moonlight as a bounty hunter?"

He laughed again. "So it seems."

"You can tell the Senator I don't tolerate harassment."

"You can tell him yourself. He'd like to have coffee with you."

"Just coffee?"

"Coffee and a conversation."

Standing taller, Dana fought the unease that crept up her spine. "Then lead the way."

38

"LOOK WHAT THE CAT DRAGGED IN!"

Jake grinned, pulling Jenkins into a bear hug. "It's good to see you, too."

The veteran agent ruffled his hair like he was twelve and patted him on the back.

"Thanks for doing this," Jake said as the two fell into step walking up to the storage facility.

"It is a bitch getting to Brooklyn this time of day, but anything for the kid that put that joyful twang back in my best friend's voice."

"Wade told you I called him?"

Jenkins arched her all-knowing blonde eyebrows. "He told me you texted him, with a promise to call when this case is over."

There was no pulling one over on this woman. She might be in her fifties, but she was as sharp as the day the FBI minted her. "How often do you guys talk?"

"Every day," she replied proudly. "I taught him how to do video calls."

"So you *can* teach an old dog new tricks?"

Joking aside, Jake was glad Wade and Jenkins were still close. His uncle had been devastated when he found out she chose the FBI over re-upping. She'd asked him to come with her, but he'd refused, using Jake and his mother as an excuse.

Jake had only been a kid back then, but now he wondered if Wade and Jenkins could've been more than friends if he hadn't been in the way. Now that he was older, it didn't sit well with him that his uncle had given up so much to raise him and care for his mother. That should've been Jake's father's job.

He pushed the thought away, hearing another of Wade's nuggets of wisdom. *Don't lose your present to your past.*

"How's D.C. treatin' ya?"

"It's a lot wetter than I'm used to."

Jenkins laughed. "Well that's to be expected after spending your entire life in one godforsaken desert or another."

Jake nodded. He'd grown up in Nevada, then spent his Army days bouncing around Iraq, Syria and Afghanistan. But the weather wasn't what made him trade his uniform for a badge. "What about you? You used to big city life?"

"Honey, I'm a chameleon. The Air Force taught me to adapt."

"Do you miss it?"

"Serving? Sometimes. But I'm doing my part with the Bureau. Besides." She popped the collar of her pristine black suit jacket. "I look a hell of a lot better in Prada than that old fart sack Wade still bums around in."

Jake snorted, thinking back on how his uncle practically lived in his old flight suits, even when off duty. "Comfortable doesn't go out of style," Jake teased in his best Uncle Wade impression.

The crease near Jenkins' blue eyes wrinkled with laughter. "That man is as stubborn as an ox. And you're not too far behind."

Jake shrugged. "Comes in handy with cases like this."

"Wanna fill me in on what you got so far?"

Jake caught her up to speed as they checked in at the front desk of the storage facility. A quick flash of their badges and they were directed to the ninth floor of the dusty red brick building.

"So you've got a Jane Doe that could pass for your MP. Same MO as Jenni James. That rules out crime of passion."

"Maybe not," Jake argued.

"How do you figure?"

"This stays between us?"

"Goes without sayin'."

"My MP was having a secret affair with a US Senator."

"Shit. You think a politician has Vega in his pocket?"

"It's not that far a reach considering the politician."

"Who?"

"Scott."

"Senator Warren Scott? This is his district!"

"I'm aware. My MP worked for Senator Scott. It's not public knowledge yet, but they were sleeping together, and he may have suspected that she was pregnant."

"So Scott hired Vega to take care of her?"

"It's possible. He told my partner he knows how to make problems disappear."

Jenkins narrowed her eyes. "You have a partner?"

"Sort of."

"Either you do, or you don't."

"It's complicated. She worked the Cramer case with me and sort of got roped into this one."

Jenkins' eyebrows bunched together like two speeding bullets stuck in suspension. "The Witch Doctor? I get Cramer and that twisted situation, but what's a civilian got to do with this case?"

"She knows my MP."

"How well?"

"They were best friends."

"Jake ..."

"I know. If it were up to me, I wouldn't let her anywhere near this, but my hands are tied. MP's parents went over my head to have Dr. Gray added as a consultant. Orders from the Assistant Director."

Jenkins gave a low whistle. "Be careful. Anyone too close to a vic tends to be a wildcard."

Jake knew that all too well, but even after everything they went through with Cramer, he had faith in Dana. She was smart and resilient, and she'd saved his life. He owed her. "One more thing, Jenks. Don't call her Witch Doctor. She hates that."

Jenkins smirked and pressed the call button for the elevator. "Roger that."

Jake took one look at the rickety old lift and opted for the stairs. Climbing nine floors would be good cardio. He hadn't gotten much in the past few days. Jenkins ridiculed him as the accordion cage closed around her, promising a bumpy ride. She might beat him up the nine flights, but there was no way he was voluntarily getting in that death trap.

Pushing through the metal door leading to the stairwell, Jake was greeted with the mundane hum of fluorescent lights. They flickered periodically as he climbed up the steps. The old brick walls were surprisingly well kept, lined with old photographs depicting the transformations the nearly two-hundred-year-old warehouse had endured.

Each flight was like walking through a time capsule as black and white images showed war-hardened warehouse workers, then smiling apartment dwelling families, then wealthy hotel guests.

Now the warehouse had returned to its roots, storing another kind of history.

Jake pushed the door marked ninth-floor open and emerged into the main hall. Jenkins stood waiting next to the elevator. "Took you long enough."

"Are all the floors FBI storage?"

She shook her head. "Just this one. NYPD has the rest. Come on, this way."

Jake followed her a short distance, their footsteps echoing off the dull vinyl tiles. "Here we are." Jenkins pulled out her key and unlocked an unmarked black door.

Inside, she flipped on a light switch, illuminating row upon row of shelves. They grew out of the dingy gray carpet like dominos. He didn't know why, but it made him think of Dana's library, and for a moment he wished he'd asked her to come.

"This should be the one." Jenkins walked to the bone-colored shelving unit labeled with the year they were looking for and began working the hand crank. The old shelving system groaned to life, rolling on the floor tracks that had been added to conserve space. Jake helped push the shelves apart while she cranked.

When there was enough space, they slipped between the rows. Jenkins went first, swiping on her phone light to read the case numbers labeling the containers of backup drives. Whoever designed the storage room hadn't accounted for the height of the shelves. They were probably ten feet tall and blocked out the track lighting that hung from the yellowing ceiling tiles.

Jenkins squinted to make heads or tails of the labels. Considering there were dozens of numeric file codes on each container, it wasn't an easy task. Jake turned his phone light on and went to work. "I'll start on the top shelves. You want to take the bottom and meet in the middle?"

"Roger that."

Jake was halfway through the first row when he felt Jenkins freeze. He looked down at her. She was kneeling on the floor, her lips pressed together in a frown.

"What is it?"

She sighed, sitting back on her heels. "You're not going to like it."

He squatted down next to her and saw the empty space where the plastic storage box should've been. Anger rushed through him like a bullet, leaving a trail of heat prickling his skin. "It's missing," he muttered, stating the obvious for no other reason than he couldn't quite believe it.

Jenkins nodded. "How much you wanna bet it's the one we came here for?"

39

CHILLS SWEPT DOWN DANA'S SPINE AS SHE PASSED BENEATH THE ORNATE stone archway.

She'd been to the Franciscan Monastery many times over the course of her research. The catacombs beneath were a national treasure, as were the replicas of other notable tombs scattered across the holy grounds. Normally, the place brought her peace, but there was something unsettling about meeting the Senator here.

As she followed Ben Riley into the church and past the altar she knew exactly where he was leading her. She'd descended the hand-hewn staircase so many times she could practically navigate it in the dark, which sometimes was necessary.

In order to preserve the fragile paintings on the tombs, the catacombs were only lit by lantern light carried by tour guides. She was about to warn Riley of that fact when she noticed something peculiar. The iron gate to the catacombs was closed. Not only that, a large chain had been draped across the earthen entrance. A red acrylic sign hung from it, announcing, CATACOMBS CLOSED TO THE PUBLIC.

Riley lifted a skeleton key from his pocket and began working the lock.

"It says closed to the public," Dana insisted.

He gave her another of his dazzling grins. "Good thing we're not the public."

She swallowed the fear that began clawing its way up her throat. There was no avoiding the cloak and dagger of it all. She was attending a secret meeting with a senator in an underground lair littered with the sacred bones of saints.

If Senator Scott was hoping to disprove his affiliation to the Priory of Bones, he wasn't off to a good start. Or maybe that was the point ... he wanted to intimidate her.

She was ashamed how well it was working.

"This way."

Fear burned in her belly, urging her to turn back as she followed Riley into the tunnel that led beneath the church. She was acutely aware of the way the sunlight faded behind her. After a few more steps, the darkness swallowed them whole.

Dana's heart pounded in her ears, almost blotting out the echoes of their footsteps. She told herself to breathe, but her lungs fought against the stale scent of loam and death that clung to the damp air.

Riley's phone was a pinprick of light amidst the darkness. But still, he walked the tunnels like he knew them better than she did. It wasn't a reassuring thought. Dana stumbled on the uneven stones. Instinct made her reach out. She caught the sleeve of Riley's suit jacket.

"Careful." His hand found hers, leading her the rest of the way.

She took no comfort in his grip. It was tight and controlling, yet the clammy smoothness of his palms did little to assure her that he could handle himself if they ran into any trouble. Though she reminded herself that he was probably on the side of trouble since he was the one who brought her here.

They rounded the corner to the crypt of St. Innocent, the child martyr. The sanctuary blazed with candlelight. A cloaked shadow stood in the center, hands clasped, head bent in prayer. The figure looked up when Dana approached, but the large black hood obscured their identity. Something about the hooded figure sent fear skittering down her spine. Even though she couldn't see the face hiding in the shadows, one thing was certain, she wasn't meeting with the Senator.

Senator Scott was a large, lumbering man. This figure was slim, average height; their movements graceful. Dana jerked her hand from Riley's iron grasp. "What's going on here?" No one spoke. "Fine. Then I'm leaving."

Riley moved to block her way. "Not until you've received the Senator's message."

"Which is?"

A smile stretched across Riley's face, ominous in the dancing shadows, but the answer came from behind her.

"It's more of a warning."

Dana whirled toward the sound. She knew that voice. Hearing it here shook her to her core. She squarely faced the hooded figure, willing it to speak again so she could be sure she wasn't losing her mind. She watched pale hands reach up and slowly pull back the black hood. Dana gasped as long blonde hair tumbled free. "Mere?"

Meredith spoke with no emotion. "I need you to stop looking."

"But ... I don't understand."

"You're not meant to."

Dana rushed forward, her fingers digging into her friend's shoulders to be sure she wasn't hallucinating. "Meredith. My God! We've been so worried. Everyone's looking for you."

"You need to make them stop."

"What? Why?"

"Because I don't want to be found."

"But I don't understand. Everyone's so worried about you. Your parents are out of their minds."

Anger flashed in Meredith's eyes. "I gave them a body! But you ruined everything."

"Mere. You're not making any sense."

"Just make them stop looking and stay out of my way!"

Dana opened her mouth to argue but an explosion of pain erupted behind her ear. Her vision went black, then white, then black again. The world tilted and the cold stone floor rose up to meet her cheek. There was a ringing. Then it stopped and the world willowed into blackness, the last bits of light crackling like the tailend of fireworks.

40

"Jake, slow down. Jake!" Jenkins jogged behind him, taking two steps for every stride of his. She was keeping up, but just barely. His long legs chewed up the corridor and then the stairs.

Jenkins swore as she followed behind him. "Don't do something stupid, Jake."

"I wanna know how much a life is worth to that little shit at the front desk. What do ya think he sold out for? One, two Gs? Maybe it wasn't even that much."

"Jacob Miller Shepard! You will not deep six your career over this. Not on my watch."

Hearing his father's name startled him, but not enough to slow him down. He huffed a bitter laugh. "What career?"

Jake hadn't signed on for this. Chasing ghosts for a corrupt government. It was Afghanistan all over again. And once again, he wasn't helping anyone. Not Meredith Kincaid. Not Jenni James. Not all the countless cases that crossed his desk. He was tired of hitting dead ends. But hitting the lazy prick at the front desk ... that was gonna feel good.

Jake tested the door's hinges as he slammed into it, full force. It collided with the spring stopper so hard, it knocked straight through the drywall. The kid behind the desk rose to his feet. *Good,* Jake thought. *That means further to fall.*

Will, as his nametag read, had the nerve to start shouting at Jake. "You're gonna have to pay for that."

Jake stormed up to the window and grabbed the scrawny punk by his shirt, hauling him through the opening like a hooked trout. "How 'bout you look the other way? Just like you did when you let someone walk outta here with the hard drive we're looking for."

"What the—"

"Stand down, Agent."

Both Jake and the wiggling prick turned their attention to Jenkins. She stood in the doorway to the stairwell, hand at her weapon belt.

"This is abuse!" Will screamed.

Jake was about to snap. "Abuse? You have no clue, do you?" He set the scumbag on his feet and shoved him against the wall. Pulling out his phone, he flipped to the photos from the ME and shoved them in Will's face. "Have you ever had your jaw removed? How about your fingertips cut off? Ever had your corpse tattooed?"

Will shook his head furiously after each question, tears and spittle leaking from him as he begged for mercy. "No. No. No. I d-didn't do anything, man. I s-swear!"

"Don't talk to me about abuse, you worthless piece of shit!" Jake roared. "You probably still live at home in your parents' basement. Tell me something. Do you get off on this?"

"I don't know what you're talking about, man!"

"Does it make you feel like a man to know you're standing in the way of justice? Making my work amount to nothing?"

"P-please ..." Will begged.

"Jake?" Jenkins wrapped a hand around his bicep, her gaze making Jake look at Will's pants. The kid had pissed himself. It snapped Jake out of his rage.

"Walk away," Jenkins ordered.

He released Will and walked silently out the front doors.

Standing in the shade of the building, Jake leaned against the brick. He watched the Brooklyn traffic rush by as he evaluated what just transpired. Had he really ripped a twenty-something punk through a security window and terrified him so thoroughly that he pissed himself?

It was a gross misconduct of power. He could lose his badge for this, or worse.

Jake closed his eyes and let his head fall back against the brick. He needed to get a grip. He knew why he flew off the handle, but he wasn't doing Meredith or Jenni or the thousands of other victimized women any good by taking his frustration out on someone else. This might get him kicked off the case and that was the last thing they needed. They deserved justice. Jake just wasn't sure he was the guy for the job anymore.

He opened his eyes, gazing up at the building. The gray stone arch over the entrance stood out in contrast to the red brick. The keystone caught his attention. Dead center was the symbol from Senator Scott's ring. Part of it anyway. Not the skull and bones, but the serpent and challis were clear as day.

Jake snapped a photo, beginning to wonder if he'd been too quick to dismiss Dana's conspiracy theories. The world seemed hellbent on rubbing his nose in the possibility of a conspiracy. Being opposed to the relevance in this case was just plain ignorant, and maybe dangerous.

Senator Scott was from New York. He was well connected. He could've easily had someone in his pocket infiltrate this building and snatch the hard drive. Probably the same person who erased the original file at the FBI field office. Dana's words echoed in his head. *The Priory of Bones were rumored to have a network so infiltrating and far reaching, nothing was off limits.*

His gut churned, that old feeling that had saved his ass a time or three woke from its slumber. He shouldn't have left Dana alone. If Senator Scott was behind the missing hard drive, then he was tying up loose ends. Dana had pegged Scott from day one. That made her a pretty big loose end.

Jake was still staring at the carving when Jenkins exited the building. Before she could lay into him about his behavior, he cut her off. "Do you know that symbol?"

She followed his gaze. "Sure. It's from the Freemasons. They built this building. Probably built most of New York, though not much is still standing. Why?"

"Senator Scott took the hard drive, Jenks."

"Jake ..."

"I know how crazy it sounds, believe me, but everything points to him."

"Even so, what you just did in there ... I think I can smooth things over, but you can't react like that."

"I know, I just—" His phone started to buzz. He glanced at it and saw Dana's office number lighting up his caller ID. "I've gotta take this." He clicked answer but didn't even get a greeting out before Claire's frantic voice erupted into sounds too high pitched to decipher. "Claire? Slow down. What's wrong?"

"Dana went to meet with the Senator."

"She what?"

"He sent his political aide over to fetch her. But that was hours ago. She said not to worry, but I can't shake this feeling that something's not right. I keep trying her phone and it goes to voicemail."

"I'm on my way." He hung up, turning to Jenkins to explain, but she was waving him off.

"Go. I'll deal with this."

His feet were already moving. "I owe you one."

"Try more than one," she called as he hailed a cab.

Jake jumped into the dirty yellow cab and threw a wad of cash at the driver. "How fast can you get me to JFK?"

41

JARRED AWAKE, THE SCENT OF SNUFFED CANDLES STILL LINGERED IN the air.

Dana was reluctant to leave the warmth of her dreams. There she was safe, with memories of her parents, sharing waffles and laughter on a snowy morning. She'd stay there forever if she could. Here ... she didn't quite know where here was, but she knew it wasn't somewhere she wanted to be.

Dana brought her hands to her face to make sure her eyes were actually open. They were. She blinked a few times and her vision started to adjust, making out shapes in the darkness. Smooth stone walls. Arched recesses. Strange red paintings. Roman numerals. A glass box.

She sat up and instantly regretted it. Pain ricocheted from her skull to her spine. Her vision went white and fuzzy at the edges as she fought the urge to vomit. Then all at once, it came back to her. Where she was. Who she'd been with.

Despite the immense effort it took, she clambered to her feet. "Mere?" The word felt like sandpaper as it scratched its way past her throat. She tried again. "Meredith?"

The only sound that echoed back to Dana was her own raspy voice. How long had she been down here? And why was it so dark?

The catacombs were eerily still. She remembered the sign she'd passed on the way down, announcing the closure. Then she remembered the very heavy chain that had been locked around the gates.

Flicking on her cellphone light, she began to run. Claustrophobia had never been a fear of hers. She worked three levels below the Smithsonian. But there was something unsettling about the idea of being locked in the catacombs. Death may be her profession, but she drew the line at sleeping in a crypt.

Stumbling in the darkness, she reached for her phone to light the way. Her heartbeat stuttered when she saw the time. Claire would be worried. But not so much time had passed that she wouldn't be able to catch up to Meredith.

The thought had her ignoring the throbbing in her head as she quickened her pace. She needed to get outside so she could get cell service. If she could get Jake on the phone, he could start tracking Meredith. Surely, she'd been caught on camera coming and going from the monastery grounds.

Energized by the knowledge that Meredith was alive, Dana tried to put together a mental timeline, but her pounding head fought her progress. The more she thought about her alarming conversation with her friend, the more confused she was. Why didn't Meredith want to be found?

Stop looking ... Meredith's words echoed through Dana's foggy mind. It didn't make sense. But at the moment nothing did. Dana couldn't breathe let alone think straight. Fresh air would help. She just needed to get outside.

Pumping her legs faster, Dana raced toward the surface. When the gate finally came into view, she felt a glimmer of hope, only to have it dashed by the sight of the chain locked securely in place. She knew it wouldn't budge, but she tried anyway, yanking on it furiously. The chain clanked against the iron with a finality that zapped her energy. Sinking to her knees Dana gripped the bars of the gate and shook it, crying out. "Help! Please! Help."

At this hour, she knew she'd need a miracle to be heard. Even though she could recite the origins and theology of just about every religion, she'd never chosen a faith of her own. If there was ever a time to pray, it was now. She yelled over and over, praying there was still someone on the sprawling grounds. Meredith's life depended on it.

As Dana knelt on the wrong side of the catacomb gates, she let her mind wander back to her brief conversation with Meredith again. Something didn't feel right. Her long blonde hair looked a bit unkempt, but her wild blue eyes were unmistakable. Dana was positive it was Meredith. Even in the dim candlelight, she was sure she hadn't been speaking to an imposter. But what possible reason could Meredith have for wanting to disappear? Especially when she knew her sister needed her.

Vindication swept through Dana as she realized the only logical explanation was that Meredith had been brainwashed by the Senator and the Priory of Bones. It wasn't uncharacteristic for cults to use separation strategies to lure members into the fold. By cutting them off from bonds to the outside world, they were easier to manipulate.

But still, there was usually some sliver of willingness on the abductee's part. Had Senator Scott told Meredith there was no way out? There was. Dana just needed to find a way to make her see that.

Dana felt even more fire to nail Senator Scott to the wall. When she got free, his office was going to be her first stop.

Angling her phone, she searched for a signal while continuing to shout for help. At this point, she'd take a miracle in any form. Her head hurt so bad she was afraid to touch it. All the yelling was making it ache more. The pain spread behind her eyes, making her nausea even worse. But she refused to give up.

"Help! Please. Someone! Anyone ..." Her voice trailed off as she realized she was wasting her breath.

The church had closed hours ago. No one was going to hear her. Trying to get cell service was her best bet. Standing, Dana reached through the iron gates as far as she could, waving the phone around as she watched the signal blink in and out. It was strongest facing the east window.

She pressed her face against the bars, breathing through the pain. One signal bar pulsed like a beacon of hope. She held the phone steady while pulling up Jake's number. She knew he was most likely still in New York, but if she could get through to him, he'd send help.

Pressing call, she watched, holding her breath as the call tried to connect. After what seemed like an eternity, CALL FAIL blinked across the screen. Dana swore and tried again and again. The result was always the same. Her battery dropped a level. She was running out of time.

Unwilling to give up, she put the phone on the floor, dialed Jake's number, pressed call and prayed as she gave it a shove. She watched with bated breath as the phone skittered across the marble floor toward the windows, and hopefully a stronger cell signal. She could still see the green icon blinking as the call tried to connect.

"Please, please, please ..."

Her heart stumbled, missing a beat when she heard ringing. A faction of a second later her prayers were answered. Jake's voice boomed through the church like the Holy Spirit. "Dana? Dana!"

She didn't waste time with a greeting. "I'm at the Franciscan Monastery locked in the catacombs!"

"Roger that." His voice was muffled for a moment before he spoke again. "Claire, she's in the church." Jake's voice became clear again. "We'll be there soon. Hold tight."

Dana's heart soared. Jake was in D.C.! He was looking for her! She knew she had Claire to thank, but at the moment, Dana could barely find the strength to stay on her feet. When her knees buckled, she didn't fight it. Clinging to the bars, she eased to the floor, letting the coolness of the iron bars quell the throbbing pain that gripped her head like a vice. Feeling woozy, she closed her eyes just for a moment.

The next thing Dana knew, Jake was shaking her awake. "Dana! Dana!"

Her eyes fluttered as she looked up at him. Claire was there too, her clear blue eyes wide with fear. "Where am I?" Dana was confused by the strange slur to her voice.

Jake's focus narrowed as he assessed her. "Can you tell me what day it is?"

"Mere was here. I saw her. We have to check the tapes."

"We will," Jake promised, reaching through the bars to squeeze her hand. "But first we need to get you to the hospital."

"No. I don't need the hospital. I need Mere."

Jake's head cocked to the side, concern lacing his voice as he spoke to Claire. "Looks like she has a pretty nasty head wound."

Dana's hand went to her head and she gave an involuntary wince. "It's just a headache."

Claire gasped. "Dana. Your hand."

Her fingers were red and sticky and kept moving in and out of focus, which made her feel dizzy. She needed her glasses. Feeling her face, she realized they were missing. "I don't feel so good."

Jake's warm hand reached through the gate to grasp her shoulder. "Can you move?"

She nodded, instantly regretting the movement. The world swayed. If Jake wasn't holding her, she might've melted through the floor. At least that's how she felt.

"Dana, I need you to move back so I can get you out. Can you do that? Can you go back down the stairs so I can remove the lock?"

"But Mere. She was here. We need to go after her."

"I know. We're gonna go get her, but I need to get you out first, okay? Go down the stairs and wait for me."

Dana tried to stand up, but the room fell dark. The cold stone floor rushed up to meet her again. Then there was an explosion of sound. It was so loud she was sure her eardrums shattered. Maybe all of her had shattered. Maybe the whole world had been blown apart because after that she saw nothing.

42

Jake pulled his Sig Sauer from his hip holster, dropping the bullet into the chamber before Dana's head even hit the ground. He squeezed the trigger. Hammer, pin, ignition. Jake exhaled with the firing sequence like it was a part of him.

The sound of the gunshot reverberated through the massive cathedral like it was return fire. But the only sound Jake was focused on was the clank of the heavy chain keeping him from Dana. It dropped to the ground, the old lock reduced to a mangled hunk of metal.

Holstering his weapon, Jake wrenched open the heavy iron gate and took the steps two at a time until he reached Dana. After she collapsed, she'd slid down them, out of sight. Reaching her, he checked for a pulse. Relief flooded him when he felt the steady beat beneath his fingers.

He yelled to Claire. "She's okay."

Claire stood at the top of the stairs, eerily still as she looked down at them. She was so pale she looked like a ghost. Seeing Dana like this was an obvious shock. So was the gunshot. Claire had screamed when Jake fired his round into the lock. There hadn't been time to warn her. Even if there had been, he knew the memory of the gunshot would haunt her. It wasn't the kind of thing to be easily forgotten if you weren't used to it. "Claire, go out front and call for an ambulance."

She didn't move. The delicate wisp of a girl looked like she was about to shatter. The last thing Jake needed was another unconscious woman on his hands. "Claire. Call an ambulance. Now."

His harsh tone snapped her out of it. She backed away quickly, her footsteps moving toward the exit. The fresh air would help. It was all he could offer at the moment. Right now, his mind was too preoccupied with Dana.

Not wanting to risk moving her, he settled next to her on the cold, hard steps. Jake gently brushed her dark hair back, avoiding the area near her ear that was slick with blood. "Help is coming, Dana. Stay with me."

Each word clawed its way up his throat, tearing through old scar tissue. Jake had said them before. To Ramirez.

He reminded himself Dana was not Ramirez, and this wasn't Afghanistan. Things were going to be different this time.

THE BEEP, beep, beep of the monitors in Dana's hospital room tried to lure Jake under, but he refused to give in to sleep.

He knew he needed it. He could count the hours he'd slept on one hand since this case began. And now, with his adrenaline depleted, he was more zombie than human. He felt like he was back on Red Team night watch. Even completely drained, Jake was determined to keep his eyes open while Dana's were closed.

Someone needed to look out for her until whoever did this was apprehended.

She was lucky he'd found her so quickly. The EMTs said her head wound was severe. The doctors were still trying to rule out a brain bleed or aneurysm.

If Claire hadn't called him ... If they hadn't been tracking her phone ... Jake wasn't someone who lived in what-ifs. It wasn't possible in his line of work. But he couldn't help imagining how differently things could've gone.

He was thankful he'd been nearby when Dana called. He'd tracked her phone to the general area but pinpointing her exact location would've been difficult if she hadn't called.

Jake leaned forward, the blue plastic hospital chair squeaking under his weight. He took Dana's hand between his. She wasn't out of the woods yet, but he had faith in her. If she would just open her eyes ...

A shadow at the door had Jake on his feet, hand at his holster. Claire sucked in a breath, taking a step back.

"Sorry," he muttered. "I thought you were ..."

"Who?" she asked.

"I don't know. That's the problem. We have no clue who did this to her."

"Do you believe what Dr. Gray said about Meredith?"

"I don't know what to believe."

Claire nodded, her inquisition over. She walked quickly into the dark hospital room, the unmistakable scent of Thai food proceeding her. Jake took the duffle from her shoulder startling her, almost like she forgot she was carrying it.

"I swung by Dr. Gray's to pick up some clothes. I grabbed her glasses, but I didn't know what she'd need so I chose an assortment. Do you think she'll mind?"

Jake shook his head. He'd known Claire as long as Dana, but the girl's odd behavior still surprised him. Right now, it was a welcome relief. "I think Dana will have more to worry about than her wardrobe when she wakes up."

"Oh. Right."

"What's in the bag?" Jake asked, though he had a pretty good idea judging from the sharp smell of Asian spices.

Claire shoved the large brown bag toward him. "I thought you might be hungry."

"Dumplings?"

She nodded.

Jake opened the bag and sighed as the mouthwatering blend of spices assaulted him. "You are an angel, Elvira."

Even in the darkness he could see Claire blush. For a moment, the webbing of blue veins in her cheeks vanished, hidden by the rush of blood beneath her translucent skin. Anyone looking into the hospital room would probably balk at the scene. An armed federal agent and a goth version of Sailor Moon.

Jake was glad Claire showed up. She understood the art of enjoying a meal without conversation. They shared the dumplings and sat in comfortable silence for a while before Claire piped up. "Do you think the Senator did this?"

"I don't know, but I have some questions for the guy who lured Dana to the catacombs."

"I swear if I knew that's where he was taking her—"

"Claire, this isn't your fault."

"Feels like it is," she muttered, picking at the overly long sleeve of her black cardigan. "I should've called you as soon as he showed up."

"You're sure he said he worked for Senator Scott?"

She nodded. "He said his name was Ben Riley, Senator Scott's congressional aide."

Anger spiked through Jake's veins. He'd eliminated the yuppie prick as a suspect at the IWP Gala. "When Dana wakes up, I'm going to have some questions for Riley."

"If she wakes up."

Jake wiped his hands on his napkin and gave Claire's slim shoulder a squeeze. "She's going to be okay." His phone buzzed in his pocket. Seeing the name on the caller ID, he stood. "Do you mind sitting with her? I need to take this."

Claire nodded and Jake briskly walked into the hall. His voice echoed off the sterile white walls. "Jenks? Any luck?"

The deep sigh that greeted him was answer enough. "I'm still trying to track down the file. Nothing so far, but I was able to smooth things over with the clerk. Turns out he had a misdemeanor charge. He'll keep quiet in exchange for expunging it."

Jake swore under his breath. Instead of tracking down a killer he was letting low-level criminals off because of his own stupidity. "That's unacceptable."

"I'm pulling the security footage, but the kid said it's erased each week."

"Not the hard drive. The deal you made with that waste of space."

"The charge was vandalism, Jake. We're not talking about a crime boss here. The kid just tagged a few buildings and was dumb enough to get caught."

Jake remained silent.

"Look, I'm sorry about the file. I want to bring Vega down, too."

"It's not just Vega." Jake filled Jenkins in about what had gone down at the catacombs.

"Shit. Is there anything I can do?"

"Send me whatever you can remember about the Jenni James case. I think between the two of us I can piece the report together from memory."

"Roger that. And Jake ..."

"Yeah?"

"We had a deal. Call your uncle."

43

A DEAL WAS A DEAL.

Jake told Jenkins he'd call Wade if she helped him with the Jenni James file. She'd held up her end of the bargain. The result hadn't been the desired one, but that wasn't her fault.

After checking that there was no change in Dana's condition, Jake walked back out into the hallway to call his uncle. The place felt too bright and public with all the hospital staff milling about, but he didn't want to wander too far from Dana.

Sucking it up, he leaned against the wall across from her room. He still had a clear line of sight. He could see Claire curled up in a chair, earbuds in. She was listening to music, her head bopping to the beat, gaze fixed on her boss.

Convinced Dana was in good hands Jake popped a piece of cinnamon gum in his mouth to ease his nerves and dialed his uncle's number.

"Jake?"

"Hey, Wade."

A booming laugh filled the line. "Damn, it's good to hear your voice!"

Jake's chest tightened. "Yours, too."

Wade paused. "Is everything okay, son?"

"Actually ..." He trailed off wondering if he should burden his uncle with the details, but before he made a conscious decision, the words began spilling out. "I'm in the hospital. My partner's not doing so well."

"Tell me." It was more invitation than command, but it broke something loose in Jake. A door he'd wedged shut suddenly opened, and he spilled the details of the past few months of his life, starting from when Dana came into it.

By the time Jake caught Wade up on their present case, he felt years lighter. He didn't expect his uncle to fix his problems but being able to share them with him had somehow lightened the weight he was carrying.

"I wish there was more I could do," Wade said when Jake was done.

"Not much you can do from Nevada."

"I'm actually heading to New York tomorrow. Walter's threatening to give my share of the hunting cabin to his son if I don't use it. Like that frogman would even know what to do on dry land."

Jake laughed. "It's good to see some things never change."

Wade and his old Air Force buddy shared a hunting cabin in upstate New York. Jake grew up going there. He had a lot of fond memories of the place. Except for the one and only time Walter and his son Mitch joined them.

It turned out the cabin wasn't big enough for four men. Especially when one of those men wouldn't stop going on about how the SEALs were the best branch of the military. The argument escalated into a shooting contest, then arm wrestling, then a full-blown drunken brawl. After that, a strict schedule was introduced so the hunting trips didn't overlap.

"Wish I could join you up there," Jake said, meaning it.

"Me too, but it sounds like you're in the weeds. Maybe another time," Wade offered, letting him off the hook.

"Wade ... I'll try harder ..." Jake trailed off, not sure what he could say to excuse the way he'd ignored the man who raised him.

"Jake, all I need is for you to know I'm here if you need me."

"I do."

“Good. Take care of yourself, son.”

“You too.”

Jake hung up, his throat tight with emotions he rarely let surface. When he’d returned from Afghanistan on a C-17 full of pine, he left the Army thinking he had to turn his back on his past if he wanted to have a future. But maybe that wasn’t entirely true. Maybe he was strong enough to sift through his memories and hold on to the good ones.

Claire’s voice broke through his thoughts. “Jake! She’s awake!”

He raced into Dana’s hospital room. Her eyes were open but unfocused as she rambled more nonsense about the Senator and Meredith. Claire handed Dana her glasses as a nurse rushed in behind him, pushing them out of the way. Claire stepped out to the hall, but Jake refused to leave in case Dana uttered anything that didn’t sound like a delusional conspiracy from a woman with a head injury.

“I’m going to give you something for the pain,” the nurse said, holding a syringe up to the IV port.

Dana screamed and batted it out of her hand. Jake was by her side in an instant, his nerves on edge. He should’ve anticipated her response. After what happened with Cramer, he couldn’t blame Dana for reacting that way around needles. He approached the nurse. “I need to see your ID.”

The nurse cocked her head, her voice full of all the attitude that went along with being questioned at this hour. “Excuse me?”

He held up his badge. “I’m sorry. Dr. Gray is under FBI protection. I can’t let you administer any medication until I can verify your credentials.”

The nurse threw her hands up. “Fine. Just don’t page me when the painkillers wear off.” She shoved past Jake, grumbling unpleasantly under her breath as she left the room.

“Thank you,” Dana whispered when he moved closer. “Needles.” She swallowed thickly. “After Cramer—”

“I know,” he interrupted, not wanting to make her relive that nightmare. He handed her a plastic cup with a straw in it. “Water?”

Jake pulled up a chair while she drank, setting the cup back on the side table when she was done. He sat down, scooting the chair even closer. "What happened?"

"I told you. I saw Mere. She's alive."

Jake sat there studying her. The burst blood vessel in her left eye looked like an ink stain, but other than that she appeared lucid. He knew she was on pain meds for the blow she took to her head, but he pulled his notepad out anyway. Flipping it open, he grabbed a pen. "Start from the beginning."

44

"So, Ben Riley shows up at your office with an invitation to see Senator Scott. You go with him. He drives you to the Franciscan Monastery and takes you down to the catacombs even though they're closed. There you see Meredith, wearing a black hooded robe?"

Dana huffed out an impatient breath. "Jake, I know how it sounds, but that's what happened."

"You said it was dark in the catacombs. How can you be sure it was Meredith?"

"Because I'm sure! I heard her voice. She pulled her hood back. I saw her face. I touched her. We had a conversation."

"Right." He ticked something on his infuriating notepad. "She told you to stop looking. Why do you think that is?"

"Because she's been brainwashed by the Senator and the Priory of Bones. We've been over this, Jake. Why are you wasting time making me repeat myself when we should be out there looking for Meredith?"

"Dana, you suffered a severe head injury. The things you remember might not have happened that way."

Panic gripped her. "You don't believe me?"

"I believe you believe that's what happened."

"Jake, please. That's what they want. For no one to believe me because of this." She pointed to her bandaged head. "I'm not making this up. Think about all the dead ends we've run into. The way that Jane Doe was mutilated. You can't tell me this is a normal missing person case."

He looked at the floor. She could see she was breaking him down. "What about the lead you were following in New York?"

"Honestly, I think it may have been a set up so whoever's behind this could get to you."

Dana hadn't thought about that, but she couldn't ignore the way the idea wrapped around her and took hold. It fit. "I'm right about this, Jake. Meredith was in the catacombs, and she needs our help." His silence frayed her nerves. "I'll take a polygraph if that's what you need, but I can't just sit here and do nothing."

"Easy, Kojak."

"Who?"

"Doesn't matter. I believe you, okay? But you're not going anywhere. That bump on your head is serious."

"I'm fine," she argued despite her head feeling like it was trapped in a vise.

"That may be, but you earned yourself an overnight. Twenty-four-hour observation. It's protocol."

"No, I—"

"It's not up for discussion."

Needing to conserve energy she decided to choose her battles. Despite her objections, she knew she wasn't in any shape to go running into the night to track down secret society members. But she also didn't need a babysitter. "Fine, but you're not going to find Meredith sitting here with me all night."

"Who said I was?"

Dana crossed her arms when she caught the hint of Jake's smirk. It always slipped out when she called him on something he'd never admit to. "So what's the plan?"

"I already have my team combing through video surveillance at the monastery and surrounding areas. They pulled feeds for the last twenty-four-hours."

"Good." That was going to be her first suggestion. Maybe she picked up more during her FBI consulting than she gave herself credit for. "What about Ben Riley?"

"My guys are gonna bring him in for questioning as soon as we locate him."

Dana nodded, wondering if there was something she was missing. Her head felt too big for her neck to hold up, yet too small for her brain. Thoughts fizzled in and out before she could grab hold of them. "What else?" she asked, hoping Jake could fill in the blanks.

"Agent Jenkins is following up on something for me in New York, but I don't expect it to yield any results."

"You didn't find what you were looking for?"

"That's putting it mildly."

Jake filled her in on his dead end in New York and his theory about the Senator's involvement in the missing case file. "You know I'm not one for conspiracies, but it's getting hard to ignore. New York is Scott's territory. He has pull there. Then I found this symbol at the storage facilities." He pulled a photo up on his phone and handed it to her.

"I like where your head's at, but this is a masonic symbol." She continued when he gave her a blank stare. "The Freemasons are responsible for most of the buildings in colonial America. An old building in New York still bearing their symbol nods more toward historical preservation than cult activity. Plus, the Masons aren't the same type of secret society as the Priory of Bones. For starters, they're not secretive. There's over two million members in the US alone."

"Did you just debunk my conspiracy theory?" Jake slumped back in his chair. "I don't like it when our roles reverse."

"Me either." She smiled, but her lightheartedness vanished when another pressing question drilled its way to the forefront of her mind. "Are you sure you can trust this other agent you met with?"

"Jenkins?" He huffed a laugh. "The woman practically raised me. I trust her with my life."

Breath she hadn't realized she was holding rushed from Dana's lungs. "She what?"

"Jenkins is an old Air Force friend of my uncle's. She moved to New York and joined the Bureau a few years before I enlisted."

"So she really is just an old friend?"

"Yeah, that's what I said." Jake's expression morphed from bewildered to amused. "Wait, who did you think she was?"

"I don't know. No one. I just ... my head hurts."

Jake's knowing grin was heart melting as he leaned in and brushed his lips against Dana's forehead. Thanks to the monitors she was hooked up to, he knew just how much the innocent gesture affected her. "Get some rest, Doc. I'm not going anywhere."

Jake moved to the small couch by the wall and settled in, while Dana worked on settling her racing pulse.

45

LOUD POPS SOUNDED AS JAKE TURNED HIS HEAD FROM SIDE-TO-SIDE trying to work the kinks out from his night on the hospital room couch.

He wondered if he was starting to lose his edge. In the Army, a night on the cheap vinyl excuse for a sofa would've been a luxury. The Bureau was making him soft. But if he was being truthful, he didn't miss having to ruck-up and rough it.

Jake's thoughts pulled him back to Dana. She was still asleep.

He'd run background checks on her nursing staff and doctors. They checked out. It gave Jake enough peace of mind that he let one of them slip something into Dana's IV for the pain.

The neurologist stopped by and spoke to him, assuring Jake that Dana was going to be fine. With the swelling down, they were able to rule out the more serious complications associated with severe concussions. She was going to make a full recovery. Though he warned that rest was the best medicine. Which she was going to get a lot of if Holt had his way.

Jake had sent in his report last night only to get a scathing phone call from his boss. Apparently, the Senator had called to complain about their little confrontation at the gala. That, combined with Jake's notes about Dana spotting Meredith in the catacombs, was enough for Holt to order the case closed.

Holt's words still echoed in Jake's ears. "She's not missing if your Witch Doctor saw her. I'm done wasting assets and burning resources on some bored Capitol Hill trust fund brat. Wrap this up, Shepard. I want the final brief on my desk by end of day."

Closing the case made sense. It was protocol. And considering Jake hadn't found any new leads to chase, there wasn't really an argument to keep digging. Though he had a feeling Dana wouldn't feel the same way. He wasn't looking forward to breaking the news to her.

Scrubbing a rough hand across his tired face, he turned his attention back to his laptop. So far, neither he nor his team had caught anything on surveillance. The only thing they had was Ben Riley entering the Smithsonian, then leaving with Dana.

Conveniently, the Monastery cameras had malfunctioned. According to their custodian there was a power outage a few days earlier that tripped the security cameras, and they hadn't been able to get someone out to service them. Nothing was recorded for more than thirty-six hours.

Jake had a team going through backlogs of footage just in case Meredith, Riley or the Senator were caught scoping out the catacombs in the weeks or months prior, but he had a feeling it wouldn't result in anything. If they'd been smart enough to disable the cameras for yesterday's rendezvous, they wouldn't have been careless enough to slip up earlier.

On top of that, Ben Riley seemed to have vanished into thin air. The agents Jake assigned to his home and office said he hadn't shown up at either place. But a search of his social media profiles revealed he was into some pretty bizarre stuff.

In particular, a role-playing game called *Memento Mori*, where players logged on to participate in virtual quests like human sacrifice, bloodletting and sexual conquests, all to earn random artifacts from the gamemaster, described as "the watcher."

It was getting harder to ignore Dana's secret society theory. Nothing about this case was adding up. Jake had a missing woman, a Jane Doe reminiscent of a prostitute cold case, erased case files, a shady political aide, a philandering senator and an angry boss telling him to stop digging.

Jake exhaled. Just another day on Capitol Hill.

Rubbing his eyes, he stared harder at the laptop screen, willing it to show him something he was missing. Dana's injury had gotten him a momentary reprieve, but he'd be expected to return to HQ soon. Holt ran a tight ship. He wouldn't let Jake run a rogue operation. If he didn't come up with a solid lead and fast, Meredith Kincaid, and most likely many other women, were going to continue getting snared in whatever trap the Senator and Vega were running.

A light knock on Dana's open door broke Jake's concentration. "Margot? What are you doing here?"

Jake's secretary stood at the door smiling brightly. "I heard what happened and thought you could use this." She walked into the room; arms full. "Coffee, two sugars," she said, winking as she handed him the cup.

He took a sip, barely able to hold back his groan of pleasure as the sweet caffeinated brew scorched its way down his throat. The two-sugars thing was growing on him.

"I also brought some chicken soup for Dana. And I figured you might need a fresh shirt," she offered, draping a dry-cleaning bag over the arm of the couch. "How is she?" Margot asked, perching herself on the arm of the chair next to Jake.

"She's tough. And lucky I got there when I did."

Margot reached over and squeezed his hand. "She's very lucky." Her hand lingered a moment too long. When Jake's gaze met hers, she pulled away, cheeks burning as she tucked her chin-length red hair behind her ear. "Anyway, I don't want to keep you from your work. Just let me know if I can do anything for you."

"Thanks, Margot. I will."

She was halfway out the door when Jake called to her. "Hey Margot, if Holt's looking for me, can you try to hold him off? I need some more time to wrap things up."

"Of course. Anything for you, Jake. You know that."

"Thanks."

Dana's hoarse voice drew Jake's attention as soon as Margot left the room. "The *anything* she means is pretty obvious."

Setting his laptop on the couch Jake rose and moved to Dana's side of the bed. "You're awake?"

"Great detective work."

Jake laughed at her sarcasm. "Someone's feeling better. Are you hungry? Margot brought you some chicken soup."

"I'm a vegetarian, and that soup is clearly not for me."

"What are you talking about?"

"Open your eyes, Jake. She brought you a new shirt because she was hoping to watch you take off the old one."

"Christ, Dana." He grabbed her IV bag reading the medication labels. "What's in this thing, truth serum?"

"Two things I'm never wrong about. The occult and the way women look at you."

"I think I liked you better when you were sleeping."

"Me too," she muttered. "Did you find anything on the catacombs' security cameras?"

"No. The cameras at the monastery were down and we lost Riley after he left the Smithsonian with you. He also hasn't returned home or to work."

"And you've just been sitting here doing nothing this whole time?"

Jake reminded himself that it was probably just the pain talking. "No, I've been looking into Riley's profile. According to neighbors and co-workers, he works long hours but seems normal."

"If he's so normal, why did he bludgeon me and leave me for dead?"

Jake cocked his head. "What happened to it just being a headache?"

She closed her eyes and exhaled slowly, clearly not amused by his sarcasm. "Can't we get a warrant to search his place if I give a statement about what he did to me?"

"We could try, but any judge worth his salt is going to challenge that warrant because of your injury."

"Great, so everyone thinks I hallucinated the whole thing! Meanwhile, Meredith is out there being brainwashed by Riley and the Senator."

"I don't think you imagined what happened, but at the risk of sounding like a broken record, we can't go after the Senator without proof. And he wasn't in the catacombs."

Dana bit her lip, her eyes watering with frustration. "What did Mere's parents say?"

Jake pulled a chair up to the hospital bed and sat down not sure how to break the news to her. Dana's mental state was fragile at best. Telling her he was being forced to drop the case might put her over the edge.

"Jake, what did they say?" she asked again, anxiety straining her voice.

"We haven't told them about the sighting."

"Oh." She started to pull the covers off her legs. "That's okay. I should really be the one to do it."

"Whoa, I don't think so." Jake grabbed her legs and swung them back onto the bed. "You haven't been released from the hospital yet. Besides, there's been some other developments."

"What?"

Jake braced himself for her fury as she propped herself up straighter against her pillows. But he couldn't do it. He couldn't tell her Holt was closing the case. He didn't want to be one more person who let her down.

Maybe there was still a way to salvage things. If he worked quickly, he might be able to find enough to keep the case open. Especially if Dana could shed some light on what his team found on the gaming platform.

He dove into that angle, filling her in on everything they'd dug up while she was sleeping. Jake grabbed his laptop and set it on Dana's lap to show her the gaming app, pointing out key elements and chats between Riley and other players. "One of my tech guys created a ghost account to get access to Riley's profile."

"This is good," Dana said, looking hopeful again. "Many cult members look for secure online chatrooms to host secret conversations."

"So do criminals," Jake added. "I can't tell you how many Al-Qaeda terrorist cells we took down thanks to these gaming chatrooms. Right now, it looks like Riley has a private chat going with three people. His avatar uses the name Perseus. We can see he's chatting with players named Charlemagne, Constantine and Ivan, but we can't access the actual conversations. They're password protected, as are the identities of the players. Everything inside *Memento Mori* is locked up tighter than Fort Knox."

Dana looked hopeful again. "Wait? *Memento Mori*?"

"It's the name of the game."

"That's also the Priory of Bones' motto." Dana pulled the laptop closer. "You said Riley goes by the name Perseus?"

Jake nodded.

"We know Meredith is Charlemagne thanks to her Facebook alias. That makes the Senator ..." She tapped her chin while squinting at the screen. "Constantine."

"How do you know that?"

"Constantine the Great was a Roman emperor from 272 to 337 AD. He was credited with restructuring government and creating New Rome which lived on for more than a thousand years. D.C. was modeled after Rome. You can see tributes to it everywhere in the architecture on Capitol Hill. If Senator Scott was going to choose a ruler's name for himself it would be Constantine; a ruler who thought he was a god. He was famous for his court of concubines. Plus, he had a church built in his honor on Jesus's tomb! There's a replica of Jesus's tomb at the Franciscan Monastery. How much do you want to bet that's why he chose the catacombs as his meeting place?"

"Okay, so who's Ivan?"

"Most likely, Ivan the III, Grand Prince of Moscow."

"I meant who is using his name in *Memento Mori*."

"Oh." Dana lost herself in thought for a moment before sparking back to life. "Considering relatively nothing has been proven about the Priory of Bones this is a bit of a leap, but I believe their fraternal order is a parallel of Skull and Bones. Bonesmen are assigned nicknames of famous rulers at their induction ceremony at the retreat house in Deer Island. Maybe we can look up the records of past members who used Ivan as their nickname to see if they correlate to any of our suspects. Traditionally they're passed down—"

"Wait. Did you say Deer Island?"

"Yes."

"That's in New York."

"Yes."

A flash of images tore through Jake's mind. Bare trees, reaching toward the sky like skeletons, leaves crunching under his feet, rifle slung over his shoulder, a white no trespassing sign. Tiny red letters spelling the words *Deer Island, NY - Scott Township.*

"What are the chances?"

Dana frowned. "Of what?"

Jake stood up. "Give me a second. I've gotta make a call."

46

There was extra vigor in Jake's step when he came back into the hospital room. "We're going to New York."

"What?"

"Get dressed, I'll explain in the car."

"I thought I had to wait to get released."

"The neurologist released you hours ago. I just wanted you to get some more rest."

"Jake!"

"Come on. We can argue in the car."

Jake was behind the wheel of his SUV, while Dana stared at his laptop screen. Scenery zipped by the tinted windows. They'd been on the road for hours and still had more driving ahead of them.

"We should've flown," Dana muttered. "Archer offered his helicopter."

"It wouldn't have saved that much time. We still would've had to get a car and drive out to the boonies. Besides, the Senator's lake house has been empty for years. It'll be there waiting for us when we get there."

"You're the one who says every minute counts."

She had no idea how right she was. But he'd made it this far without telling her they weren't officially working a case. If they could find new evidence in Deer Island, he wouldn't have to. "Driving is safer after a concussion."

"Oh, I'm sorry. I didn't know you had 'Doctor' in front of your name, too."

"You don't have to be a doctor to know your way around a concussion."

Dana crossed her arms. "They wouldn't have discharged me if I was in danger. Plus my nurse said I was fine to resume normal activities."

"Is flying a normal activity?"

"No, but neither is hunting down secret society members at their lake house."

Jake frowned, tightening his grip on the wheel. "Mock me all you want, but I'm not willing to endanger your safety more than this case already has." The conviction in his comment shocked Dana into silence long enough for him to change the subject. "Can you check under the front seat for a map? The cell service is spotty out here. I want to have a backup in case we lose GPS."

Dana located the *Rand McNally Road Atlas* and started flipping through it. "What did your uncle say about Senator Scott that made you want to drive all the way up here?"

"When I remembered that his hunting cabin is in Scott Township, I knew it couldn't be a coincidence. I asked Wade, and he said Senator Scott's family basically founded the whole upstate New York area. He still owns one of the original lake houses on Deer Island. It came back to me when you mentioned the Skull and Bones house."

"What did?"

"There was a case up here when I was about sixteen. Young woman drowned in the lake near our cabin. I remembered seeing it on the news. Wade said she was found on the banks of Scott's lake house."

"That seems suspicious. Can't we use that to bring him in for questioning?"

"No way. One more complaint from Scott and we can both kiss our careers goodbye."

"What are you talking about?"

"He called Holt. Apparently, our discussion at the gala made an unfavorable impression."

"Scott is trying to strong arm the FBI? That means we must be getting close."

"Maybe, but we're still not gonna be able to make an eighteen-year-old crime stick to a US Senator with an alibi. Anyway, the drowning was ruled accidental."

"What was his alibi?"

"He was in Connecticut, visiting an old college buddy."

"How convenient." Dana's finger tapped anxiously on the door. "So why are we even driving up here if you don't think he did it?"

"Ever hear of the term Hail Mary?"

She rolled her eyes. "So you're just winging it now?"

"Something like that." When she didn't respond he continued. "Eighteen years ago a body washed up on Scott's lawn. It's a long shot, but it's a trail worth following. Maybe poking around, talking to neighbors can turn up something new."

"Do you really think anyone still remembers what happened?"

He gave her a knowing look. "You tell me."

When Dana spoke again her voice was sullen. "What happened to my parents was different."

"Maybe, but we need something to link Scott to the body in the Basin or he's gonna walk."

"Then I guess I'll start researching the drowning and the Senator's family history while we drive."

"It's a long trip. Why don't you get some sleep?"

"I'll rest when you do."

47

Dana related to Jake's words more than she wanted to admit. He knew her secrets about her parents, but it was still hard to talk about. After what happened to them, chasing down a corrupt politician seemed like a cakewalk. It was also probably why she didn't blink at spending her days researching the graphic occult rituals of death.

Since meeting Jake, dead bodies had jumped off the pages and into her real life. It wasn't something she enjoyed, but she liked the way it validated her research. Because of her acute knowledge in her field, she'd helped catch a serial killer. If this trip panned out, she'd help catch one more monster.

Dana's mind wandered to her interaction with Meredith in the catacombs. She couldn't wrap her head around what would make a smart, capable woman like Mere fall prey to whatever spell she was under. Dana was spiraling down a rabbit hole of Stockholm syndrome studies when Jake's voice broke through. "Are you hungry?"

"Actually, yeah. I'm starving."

He grinned. "I was hoping you'd say that. There's this great diner my uncle and I used to go to a few miles North. You're gonna love it."

"Why?"

"Just trust me."

"I don't know."

"Oh come on. You let Claire pick where you're gonna eat all the time."

"It's not that. I feel guilty stopping to enjoy a meal knowing Mere is still out there."

"Place the mask over your own mouth and nose before assisting others."

"What?"

A wistful look passed over Jake before his grin erased it. "It's something my team and I said to each other before each mission."

"The thing the flight attendants say before take-off?"

"Yeah. The Army uses a similar philosophy. You can't take care of anyone if you don't take care of yourself." He gave her a wink. "Which means we have time to eat."

THIRTY MINUTES later Dana sat in front of the largest stack of waffles she'd ever seen. "Okay, you were right. This was worth the stop."

"Right?" Jake mumbled around a mouthful of food. "I know waffles are your thing, but you're missing out if you don't try the patty melt."

She turned her nose up at the grease dripping down his hands. "Vegetarian, remember?"

"What, you never take a cheat day?"

She snorted and dug into her mountain of buttery waffles. She'd drenched them with maple syrup the moment they arrived at the table and waited the allotted time to ensure the sticky sweet syrup had been fully absorbed into the golden pastries. When the first bite hit her tongue it instantly transported her back to that safe place she held deep inside her heart. Closing her eyes, she let the memories melt in her mouth holding onto the echo of her mother's laughter.

When she opened her eyes, she was acutely aware of Jake's watchful gaze. "What?"

He swallowed, snapping out of his trance. "Nothing." He quickly took another large bite of his patty melt.

"Doesn't your uncle live in Nevada?"

"Yep."

"Then why does he have a hunting cabin in New York?"

"Long story. Basically, he owns a share and comes out a couple times a year for different hunting seasons."

"And you used to come with him?"

A rueful smile crossed Jake's unshaved face. His five o'clock shadow added a ruggedness to his chiseled good looks that made him even harder to resist. "Yeah. I practically grew up in these woods. It's where I learned to shoot."

Dana nodded, taking another bite of waffles, trying not to think about a young Jake sitting in this very booth, his whole life ahead of him. She wondered if everyone felt so much sorrow when they looked back. Maybe for some people, childhood memories were a source of comfort.

Even though her brief time with her parents had been happy, looking back at those memories only served to remind her of the great gaping hole their absence left.

Did looking back cause Jake the same kind of pain?

If the young, fresh-faced version of him had known the horrors he'd face in the Army, would he have enlisted?

He was the only other person she'd met who seemed as scarred and burdened by his past as she was. It made her feel a connection to him she couldn't quite explain. It was a possessive magnetism that she didn't all together enjoy but didn't want to give up.

What did that say about her?

The waitress brought the bill. She leaned over to make sure Jake got a full glimpse of the breasts her pink uniform did nothing to hide. The name tag that hung from the mostly unbuttoned top read Honey.

Either available men never visited the greasy spoon or Honey was hard up. All lashes and giggles, she reached for the cash, practically eyefucking Jake in the process.

Dana was disgusted that such a vulgar word had just come to her mind. Claire was rubbing off on her, and not in a good way.

After the short walk through the gravel parking lot, Dana climbed back into the SUV. She gave Jake a healthy dose of side eye as he pulled back onto the deserted country road. "Do you really not notice the way women look at you?"

"I notice the ones that count."

Well, damn. She didn't have an answer for that, or the blush creeping up her neck.

She caught the cocky smirk he wasn't trying to hide as he winked pointedly at her. "Keep your eyes on the road, Shepard."

He gave her a jaunty salute. "Roger that, Doc."

48

Immediately, Jake knew something was off.

Despite the gate that was chained shut, Senator Scott's lake house had more tire tracks than a truck stop. A place that was supposedly a seasonal vacation home shouldn't have signs of this much activity.

"This can't be it," Dana said, walking up beside him. She tented her hand over her eyes and squinted into the setting sun. The boarded-up house was just visible in the distance. "The place looks deserted."

"I think that's the point."

"What do you mean?"

"It's a great cover. No one would look twice at a vacation home boarded up for the season. But look at the tire tracks. They're fresh. And there are a lot of them."

Dana knelt down to inspect the wide tracks. "Why are they so large?"

"Probably from a bus or moving truck. Something that can easily move a lot of people at once."

He snapped a few photos of the tracks, then moved to the gate. Slipping on a pair of gloves he gave the chain a solid tug. It didn't budge. For once he found himself wishing he had Dana's luxury of working around the law.

He hadn't come all the way out here just to be turned away by the "no trespassing" signs posted on the brick wall surrounding the property. Dana seemed to feel the same way. "There has to be a way in somewhere."

They poked along the property's perimeter. Ivy climbed the seven-foot walls, disappearing as it spilled over the faded red bricks. As much as he wanted to climb over for a closer look, Jake knew that wasn't the way. If this was the place Scott was hiding his secrets, they needed to do this right. "Come on," he said, walking back toward his SUV.

"You're leaving?"

Dana's tone was more than accusatory. He didn't blame her. His gut was telling him this was the place too, but there was nothing they could do without a warrant or a pair of bolt cutters.

"I don't want to spook whoever's been making these tracks. We passed an access road a little way back. We'll park there and see if there's any action."

Appeased, she got in the vehicle, riding in silence to the access road. The quiet gave his mind space to rearrange the puzzle pieces. It smelled like a cover up. And this was the perfect place to pull one off.

Jake parked and scrubbed his hands over his face, stubble scraping his rough palms. He ran over his notes while they waited but couldn't find a way to make all the parts fit together. Somehow, they'd led him back to New York; the state where Scott was king.

That had to mean something.

"What are you thinking?" Dana asked after they'd been sitting there long enough to watch the sun set.

"It's too early to tell."

She gave him an impatient look. "I know you have a theory."

"I'm working on one."

"Care to share it?"

"I think this is bigger than we suspected."

"What do you mean?"

"I think Senator Scott and Terrance Vega are in league. I think this place is their hen house, where they hide the women they're trafficking. Vega's clubs could be the way they show the girls off and launder the money. Jenni James was going to blow the lid off a few years ago, but they got to her first."

"Mere would never be complicit in something like that."

"I'm not sure how Meredith is involved, but I think we weren't meant to figure out she wasn't the Jane Doe. When you did, whoever's in charge told her to get you to back off, or next time it wouldn't be a look-a-like in the Basin."

"If you're right, then someone is threatening her. We can't stop looking."

"We won't. But I think Meredith's relationship with the Senator got her more involved in whatever scheme he's running than she planned. You have to be prepared for every outcome."

Dana swallowed. "Is there any chance she's safer if we stop looking?"

"Probably not."

"Then we keep pursuing our leads."

It was the right call but having Dana on board still didn't make Jake feel any better. She'd lost enough people in her life. If Meredith was added to that list because they ignored her warning, it would hit Dana hard. He knew how difficult it was to carry around the weight of a bad decision.

His hand reflexively went to the dog tags at his neck. Dana didn't miss the move. Mercifully, she didn't bring it up. Instead she asked, "What do we do next?"

"It's getting late. I say we get an early start tomorrow. Stake out the area some more. We don't see anything, we start talking to neighbors. If they can paint a picture of suspicious activity, it might be enough for a warrant."

"Okay. Are there any hotels around here?"

"I have a better idea."

49

Driving up to the old hunting cabin filled Jake with a mix of emotions. He rolled his window down, letting the symphony of night insects fill the SUV. The smell of wet leaves under his tires mixing with the unmistakable scent of campfire welcomed him.

Nevada was where Jake was born and raised, but something about these woods had always felt like home. Here he wasn't a boy with no father or a son with a broken mother. Hell, he didn't even know what it meant to be a soldier when he last set foot here.

The only thing he had to be when he was here was himself. That was always enough for Wade.

His uncle brought him here to give him a slice of normalcy. To teach him how to hunt and track and live off the land. All skills which later made Jake a good soldier and ultimately led to his survival, even when he wasn't so sure he wanted it.

So why did it feel so wrong to be here now?

It was too late to turn back. Jake had already called Wade to let them know they were coming. As his headlights caught the small log cabin, his stomach knotted. Looking Wade in the eyes after knowing he'd disappointed him wouldn't be easy. But Jake wasn't someone who ran from his problems. At least he hadn't used to be.

Immediately after the headlights passed by the window, the screen door swung open and his uncle's lanky frame appeared. It was like he was stepping out of Jake's memory. Wade looked like he hadn't aged a day. He was still wearing his favorite military issued paratrooper jacket and his dirty blue Air Force ball cap that proudly displayed his unit patch.

The sight brought Jake back, a mix of melancholy and nostalgia washing over him as Wade waved Jake into the parking spot next to his beat-up pickup truck with the precision of a ramp marshal directing an F-16.

Jake shook his head, his shoulders shaking with laughter despite his nervous energy. "I can't believe he still flags me in like I'm piloting a bone."

"What?"

There was no time to explain. Wade was already moving toward them. There would likely be a lot of military jargon Dana wouldn't catch. Jake would clear up her questions later if that analytical mind of hers didn't figure it out first. "Doesn't matter. It's just good to see him."

Wade jogged toward them, his gait unhindered by his nearly sixty years. Jake's chest constricted as his uncle wrenched the driver's door open. He didn't even get a chance to undo his seatbelt before the dome light lit up Wade's sun-weathered face. "Well I'll be. You are a sight for these sorry eyes."

"It's good to see you too, Wade," Jake said, shaking his uncle's hand.

"I was talking about the beauty sitting next to you." Wade winked in Dana's direction.

Jake beamed. "Dr. Dana Gray, meet Wade Shepard, my uncle."

"That's Master Sergeant Wade Shepard to you, G.I Joe."

"Retired, Master Sergeant," Jake amended.

"Yeah, yeah. Don't remind me. Come on, you two must be starving."

Wade was already moving, talking a mile a minute and acting as if this wasn't the first time they'd been together in years. He didn't know if it was for Dana's benefit, but he'd take it.

Walking toward the roaring campfire, he felt like he was home for the first time in a very long time.

50

"Have a seat, darlin'," Wade instructed, adding another ancient folding chair to the mis-matched collection around the campfire. "I'll put burgers on."

"She doesn't eat meat," Jake corrected.

Wade spun around. "No meat?"

Dana raised her hand. "Vegetarian."

"What?" Wade glared at his nephew. "Jacob Miller Shepard! What's the one rule I taught you? Never date a woman who won't eat meat!"

"We're not dating, Wade. I told you, she's consulting on a case." Dana enjoyed the crimson creeping up Jake's neck as he faced her. "He's just joking. He thinks he's funny."

"He made *me* laugh."

"See," Wade called from the grill. "You're the only one with no sense of humor, Jake."

She couldn't fight her grin. "It's true."

Wade shook his head. "I don't know where I went wrong with him. He picked Army over Air Force. Then took a job with the Feebs. I could've dealt with it if he'd at least inherited my sense of humor."

Dana nodded. "Or your good looks."

"Oh!" Wade shouted as he pointed a spatula at her. "Jake, I like this one."

Jake crossed his arms, glaring at her. "Really? You're getting in on this, too?"

She laughed. "Why not?"

Honestly, she wasn't known for her sense of humor either, but Wade's teasing was keeping her from feeling frustrated about how things had gone down in the catacombs.

If she hadn't let Riley knock her out, Meredith would be safe, and this whole thing would be over. Dana knew she needed to let it go if she wanted to make progress tomorrow. She had to recharge if she was going to be at her best. And right now, that meant welcoming the pleasant distraction Jake's uncle was offering.

Wade flipped the burgers on the grill and piped up. "I think I've got something for your vegetarian girlfriend in the house. Give me a minute." He trotted up the two front steps, crossed the narrow porch and disappeared into the cabin. The screen door slammed shut behind him, leaving Jake and Dana in the crackling silence of the campfire.

"He's a livewire."

Jake chuckled. "I wish I could say he's not always like this, but I'd be lying."

"I like it. I can see where you get your charm and wit."

"Don't let him hear you say that. His head's already too big."

She grinned. "I can see that. But I mean it. It's kind of great to have family like him around."

Shadows danced in Jake's eyes, disappearing when Wade reemerged. He carried a large plate and a bag of marshmallows, grinning from ear-to-ear. "How do s'mores sound, Dr. Gray?"

"Please, call me Dana. And s'mores sound great."

Jake jumped up from his chair, intercepting the bag of marshmallows. "How old are these?"

Wade shrugged. "I don't know. Does it matter? Marshmallows don't go bad."

"There's an expiration date for a reason, Wade."

Dana snatched the bag from Jake. "I'm sure they're fine."

He sighed and held up his hands, clearly outnumbered.

"They can't be that old," Wade argued, manning the grill again. "Walter brought them up when he was here with his grandkids not too long ago."

"Walter. Is that the guy you won the cabin from?" Dana asked.

Wade grinned, his eyes dancing with joy in the firelight. "Jake told ya about that, did he?"

"Not really. He just said it was a long story."

"Ha!" Wade wheezed a laugh that made the leathery wrinkles around his eyes deepen. "It's a short story. I have better aim than Walter Kaminski. Always have, always will."

Jake grunted. "More like you can hold your liquor better."

"There may have been some Jameson involved, but that didn't stop me from knocking every tin can off that log," he said, pointing his spatula into the distance.

It was too dark for Dana to tell if he was pointing to a physical log or a metaphorical one that existed in his wistful memories.

Jake cleared it up. "The two newly minted GIs came up here for some R and R and got so sauced on their first leave from Plattsburg, they couldn't remember who won the shooting contest for the cabin, so Walter demanded he get to keep half the share since it was his to begin with."

"I won, fair and square. Walter knows damn well I'm the best shot in the unit," Wade announced, tapping the patch on his hat.

"It must run in the family," Dana said. "Jake's teaching me to shoot."

Wade's bushy gray eyebrows stretched up his forehead like two caterpillars waking from a long slumber. He passed Jake a paper plate with a fat burger on it, grabbing one for himself before taking a seat. "Is that so?"

"Just want her to be able to defend herself," Jake muttered. He took a huge bite of his burger, looking uncomfortable about the topic. Dana couldn't imagine why. He was a great shot. Plus, the shooting range had been his idea. Of course, he probably never would've suggested it if she hadn't fired a weapon at the back of a fleeing assailant a few months ago.

But that was water under the bridge. At least she wanted it to be. Sometimes she awoke in a panic, sheets soaked with sweat from nightmares of Cramer. She knew he couldn't hurt her now, but she couldn't convince her sleeping mind that she was safe. "Who's the better marksman in the family?" she asked, hoping to keep the conversation going.

Wade's attention moved to his nephew, his eyes brimming with pride. "No one's better than Jake."

Jake looked down at his feet, digging the toe of his boot into the dirt. "Well, you taught me everything I know, so ..."

"Shoot." Wade pulled his hat off, running a hand through his thick salt and pepper hair before putting it back on. "Don't be modest, son. Your SFSC record still stands."

"SFSC?"

"Special Forces Sniper Course," Wade recited proudly.

Her gaze met Jake's. The shadows were back in his eyes, poisoning the lightness that had been there a moment ago. "I didn't know you were a sniper."

Jake stood abruptly, throwing his empty plate into the fire. "I'm gonna get more firewood."

51

"What just happened?" Dana whispered when Jake was out of earshot.

Wade shook his head. "I'm afraid that was my fault. It's been so long I hoped maybe he'd started to let go of those things."

"What things?"

"Jake's last tour in Afghanistan ..." Wade trailed off. In the distance Dana could hear Jake stomping around in the woods, snapping branches. "He's never really talked about it, but what happened to him and his team ..."

"To Ramirez?"

Wade's bushy eyebrows were shocked awake again. "Jake told you about Danny?"

"Barely."

"Darlin', barely is more than most of us get when it comes to that boy. I'm glad he has someone like you in his life. I worry about him being all alone in that city."

So do I. Dana kept the thought to herself. "I'm glad he's in my life, too."

"It's good ya both came here. It'll put his mother at ease to know I've laid eyes on him."

"Does she live in Nevada ,too?"

"We live together," Wade clarified. "I'm her primary caregiver. It's a long story, and it's not really mine to share."

"Oh. I'm sorry. Jake didn't mention it."

Wade offered her a kind smile, but his eyes were full of sadness. "I'm not surprised. They haven't spoken in years. Actually, this is the first time I've seen Jake since he left the Army."

Dana's heart slid to her feet. "But that was years ago."

"Probably almost five by now."

She shook her head. Outrage clogged her throat making her voice tight. "That's a tragedy."

"Couldn't have said it better myself."

Jake trudged over, breaking up their conversation as he threw logs onto the fire.

"Well this one is a lot better than Angela," Wade added, smiling up at Jake as he jerked a thumb toward Dana.

She tried to sound casual. "Angela?"

Jake continued stoking the fire. "Yes, Wade, we all know you didn't like my high school girlfriend."

Dana's interest piqued. She knew a guy as good looking as Jake had to have a long line of women lusting after him. She'd seen it with her own eyes. But in the time they'd known each other, she'd never once seen him return the favor. There had to be a reason. Had there been one woman who ruined him for all others? Was it Angela?

Wade was the source to satisfy her curiosity.

She told herself it was reasonable to want to get to know the man who was watching her back, but her interest ran deeper than that. "Did Jake bring a lot of women around?"

Wade whistled. "Since he was a boy, he's had girls batting eyes at him like toads in a hailstorm. But our Jake just isn't the settlin' kind. Guess none of us Shepard's are. I blame it on the name. We descended from sheep herders, ya know? We're a nomadic people."

"All right, all right," Jake interrupted. "Dr. Gray doesn't need a history lesson."

"I actually agree with Wade. A great deal of truth can be found in a person's name. Historical links have proven that people who can trace their family name back five generations or more live twenty percent longer due to that connection."

Wade gave Jake an impressed look. "And she's smart, too."

"Yep, and she'll remind you of it."

Dana was armed with a comeback, but Wade cut her off. "Speaking of names. Did you find anything helpful at the Scott place?"

52

Jake filled Wade in on what they'd found at the lake house. "Basically, we found a whole lot of nothing," he summed up. "Or nothing we could access anyway."

"I'm so tired of running into dead ends," Dana muttered.

Jake stared at her. "We have a plan for tomorrow."

"And if that doesn't work?"

"We make a new plan."

There was that aloofness again. He knew a woman's life potentially hung in the balance, but he sounded like he was talking about something as mundane as home renovations. It was a coping mechanism he used to get through the job, but sometimes he wondered if it bled over into other aspects of his life where it shouldn't.

Sitting there, listening to his uncle and Dana discuss the case, made Jake feel more alive than he could remember. He knew it was because the careful line he'd drawn between his past and present were getting dangerously close to blurring. But maybe he didn't care. Maybe it was better to feel the pain than nothing at all.

He looked at Dana in the firelight, wondering if he was brave enough to let her in. She looked so goddamn beautiful. Hair down, golden flecks glowing in her brown eyes, her lips pursed in thought. For a moment he let himself imagine he was the kind of person who could start over in a place like this with a woman like her.

Wade's voice cut through Jake's daydream. "You could always check township records to see if the Senator has any other properties he's hiding. The Scott name is everywhere up here. Those people think just because they settled this place they can get away with murder."

Dana perked up. "What do you mean?"

"I suppose you know about the girl who drowned at their place?"

She nodded. "Ruled an accident."

"Accident my ass. She had writing all over her body and was missing her spleen."

"Her spleen?"

"Yep. And she wasn't the first one."

"Then why was it ruled an accidental drowning?"

"Because the Scotts have more money than god. They make the law in these parts. It doesn't hurt that Powell Scott is the sitting judge either."

Dana looked at Jake. "This has to be the place. If Scott's hiding something, it's here. Wade's right. Scott could literally get away with murder with a family member as the local judge."

"Not just any family member. Powell Scott is Senator Warren Scott's great uncle. He was very involved in Warren's upbringing. Probably passed down a few of the nasty family legends, too."

Dana's eyes widened. "What legends?"

Jake held up a hand. "We have enough conspiracy theories as it is."

"What legends?" she demanded, sending a glare his way.

Wade dove into the tale. "The year was 1890. Elder man Hudson Scott III, called upon the legendary Fox Sisters to entertain guests at the town hall anniversary. The Fox Sisters were famous for their séances and Hudson Scott III wanted to contact his ancestors, namely the town's founder and his great, great grandfather, Hudson Scott the first.

"The show went off without a hitch as the three sisters were seemingly able to answer all the questions the towns folk had for the spirits through their rapping. Once for yes. Twice for no. By the time the event was over, Hudson Scott III was so taken with Catherine, the youngest Fox sister, that he invited her back to his home. The sisters said they had another engagement and left, but Hudson, not used to being turned down, continued to call on her until Catherine finally accepted his invitation.

"She arrived at his house in secret, under the cover of night, only to find that he hadn't invited her there for an evening of romance, but one of sinister intent. Hudson took her to his cellar where a secret meeting of cloaked men was taking place. They needed a priestess to preside over their sacrificial rituals.

"When she saw the poor lamb tied to the stone altar, she came clean, telling Hudson that the séances that made the Fox Sisters famous were merely a well-rehearsed act. Mortified he'd been duped by a woman, Hudson slit her throat, filled a challis with her blood and drank it. Then he cut out her spleen and—"

Dana cut in. "And divided it into equal pieces to distribute to the rest of the members."

Wade's dark eyes widened. "You know this story?"

"I know a very similar one. Please, continue."

"Legend says each of the men in that room prospered, living a life of wealth and achievement. They formed an elite society which they held in supreme secrecy, only surfacing every few years to choose another woman to sacrifice, ensuring their wealth and success continued."

Dana sat up straighter, her brown eyes ablaze in the firelight. "Who else does that sound like?"

Jake knew the question was directed at him and that it wasn't rhetorical. "I don't have the energy to argue conspiracy theories with you right now."

"The Priory of Bones isn't a theory. They're very real and they got their start right here, at a lake house on Deer Island, very similar to the one we were just staking out."

"Which is it? Skull and Bones or the Priory of Bones?"

"I don't know. Maybe both. Skull and Bones has an origin story very similar to the one Wade just told."

"It's a legend, Dana. A campfire story."

"Maybe not. Senator Scott got involved in this somehow. If we can prove his ancestors founded the Priory of Bones—"

"We're trying to solve a missing person case, not decode secret societies," Jake argued.

"I know that."

"Really? Because I need facts to keep this case open, and I haven't heard one yet."

"Fine. Call Dr. Fletcher and find out if our Jane Doe is missing her spleen."

"She was missing her jaw and fingertips too. What's a missing spleen gonna prove?"

"It's something."

"It's not enough."

"What about Ben Riley's conversations in *Memento Mori?* It points to a group of elitists that fit the profile. While we're up here we should visit the Skull and Bones retreat house to see if it sparks any leads."

"I don't have the time or authority to go snooping around some phony secret society house."

"It's not fake. We've been over this."

"Yes, and you know where I stand."

She glared at him. "Yeah, you've made it perfectly clear that you think my best friend drank the Kool-Aid so we should just give up."

"Former best friend," Jake clarified.

"Why do you keep bringing that up?"

"Because you need to face the fact that she may not be the person you remember. From what went down in the catacombs, it sounds like she's made her choice."

"What are we doing here if you're not invested in trying to save Meredith?"

"I'm risking my career to be here right now. I think it's obvious I'm invested."

Dana blinked, confusion overriding her offended expression. "What are you talking about?"

"Hold on." Wade interrupted the stand-off. "Why would your career be at stake?"

Jake ran a hand through his hair, squeezing the back of his neck. "My boss told me to close the case. We're here unofficially and without jurisdiction."

"Jake ..." Dana's eyes burned with questions.

Wade cleared his throat. "It's getting late, and it seems like you two have some things to discuss."

Jake stood up, wanting to explain, but Wade waved him off, disappearing into the cabin.

53

JAKE POKED THE FIRE, SENDING GLOWING EMBERS DANCING INTO THE night sky like fireflies. Dana watched, waiting for him to calm down. She had questions, but she knew better than to push while his temper was unleashed.

Elbows on her knees, she held her chin in her hands, the weight of the last few days finally catching up. This was a mess, and she needed to fix things before they got worse. "Why didn't you tell me Holt was closing the case?"

"Would you have listened?"

"You would've made me listen."

He gave a bitter laugh and picked up a shovel to stoke the fire again.

Dana sighed, realizing he was right. If he'd told her there was nothing more to do for Meredith at the hospital, she probably would've charged out of there trying to figure it out on her own. "Okay, so maybe I wouldn't have listened, but I would never ask you to jeopardize your career."

"But you have. In every case we've worked you go off on your own, handle things the way you see fit. There's a price for that, Dana. So far you've been lucky it's not your life."

"I know." Her voice was soft. "But I'm doing what I think is right. I didn't mean for it to put your job in jeopardy or upset your uncle."

"He's not upset. He's disappointed."

"In you?"

Jake jammed the shovel into the soil, resting one foot on the few inches he hadn't buried. "I know it doesn't mean a lot to you, but we respect protocol and procedure. We're military. We follow orders. It's how Wade was brought up and how he brought me up. The fact that I disobeyed a direct order from a superior makes him feel like a failure."

"Then why did you?"

"Because I didn't want to let you down."

His words speared deep. Emotions strangled her. The only word she managed to get out was his name. "Jake ..."

She was on her feet, moving toward him. His eyes locked on hers as she approached. He watched her like a predator watched its prey. As she rounded the fire, his eyes mirrored hers; fear, anticipation, desire.

She wanted to unleash it all. To tell him he was the one person in her life who'd never let her down. She wanted to convey how grateful she was, but she didn't know how. She only knew it would involve pressing her lips to his, but that was possibly the only thing in this world that terrified her more than not finding Meredith.

Reaching him, she gripped his jacket just below the collar, ensuring she had his attention. "You haven't let me down, Jake. You never do. But you don't need to take this kind of risk for me."

Jake's chest rose and fell, the powerful beat of his heart pounding against her hands. "I did let you down, Dana."

His eyes fell to her shoulder. The wide neck of her sweater exposed the pale edge of her scar. Jake's hand slid up her arm, sweeping her hair over her shoulder. He tugged her sweater, exposing more of the scar. His thumb traced the sensitive skin from collarbone to sternum, sending a chill rippling through her.

She tried to step back and break the connection, but he held her in place. He pulled her closer, his breath on her neck as he tugged the sweater again. His hands slid up her back until he reached the exit wound, where his bullet had torn through. The memory of scorching pain echoed inside her when she closed her eyes.

Jake pressed his palm flat against the scar, his eyes burning with regret. “I let people down, Dana. It’s what I do. Wade. Danny. You.”

“Jake, you saved me.”

“I shot you,” he growled.

She grabbed his face. “And I’d tell you to do it again.” She ignored the rough stubble that pricked her healing palm, forcing him to look at her. “It was the only way. You know that.”

He eyed the silvery patch of flesh that seemed to glow in the moonlight. “Does it still hurt?”

She slipped a hand beneath his jacket, placing it on his chest over the patchwork of scars she knew lay beneath the thin fabric of his shirt. “Do yours?” She could feel the dog tags pressing into her hand with every pump of his heart.

His stormy gaze bore into hers. “Every. Single. Day.”

“Good. It’s a reminder to live.”

Jake’s hands moved to her waist again, his forehead meeting hers. His breathing was shallow and fast. He shook his head, battling against the same internal struggle she was. This was a line they weren’t equipped to cross.

She watched his throat roll before he spoke. His voice sounded as strangled as her heart. “Dana ... I can’t make you any promises.”

“Who says I want any?”

Jake’s hand roamed to the back of her neck, and Dana let her eyes close. Her heart leapt to her throat as she forced her mind to stop thinking of all the reasons this was wrong.

Jake said her name again, dripping with so much desire she couldn’t have stopped her lips from crashing into his if she wanted to. But the bullet that whizzed by her head certainly did.

The sound of the gunshot ripped them apart, raining splinters into the darkness as the bullet exploded into the side of the cabin. Dana’s mind was still working out where the hell it’d come from when Jake shoved her to the ground.

54

Jake's heavy frame crushed Dana, the scent of damp earth and smoke filling her lungs as they took cover behind the firepit. "On my signal, we move," Jake commanded.

She gave a quick nod and waited. Something creaked on the porch. Two more shots rang through the night. But these came from the cabin. They were answered promptly by a volley of gunfire from the woods. The shooter on the porch responded in the lull that followed.

"Now!" Jake roared.

Yanking her to her feet, they scrambled to the porch. Wade tossed a shotgun to Jake. He caught and cocked it midstride. In one more step he was in shooting stance, unleashing hellfire alongside his uncle.

Dana made herself small, standing behind one of the wide timbers framing the porch.

"Get inside," Jake yelled.

"You first."

He fired his weapon in answer. Smoking shells ejected all around her faster than she could count them. Wade hollered over the mayhem. "You know how to load a shotgun?"

She shook her head. "Only a Sig Sauer."

"Why didn't you say so?" He kicked a large metal box in her direction.

Dana willed her hands to stop shaking long enough to open the latches. Inside was a small arsenal of handguns. A black Sig Sauer 9mm gleamed back at her like the grin of an old friend. She grabbed it, ejected the magazine, checked the load and snapped it back into place. "Should I go around back?"

Jake shook his head. "Only one way in and we're guarding it."

"Where do you want me?"

"Inside would be best. But since there's no time to argue, take my right."

Dana moved into position. Wade was on the left. Jake in the middle. Each in a crouched position behind a large timber. Dana leveled her weapon, the muzzle only inches above the porch rail. "What do I shoot at?" she whispered.

"The flashes."

Just as Jake answered the forest exploded with gunfire again. Aiming toward the muzzle flashes was easy enough but she had no way of knowing if she'd hit her target. The continuation of return fire told her she hadn't.

"Five shooters," Jake yelled.

"Round Robin?" Wade asked.

"Works for me." Jake turned to Dana. "Three round bursts. Wade starts. I go as soon as he finishes. You go right after me."

There was no time for questions. Wade was already firing. Jake was next. Then it was Dana's turn. They continued like that until the shots in the woods became more scattered.

"We got 'em on the run!" Wade hollered.

"Keep pressing," Jake ordered, filling his pockets with ammo.

Their chorus of gunfire continued; the pattern so syncopated you could set a watch by it. Jake stood, moving from his protected perch into the open. "Cover me."

He descended the steps without looking back. Dana blinked. There wasn't time for her to let the overwhelming notion of that kind of trust sink in. It was her turn to shoot. She kept a running count of her remaining bullets. She'd have to reload soon. They went through one more round. Only three shots were returned.

Another round. Two shots returned.

Jake moved further into the woods.

Two more rounds. One shot returned.

She couldn't see Jake anymore.

Another round. No shots returned.

She needed to reload, but she wouldn't be fast enough. It would leave Jake exposed. Dana signaled to Wade and pointed to the box. He jogged toward her, pressing the shotgun into her hand. "I'll load. You shoot."

"But."

"Just pull the trigger."

Jake's three round burst echoed through the woods. She was up. She aimed the rifle far away from the direction Jake had gone, switched off the safety and squeezed the trigger. The first shot ripped through her like a wave of thunder. She didn't have time to think about the shockwave of pain it sent to the back of her head. She pumped the weapon and fired again. She was prepared for the power behind it this time. By her third shot her shoulder was numb with pain.

Wade shoved the Sig at her. "Shoot while I reload, then we'll pick up the pattern."

Dana nodded, grateful to have the familiar steel back in her hands. She fired and fell back into the pattern. It felt like an eternity before Jake reappeared holding up a hand.

"Hold your fire," Wade directed.

Jake walked onto the porch, his footsteps heavy. "They're gone."

Dana didn't lower her weapon. "Are you sure?"

"For now."

She rushed forward not sure whether to kiss or kill him. Her hand settled the argument, slapping him instead. "You could've been shot!"

Jake massaged his cheek. She knew she hadn't hurt him because he was already grinning. "Not with you two watching my six."

Wade was smiling too, thumping his nephew on the back. He slung his shotgun over his shoulder. "We still got it."

Dana glared at them, her adrenaline pumping. "You're both insane!"

"I'll take first watch," Wade offered.

Jake shook his head. "I've got it. You two try to get some rest."

"Rest?" Dana could feel her anger building. "Someone just tried to kill us. How are we supposed to rest?"

"There's not much we can do until daybreak. I'll head out at first light and see what the shooters left behind."

"I don't get how a firing squad found ya all the way out here," Wade added. "Were you followed?"

"No." Jake spoke the word with finality.

"We don't know that," Dana argued.

"Actually, I do."

"Jake can spot a tail better than an eagle," Wade boasted.

Dana crossed her arms. "Then how did they find us?"

Without a word, Jake stalked off the porch and back to his SUV. The dome light came on and Dana watched him dig around inside. He returned with their duffle bags over his shoulder and her purse clutched in his big hands. He held it up as he walked back up the steps to the bullet riddled porch. "This is how they found us."

He flipped on the porch light and dumped the contents onto the small table by the front door. Keys. Wallet. Lip balm. Phone Charger. Gum. Prescription bottle. Sunglasses. Pen. Change. A button.

Dana cringed, her fingers itching to snatch her bottle of Xanax. She didn't like having her personal life on display, but Jake didn't seem to care. He rooted around in the contents on the table like he was at a flea market carelessly scouring through the trinkets of someone else's life.

"Here it is." He held up a tiny silver circle. It was flat and round, smaller than a dime.

"Tracking device?" Wade asked.

Jake nodded. "Must've put it in your purse at the catacombs."

Heat flushed through Dana, again embarrassed by her stupid move to accept Ben Riley's invitation. "The Senator sent those men here?"

Jake's eyes met hers. "That's what we need to find out."

55

THE MOONLIGHT FILTERED IN FROM THREE SMALL WINDOWS ABOVE THE bed. They were each only a few inches wide. The perfect size for the muzzle of a shotgun. Jake hadn't been kidding. There was no other way into the cabin. It was a fortress, almost like it had been built to withstand the kind of assault they'd just faced.

A chill rippled through Dana as she thought about how differently the night could've gone. She'd showered and changed into the ridiculously thin tank top she found packed in her hospital bag, courtesy of Claire. The only other option was a black lace negligée. Dana's cheeks heated the moment she saw it in her bag. She needed to have a conversation with Claire about boundaries and appropriate attire. Or at least ban her from ever being responsible for her wardrobe again.

Dana slipped her hand from under the heavy quilt to check the time on her cell phone. Time was about the only thing it was good for since she had no service this deep in the woods. Dawn was still a few hours away. She knew she should try to get some sleep, but there were a million thoughts running through her mind, making sleep impossible. Not to mention she nearly jumped out of her skin every time she heard a noise outside the cabin.

Jake was still on watch. That gave her some solace but watching the eerie shadows creep across the bed made her imagination run away with her. She knew the swaying limbs that looked like arms reaching out for her were just shadows from the trees, but it made her want to reach for her Xanax. She resisted, wanting to be alert in case whoever'd been shooting at them came back.

She tried to practice deep breathing techniques to relax, but halfway through counting to ten she heard the screen door open. The sound made her bolt upright. Her heart remained in her throat until she heard Jake's deep voice speaking to Wade in the hall. The conversation between the men was too muffled for her to make out. It only lasted a moment before the screen door opened and shut again.

Dana listened to the footsteps getting closer to her door. They were Jake's, but that only made her heart pound harder. She wondered what it meant that she'd memorized the cadence of his footfall. The door to her bedroom creaked open, and he poked his head in. "You asleep?"

"No," she answered quietly.

"You should be."

"Easier said than done."

"Did you take anything?"

There was no accusation in his tone, but she still hated that he had to ask. "No."

"You should've told me."

"Told you what?"

"About the Xanax. You're still having the nightmares?"

Dana's cheeks burned. Her mind flashed back to the first few nights of her recovery after the Cramer case. Jake and Claire had been caring for her around the clock. Claire took days and Jake had nights. Which meant he was the one who witnessed the night terrors that left her sweat-drenched and screaming.

"They're getting better." *They weren't.*

In a quest to find her parents' killer, she'd traded one nightmare for another. And after tonight she knew there would be a new threat waiting in the shadows to haunt her when she closed her eyes.

She didn't know if Jake could sense her lie, but he shut the door and crossed the room to sit on the edge of her bed. His hand brushed hers, and he flinched. "Christ. You're freezing."

Jake pulled his shirt over his head, handing it to her. She begrudgingly sat up and put it on because she *was* freezing, and his shirt was still warm from his body heat.

Pulling the covers back around her, she sat against the headboard, pulling her knees to her chest for warmth. Jake sat bare-chested on the edge of the bed, watching her quietly. There was a mix of emotion swirling behind his stormy eyes. That electric spark that ignited between them just before the woods erupted with gunfire was back. For a moment she thought he was going to move closer and pick up where they left off. But then he shifted so his back was to her, his eyes fixed on the door.

The moonlight made the scars on his back glow silver and white. She couldn't stop from reaching out to boldly trace one. She let her hand fall away when she noticed he was holding his breath. "Do they ever stop?" she whispered. "The nightmares?"

Jake never admitted he had them, but she knew the scars he carried on the outside were likely nothing compared to the mental anguish he suffered. He finally shook his head.

Dana felt her chest tighten with disappointment. "Then how do you keep going?"

"What other choice is there?" He stood up. "Wade's on watch. I'm gonna get some shut eye on the couch."

He was across the room and stepping back into the hall when Dana spoke. "Jake, I'm sorry."

He turned around. "For what?"

"For bringing this fight here. For putting your job in jeopardy. For all of it."

He paused, turning fully to look at her. The wind howled outside, sending a shiver through the trees that made the shadows dance across the room. The moonlight caught the silver of Jake's dog tags.

She wanted to know more. Her curious mind was difficult to tune out, but she knew now wasn't the time for questions about the past. The present was giving her more than enough to deal with.

Jake's voice drew her back. "What happened tonight wasn't your fault. If anything, it's a reminder that life's too short for apologies or promises."

She stiffened. "I don't believe that's true."

"For me, it is." He stepped through the door and pulled it shut behind him, taking temptation with him. Maybe it was for the best. Jake and her... that was just one more disaster she'd narrowly escaped tonight.

56

WADE HELD THE TINY SILVER DISC BETWEEN TWO FINGERS. "IT COULD just be a tracker."

"Or it could be a bug," Jake replied, shoveling another bite of soggy bran cereal into his mouth. "We have to operate under the suspicion that they know everything."

He watched Dana wrap both hands around her mug. She stared into the steaming tar Wade called coffee, completely zoned out as he argued surveillance technology with his uncle.

The watery light of dawn hadn't brought the renewal of energy he'd hoped for. None of them had gotten much sleep. Canvassing the forest at dawn had zapped the little reserve Jake had left. He'd functioned under worse conditions, but Dana looked like she was running on empty.

No sleep. No leads. No hope. He couldn't blame her. He also couldn't stop wondering how much he'd contributed to the worry lines creasing her brow.

Last night had been dangerous on many levels. Truthfully, Jake was more comfortable facing gunfire than the prospect of crossing into unexplored territory with Dana.

It's not that he hadn't thought about it. He had. A lot. But that was the problem. Jake was a man of action. That's why he'd almost let things go too far. It had been all he could do to stop himself from climbing into bed with her last night. But he was no good for her. That's all there was to it.

He meant what he said. He didn't do apologies or promises. Dana deserved someone who did. Preferably someone who didn't spend their life paying for past sins by running headlong into danger.

In the short time they'd known each other he'd lost track of the times his job had almost gotten her killed. If anyone was owed an apology, it was Dana. The best he could do at the moment was to keep working this case. That meant following the clues.

Their early morning search of the woods confirmed his guess. There'd been five shooters. From the tracks, they'd fled east after ambushing the cabin. Back toward the Senator's lake house. Other than that, the only evidence left behind was bullet casings and tree bark that looked like Swiss cheese. Jake spotted blood among the trodden leaves, so they'd hit at least one of the shooters. It was most likely the reason they'd retreated.

He'd gotten lucky.

His gaze found Dana again. She shivered as if she was reliving the close call they'd faced last night. She lifted the black coffee to her lips and drank. He gave her credit. Half the guys in his unit wouldn't have been able to stomach Wade's brew. But she seemed to be savoring the bitter flavor. The only thing Jake liked about his uncle's coffee was it was so hot it scorched the taste buds off his tongue. He didn't mind the way it burned a trail of heat down his throat to his belly either.

Speaking of, Dana needed to put something in her stomach. Unlike the two men she shared a table with, she didn't seem to have an appetite. She didn't touch the cereal in front of her. She just clutched her mug with a white-knuckle grip, periodically sipping coffee, her knees bouncing beneath the table.

Jake nudged her. "You should eat."

"I'm not hungry."

"I didn't ask if you were hungry. I said you should eat."

She glared at him. "I can't. All this sitting around doing nothing is making me anxious. We need to go back to the Senator's house."

Jake glared right back. It wasn't the first time she'd brought that hairbrained idea up this morning. "I told you, I'm not walking into a trap. We're outmanned. We wait for backup."

"We don't have backup or time," she reminded him. "This isn't even an active case anymore."

"I'm aware."

"So what? We just sit here and do nothing?"

"No, we wait for Jenkins and her team to make good on that favor I called in."

Dana shoved back from the table and stood. "We don't have time to wait!"

Jake stood up to follow her when she grabbed her jacket and strode out the front door. He caught up to her at the SUV. "Dana, wait."

"You said we'd go in the morning. It's morning! We need to go back to the Senator's house."

"We will, but we don't have jurisdiction here. Not to mention there's only three of us and at least five of them. I don't like those odds. We wait for backup."

"It'll be too late by then. We're close. We have to be, or people wouldn't have been shooting at us. The longer we wait the more time they have to gather their own back up or cover the trail leading to Meredith. If we don't go now, we could miss our chance. Plus, you said we injured at least one of them."

"So."

"So, we're not that outnumbered."

Jake shook his head. "You're a pain in the ass, you know that?"

Seeing she'd won him over, she dangled the keys. "Are you gonna drive, or am I?"

57

THE SMOKE WAS VISIBLE LONG BEFORE THEY TURNED ONTO THE ROAD THAT led to the lake. Dana rolled the window down to get a better look, but the thick scent of charred wood and sulfur stung her nose. Closing the window didn't help. The odor filled the interior, clinging to her like a veil of regret. It wasn't the acrid smell that made her eyes water; it was her mistakes.

They were too late. Whatever had been at the Senator's lake house was gone.

Jake took the final turn, driving straight through the wide-open gate to the smoldering remains of the house. Fighting the urge to say, "I told you so," Dana wrenched the door open and exited the SUV. She couldn't explain the intensity of her pace as she charged up to the smoking skeleton of the house. It was obvious there was nothing left for her to find. At least she hoped that was the case. A part of her was terrified that Meredith had paid the ultimate price.

If Meredith had ever been here, Dana prayed she wasn't now.

"This is fresh," Jake said from behind her, kicking over a still glowing section of porch railing.

"I told you we should've come earlier!"

"Not that fresh. This fire was most likely set right after our attackers fled."

"So the Senator could destroy the evidence."

"We can't prove that."

"We have the bug."

"Which means we have nothing. Wherever it came from, it's top of the line. We won't be able to trace it."

"Maybe they're still tracking the device. We could use it to lure Riley or whoever's behind this back out into the open."

Jake shook his head. "I think it's safer to flush it and move on."

Dana swore loudly, kicking the charred debris at her feet. "I'm so tired of being one step behind!" She kicked another piece of rubble, spraying ash into the air.

"We're not out of this yet."

"Look around, Jake. There's nothing here. We're out of time. Your boss is probably clearing out your office right now so he can get Senator Scott off his back."

"Then let's make it count."

"How?"

"We're here, aren't we? Let's walk the property. See if anything got left behind."

Defeated, Dana was too tired to argue. They grabbed masks from the crime scene kit he kept in the SUV and shared a pair of work gloves he found in the glove box. Jake snapped two limbs off a nearby tree so they'd each have something to dig through the smoking debris. They worked from the outside in. Or at least as far as they could without the soles of their shoes melting.

The change in temperature was staggering. That combined with the smoke laden air made Dana feel like she was back in Mexico, excavating artifacts from the Mayan ruins. She'd done an undergrad semester there, assisting a team of archeologists that thought they'd discovered mummified remains. It turned out it was just a tourist who'd met an untimely end. The perfect combination of dry heat where the body had been wedged, caused it to naturally desiccate.

Dana imagined that was happening to her now.

She'd already stripped down to her last layer. The thin tank top she'd slept in and the pair of jeans Claire packed. Dana lowered her mask to steal a deep breath. Wiping the sweat from her forehead with her arm, she put the mask in place and went back to work clearing a path.

The task felt useless. There were bits of stone and metal, but everything else had been reduced to a smoking pile of ash. The smell of gasoline or some other type of accelerant was pungent in the wreckage. Whoever set this fire had made sure nothing would survive.

Still, she pressed on. When she tried to move the remains of a window frame, the brittle glass shattered. Something glittered beneath the glass. Dana bent down to examine the shining gold and red speck. It stood out in contrast among the embers and ash. She pushed the glass aside with her gloved hand and dug out the trinket. It looked like a piece of jewelry. When she held it in her palm, her stomach dipped. It was a ladybug. Meredith's ladybug.

"Jake! I found something."

58

The cloud of dust the Yukon kicked up told Jake he still wasn't in signal range. He accelerated, gripping the wheel as they bounced down the rural dirt road.

"You're sure it's hers?" he asked again.

"Yes. I gave it to Meredith when she graduated from Georgetown. She thought ladybugs brought luck."

"She can count herself lucky you found it."

"You think it's enough to get Holt to reopen the case?"

"It's the best shot we have."

Meredith's warning in the catacombs. Her jewelry found at a smoldering arson scene. Five mercenaries shooting at them. It wasn't solid evidence, but it was enough to warrant further investigation. At least in Jake's opinion. He just needed to get into cell range so he could call Holt and convince him.

"She could've left it behind," Dana said. "Like a clue to tell us to keep digging."

Jake nodded, but he didn't necessarily agree. He'd dealt with enough victims who couldn't differentiate between love and abuse; right and wrong. The Meredith Dana remembered was most likely long gone. But he didn't want to take Dana's hope away. She needed something to cling to.

"I still can't believe she was there. We were so close. I should've told you I was going with Riley. We could've ended this already."

"Wallowing in shoulda, woulda, couldas isn't going to change anything. Trust me."

"I'm not wallowing."

Jake raised an eyebrow.

"I'm angry," she argued. "Mostly at myself."

She added the last part quietly, but Jake heard. He reached over and grabbed her hand which was steadily picking her seatbelt apart one thread at a time. "Have faith."

"That's usually what I say."

"I know."

"Are you saying I'm right?"

"I'm saying we're going home to rally the troops. You need to be ready for the fight."

"I am."

Jake nodded, fighting his grin. He half expected her to say she was born ready. That was the kind of determination she exuded as he fishtailed back onto the first paved road in miles. It was hard not to admire that quality in a woman.

A few miles later the tell-tale sound of cell service chimed through the SUV as notifications started coming through to his phone. Jake pushed the call button on the steering wheel and dialed Holt's number.

His superior answered immediately. "Shepard! Where the hell are you?"

"I'm on my way back to the city."

"From where? And where the hell is the Kincaid report I asked for?"

"I was tying up a loose end, sir. But I ran into a problem."

"What kind of problem?"

"It's a mistake to close the Kincaid case. There's something there. We were ambushed last night, and someone set Senator Scott's lake house on fire. Based on what I saw there, we need to bring him in for questioning."

"Good luck with that."

"Sir?"

"You're not getting anywhere near that man thanks to the photos your so-called partner leaked."

"What are you talking about?"

"Are you on some kind of vacation I don't know about? Turn on any news outlet. The Scott-Kincaid sex scandal is going to break the internet."

Dana gasped beside him and held up her cell phone. Jake swore and pulled over, parking on the shoulder. "What makes you believe Dana leaked the photos?"

"Multiple sources confirmed it."

"Holt, she wouldn't do that."

His laughter was cold. "And I suppose you're going to tell me she wouldn't burn his house down either."

"She's being set up. I can vouch for her. She's been with me since she left the hospital. We were at the lake house, someone followed us and shot the cabin we were staying at to hell."

"I know you were at the lake house. It belongs to a US Senator. There's surveillance. Surveillance that caught you two snooping around hours before the place went up in flames."

"Holt, you don't seriously believe we're involved?"

"I believe your little Witch Doctor is pissed Scott is sleeping with her friend. Revenge is a pretty solid motive."

"You're making a mistake. Scott is trying to cover something up. Something big. Meredith may be helping him. Just give me some time and I can prove it."

"Times up, Shepard. This case is closed."

"What about the fire?"

"Not our problem. Now get your ass back to HQ if you want to keep your job."

"The Kincaids aren't going to let this go."

"The Kincaids can kiss my ass."

The line went dead and Jake stared at the open road for a solid minute trying to wrap his mind around what just happened. Dana sat next to him, silently scrolling through the media shitstorm the photos of the Senator and Meredith had unleashed.

"Jake, what do we do?"

He didn't know. But one thing was certain. They were officially on their own. Not that it mattered. Even with a badge he wouldn't get close to the Senator now. His PR team probably had him on lockdown, ready to slap a defamation suit on anyone who looked at him wrong.

"I didn't leak those photos."

"I know."

"Who else had access to them?"

"A very small and trusted team."

"How trusted?"

"It wasn't them."

"If it wasn't one of your team, then who?"

Jake was wondering the same thing. "Who had something to gain?"

Dana was quiet for a moment, continuing to scroll through unflattering headlines about Meredith and the Senator. "What if he did it?"

"What?"

"What if Scott leaked the photos?"

"Why would he do that? Those photos could ruin him, not to mention make him a suspect in Meredith's disappearance."

"For this very reason." Dana's eyes drifted to that faraway place her brilliant mind went when she was working out a problem. "This could've been his safety net. We can't get near him now and he knows it. Every reporter trying to make a name for themselves is going to be doing anything they can to get access. It's the perfect excuse for him to go into hiding."

Jake had to admit it was a viable theory. He wouldn't be surprised to find Scott pulled a stunt like this. He sent hit men after them and ordered his own home be destroyed. There wasn't much he wouldn't do. But why?

Was Dana right? Was Scott wrapped up in his ancestors' secret society obsession? Had he taken it too far?

Jake thought about the clues they'd uncovered so far. The one that bothered him, the one he couldn't make fit, was Ruby's. Why had

Meredith been there? And why did a dead woman surface dressed like her? He couldn't shake the feeling that it was connected to Jenni James.

The cold case ripped from his past kept scratching its way to the forefront of his mind for a reason. But he couldn't see how the two cases—or worlds—would ever overlap.

Meredith Kincaid was a Capitol Hill princess. Jenni James was a prostitute. Their paths would never cross in a million years. So why had someone dumped both bodies in the Basin, dismembering them the same way? It hadn't actually been Meredith's body, but it was certainly supposed to look that way. A gut churning thought gripped him. Did that mean Jenni James was still alive? Maybe the body he'd been sure was hers was a look-alike, too.

Dana's voice drew him from his spiraling thoughts. "I know how you feel about following orders. I get it if you can't see this through. But I have to."

Jake turned toward her. "These guys don't play, Dana. You saw what happened at the cabin. This is dangerous."

"I'm not asking your permission, Jake. I know you don't think Meredith is the friend I remember. But that doesn't mean she's not worth saving."

"I never said she wasn't."

Dana stared at him, those bottomless brown eyes of hers sucking him in. She wasn't asking for his help, and that made him want to give it. He knew she was capable and could probably get pretty far on her own. Truth be told, he was okay with Meredith staying gone if that's what she wanted. But Dana would never let this go, and that stubborn loyalty might get her killed. That wasn't something Jake was okay with.

He didn't know why he was even hesitating. Despite all the excuses he gave himself, he couldn't walk away from her any more than he could walk away from his past. Some things just got under the skin, destined to haunt a man.

Jake reached across the console and grabbed her chin. "If we're gonna do this, we do it my way."

Dana stared back at him, absorbing the weight of his words. "What about your job?"

He grinned. "I already have a reputation for not following orders. Might as well see this through."

She tried to hide it, but her relief was evident. Her throat bobbed before she spoke. "I think we should go to the Kincaids. If we tell them what we know, they'll help us."

He put the SUV back in drive. "Seems like a good place to start."

59

The antique bone China rattled in Elizabeth Kincaid's hands. "You saw her?"

Dana and Jake had filled the Kincaid family in on all they'd missed in the last few days. Spotting Meredith in the catacombs, Dana's brief hospital stay, the shootout at the cabin and what they'd found in the ashes at the Senator's lake house.

Everyone had authenticated the ladybug charm, but Elizabeth couldn't seem to get past the idea that Meredith had been within reach. "She was here? In D.C.? You're sure?"

"Yes." Dana kept her voice calm and collected, like Jake instructed. He said it would be the best way to get the Kincaids to slip up if they knew something. He said guilty people tended to feel the need to fill the silence. Dana paused before speaking again. "I'm positive it was her."

Archer Kincaid looked ashen, his authoritative attitude from their last encounter long gone. He grabbed his wife's trembling hands and helped her put the teacup down. "Did Meredith say anything?"

Dana nodded. "She did."

Elizabeth gasped. "Well what was it?"

Dana delayed her response deliberately so Jake could watch the reactions of everyone in the room. "Meredith told me to stop looking. She said, 'make them stop looking and stay out of my way.' Do you have any idea why she'd say that?"

Elizabeth dissolved into sobs, but Abby spoke up. "Because she's as done with this family as I am."

"Abigail." Archer's eyes flashed with disapproval, but his youngest daughter remained unphased. Abby stood. "I'll be in my room if you need me."

After she left, Archer got up, resuming his earlier pacing. They were in a part of the house Dana had never visited before. It seemed to be Archer's private office. The walls were dark green with walnut wainscoting. There was so much oiled wood and leather in the space, for a moment it was as though she'd been transported to an old Irish pub.

Archer had insisted they speak in this room, where he was sure their conversation would remain confidential. Apparently, she wasn't the only one concerned with unwanted surveillance.

If Dana thought the media presence was bad when Meredith first disappeared, now it was reaching Lady Diana proportions. Not only did she and Jake have to fight the mob of Press and protesters to get to the Kincaid residence, but they'd endured an excessive pat-down by the new security detail manning the estate.

"How did she look?"

Archer's question surprised Dana, but she wasn't familiar enough with such situations to know if it was normal. Maybe Archer was just a concerned father, worried about his daughter's safety. She looked to Jake, who nodded, so she answered. "She looked upset, but uninjured."

"She didn't say anything else?" Archer asked.

"She did say one thing. I'm not sure what it meant."

"What is it?"

It was the part of their conversation that Dana had gone back to the most. "Mere said, 'I gave them a body. But you ruined everything.'"

Archer dropped the glass of Scotch he'd been holding. Elizabeth jumped up, rushing out of the room only to return with a member of her housekeeping staff to clean up the mess. The glass was whisked away in moments, but the scent of alcohol lingered even after Elizabeth followed her housekeeper from the room.

That left Jake and Dana alone with Archer. Maybe now they could get somewhere. Because as much as she hated the idea, she had a feeling Meredith's father knew more than he was saying.

"I've never seen this photo before," Dana said, moving to the wall of built-ins. She removed the small gold frame from its place on the bookshelf. "This is you with Dr. Fredrick and Senator Scott, and who's the fourth man?"

Archer barely looked up from the new glass of Scotch he was pouring. "My cousin, Walter Riley."

Jake was already looking at Dana when she turned to catch his eye. He'd heard the last name, too. She turned her attention back to the photo, scrutinizing the background while Archer sipped his drink.

The gothic stone building behind the younger versions of the men was unmistakable. So was the gold ring partially visible on Elias Fredrick's hand. Dana's heart began pounding faster. If she was right, the deception went deeper than she'd ever imagined.

She looked at the smiling men in the photograph, arms slung over one another's shoulders. They looked young and carefree, but had they already begun their spiral into the occult?

She held the frame out to Archer. She knew the answer, but she asked anyway. "Where was this photograph taken?"

Archer's attention sharpened. "Yale."

"I thought you went to NYU?"

"I did. My cousin went to Yale. I visited him often."

"Walter Riley?"

"Yes."

"Are you two still close?"

"Considering he's dead, no, we're not close."

Dana's mind raced. Was Walter Riley the Senator's alibi for the drowning at his lake house? Had he been permanently silenced? It couldn't be a coincidence that his last name was Riley. Ben had to be his son. Called up to take the place of his father in the Priory of Bones.

She started to feel ill as the pieces clicked into place. She didn't want to believe it, but this proved Archer Kincaid was involved. The men he was photographed with were all Bonesmen. She could feel it. They'd met at Yale, made connections in one secret society or another, then were tapped to a higher order.

But what were they playing at? And how had Meredith gotten mixed up in it all?

The final question made Dana's stomach flip with revulsion. Two of the men in the photo were responsible for her job at the Smithsonian. Was it happening again? Was she being set up by the people she trusted?

Her thoughts fractured as images of Cramer emerged from the shadows of her exhausted mind. She blinked rapidly, reminding herself her eyes were open. Cramer couldn't get to her here, in the present. His body was cold and dead, rotting six feet under in Glenwood Cemetery. She'd watched his casket lowered into the ground.

But even that hadn't stopped the nightmares.

Her hands began to tremble. She set the frame down, craving a Xanax or a run. It was the best way she'd found to deal with the aftermath of surviving a serial killer. Since she could do neither at the moment, she focused on her breathing. Slow deep inhales through her nose and out her mouth.

She thought she'd been discreet about her anxiety, but Jake crossed the room to stand beside her, ready to jump into hero mode. It pissed her off. Both her weakness and his ability to enable it. She held on to that anger, turning to face Archer Kincaid. "Anything I should tell Meredith when I see her again?"

"Do you know where she is?" he demanded.

"No. But I found her once. I'll find her again."

Archer's eyes narrowed, his assertiveness slipping its leash. "Tell her to stop this madness and come home."

"And you sure there's nothing you haven't told us regarding her disappearance?" Dana pushed.

Archer stepped closer, his anger bubbling over. "What could you even do about it if there was? The FBI called me this morning to inform me that they're no longer handling this case."

Dana balked. She hadn't expected that. She and Jake had decided to leave that minor detail out. He said it would keep the Kincaids calm and cooperative. Right now, Archer was neither.

Jake spoke up. "If you knew that, why'd you let us in?"

Archer fixed his glare on Dana. "Professional courtesy. But I think that's worn out. You should leave."

"We're the only ones still looking for her. If you know something, now's your chance to help us." Dana held Archer's stare praying he would crack. She was convinced he knew more than he was sharing. But Archer Kincaid was a man who knew how to handle pressure. He wouldn't hold a seat under the President if he didn't.

She wished he loved his daughter enough to spill his guts, but if he wanted to stay tight lipped that was fine. She knew someone who wouldn't.

60

"It makes sense. Look." Dana could barely contain herself when she held her phone up to Jake. The photo she'd snapped of the four men before they left Archer's office was blurry, but it was clear enough to blackmail Dr. Fredrick if necessary.

"They met at Yale and joined Skull and Bones. You can clearly see the ring on Elias's finger. Archer got wrapped up in it thanks to his cousin. It explains how they all ended up in such high-powered positions. Especially Archer. He didn't come from money like the rest of them. I always thought he married into it with Elizabeth, but maybe it was the Priory of Bones who put him in his position. But I still don't get why he's protecting the others if they have something to do with Meredith's disappearance."

She glanced at Jake. His eyes were glued to the road which was probably a good thing considering he was breaking about five different traffic laws as he swerved in and out of lanes at breakneck speed. Even with his lights flashing, drivers weren't moving fast enough.

"Jake, this is usually the point where you tell me I'm wrong."

"Yeah. But this time, I think you're right."

"You do?"

"I know that mentality. Protect your brothers at all costs. It was practically drilled into me from the moment I enlisted."

She grabbed the door handle when Jake slammed on the horn, nearly clipping a car when he changed lanes. "Slow down. We're not going to be able to help Meredith if we're dead."

"Dana, one of the men in that photo won't talk, one is dead, and the other one is off limits. Elias is the last one left who can help us make sense of this mess. Kincaid knows that. Which means we need to get to Elias first."

"Well in that case, step on it."

A few harrowing miles later, they screeched into the parking lot of the Smithsonian. Dana jumped out of the SUV, her feet pounding the pavement alongside Jake's. She caught a familiar black-clad silhouette standing outside the employee entrance. Even from a distance she could see her intern's clear blue eyes widen behind her cat-eye frames.

Claire hurried to meet them at the doors. "What the hell happened to you?"

They'd washed up at a rest stop before going to the Kincaids', but both she and Jake still looked like the walking dead in their torn clothes, covered in ash. She had spare clothes in her office, but there wasn't time for that.

"Is Elias in?" Dana demanded, using her key card to open the door.

"Dr. Fredrick?" Claire looked confused. "Yes, I just saw him talking to Tammy at the front desk."

Jake held the door open, rushing both women inside. "Let's move."

"What's going on?" Claire called as they raced down the corridor toward the lobby.

"No time to explain!" Dana yelled.

Elias wasn't at the front desk, or in his office, but they lucked out when they literally collided with him in the hallway. He'd just come out of the men's room, his watery eyes bulging when he saw the state of them.

"Dr. Gray? What's happened?"

Jake grabbed him by the collar, popping buttons off of his dress shirt as he hauled the older man off his feet. "We'll ask the questions."

Jake shoved Elias back through the men's room door, giving Dana no option but to follow. She'd only wasted a split second in her decision, but already, Jake had her boss shoved against the mirrored wall. Large cracks were spiderwebbing out from behind Elias's head.

"Where is she?" Jake demanded, spittle flying from his lips as he invaded Elias's personal space.

"I-I don't know what you're talking about."

"Dana, grab his phone," Jake ordered.

Dr. Fredrick trembled as she searched his pockets, but she had no mercy for him. She quickly located his phone and showed it to Jake.

"Turn it off and flush it."

She followed his orders and returned to stare into her co-worker's eyes. He was blubbering with fear. "Dr. Gray? Please, I don't understand."

"I think you do understand." She pulled her own phone out and held up the photo she'd taken.

He shook harder. "I don't know what they told you, but I didn't do anything wrong. They all wanted to be there. It was a privilege."

"Who?" Jake snarled.

"The girls. They told us they were legal. If they weren't, I didn't know. I didn't hurt anyone."

"What about Meredith?"

"Meredith?" There was genuine surprise in his voice. "She was never there."

Jake shook him. "Start talking."

61

"So you admit it?" Dana reiterated, just to be sure she understood. "You were in Skull and Bones?"

Elias's bushy gray eyebrows rose wistfully. "Yes. It was an honor to be tapped."

Dana's skin crawled. She wished she could feel vindicated about the secret society's involvement, but for once, she wished she was wrong.

"The cult is where you met Warren Scott, Walter Riley and Archer Kincaid?" Jake asked, his notebook in hand. He'd calmed as soon as Elias started to talk.

"Not Archer. He's not a member. And it's not a cult. We're a fraternal brotherhood."

"Sure," Jake muttered. "I'm sure that's what Manson told his followers, too."

Dana tried to steer the conversation back on track. "But you met Archer at Yale?"

"Yes. He came to visit his cousin, Walter, every few weeks. They were close. The only family he has, I believe. Well apart from Elizabeth and the girls."

"When did the women become part of this?" Jake demanded.

"They'll kill me for telling you this."

"I'll kill you if you don't. And I promise, my way will be worse."

Elias swallowed. "The girls were always a part of it. Dates were brought in for each of us at our initiation."

"Dates? That's what you call the women you abused? It's called human trafficking, you piece of shit. They weren't there willingly. Each and every one of them were forced there and served to you on a platter because you think you're better than them. Let me tell you, you're not!"

Dana put a hand on Jake's chest, forcing him to take a step back. "Maybe I should ask the questions."

He caught the warning in her voice. They only had a little time and needed to get answers. Every time Jake snarled at Elias the man looked like he was going to have a stroke.

"So the brotherhood set up dates for you, what else?"

"Anything we wanted. Cars, jobs, homes. With their network, the sky's the limit."

"When did it change?"

"What do you mean?"

"When did women like Meredith start disappearing?"

"I told you, Meredith isn't involved in this."

"We know she is. Meredith, Senator Scott, Ben Riley, Archer Kincaid and you."

"Yes, Ben and Senator Scott are Bonesmen, but I already told you, Archer is not. And Meredith certainly isn't."

"Elias, I saw the ring. I know you're more than just a Bonesmen."

"What are you talking about?"

Dana showed him the photo on her phone again, zooming in on the ring. "You're a Priory member."

Elias laughed. "That old thing? Warren gave it to me senior year. He has one, too. He made one for each man in that photo. It was a joke. Our own personal brotherhood."

Dana glanced at Jake. She couldn't tell if Elias was telling the truth. Her gut told her he was. She'd worked with the man for years, and always thought he was dull; dedicating his time solely to the museum. He didn't seem like the type to live a double life. But how well did she really know him if he'd hidden this from her?

She continued with her questioning. "Have you ever been to Senator Scott's lake house?"

"Which one? He has quite a few."

"The one in New York where a girl drowned." Jake's tone made Elias stiffen. "The same one that he burned down yesterday."

Elias's eyes widened. "Is he … is Warren dead? Is that why you're here?"

"What did I tell you?" Jake demanded. "We ask the questions. Warren Scott isn't your concern right now."

Dana could see the fear turning to panic in her boss's eyes. She needed to wrap this up quickly and get out before someone came looking for him. "Have you ever been to that house?"

"No."

"And you're telling me you're not involved in another secret order like the Priory of Bones?"

"No. Just Skull and Bones. I'm just a Bonesmen. I swear."

Dana had an idea. She grabbed Jake's notebook and flipped back a few pages. "You got nicknames at your induction ceremony, correct?"

Elias nodded.

"What was yours?"

"I'm Geronimo."

Dana's gaze met Elias's. She knew why he'd chosen that name and why it was significant in both the occult and conspiracy circles. Geronimo's skull was stolen from his grave, allegedly by Skull and Bones members. The FBI investigated the case, but the skull was never recovered.

Maybe Dr. Fredrick wasn't as dull as she thought. She looked back at Jake's notepad. "Do you know members that go by these names? Constantine, Charlemagne, Perseus, Ivan."

"Scott is Constantine. Perseus was Walter Riley's moniker, passed down to Ben. I don't know the others."

"Why'd you say, 'I'm Geronimo' like you're still a Bonesmen?" Jake interjected.

Elias picked the wrong moment to be brave, lifting his chin as he responded. "Once a Bonesmen, always a Bonesmen."

Jake stalked forward, grabbing Elias by the throat. "Are you telling me you still participate in this shit?"

Elias's cheeks hollowed as he looked anywhere but at Jake. His lower lip trembled when he spoke. "Yes."

Jake's temper unhinged. He punched the mirror beside Elias's head. Glass rained down slicing the man's face. He cried out. "I didn't know. I didn't know they were ... were."

"Yes you did!" Jake yelled. "You knew they were there against their will. But you didn't care. You did what you wanted anyway, then discarded them like trash!" Jake's face moved even closer to Elias's as he tightened his grip. "Maybe someone should treat you like that so you can experience the psychological damage." His knee connected with Elias's groin.

"Jake!" Dana wedged herself between her boss and the green monster that had temporarily taken over the man she knew and trusted. She grabbed his hands doing her best to pry his fingers from around Elias's throat. The last thing they needed was another dead body.

"Jake! Stop! Let him go!" But Jake was somewhere else. Her words fell on deaf ears as Elias thrashed, gasping for air.

Dana shoved her way between the men and grabbed the thin chain around Jake's neck. She yanked, pulling the dog tags loose. She held them in front of him. Jake blinked, coming back to the here and now. "This isn't the way, Jake. Let him go."

This time, he listened, and Elias collapsed to the floor. When Dana saw he was still breathing, she shoved Jake toward the door. "We need to go."

62

Jake held his hand out to Dana in the elevator. She gave him a concerned look but placed his dog tags in his open palm. He slipped them back around his neck, feeling some of the tension ease.

They rode to the lobby in silence. The doors rolled open, revealing Claire, her agitation clear. She rushed toward them. "Where were you? What's going on?"

"I'll explain when I can," Dana said as Jake breezed by her without a word. "Can you do me a favor and send someone down to check on Dr. Fredrick? He's in the men's room outside his office."

"Uh-okay. But where are you going?"

"It's better if you don't know." Dana pushed through the exit door behind Jake.

Claire followed them outside. "I want to help."

"Stay out of this," Jake ordered.

He looked back to see Dana mouthing, "I'm sorry" to Claire.

The girl stood on the sidewalk, arms crossed tightly around her thin frame. Jake could already hear the blare of sirens in the distance. He wanted to tell her to make herself scarce. She didn't need to get tangled up in the shitstorm that was about to descend on the Smithsonian.

He didn't know whether it was Kincaid or Fredrick who called the cavalry. It didn't really matter. Thanks to his temper, he needed to lay low. He'd already taken Dana down with him. He didn't need to involve Claire, too. She was a smart girl, resilient. She had to be. Fragile women didn't survive in a world this twisted.

He pulled onto Madison and made a left on Seventh. They needed to stay off the main roads in case Kincaid's security team put an APB out on his vehicle.

"Where are we going?" Dana asked.

"I don't know. We just need to get out of the city."

"What was that back there?"

"Nothing."

"Don't tell me nothing. I was there. You would've pounded Dr. Fredrick's face in if I hadn't stopped you."

"Yeah, and that wouldn't have been enough." He shook his head. "I can't stand men who prey on women."

"I'm not okay with his complicity either, but one problem at a time. We're not going to dismantle an entire society of sexual deviance in an afternoon. We need to focus on how the Senator is involved in this so we can get to Meredith."

"Yeah, and I think I know where to start."

THIRTY MINUTES later Jake parked his SUV across the street from Ruby's Slipper.

Dana looked at him. "What are we doing here?"

"Terrance Vega owns this bar, though brothel is probably a better word. Scott needs women for his little cult gatherings, and I'd bet money that Vega is his supplier."

"That could be why Mere's in hiding. Maybe she found out, and Scott threatened her?"

Jake thought it was more likely Meredith was just as involved as the Senator but mentioning that to Dana would get him nowhere. "We can't get near Scott right now, so working Vega is our best angle."

"Do you think anyone in there will talk to us?"

"Not us, you. I got stonewalled by the bartender the last time I came. You might have better luck chatting up the women."

"Okay. What am I looking for?"

"Nothing specific. Keep the conversation light, casual. Any hint that you're fishing, and they'll clam up. And keep an eye out for an Ivy leaf tattoo on any of the girls you talk to. That's Vega's brand."

"He brands his women?"

"They're not women to him. Vega thinks of them as commodities to be bought, sold and traded. They're sex slaves in every sense of the word."

"If you know all of this, why can't you stop him?"

"No one will testify. They're too scared. Jenni James was the only one willing to flip, and you saw how that ended."

Again, Jake felt the nagging question return to him. Was Jenni really dead? They hadn't been able to ID the body, and even though he was 99.9% sure it was her, and that Vega was behind the body dump, they couldn't prove it, and that left room for doubt to creep in. Especially after the Jane Doe matching Meredith's description was found in the same place.

Maybe Vega just wanted to make it look like the girl who crossed him was dead to send a message. If that was true, why keep her alive? Was she more valuable that way? Or did he have a fate worse than death in mind for the women who betrayed him?

Dana's hand was already on the door. Jake reached over to stop her. Her big brown eyes flashed in alarm. "What are we waiting for?"

"Nothing. I just ... what happened back there ..."

"Jake," she interrupted, her expression unreadable. "No apologies or promises. Let's just get these bastards."

63

Dana didn't know what was more shocking, the fact that Jake almost apologized or the seedy world of prostitution that existed only minutes outside Capitol Hill.

The moment she'd walked through the red door of Ruby's Slipper, she'd descended into a different realm. Women in every stage of undress teetered around on stilettos like zombies doped out of their minds. No wonder no one ever spoke up. They all seemed too drugged to even know where they were let alone what was happening.

Talking was out of the question. The women only ambled over to Dana for a moment, moving on when they realized she wasn't a potential customer.

Jake ordered them each a beer. He handed her one and told her to drink it, so she didn't look suspicious. Putting the cold bottle to her lips, Dana couldn't bring herself to enjoy it. It felt wrong to be here, free to come and go when these women weren't.

Revulsion churned in her stomach every time she watched a sad man lead an even sadder woman through the door in the back. A red neon sign blinked the words "Private Rooms" above it, the red glow adding to the hellish conditions of Ruby's.

Dana slid into a booth while Jake made his rounds. The bar was dark and much too warm. The flickering neon was making her dizzy. She put her hands on the table to steady herself, but immediately regretted the decision. She didn't know why the surface was so sticky and she didn't want to. Pulling her hands back, she wiped them on her pants, which were still stained with soot.

In a normal D.C. bar, her appearance would make her stand out, but here she almost looked like she belonged. Why had Meredith ever visited this place? Could anything in her life make her desperate enough to turn to this kind of lifestyle?

Dana nursed her beer for the next hour making unsuccessful small talk with the women. It didn't look like Jake was doing any better. He sat at the bar so they'd each have space to work. The bartender ignored him and so did the women when he didn't bite at their offers.

Coming to Ruby's felt like another dead end. The only thing it accomplished was filling Dana with a crushing helplessness. No one should have to live like this. Jake was right, Elias had to know what he was doing if these were the women entertaining him and the other Bonesmen.

Finally, Jake signaled that it was time to leave.

Dana couldn't get out the door fast enough. The afternoon air tasted like freedom, and she drank it in as they jogged across the street to the parking lot.

"Get anything?" he asked, once they were in his SUV.

"No. You?"

He shook his head but held up his phone. "Sorry I cut it short, but I got a message I need to follow up on. I didn't want to leave you in there alone."

"No complaints here."

Jake's jaw flexed. "That's why I hate working sex crimes. Shit's hard to take."

"Is it about the case? The message?"

"It's from Evans. His team was running codes to backdoor the *Memento Mori* chatroom before Holt shut us down."

"Did he get in?"

"We're about to find out."

Jake dialed a number and put the phone on speaker so Dana could hear. After two rings, someone answered. "Evans."

"It's Shepard."

"Hey, Shep. You okay?"

"What'd you hear?"

"More like what didn't I hear. Holt's on the warpath, banging down every door in the building looking for you. He sent a burn notice for the Kincaid case. Which in my experience means we're on to something."

"My thoughts exactly."

"If I know you, you're still working this, off book."

"Depends. You got something for me?"

Evans gave a gruff laugh. "Wouldn't be risking this call if I didn't. You got your laptop with ya?"

"Yeah."

"Holt shut things down before my worm could break in, but I'm gonna send you a file I extracted. It looks like a bunch of gibberish to me, but maybe it means something."

"Holt's probably flagged my account. Send the file to our league chat."

"Done."

"Thanks, Evans. Appreciate it."

"Yeah, how 'bout you don't mention it. Don't wanna lose my job, but I got a daughter. I can't sleep withholding evidence that could help that Kincaid girl."

"You did the right thing," Jake said.

"Let's hope."

Evans hung up and Jake twisted around in his seat to grab his laptop from the back. He powered it up and logged on, opening up a browser displaying a scoreboard with sport stats. Dana raised her eyebrows. "League chat?"

"Fantasy Football." He shrugged. "Got talked into it."

She scoffed, imagining Jake at the office watercooler pretending to care about the score of some game he didn't watch. There wasn't even a television at his house. "Do you know fantasy sports leagues technically meet the criteria to be classified as cults?"

"I'm not surprised. Here we go."

Dana was immediately thrown back into the case as she leaned over the console to look at Jake's screen. The file was a screen shot from the *Memento Mori* chat between Perseus, Constantine and Ivan.

"It's just more garbage," Jake grumbled.

Dana was still scanning the screen. "Maybe not."

"They're just talking about collecting stupid tokens in the game. Gemstones and candlesticks? It's got nothing to do with sex trafficking."

She read the lines again.

Ivan: Need a new vault. My gems aren't safe.

Constantine: Working on it. Need time.

Ivan: Don't got time.

Perseus: Diversify. You have other artifacts.

Ivan: Already lost my emerald. Not leaving my ruby behind too.

Constantine: This is bigger than one stone.

Ivan: Have terms been negotiated?

Constantine: We're close. For now concentrate on the candlestick.

That was it. All they had to go on. Dana read the lines over and over. The answer taunting her. She was sure it was hidden somewhere in those lines if she could only decipher the code.

Her mind flipped through a mental catalog of occult research as she recounted everything she knew about Memento Mori. The phrase sparked a series of macabre paintings from the Renaissance period when artists were obsessed with the idea of capturing death on canvas.

They often added subjects into their paintings that could extinguish or decay, like fruit, flowers, candles. There was always a skull to represent death. And treasures, like gems and gold to represent wealth.

In the chat, Perseus, aka Ben Riley, Constantine, who she presumed was Senator Scott, and the unknown figure, Ivan, were all talking about the gemstones: the wealth.

Dana let her gaze wander as her mind whirled through a myriad of possible scenarios. Across the street, the red door opened and closed, drawing her attention back to Ruby's.

Realization hit her so hard she gasped for air.

Jake tensed. "What is it?"

"Could it be that simple?"

"What?"

Dana ignored Jake's question and dug under the seat, pulling out the atlas she'd used to help them navigate the back roads of Deer Island. She flipped to the section highlighting the chain of finger lakes that dotted the isolated woodlands of upstate New York. There it was, shining back at her like a beacon of hope.

Candlestick Lake.

"Jake, I don't think they're talking about artifacts. They're places. Candlestick." She pointed to the lake on the map. "Ruby!" she pointed across the street to the club. "I don't know what the Emerald is, but—"

Jake punched the steering wheel. "I do. Emerald Heights."

64

TEN MINUTES LATER THEY WERE PARKED OUTSIDE EMERALD HEIGHTS.

The condemned apartment building looked worse than Jake remembered. When he'd worked the Jenni James case, this block of Deanwood had been a hub for illegal activity. Prostitutes, drugs, gangs. Now it was dead quiet, but that didn't stop the anger simmering just below Jake's skin.

Emerald Heights was the last place Jenni James was seen alive. It was also owned by Deanwood's king slumlord, Terrance Vega. In Jake's mind, that wasn't a coincidence.

Vega hadn't cooperated with the FBI during the investigation into James' disappearance, so shutting down one of his establishments was its own form of vindication. One Jake hadn't lost a wink of sleep over. He wished he could say getting Emerald Heights condemned was a win, but Vega had dozens of other properties with reputations just as despicable.

It drove Jake crazy that a guy like Vega wasn't behind bars. Everything he threw at him in the James case slid off like the man was made of Teflon. Jake reminded himself he was playing the long game. Taking down someone like Vega was like a game of chess. It required skill, finesse, patience. He couldn't explain it but sitting outside Emerald

Heights made it feel like it was his move. He just needed to spot an opening.

"What are we doing here?" Dana asked.

Jake could tell she was getting antsy, but something told him coming back here would help him connect the dots. They were getting close, he could feel it. Dana's interpretation of the chatroom conversation was spot on. It had to be. This was the Emerald.

He stared out at the quiet street. There was no movement in the boarded-up building. No one even walked on the same side of the street, like getting too close would call out the ghosts who dwelled there. Countless people had OD'd inside those walls. Not to mention the other unspeakable acts that happened to the women who were forced to live there.

"Jake?" Dana pulled him from his thoughts. "Why are we here?"

"Making sure the Emerald isn't in play."

She took her glasses off and rubbed her eyes. Putting them back on she shook her head. "It doesn't look like anything's happened here in a long time."

He agreed, but he wouldn't be doing his job if he didn't at least check it out. "Vega owns this property. And Ruby's. He names his properties after things he thinks sound expensive. Emerald Heights, Ruby's Slipper. He's got Diamond Park Apartments on 46th. There's more clubs, too. He's building his sex trade empire right here in Deanwood."

"What about Candlestick Lake? Does he own anything up there?"

"I don't know."

"Well, let's go find out," she insisted.

"I want to scope out the Emerald first."

"Jake, no one's here."

"We don't know that."

"Yes we do. Ivan said he lost his Emerald."

"We need confirmation that Ivan is Vega."

"He has to be. You said he owns Emerald Heights and Ruby's Slipper. He also fits the profile of someone who would use a Russian Czar as a nickname."

Jake gave her a quizzical look that he regretted the moment she started spouting off Russian history. A school bus rumbled by, drowning her out. Jake watched it roll to the corner and stop.

Dana paused her history lesson and cocked her head. "Who would put a bus stop so close to a place like this?"

Jake watched the stop arm slide out as three children exited. Something itched in his mind. He looked at his dash screen. The time and date were boldly displayed. Wednesday, 2:46 pm.

The memories swirling in the dark corners of his mind began to take shape, pulling him back to the last time he'd been in Deanwood.

It was raining. He sat in his SUV outside Ruby's. A school bus cruised by, brake lights glowing as it stopped a few blocks up. Three figures got off the bus, their shapes distorted by the rain coating his windshield. They were female by his best estimate.

He closed his eyes recalling as many details as he could about the scene.

Something was off. But what?

That bus was older than this one. And the stop arm didn't slide out. He was sure of it. At the time he hadn't noticed. His mind was too preoccupied with details of the Kincaid case. But now that he saw this bus, the one from his memory struck him as odd. The stop arm was protocol, meant to protect the children getting on and off from traffic.

He thought about those three figures again. Were they children? Or could they have been women?

Jake stared at the bus in front of him. It was starting to pull away. He swore, unbuckled his seatbelt and raced after it on foot.

Less than a minute later he was heading back to the SUV, phone in hand, lips pressed together in fury. Dana stood outside the car, her eyes wide as he approached. "What the hell?"

"I can't believe I missed it."

"Missed what?"

He held up his phone. "The school bus. That's how they're getting girls in and out." He was close enough for Dana to see the photos he'd taken. "The tire treads match the tracks we saw at the lake house. Vega is using school buses to transport the women he traffics, and Scott is helping him."

"Are you sure?"

Jake pulled up the photos of the tire tracks from Scott's lake house. "They're an exact match."

Dana's voice vibrated with the same eagerness he felt. "Is this our smoking gun?"

Jake grinned. "I think it is. And I know exactly what to do with it."

He ushered Dana back to the SUV and turned on his blue and reds, determined not to be too late this time.

65

DANA WATCHED JAKE TIGHTEN THE STRAPS OF HIS FLAK VEST. A FEW months ago, she didn't even know the word and now she was trying to figure out how to put one on.

She stood on the outskirts of the chaos that had taken over Wade Shepard's hunting cabin. Agent Jenkins had come through for Jake. She had a small army ready to storm the Senator's house on Candlestick Lake.

Dana could see why Jake and his uncle were so fond of the woman. Jenkins had a no bullshit attitude that got things done. Jenks, as her subordinates called her, ordered the agents and tactical teams around with precise authority, spelling out exactly how she wanted things to go down.

Dana did her best to stay out of the way. It was hard to believe just a few hours ago she'd been in D.C.

After leaving Emerald Heights, the plan fell together seamlessly.

Agent Jenkins opened a new investigation thanks to Jake's photo evidence. Since she was the senior agent in charge, she had no trouble getting Jake assigned to the case. His next call was to his uncle to secure the cabin as a command post once Jenks identified a property on Candlestick Lake owned by a trust in Senator Scott's name.

A drone gathered aerial footage of the property. What came back warranted the HRT members who were readying their weapons as Jenks laid out the impending siege. Jake watched with rapt attention.

From the moment his badge was no longer sidelined, he was in mission mode. He hadn't stopped moving since they left Emerald Heights. Go-bag ready, he rushed Dana to the FBI's private plane.

Holt, who was even more intimidating than Jake made him sound, had been waiting on the tarmac. Thanks to Jenks, Jake was back in his boss's good graces. Dana wasn't as lucky. The FBI assistant director didn't so much as look at her the entire flight, but she was more than okay with that considering the way he'd acted when she'd tried to get on the plane.

She could still see the veins bulging in his neck when he shouted at Jake. "What the hell is she doing here?"

"She's my partner."

"I closed that investigation and as far as I'm concerned, she should've never been brought in. She's caused enough damage to the FBI."

Jake's chest bowed up as he squared off with his superior. "We should be thanking her for Cramer."

"If you see it that way, you're softer than I thought."

More was exchanged between the two men; mostly Holt grumbling his discontent, but it was Jake's words that stuck with Dana. "She's the reason we have a lead to chase. But more importantly, she's my partner. She gets on the plane, or I don't."

Before that moment, she'd been slightly terrified about the idea of racing into battle alongside an FBI Hostage Rescue Team. She wanted to be there to help bring Meredith home, but she was doubting her place until Jake's unwavering belief sent her skepticism slithering back into a hole where it belonged.

She was the reason they'd still had a fighting chance to save Meredith and countless other women. If Dana hadn't been relentless about being involved in every facet of this investigation it would've been over the night of the gala when the body was found. She was the one who debunked the doppelganger in the morgue. She followed

Riley to the catacombs and confirmed Meredith was alive. She found the charm in the ashes. She cracked the code hidden in the chatroom message.

She belonged here. She knew it and so did Jake. Even if no one else did. That was enough.

"Dr. Gray." Dana's head snapped up at the sound of her name. Agent Jenkins waved her over to the group. "You'll hang back in the tact bus in case we get into a hostage situation. Where's my negotiator?"

An aging man wearing a navy-blue jacket with FBI printed on the back in big yellow letters raised his hand. "Agent Simms."

"Simms, you'll be on com if we need to handle hostage negotiations." Jenks turned her attention back to Dana as she addressed the unit. "This is Dr. Gray. She has extensive knowledge of the potential cult mentality driving the members of this cell. She's our ace in the hole if things go south, and we need someone to talk sense to these yahoos. Get acquainted."

Dana felt too many eyes on her as a few dozen men looked her up and down. They didn't need to speak. She knew what they were thinking. *You don't belong.* It was something she'd been told her whole life. And in one respect it was true.

All the men here had paid their dues, earning their badges in the military or some other form of mercenary work she didn't want to know about. But she'd paid, too. She may not have sworn an oath to protect and serve, but she'd dedicated her life to understanding death. She studied cults and rituals so obscure they were either forgotten or said to have never existed in the first place.

Maybe she hadn't fought the same kind of battles as these agents, but she knew it was ignorance that caused more senseless death than anything. Stopping it was her war.

66

"ALL RIGHT, TEAM." JENKINS' VOICE ROSE OVER THE BUZZ OF ACTIVITY IN the woods. "You know the drill. We roll at twenty-one hundred. Round up in thirty."

Jake moved through the crowd as the teams disbursed to gear up and make final weapon checks. He'd done all his prep work on the plane. Right now, the only thing on his mind other than the success of this mission was getting Dana through it in one piece.

He wished she'd sit this one out, but he knew better than to hope for that kind of miracle. She was as liable to stay on the sidelines as Jenkins. Jake shook his head, wondering how the hell he'd ended up with two take-charge women bossing him around.

He'd expected Dana to be a pain in his ass, asking a million questions as that brilliant mind of hers got lost in a maze of what-ifs. But she'd been uncharacteristically quiet since they'd boarded the plane.

That was Holt's fault.

Jake could've punched the man's teeth down his throat for speaking to a woman like that, but his chivalry probably would've pissed Dana off more than anything Holt said. He wished his boss hadn't decided to play babysitter. Holt's wrinkly ass belonged in a cushy office chair, not out in the field.

Lucky for everyone involved, Jenkins was running this show. That meant the only punks spitting teeth would be the Senator and his crew. Holt would be in the tact bus with Dana. It was the safest place she could be. Even so, Jake wanted to get some things off his chest.

Pushing his jackass of a boss out of his head, Jake made a beeline for the mobile tactical office they referred to as the tact bus.

He spotted Dana standing outside the giant vehicle that would take her to the scene. She was chewing her nails, a sure sign of her nerves. "You okay?"

She jumped at the sound of his voice. "Yeah. Just a little nervous."

"I'd be worried if you weren't."

"Do you feel like this every time?"

Jake suppressed his chuckle. This wasn't war, but to someone who spent their life in a library, it probably seemed that way. "It's how you know you're alive." He winked. "Speaking of ... let's keep you that way." He grabbed the extra handgun he'd tucked into his weapon belt. Double checking the safety, he handed the military issue Sig M17 to Dana.

"What's this for?"

"Just in case."

"But I'm going to be in the bus."

"I know."

Her brown eyes glittered with alarm. "You think something's going to go wrong?"

"No. I just like to be prepared."

"Did you see something on the drone footage that I didn't? What aren't you telling me?"

"That's not why I came over here."

"But there's something you're not telling me."

Jake was shaking his head, but he could see Dana was already in panic mode. This wasn't the right time to bring up what was troubling him. Especially with so many people around. He pressed the gun more firmly into her hand. "It's loaded."

"How many bullets?"

"Twenty-one round magazine. That's more than enough."

"You sure that's a good idea?" Jenkins asked, walking up behind Dana.

"She knows how to use it," Jake defended.

Jenkins grinned. "That's what I'm afraid of."

"I'd let her cover me any day of the week," Wade called, ambling over to join the conversation.

Great, just what Jake needed, an even bigger audience.

Jenkins' eyes twinkled as she barked a laugh in his uncle's direction. "Well, those words carry weight coming from a stubborn old fart like you."

"No more stubborn than you, Remi."

Jenkins growled. "What'd I tell you about calling me that?"

Jake watched the two ex-airmen exchange banter. The love between the old friends was clear. Not for the first time, he wondered why they'd never become anything more. Jenkins was a formidable woman, but Wade was never one to back down from a challenge.

Speaking of challenging women. Jake turned his attention back to Dana. She was still looking at him with that questioning gaze that cut him to the quick. He needed a moment alone with her before taking his spot on the Alpha team.

Jake would be going in with the first wave to eliminate the Tangos they'd spotted with the drone. He glanced at his watch, wanting more time to sort out the emotions crowding his chest. He needed to stop wasting the moments he had left.

Jake stuck his hand out to Jenkins, hoping she'd take the hint. "Thanks for backing me up with this."

She clasped his hand tightly. "Always."

Jake turned to his uncle. "Wade, thanks for letting us assemble here."

"I already told ya, this place is as much yours as it is mine."

"Thank you. I'll make you proud out there."

Wade grabbed the hand Jake offered, shaking it hard. "You always do. Take care of yourself." His keen eyes traveled to Dana. "Both of you."

When Wade and Jenkins finally headed off in the direction of the cabin Jake could breathe easier. He couldn't afford to be distracted on this mission. That's why he needed to get the words out before they ate him alive. But Dana beat him to the punch.

She shoved his shoulder. "I thought we were a team?"

"We are."

"Then what aren't you telling me?"

"Christ, you're relentless, you know that?"

She crossed her arms, glaring at him in a way that turned him on as much as it pissed him off. He grabbed her by her vest, pulling her toward him so unexpectedly she gasped.

"Jake! What the—"

He yanked the Velcro straps at her ribs, tightening both sides. "This doesn't work if you don't wear it right."

Dana looked up at him, her hands gripping his vest for balance. She was wearing contacts today. He wanted to look away, because the determination he saw in her gorgeous brown eyes was going to be his undoing. That and those damn pouty lips. The thought of owning them made him ache.

They stood only a few feet from where it almost happened. And here they were yet again, like kissing her was unavoidable. He wished he was better with words. Hell, he wished he was better, period. Dana deserved more than he could give her, but that didn't stop his selfish desires. Not when moments like these put life in perspective.

Time was short. Tomorrow wasn't guaranteed.

He saw Ramirez in his mind, grinning from ear-to-ear as he threw Jake the YOLO hand signal before leaving some piss poor excuse for a bar with the hottest girl they'd seen in miles.

"Jake?" Dana's voice was a beam of sunlight bursting through his painful memories, forcing him to push away all thoughts of his best friend. He met her searching gaze, hating the way she made him want to be the guy he was before he let the Army chew him up and spit him out.

The warning whistle blew in the distance. The teams were mounting up. It was now or never. Jake's hands moved from Dana's vest to her neck, until he was cupping her cheeks. Words failed him so he pressed his lips to her forehead.

She stilled, her breath warm against his neck. He let himself inhale her scent, craving more but there wasn't time. He pulled away, pausing to drag his thumb across her lower lip. Watching the delicate skin part sent blinding lust ripping through him as he imagined the release those lips could grant.

The sounds of engines roaring to life echoed around them.

"Jake. You should go."

"I know." He exhaled slowly. "Dana, if things don't go as planned. If I don't make it back, I need to tell you—"

"No!" She scrambled back so quickly her back collided with the tact bus in a dull thump. "No way. Don't you dare give me that 'if I die' bullshit!" The fierceness in her eyes was unwavering. "Whatever you have to say to me, you can tell me when this is over."

He gave her a long, hard look, committing her obstinate features to memory before turning away to the shrill cry of the final whistle.

"Jake." Dana grabbed his hand, pulling him back. "Place the mask over your own mouth and nose before assisting others."

He grinned, his chest tightening hearing his old team's mantra. He gave her hand a meaningful squeeze before letting go. Resolve spread through him as he executed a salute. "Yes, ma'am."

67

GHOSTLIKE WHISPERS RATTLED THROUGH THE TREES IN THE DARKNESS AS the wind picked up.

Dana stared out the viewing window of the tactical bus into the inky darkness. She knew Jake and dozens of other agents were out there somewhere, armed to the teeth, but she couldn't see them.

She knew they were using the darkness as cover, but she wished they'd waited until first light. Everything felt more desperate in the dark.

Someone opened a window to increase airflow in the stuffy command center vehicle. It didn't help. Dana could smell the eggy dampness of the lake. It mixed with the tangy odor of sweat and anxiety inside the cramped space making it hard to breathe.

She watched the red numbers race by on the large scoreboard-esque display above the deck of monitors. The timer had started the moment the mission was under way. They were rapidly approaching the marker when the teams would make their move. She held her breath and watched the clock. Five, four, three, two—

Shots rang out, piercing the calm night. The darkness erupted into bursts of light and chaos as gunfire lit up the area leading to the large colonial lake house. It glowed like a monster cut out of smoke the tear gas left behind.

Through the barrage of bullets Dana was glued to the monitors. There she could watch the attack from every angle. GPS trackers showed team movement; each member depicted by a blinking yellow dot. Other monitors showed actual footage from body cams.

Jake wore one and Dana's gaze moved from screen to screen trying to determine which footage might be his. The only thing that kept her calm was seeing all the cameras were functioning. None were down or still. That meant they hadn't lost anyone—*yet.*

Staring at the jumpy footage was making her queasy. Dana moved back to the viewing window at the front of the bus, waiting for the signal. When the series of clicks finally came through the radio, a fresh-faced tech at the controls hit the lights, flooding the lawn with enough wattage to light up a football stadium. The whomp-whomp-whomp of the FBI helicopter grew louder until the concentrated beam of its searchlight joined the siege.

Dana could see the action now. There were no shadows left to hide the atrocities of the terrifying scene unfolding on the lawn of the lake house.

Two school buses were parked in the circle drive. Women cowered, huddled together near them, coughing and clutching each other as mercenaries and HRT squared off. It only took a matter of seconds for Jake and Jenkins' unit to take control. They outnumbered the security detail at the house, just like their drone recon predicted.

The pop-pop of gunfire ceased as suddenly as it started. Bodies lay scattered on the lawn. Dana could make out three unmoving heaps. Her heart pounded as she tried to find Jake in the fray.

She knew the potential for casualties. Jenkins had been explicit about it when Dana insisted on coming along. She told the gruff New York agent she could handle it, and Jake vouched for her. But he was wrong. This felt different from the other crime scenes she'd witnessed.

Her mind flashed back to the D.C. alley where she'd watched the life drain out of a pair of cold, hateful eyes. Dana's stomach clenched violently. She staggered out of the bus with her hand over her mouth.

Gunpowder clung to the air. Charred metal mixed with a hint of sulfur; the scent was unmistakable. It burned her lungs as she choked back the bile scorching her throat.

She didn't want to see death claim anyone like that again. Especially not someone she knew and cared for. She sent up a silent prayer for Jake, Meredith and the agents she'd met briefly before they bravely ran into battle.

Jenkins' voice sounded over the com. "This is the FBI. Put your weapons down and your hands up."

Dana could hear the teams checking in. Deep voices crackled over the speakers inside the bus, barely audible through the open windows. She listened intently as the tech verbally confirmed each call. "Bravo team, clear. Delta team, clear. Charlie team, clear. Echo team, clear."

Please, please, please ...

"Alpha team. Clear." Dana crumbled to her knees when Jake's voice came over the radio.

"Alpha team, clear," the tech repeated.

Jake's voice crackled over the radio again. "Three Tangos down."

Three targets? Dana scrambled to her feet and back onto the bus needing to know who the casualties were. She prayed Meredith hadn't been caught in the crossfire. They weren't able to confirm she was at the lake house during the drone sweep, but they knew Ben Riley was, and they needed him alive for questioning.

Back on the bus, Dana found the nearest monitor, recognizing Jake's hulking form in an instant. "Can you zoom in?"

The tech supervising the screen looked to Jenkins for confirmation. She gave a curt nod. Dana held her breath as the camera zoomed in on Jake and the figure he loomed over. The man was on his knees, hands secured behind him. Jake held on to him while barking orders she couldn't hear.

When the image cleared enough for her to make out the man's features, she gasped. Her head throbbed with recognition. "That's him. That's Ben Riley."

Her eyes scanned the rest of the people on screen. She needed to find Meredith. "Zoom out," she commanded. "I want to see the women."

The tech obeyed without checking for approval this time. By Dana's estimate, nearly a hundred women huddled together on the ground near the school buses. It appeared Riley and his crew must've been trying to load them when Jenkins sent her unit in.

Dana studied the terrified faces searching for Meredith. The women were too close together, some of them bound to one another by their wrists. She needed to get closer.

"Can I see Agent Shepard again?"

Jenkins spoke up. "I've got eyes on him over here."

Dana moved between the screens. Jake still had Riley at gunpoint while other agents rushed across the lawn. Some moved into the house, others continued rounding up the subdued targets.

"What's Jake waiting for?" Dana asked. "We need to question Riley and find out where Meredith is."

"We're clearing the house first," Jenkins replied. "Jake will bring Riley in once it's safe to do so."

Dana's heart was in her throat. She expected her adrenaline to fade after the initial attack but waiting to find out if they'd finally found Meredith was killing her. Her eyes bounced between the screens looking for any signs of the face that used to be as familiar as her own. She couldn't shake the feeling she was missing something.

She caught Riley's mouth moving on the screen. "What's he saying?"

Jenkins leaned in. "Get me audio on Alpha team leader."

A moment later Jake's voice boomed through the bus. "Save it, Riley."

"I swear," Riley sniveled. "This wasn't my idea. I'll spill everything if you cut me a deal, but you gotta get me out of here. It's not safe. She's not gonna let me walk away."

"Who?"

"Meredith Kincaid. She's as much to blame as Scott and Vega."

"Terrance Vega? Are these his women?"

"Yes. And it's not just him. I'll give you a list of all the big players. Just please get me out of here."

"Don't worry, we've got a prison cell with your name on it, buddy."

"Good. Let's go. What are you waiting for?"

"Just gathering all your friends inside."

"There's no one else in the house. We were putting the gems on the bus when you busted us."

"Gems?"

"It's what we call the girls."

"Like in the video game?"

Riley paled.

"Yeah, we know about your little chatroom. That's how we found you. Whose idea was *Memento Mori*?"

"Meredith's."

Jake laughed. "A Capitol Hill princess is a closet video game freak? You're gonna have to do better than that if you think you're getting a deal."

"She's not who you think. This whole disappearing act was her idea. She's the one who wanted to blackmail her father to get more funds."

"Archer Kincaid is involved?"

"She said he'd go along with it, but it turns out he's the only honest one in that family."

Jake frowned. "Keep talking."

Movement on the other screen caught Dana's eye. She watched as a woman stood from the group cowering near the buses. Her hair was blonde and dirty. It hung in a face that was barely recognizable under all the filth and rage, but Dana would know it anywhere.

"Mere." She whispered her best friend's name, horror-struck as she watched the woman on the screen pull a pistol from the waist of her jeans.

68

DANA FELT TIME SLOW WATCHING MEREDITH DRAW HER WEAPON. SHE leveled it at Riley, her voice guttural. “Shut up, Perseus!”

Meredith’s rage took on a physical presence.

“Shit! Shit! I told you,” Riley blubbered as he tried to crawl behind Jake.

Chaos erupted behind Dana as Jenkins commanded the teams to train their weapons on a new Tango: Meredith Kincaid.

Agent Simms shoved Dana aside to get to the com. “Meredith, this is Frank Simms with the FBI. I know this has been hard on you—”

“You don’t know anything!” Meredith screamed, the gun shaking in her hands.

Simms pressed the com button and spoke slowly. “You’re right. You’re right. Can you help me understand, Meredith? Can you do that, sweetheart?”

Dana watched Meredith’s gaze turn toward the bus. Her blue eyes burned straight through Dana on the monitor. She could tell Meredith was on the verge of losing it, and Simms’ negotiating tactics were only making things worse.

Dana grabbed his arm. “She speaks four languages and graduated first in her class from American Law. Don't speak to her like she's a child."

Simms turned his patronizing glare on Dana. "She *is* a child. A child throwing a tantrum with a deadly weapon. Now back up and let me do my job." He shook Dana off and hit the com button again, his voice booming through the speakers to Meredith. "Why don't you put the gun down so we can talk about it."

Meredith wasn't listening. Her eyes were back on Riley, her hands no longer shaking as she whispered a phrase over and over.

Simms swore. "Who's on audio? I can't hear what the hell she's saying."

"Memento Mori." No one heard Dana. She cleared her throat and spoke louder. "She's saying Memento Mori."

"What the hell does that mean?" Simms demanded.

"Death comes for us all."

Simms sucked in his scarred cheeks, giving the impression of a bruised potato. He flipped through his notebook obviously out of his depth, while everyone on the bus scrambled to anticipate the next move.

Dana was done being pushed aside. She lunged forward pressing the com button. "Mere? It's me. It's Dana."

Meredith's lips stopped moving, her gaze swinging wildly as she looked around.

Agent Holt stepped up behind Dana, warning in his tone. "Dr. Gray."

Dana ignored him and pressed the com again. "I'm right here, Mere. And we're going to get through this. Together."

Dana's feet were moving. Carrying her off the bus before anyone could stop her.

69

DANA'S STEADY VOICE CUT THROUGH THE TENSE SCENE LIKE BLUE SKY IN A hurricane. Her words seemed to affect Meredith in much the same way they did Jake. When Dana said "we're going to get through this together," the fire in Meredith's eyes guttered.

Jake used the momentary distraction to widen his stance, edging slightly in front of Riley. The little prick wasn't going anywhere. He didn't pose a threat. Jake had searched him after the initial attack. The preppy little prick hadn't even been carrying. With his hands cuffed and a few dozen agents in the shadows, Riley had no chance of escape.

He would, however, get himself shot if he didn't keep his mouth shut.

"I told you this would happen," he hissed. "She's crazy, man. I didn't sign up for this shit. This is all my father's fault. I had to take his spot."

"Your father's dead."

"Yeah, but I'm a legacy. I had to join. He always said it was my divine right or something, but he never said anything about this shit. I didn't sign on for sex trafficking and shootouts. It's all that bitch's fault. The spoiled princess had daddy issues. It was her idea to blackmail him to get funding for transportation so we could expand." Riley peeked around Jake and screamed at Meredith. "Thought she'd stick it to her old man for never paying attention to her. But looks like he stuck her."

"Shut up, you coward!" The fire was back in Meredith's eyes. "You took a vow to the brotherhood!"

Riley sniveled on his knees. "Please, man. You need me. I'll tell you anything you need to know. Just don't let her near me."

Justice had always been simple to Jake. Protect the innocent, punish the wicked. It pissed him off that the little snake was right. He *did* need Riley. A guy like him wouldn't survive in prison and he knew it, which meant he would spill his guts to the feds for the right deal. He'd probably end up in witness protection in Florida or somewhere cushy.

It was the thing Jake hated most about his job. Letting little fish go to catch larger ones. Fascism at its finest.

Jake let his gaze travel over Meredith, sizing up where she measured on the scale of justice. It was obvious Riley would squeal like a stuck pig. Meredith on the other hand ... he wasn't sure.

In another life, Jake had interrogated more men than he could remember. He could spot weakness and exploit it. But with Meredith, her rage went deeper than anything he'd seen stateside. Her fury was tinged with delusion, a pure zealot belief that defied reason. Those were the people who would never break, because something in them had broken a long time ago. There just wasn't enough left to salvage.

That made them dangerous.

Riley continued to whine until Jake grabbed him by the collar. "Do exactly what I say, and you might just make it out of here alive."

The com in Jake's ear crackled before he heard Jenkins speak. "Hold your fire. I repeat, all units hold your fire. Friendly on the field."

Jake kept his weapon on Meredith as he swept the area, expecting to see Simms cresting the hill. When he recognized Dana's silhouette, his heart jumped into his throat, throbbing so hard he thought he would choke.

Her long brown ponytail lashed her cheeks as the wind gnashed at her back. Her pace was fast, determined, matching Jake's pulse.

Shock turned to anger, then frustration until his training quickly overrode his emotions. He channeled his anger to sharpen his focus.

Every disadvantage had an advantage. Dana's appearance distracted Meredith and he wouldn't let that go unrewarded.

Moving slowly, he unstrapped his Kevlar vest and slipped it over Riley's head. With his hands bound Riley wouldn't be able to tighten the straps for maximum protection, but it was the best Jake could offer at the moment.

He took another step away from the snake at his feet. With Dana in play, he kept Meredith squarely in his sights. Holt's voice sounded in his earpiece, barking some order or another. Jake didn't have time for his boss's hot air. He switched off his com. There was too much on the line to be distracted by something as trivial as his career.

He exhaled deliberately, working to slow his heart rate as he counted each step that drew Dana within range of Meredith's Ruger.

70

DANA CLENCHED HER FISTS, HOPING TO SQUEEZE OUT THE TINGLING IN HER sweaty palms as she crossed the trampled grass. The scene was surreal. This must be what it was like to walk onto a film set of a movie.

Men dressed in black stood along the edges of the shadows, automatic weapons drawn and waiting for action. A helicopter swooped above, its searchlight still probing from treetops to lake. The tension was palpable. Dana forced herself to focus only on Meredith.

She knew Jake was there, in her periphery, ready to do his job if she didn't succeed. If she couldn't talk Meredith down, Jake would be forced to eliminate the threat, one way or another.

Dana stopped fifteen yards away from the situation unfolding on the lake house lawn, creating a triangle between her, Meredith, Jake and Riley. Meredith stood to her right, among a group of terrified women who were doing their best to lay flat to the ground. Jake was on Dana's left, with Riley kneeling beside him.

The cold steel of the M17 pressed into the small of her back. It added to the weight of the situation. Jake had given it to her for protection, but she never imagined Meredith would be the threat. Dana took another step forward, splaying her hands at her sides. "Mere, what's going on?"

"I'm defending an oath."

"You don't have to do this."

"You of all people should know that I do. The Order requires it."

"This is about the Priory of Bones?"

Meredith's eyebrows knitted together, recognition burning in her eyes. "I finally have a family. One who would die for me."

Dana's heart pounded as Meredith confirmed the truth. Proof of the most secret society in the world. The Priory of Bones was real. And they'd recruited her best friend. It was almost too much to absorb, but the direness of the situation required her to focus on the immediate. "Mere, you've always had a family."

A bitter smile spread across Meredith's cracked lips as she shook her head violently. "No. This is real family. Not that shrewd group of self-serving capitalists who share my blood."

"Meredith, your family loves you. I've been to the house. They're worried about you."

"Ha! The only thing they've ever worried about is money. Do you know my father could've stopped this whole thing? All he had to do was fund Scott's agenda, and I could've come back before anyone even knew I was missing. My father certainly wouldn't have noticed I was gone. But he refused. He made his choice. So I made mine."

Meredith was extorting her father! The final pieces of the puzzle began to take shape. Archer Kincaid's position made him a target. There were measures to protect members of the Presidential staff, but he never would've seen a threat coming from his own daughter. Much like Dana hadn't thought her friend would ever betray her the way she had in the catacombs. But she still had hope of getting through to her. Meredith was still in there, buried beneath layers of propagandized occult influence.

Dana tried a new strategy. "What about Abby?"

Meredith's face contorted with rage. "Abby might be the worst of them. Do you know she's pregnant?"

Dana nodded. "She told me."

"Did she tell you she came to me for help getting rid of it? Not because she's scared but because she doesn't want to lose her precious inheritance. Money! She'd rather have wealth than the infinite abundance of creating a life! What I wouldn't give for that gift!"

Suddenly Dana understood; how Meredith could've fallen in with such a volatile cult, how she could've turned on her father, abandoned her sister and mother. It was a fear that crushed everyone. Meredith thought she was alone.

The Priory of Bones had given her a home, one where she had a place at the head of the household. Where her voice was heard. She most likely saw herself as a mother-figure to the cowering women she stood over. It gave Dana a new perspective as she beheld her friend's position, wielding a gun above the heads of the women huddled near her. She thought she was protecting them.

A piece of Dana's heart broke for her friend, but now that she knew Meredith's fear, she started to chip away at it. "What about me, Mere. You have me."

"I thought I did. But you're a liar, like everyone else."

"I didn't lie, Mere. You did. You could've told me about the Priory. We could've found a home with the Order together."

Meredith shook her head. "No. No, you would've tried to change my mind. I know how you work. You see things in black and white. We have to operate in the gray."

"You're wrong. I know what it's like to have no family. To be so isolated from the world that you start to see loneliness as a companion. That's where I was when I found you. But you gave me hope. You gave me a place to belong. We can be like that again. Just put the gun down."

Meredith shook her head harder, pulling her hands to her ears, gun and all. "No. No. No!"

Dana was getting through to her. She risked a step closer. Meredith flinched, aiming the gun at her chest. "Stop lying to me!"

"I'm not lying, Mere. I care about you. And I know you still care about me. You wouldn't have arranged that meeting in the catacombs if you didn't."

"Do you know what I compromised to do that? I was trying to protect you. You should've let me go."

"You were trying to protect me because deep down our friendship still means something to you. You still have ties to this world, ties to me. That's why you left me this, isn't it?" Dana slowly reached into her pocket and pulled out the ladybug charm, holding it between her thumb and forefinger. "You didn't want me to give up on you, and I won't."

Meredith's blue eyes swam with tears and regret. "It's too late."

"No, it's not."

"Yes. They know too much. *He* knows too much." She swung the gun toward Riley again.

Dana followed her stare, her eyes locking with Jake's for the first time since the standoff began. That's when she noticed he wasn't wearing his vest. It was on Riley. The cowering man began babbling. "No. I-I never wanted this. I-I want out. This was all her. Her and Scott. They killed that girl you found in the Basin. Vega set the whole sick thing up. I'll tell you everything, just get me out of here."

Meredith's eyes flashed with wild fury. "You traitor!"

"Mere, look at me." Dana tried again. "Mere, don't look at him. I know he's lying. I know you would never do something like that."

Meredith angled her head, the move almost feline, just like the Cheshire grin that carved her cracked lips. "He's not lying. Warren let me pick her out. My very first offering. Her blood tasted like honey. I hated to spill it. Her death is your fault, Dana. I wouldn't have slit her throat if you would've just listened to me."

"I told you!" Riley yelled. "She's a fucking psycho!"

"She was so pretty." Meredith giggled. "She looked just like me. That's why I chose her. I wish I could've kept her, but she'd not really gone. Her blood lives on inside us. In the Order. Her blood binds us." Meredith's wild aim found Jake. "So does Jenni's. But you know all about her, don't you?"

Dana's heart twisted with anguish. Her gaze met Jake's again. He gave the tiniest shake of his head, as if he knew the decision she'd just come to. Her last resort.

"That's a confession!" Riley shouted. "Shoot her!"

Meredith laughed. "The only way out is death, Perseus. Death comes for us all."

"Mere, no!" Dana yelled, pulling the gun from the small of her back and aiming it at the woman she once would've died for. "Don't do this."

"I have to."

"No, you don't. If you shoot Riley, the FBI agent standing next to him will shoot you."

"You chose your side. I chose mine." Meredith's jaw tightened as she leveled the gun.

The world stood still as Dana watched Meredith's finger move to the trigger. "Please, Mere. Don't do this."

She begged her friend not to say the words that would seal her fate, but Meredith's mouth formed them anyway. "Memento Mori."

The gunshot was deafening. It snapped the world back into focus. The recoil ripped through Dana, snapping her teeth together as she tasted the burnt metal in the air. She stared at the bloom of crimson staining Meredith's dirty white t-shirt, then she searched out Jake and Riley. Only one of them was still breathing.

71

JAKE BRACED FOR AN IMPACT THAT NEVER CAME.

Two bodies fell. Two smoking guns. He was responsible for none.

Flipping on his safety, he checked his weapon just to be sure he hadn't fired on impulse.

He hadn't.

Looking down he saw Riley sprawled face up, dead eyes staring at nothing. A single bullet hole pierced his forehead. The entrance wound was small and dark, but Jake knew the back of Riley's skull had split open like a watermelon.

Jake ignored the brain matter and gore covering the grass. He was too busy tracing the scene.

Meredith lay on her back, almost twenty yards away. Considering the distance, hitting Riley right between the eyes was one hell of a shot. But he was more impressed with Dana's aim.

His stare fixed on her. She still held the M17 in a white knuckled death grip. Realization punched him in the gut harder than any bullet. Dana had shot Meredith so Meredith couldn't shoot him.

Christ! She'd chosen to protect him over her best friend. He didn't want to think about the devastating ramifications that decision would have. Jake holstered his weapon, one hand feeling his chest, still trying to process there wasn't a bullet lodged there.

There was only one reason he was still alive—Dana. She'd fired first, not knowing who Meredith's bullet was meant for.

His chest burned like he'd swallowed a cigarette. Something he couldn't explain made him want to run toward Dana and away from her at the same time. He chose the former, his feet moving before he knew he'd made the decision.

He picked up speed as HRT shook off their shock and fell into line. Agents shouted commands, medics rushed up the hill, women shrieked, rushing away from where Meredith lay. Holt was on the horn, ordering Dana's head on a platter, but Jake kept moving.

"Over my dead body." He picked up his pace. He had to get to Dana first.

He called her name, snapping her out of her trance. She dropped the gun. A shriek tore from her lungs as her feet began to move. She was running too, but not toward him.

She was running toward Meredith.

Jake changed course, pumping his legs harder to cut her off before she covered the distance to where Meredith lay motionless. What Dana had done, saving him over her friend, would shatter her. She didn't need to see the aftermath on top of that.

He knew all too well that some things could never be unseen.

"Dana!" Jake slammed into her, clamping his arms around her like a vice as she screamed and clawed at him.

"Let go! Mere! Mere, I'm sorry. Mere!" She struggled like a feral cat, but he held her tight, until her fight gave way to fear. "What have I done? Jake, please, I need to see her."

He shook his head. "It's better if you don't."

She turned those dark brown eyes on him, her glare cutting him deep. "You don't get to make that call."

He exhaled and let her go, knowing this wasn't a war worth waging. Dana would never be someone who accepted protection, no matter how much she deserved it.

She slipped from his arms and covered the ground quickly, coming to a stop at Meredith's side. Jake followed a few steps behind, trying to remember how much space he'd needed that day in Ghazni.

Loss hit everyone differently, but eventually it broke even the strongest of them. Dana would crack. She needed to if she had any hope of healing. Until then, he would hang back.

She let out a sob and sank to her knees, grabbing Meredith's shoulders. She shook her, sobbing into Meredith's blood-soaked shirt. Dana's hands came away red, and she began to shake. She cried harder, whispering apologies to her friend.

A team of paramedics arrived on scene. They split up, between Riley and Meredith. Jake wanted to tell them Riley was a lost cause, but he let them do their job. They'd come to that conclusion soon enough.

He focused on the three medics who joined Dana. She was quickly pushed out of the way so they could assess their patient. Backing a few feet to give them space, she trembled uncontrollably. Jake finally stepped in, unable to do nothing while she unraveled.

He walked over and put an arm around her shivering shoulders. This time she didn't fight him. She turned into his chest and let him pull her into his arms. Jake held her tight, his heart crashing against his ribs. This was his fault. Because of him, Dana would carry this stain on her soul forever.

She'd taken a life to spare his. He didn't deserve it.

"I had to," she whispered. Her big brown eyes stared up at him, ripping apart his soul. "I had to, Jake. She would've shot you. I had no choice." Fat tears rolled down her cheeks as she blinked up at him, waiting for him to say something, anything to tell her that she'd made the right choice, saving him over her friend.

All he could say was "I'm sorry." It was a word he never said, but once it was past his lips he couldn't take it back. He said it over and over, making up for a lifetime of apologies, holding her together as she fell apart.

He didn't know how long he stood there, a boulder in a river, as the world rushed around them. He'd stand there as long as Dana needed him to, sheltering her from this storm. After what she'd done for him, there was no alternative. He would eternally be in her debt.

At some point he knew Jenkins would need to debrief him, and Holt would have plenty to say. But for now, Jake's only duty was to Dana. He had a feeling there wasn't much that could shake the loyalty he felt for her now. Which meant he was royally fucked.

A medic's voice burst through Jake's torturous thoughts. "We've got a pulse."

Another medic spoke up. "Bradycardic. Push three milligrams of atropine and get her on the bird. Let's move, people."

Dana lifted her head from Jake's chest, her eyes wild with hope. She grabbed the arm of a medic who rushed by. "Is she alive?"

"For now, but it'll take a miracle to keep her that way."

Dana let go, and the medic ran to join the team carrying Meredith's stretcher toward the helicopter. Jake looked down at Dana, her hopeful expression more crushing than her grief. For the first time, he felt himself truly thinking like a Fed as he wondered what side of the scale Meredith's survival fell on when it came to the greater good.

Surely one less deranged criminal was better for society. But what was better for Dana? And why did her approval hold more weight than the moral justice Jake lived by?

72

THE COOL, CLEAR WATER SWIRLED AROUND THE WHITE SINK BASIN LIKE A tiny cyclone before gurgling down the drain. The water was clear. Dana knew it was clear, but she couldn't stop seeing the pink tinge of blood every time she washed her hands.

She splashed some water on her face and left the faucet running as she grabbed both sides of the sink for support. Waves of dizziness snuck up on her every time she remembered this wasn't a dream. She stared at her reflection in the small bathroom mirror. She knew Jake was right outside the door. She needed to pull herself together or he would barge in soon.

He hadn't left her side since the shooting. It was making her claustrophobic. So was being cooped up inside his uncle's cabin.

It was hard to believe only a few hours ago she'd been aiming a gun at Meredith. It felt like a lifetime had passed in a blink of an eye. But she presumed that was because she'd just been interrogated by two high-ranking FBI officials.

Jenkins had been sympathetic, acknowledging that Dana had just shot and possibly killed a woman who at one point she considered her best friend, but Holt was relentless. He'd grilled her for almost an hour, making her relive the entire traumatic event.

It'd happened so fast, but at the same time, she could recount every detail like she was watching a movie in slow motion.

The gun in Meredith's hand. The way her cracked lips tightened as she pulled the trigger. Dana hadn't hesitated. Meredith's shot could've been for Jake. And as much as she hated it, as much as it killed her, she knew she would do it again. There'd never really been a choice. If the roles had been reversed, Jake wouldn't have hesitated either. In the end she was cleared of any charges.

But if she'd made the right call, why did everything feel so wrong?

Another wave of bile assaulted her throat and she ran to the toilet to wretch the contents of her empty stomach. She'd just finished washing her mouth out when there was a knock at the door. "Dana? You good?"

She wiped her mouth with the back of her hand. "I need a minute."

Checking her watch, she wondered if Meredith was out of surgery yet. Jenkins promised to keep her updated. Besides Jake and Wade, Jenkins was the only other person who seemed to remember Meredith even existed.

The rest of the FBI had already moved on to the next mission: Senator Scott.

Dana washed her hands again, splashed some water on her face and turned off the faucet. She dried off with the fresh white towel on the back of the door. Someone had replaced the one she'd ruined scrubbing the dried blood off her hands.

With a deep breath she opened the door, confronting Jake's concerned stare. The storm clouds were a permanent fixture in his blue eyes, and he was chewing gum like it was necessary for survival. At least the cinnamon scent soothed her nausea. "Any news?"

He shook his head and fell into step with her, not noticing that his presence made the crowded cabin even more cramped. An agent sidestepped them before Jake bowled him over as Dana headed for the door.

"Where are we going?" Jake asked.

"*I'm* going outside. I need some air."

Jake ignored her use of the singular and followed her to the porch.

There were three agents out there. One look at her and they immediately made themselves scarce. "I guess that's one plus," she grumbled. "People get out of your way after you kill someone."

Jake didn't crack a smile. "She's not dead, Dana."

"Yet. Isn't that what you told me?"

"Just trying to prepare you for all the possible outcomes."

"I pulled the trigger, Jake. I knelt in her blood and spent half an hour scrubbing it from under my nails. I'm completely aware that Meredith might die and that it's my fault."

"It's not your fault. She made choice after choice that led her here."

"Yeah," Dana said quietly. "So did I."

The screen door squeaked on its hinges, and Jenkins poked her head out. "There you are. We're moving on Scott. Wheels up in twenty. You in?"

Dana nodded, since she was pretty sure Jake wouldn't go if she didn't. It was infuriating. She wished he would just yell at her for leaving the bus or tell her he should've never given her that gun or do anything other than stare at her like she was made of glass.

Jenkins was about to disappear back inside when Dana spoke. "Are you coming to D.C.?"

The senior agent paused, looked inside, then stepped back onto the porch, letting the door shut behind her. "No. I've gotta wrap stuff up here; sort out getting statements from all the women, see what else shakes loose. Holt's heading up the D.C. raid. Should be an easy in and out. They've already got eyes on Scott's house. He's inside, alone as far as anyone can tell."

Dana chewed her nails, staring down at the floor. Buckshot peppered the floorboards, reminding her how close she'd come to death even before rushing onto the lake house lawn. She heard Meredith's last words in her mind again. *Memento Mori.*

Dana seldom needed a reminder that in the end, death claimed everything. A reoccurring undertone in occult studies was that without death, life had no meaning. She used to believe that was true. It's why she'd spent nearly twenty years trying to solve her parents' murders. She thought the truth about their deaths would give her life more meaning. In reality, all it did was bring more death into her life.

And yet, each brush with her mortality didn't make her feel more alive. If anything, she was more lost than ever.

Jenkins' voice pulled Dana from her spiraling depression. "I know it may not feel like it now, but we did good here. We saved more than a hundred women from the hellish existence of sex trade. Senator Scott is going to go away for a long time, and thanks to the recording we got off Jake's body cam, we can use Riley's and Meredith's confessions to go after Vega."

"Yeah, once we find him," Jake muttered.

Jenkins raised an eyebrow at him. "This job is done one day at a time. Remember that." She looked at Dana. "Both of you."

73

THE RUNWAY SHIMMERED IN THE AFTERNOON HEAT.

Jake had no doubt he could fry an egg if he dropped it on the pock-marked asphalt. It was one of those early heatwave days that fooled Washingtonians into thinking they could dust off their swim trunks. He'd witnessed enough of the fickle weather to know better.

Wiping his forehead with the back of his hand, he adjusted his shades. He stood on the tarmac, shoulders back, hands clasped behind his back. It was a habit thanks to his time in the military. He glanced over at Dana. She slouched next to him as the rest of the agents deboarded.

The team being sent in to apprehend Scott was small, but that was deliberate. Holt didn't want news of the siege leaked. That's how it always was with government officials. Nothing flashy that would attract too much attention.

Another politician in handcuffs. It would barely register on the six o'clock news.

Jake wished they could go in full force like they had at Candlestick Lake. It might make other Capitol Hill deviants think twice before forgetting the oath they swore to uphold justice.

Holt exited the plane, and everyone moved to the hangar to divide into their assigned groups. Six black Yukons with tinted windows waited to transport them to Scott's house, where they'd arrest him.

Dana had special clearance to come with them. Jake owed that tiny miracle to Jenkins. He'd asked her for the favor, knowing as soon as Dana's feet were back on solid ground, she'd go straight to visit Meredith at the hospital.

There'd been no updates since she went into surgery. Jake didn't know if that was good or bad. Either way, he wanted to be with Dana when she got the news. He told himself he wasn't just dragging her on this mission to babysit her. Her expertise would be invaluable as they combed the Scott residence. If there was anything related to the shocking secret society that Meredith had admitted to, Dana would spot it.

At least that's what Jake asked Jenkins to tell Holt.

Jake's boss had been uncharacteristically quiet prior to the short flight back to D.C. Thankfully there hadn't been enough room for everyone on the FBI's private plane. Jake volunteered to ride in the additional puddle jumper that had been chartered, along with Dana and three other agents. He would've flown in the cargo hold if that spared her from Holt.

The prickly assistant director had used up all his free passes as far as Jake was concerned.

Though it was unlikely Holt would get in his way during the siege, he was still steering clear of the man. Holt was only tagging along on the mission for appearances. Jake still believed he had no business in the field at his age, but perhaps he thought his presence would garner some good press for the Bureau after the dark cloud that Cramer had cast on the department.

Following Dana, Jake climbed into the backseat of one of the identical SUVs in the hangar. Hayes took the wheel. Whitley rode shotgun. Jake didn't know the HRT agents well, but they'd had his back in NY, and that was good enough for him.

The teams had been organized and briefed before leaving the cabin. That was another advantage of using a small group. They'd all just been through hell together. Rounding up an overweight senator would be a cake walk. Plus, there was no reason to waste time going over things again in D.C. with new agents. Everyone here was on the same page.

The car ride was too quiet for Jake's liking. He glanced over at Dana. She stared out the window, knees bouncing as she restlessly chewed her nails. They were going to be bloody stubs soon. He wanted to reach over and stop her, but the gesture felt too intimate with the other agents in the front seats.

Jake wrestled with his hang-ups over emotional intimacy. He'd been ready to kiss Dana in front of everyone back at the cabin. So why couldn't he reach over and grab her hand to comfort her now?

After what she'd just done, he should be willing to take a bullet for her. Actually, that he could do. It was the idea of letting her in that was paralyzing. Which was exactly why they would never work.

Truth be told, there were a lot of reasons why they wouldn't work.

Wade's voice found its way into Jake's mind just then. *You can't just dip your toe in. You gotta dive in headfirst, straight into the deep end and be willing to drown. That's what love can do, son. It can pull you under if you ain't able to give it everything ya got.*

It was another of his uncle's strange Nevadan expressions he'd rattled off ages ago when Jake thought his high school girlfriend was the one. He had no idea why the absurd advice had come back to him now.

He didn't think of Dana that way. He didn't think of anyone that way anymore. But even if he did, he knew better than to try to build something on such a damaged foundation.

Jake silenced his idle thoughts and stared straight ahead, focused on what was important. In a few minutes they'd be at the Senator's house and he would have another opportunity to do what he did best —serve justice.

74

Dana's heart pounded as they pulled onto Senator Scott's block.

Agents already on the scene had blocked off the street leading to his private residence. The FBI convoy roared by rows of angry residents who hadn't been permitted past the blockade to the homes inside the posh gated community. Not used to being denied, the stone-faced agents had their hands full keeping the residents sidelined.

Beyond the blockade, the streets were quiet. Too quiet. It seemed even the birds knew what kind of monster dwelled here. Dana gawked at the ornate wrought iron gates they passed through. They were tall and foreboding in the traditional gothic style, with a large S emblazoned in the center. It made the place look otherworldly.

The house was set too far back to see beyond the hedges and winding drive, but her mind conjured up images of Transylvanian castles, rather than the Georgian Colonial that probably stood just out of view.

Doors opened and closed in the SUV, making her jump. She turned to look at Jake. His door wasn't open yet. He was donning a generic FBI jacket over his bulletproof vest. Her mind flashed back to the last time she'd seen him wearing the vest; before he gave it to Riley, before she'd been forced to choose between him and Meredith.

Dana closed her eyes. Inhaling deeply, she reminded herself there was no going back.

The sound of Jake's car door opening made her glance in his direction. He was still sitting there staring at her.

"What?"

"You're going to stay in the car, right?"

"Yes."

"You said you'd stay on the bus ..."

Anger flooded her as Jake's words trailed off. "Yeah, well I guess you're not the only one who's no good at promises."

His jaw muscles twitched, like he wanted to say more but he thought better of it, turning toward the door instead. Dana's hand shot out. She grabbed his arm and he paused, turning to face her, his eyes stony. "Be careful, okay?"

He gave a curt nod before shutting the door.

Dana sank back against the black leather seats. Her head fell against the rest, and she closed her eyes, regretting her words. She was angry, but at herself, not Jake. None of this was his fault.

She checked her phone again. Still no updates on Meredith. Dana wanted to be at the hospital with her. No one deserved to be fighting for their life all alone.

As far as she knew, the Kincaids still hadn't been notified of their daughter's fate. All Dana knew was that Meredith had been life-flighted to Geneva General and rushed into surgery.

Jenkins sent two of her agents to accompany Meredith. Dana knew the move hadn't been out of kindness. Meredith had admitted to a multitude of crimes. If she survived surgery, she'd go into FBI custody.

Still, Dana couldn't quite accept that Meredith would have willingly done those things. The woman she used to call her best friend had to be in there somewhere. Maybe, with the right guidance, Dana could find her again.

She pulled up the hospital's webpage on her phone. Her finger hovered over the phone number. Jenkins promised to keep Dana updated, but she knew the other agent had a full plate back in New York. One phone call just to check Meredith's status wouldn't hurt.

Dana hit the call button at the same time Agent Whitley banged on her window. She jumped, bobbling the phone. When her heart started beating again, she rolled down her window. "What's wrong?"

"Holt's asking for you."

"Me? Why?"

Whitley didn't answer. He just opened the door and gestured for her to exit the vehicle. Dana scrambled after him, heart in her throat, phone call forgotten.

"Did something happen?" she asked, jogging to keep up with Whitley's long strides. "Is it Jake?"

"Your boyfriend's fine."

If she'd been wondering what the other agents thought of her tagging along, the snide comment gave her an answer. But she didn't care what they thought. She was here to do a job. She didn't let the opinions of others get in her way.

Ignoring Whitley's dig, Dana let relief clear her mind. She hadn't heard any gunfire. Not even a single pop. Jake specifically made sure she didn't have a radio so she wouldn't know when the signal was given to invade the house. *As if keeping her in the dark would somehow protect her?* She scoffed at the idea. Thanks to what happened to her parents, she'd lived half her life in the dark. Look how that turned out.

Trailing Whitley down the driveway, she tried not to picture every worst-case scenario her mind conjured. Instead she occupied her runaway thoughts by mentally recalling the tactical briefing she'd sat in on at the cabin.

The plan for securing Scott's home was simple. There were four points of entry. Four teams of two would cover each one until the signal was given to make a united attack while the D.C. agents kept eyes on the perimeter. Jake was on the team tasked with taking the front door, the very place she was walking toward now.

The house was a large brick Colonial with a white columned entry, black shutters and thick Boston Ivy creeping up the walls. Agent Hayes stood outside on the flagstone steps leading to the front door. He looked green around the gills. Dana tried to walk past him, but he held a hand up to stop her. "Here. You're gonna need 'em."

She looked at the crumpled pair of blue rubber gloves and paper booties briefly before putting them on. Whitley was doing the same, but she didn't wait for him. Dana rushed ahead to open one of the massive oak double doors.

75

It was the smell that hit her first.

Death dwelled here. But it wasn't recent.

She spotted more than half the agents huddled inside the large vestibule just beyond the foyer. Jake crouched near them, examining something on the floor. Dana's attention followed the Herringbone pattern of the beautiful parquet floor until she reached the object occupying Jake's attention.

There was a large brown leather suitcase, laying on its side. The antique kind with straps and buckles. Both were undone, partially displaying what was inside. She took a step closer, noticing the suitcase wasn't large enough to fit the object from the way the silver zipper yawned open like rows of glittering teeth.

That's when she saw it. The hand. Or at least what was left of it. "It's Scott, isn't it?"

Jake glanced up at her when she walked fully into the scene. "Yeah."

Taking a deep breath, Dana crouched next to Jake to examine the remains. What she'd first thought was a shadow from the suitcase was actually a pool of blood that had seeped through the leather onto the floor. The hand that hung partially from the unzippered portion was missing its ring ringer; a clear sign of who'd done this. In case there was any doubt, they'd left their calling card behind.

The Priory of Bones symbol had been branded into the leather. Dana stared at it, letting the implications sink in. She'd been fascinated by the speculations surrounding the secret society for most of her career. Now here she was, staring at hard proof of their existence. She expected to feel elation at the discovery, but she was too repulsed to be anything but devastated.

The cult that had stolen her best friend was still out there, operating in the shadows, luring in more innocent victims.

Holt appeared; another agent trailed him carrying a laptop in an evidence bag. "Dr. Gray. There you are. We recovered Senator Scott's laptop. I'm sure we'll find everything we need on here." He sneered. "Looks like we won't need your *expertise* after all."

"You won't find anything on the laptop."

"How could you possibly know that?"

"The Priory of Bones hasn't survived in secret for hundreds of years by being careless. Whatever Scott had on the Bonesmen is already gone." She pointed to the missing finger. "We should've kept his ring."

Holt glared at Jake. "What's she talking about?"

"Senator Scott wore a ring that may have hidden a flash drive."

"And you had possession of it?"

Jake gave Dana a look that would've sent Hades slithering back to the depths of hell. "No."

"Well?" Holt prompted, turning his impatience on her. "You're the expert. Where do we find the ring?"

"We don't. It's gone. The Bonesmen took it when they slit Scott's throat."

Suspicion danced in Holt's stern eyes. "How do you know that?"

"It's my job to know. Isn't that why you brought me here?"

"I brought you here to help gather evidence to put a corrupt politician behind bars, not spout off fairytales about secret societies."

"It's not a fairytale. The Priory of Bones is alive and well. What more proof do you need?" she yelled, pointing to the suitcase. There were two more by the door. They showed no signs of human remains.

"He was obviously going to run, but the Bonesmen got to him first. Senator Scott was executed by the secret society he belonged to. That's their seal branded in the leather. Open the suitcase, you'll find the same symbol burned into his tongue in retribution for exposing their secrets."

Holt's eyes flashed with anger. "Open the suitcase."

Another agent spoke up. "We should wait for forensics."

"That's an order," Holt demanded.

Dana looked at Jake, her throat rolling as she tried to swallow her fear. She didn't know if she could stomach what was inside. Jake spoke quietly. "You don't have to do this."

"I think I do."

Together, they slowly unzipped the suitcase. When Jake flipped back the lid, a vortex of silence swallowed the room. Dana stared at the mangled body, sickened by the shocking brutality. There was so much damage she didn't know where to look. In order to fit Scott inside the suitcase, he'd been partially dismembered. As she'd predicted, his throat was slit. She didn't have to see his tongue to know she was right about that, too. She was close enough to smell the charred flesh.

Jake stood and offered her a hand. She took it, eager to get away from the corpse. Holt and the other agents moved in to get a closer look, but Dana couldn't get far enough away. She backed up until she collided with the wall. She leaned against a sturdy piece of antique furniture to stay on her feet.

Jake joined her. "You good?"

She shook her head. "How can people do this to each other?"

He didn't answer, but the hard set of his jaw told her he'd seen worse. Turning away, Dana tried to blink the burning emotion from her eyes. She focused on the precise carving of the furniture. She rested both palms atop the vintage sideboard and closed her eyes. The suitcase came back to her. But so did something else.

Dana's eyes flew open. "Jake. What if someone didn't do that to him?"

"What?"

"I mean not all of it. The finger." She crossed the foyer to the body. "Look how clean the cut is. The other injuries are jagged, brutal."

"What are you saying?"

"What if he cut his finger off before the Bonesmen came to get him?"

Holt faced her. "Why would he do that?"

"Look around. History was important to Warren Scott. His ancestors founded the Priory of Bones. He'd want to make sure the legacy didn't end with him."

Jake touched her elbow, drawing her out of her staring contest with Holt. "You think the ring's still here?"

"I do." Dana turned in a slow circle, surveying what she could see of the colossal home.

"It'll take months to catalog all the evidence in here," Jake grumbled.

"We might not have to." Dana was moving back across the foyer, her words from the IWP Gala echoing back to her. *Did you know many sideboards like the one you're using tonight often had secret compartments?*

She ran her fingers along the elaborate carvings, opening drawers and feeling inside. She worked her way over the surface, rapping on the wood, listening as she moved. When she got to the left side, all at once, the solid tone turned hollow. Dana caught Jake's eye and grinned. She pulled the nearest drawer open again, removing it completely so she could access the cedar interior. She knocked along the paneled lining until she found the hollow spot again. Dana pushed her hand firmly against the thin strip of cedar and slid it out, revealing a small compartment that had been hollowed out of the frame.

She reached inside, her heart in her throat when her fingers wrapped around something solid. The gold glittered as Dana held the ring up to Jake. "Our smoking gun."

Taking the ring from Dana, Jake skillfully located the micro drive. Holt walked over, palm outstretched. "There, that wasn't so hard, was it?".

Jake handed everything over, as Dana objected. "That ring belongs in the Smithsonian."

Holt gave her an oily grin. "Right now, it's evidence."

"This isn't over," Dana warned.

Holt regarded her. "We have the flash drive. If it's as important as you say I'm sure we have what we need to end this."

She shook her head. "We're too late. The Bonesmen will be long gone by now, and it's your fault."

"You're blaming this colossal disaster on me? That's rich."

"If you'd listened to Jake from the beginning, we could've brought the Senator in and stopped all of this senseless death."

Jake placed a hand on her shoulder. She shook him off. She wasn't done with Holt yet. "You had a chance to stop this, but your incompetence got in the way. Now countless others will be victimized. Their fate is on your conscience. And so is Meredith Kincaid's."

DANA MARCHED BACK out the door she'd come through, tearing off her gloves as she walked. She sucked fresh air into her lungs in gulps, her pulse pounding behind her eyes. She wanted to close them and sleep for a thousand years, but even that couldn't rid her of that image.

If Meredith survived surgery, would there be a suitcase waiting for her?

Jake found her outside. One look at her panic-stricken face was enough for him to silently usher her back to the SUV. He opened the hatch and made her sit on the tailgate. He left momentarily, coming back with a bottle of water. "Drink."

She tried, but she was breathing so fast she choked. Jake took the water while she coughed, fighting to catch her breath. The SUV dipped under his weight when he sat down next to her. His hand was on her back, rubbing slow circles. "Breathe."

"I—can't." She gasped, at a loss over the sudden panic attack. Something inside her had cracked inside that house and everything she'd been bottling up was rushing out.

Nothing made sense. She'd just screamed at Jake's boss, one of the most powerful men in the FBI, her own boss was part of this crazy conspiracy, Senator Scott was dead, Meredith was in the hospital fighting for her life because of the bullet Dana put in her chest, and Jake was looking at her like he'd kiss away all her problems if she'd just let him.

She reached for the water bottle and drank deeply, managing not to choke this time. Capping it, she took a few more shaking breaths, trying to get hold of her emotions. "What the hell is wrong with me?"

The question had been rhetorical, but Jake stood so he could take her face in his large hands. "Cut yourself some slack."

"Why? This is a disaster."

"Yeah, and without you, it would've been a bigger one. Scott can't hurt anyone anymore. That's a win. Archer Kincaid is no longer being blackmailed. That's a win. Your boss is cooperating. That's a win."

Dana blinked. "Dr. Fredrick? Since when?"

"Holt sent someone over to detain him after what went down in New York. Fredrick helped us compile a list of members to investigate. Holt's putting a task force together. I guess he's not completely incompetent."

Dana wasn't in the mood for humor. She tried to pull away, but Jake had other ideas. He tugged her to her feet and against his chest. With his arms tightly around her, she closed her eyes, hating the comfort she found in his embrace. She didn't deserve comfort while Meredith's life hung in the balance. And Jake didn't deserve her indecisiveness.

After everything they'd been through, it was clear they meant something to each other. But their bond had been forged by trauma. Could anything good ever come from that? Did she even want it to?

How could she let herself need him if it meant choosing his life over someone else's?

The sound of a phone ringing jolted Dana from her impossible questions. She pulled away from Jake, instantly missing his warmth. He answered his phone, pacing a few feet away. The conversation was brief and dominated by the caller. Jake didn't say more than two words before hanging up. "That was Jenkins. She just spoke to Meredith's surgeon."

"And?"

"She made it through surgery, but it doesn't look good."

"What do you mean?"

"All I know is that she's in the ICU. But they don't expect her to make it through the night."

Dana pushed her glasses into her hair. She thought tears would come but they didn't. She was too full of disbelief. She pushed her palms into her eyes shaking her head as reality set in. Jake tried to pull her back into his arms, but this time she pushed him away. Setting her glasses back in place she spoke. "I need to go see her."

"I'll come with you."

"No. I'm good."

Jake grabbed her hand. "Dana, you don't have to go through this alone."

She closed her eyes, but it was no use. Every time she looked at Jake, she saw herself choosing him over Meredith. It was tearing her in two. She opened her eyes and squeezed his hand. "Thanks, but I want to."

76

TEARS STAINED DANA'S CHEEKS AS SHE LOOKED UP AT THE BLUE SKY. Birds soared above, riding the warm breeze caressing the trees. The sun elongated her shadow. Sunny days never felt right during a funeral. People shouldn't have to grieve in the sunshine, watching the world continue to turn as though death was insignificant.

Dana stood beside the fresh grave site with Jake and other mourners. Fewer people had turned out than she'd expected. It reinforced her decision to come. Being here was difficult, but it was the right choice.

The service was short and to the point. When it was over, she hung back as the funeral goers dispersed. Jake waited with her while Margot hung back, looking awkward and uncomfortable. Dana was touched that Jake's secretary showed up. Her presence made the poor showing less depressing.

Dana had a feeling Margot was only there to win points with Jake. The woman clearly adored him. It was cruel that he didn't seem to notice her. But that was often the way the world worked. Overlooked by the ones we desire, desired by the ones we overlooked.

It was Dana's turn to approach the grave. She stepped forward, studying the inscription beneath the name on the headstone. *Beloved son. Your memory shall live on.*

She touched the cool stone and closed her eyes, releasing any lingering malice. Ben Riley had paid for his crimes with his life. That was enough. She had too much weighing on her as it was. She needed to close this chapter and focus on what came next. Grabbing a handful of earth, she tossed it into the grave.

Without looking back, Dana walked to where Jake and Margot waited.

"Ready to go?" Jake asked.

She looked down the rows of tombstones in the distance. "In a minute."

Tension stretched out between them as Jake bit his tongue. There was one more grave Dana wanted to visit, and he'd already given his opinion on the matter. Margot cleared her throat. "Well, I think I'm going to head home."

"Thank you for coming," Dana said, meaning it.

"Of course. I know you've been through a lot." Margot looked at Jake, adoration consuming her expression. "You both have."

Dana said her goodbyes and began walking down the rows of simple tombstones. She couldn't help thinking they looked like brittle fingernails clawing their way up from underground. Jake fell into step beside her.

"You don't have to come with me."

He stuffed his hands in his pockets. "I know."

Dana kept walking. "You two would be good together."

He laughed. "Me and Margot?"

"Yeah. Why not?"

Jake scoffed. "We work together."

"So do we."

Seeing where the conversation was headed, Jake changed the subject. "I still don't see why you wanted to come to Riley's funeral."

"Every life deserves to be remembered for more than how they died."

They walked in silence a bit longer before Jake spoke. "How's Meredith?"

"Better, I think. I've been to Geneva General every day, but I only get to see her through her viewing window."

"But she's stable?"

"Yeah. They're moving her out of ICU, and then she'll be transferred to John Hopkins. It'll be good for her to be closer to home. Easier for her family to visit."

"Does that mean you're coming back to D.C.?"

She shook her head. "I was thinking I'd find a place by John Hopkins. It's only about an hour and a half drive into the city. I'll just commute."

Jake stopped walking. "I don't know if that's a good idea. You're running yourself ragged."

Dana faced him. "I'm fine. The important thing is Meredith. It looks like she's going to pull through."

"And what about you? Are you gonna pull through?"

She forced a tight-lipped smile despite the emptiness gnawing at her. "I always do."

"What about us?"

She was surprised he'd come out and asked the question he'd been dancing around for the past few days. Staring at her feet, Dana pushed back the tidal wave of emotion that surged through her whenever she thought about her decision. "I think I need some time."

Jake nodded. "Take all the time you need."

She looked up at him, relieved to see he meant it. There were no storms clouds blocking the bright blue sky of his eyes. Instead he smiled and offered her his arm. Dana hesitated, looking past him to the tombstone she'd tried to visit too many times.

She could read the name from here. *Thomas Cramer.*

Just knowing he was where he belonged gave her the strength she needed to face him in her nightmares. Besides, she'd battled enough demons today. She met Jake's gaze, slipping her arm through his. "This is close enough."

"Yeah?" He looked around. "This is closer than last time. I'd call that a win."

She grinned, and this time it didn't feel so forced. "Me too."

Epilogue – Dana

The scribbled black letters stared back at Dana, stark against the white paper.

She ran a hand over the cover page. The handwritten report was thick, more than two hundred pages. She'd purposely avoided typing it. That would make it too accessible.

As important as this research was, she planned on burying it.

She'd spent the last few months compiling everything she'd learned about the Priory of Bones into these pages. It was a shame no one would ever get to read them, but it was the right call. Some secrets were better left undiscovered.

Claire poked her head into Dana's office. Her intern lit up seeing the stack of papers. "Are you finished?"

"Yes." Dana slipped thin cotton twine beneath the pages in opposite directions, tying them in the center before carefully placing the manuscript into a box and shutting the lid.

"Wait," Claire protested. "Don't I get to read it?"

"No, it's safer if you don't."

Claire crossed her arms. "I don't need you to protect me. I'm aware of the darkness that exists in the world."

"I know you are." That was partly Dana's fault. She shouldn't have brought Claire into her world, exposed her to the death and darkness she called a profession.

Dana placed the box in the safe behind her desk and locked it. She stood, grabbing her coat. Claire spoke as she passed. "You're really not going to share what you uncovered about the Order?"

"I'm really not."

"What happened to our research making a difference? You told me we're the ones who shine light into the darkness."

A crushing sadness gripped Dana hearing her own words thrown back at her. Her mind snagged on an exhibit the Smithsonian housed upstairs. *The Darkest Part of the Universe.*

It explored the depths of Boötes void, a black hole more than seven-hundred million lightyears from Earth. Sixty galaxies had been swallowed up by its unfathomable darkness. That's how Dana felt in the face of the Priory of Bones.

"Claire, in this case, we're just a flashlight in a void."

Her intern's nostrils flared. "Sometimes that's all it takes."

"Sometimes. But not this time."

Jake and the task force Holt organized hadn't been able to make anything stick to the people Elias Fredrick named, and Terrance Vega had vanished into thin air. That left Meredith to take the blame.

She was being transferred to a federal psychiatric facility at the end of the week. This was Dana's last chance to see her. "I'll be at the hospital if anyone needs me."

She knew no one would. Dr. Fredrick's replacement had yet to even introduce himself. He, along with the rest of Dana's colleagues, all seemed to believe the rumor circulating through the Smithsonian. Sublevel three was cursed.

Dana couldn't blame them. She'd been at the center of two of the largest crimes Washington D.C. had faced in recent times. And since this last one had destroyed the reputation of the museum's beloved Dr. Fredrick, everyone was steering clear of her.

But she had no room to talk considering she'd been using the same avoidance techniques with a certain brooding FBI agent.

Jake had his hands full with the task force investigation, but he still made time to call or stop by her office when he could. Their conversations were always civil. He gave her updates about the case, asked about Meredith, traded Thai restaurants recommendations with Claire, but Dana knew he was still waiting for an answer to his graveside question. *What about us?*

She didn't have an answer. Right now, Meredith needed her.

DANA GREETED the lobby nurse by name. She was at the hospital often enough that she knew most of the nurses and doctors on Meredith's floor. Even worse, she knew the FBI agents who stood guard outside her door.

For months Dana hadn't been allowed inside the hospital room while the Bureau psychologists worked with Meredith. Finally, they gave up on getting a statement from the catatonic woman and made arrangements for Meredith to be transferred to a psychiatric facility.

The agents remained on duty, but with the transfer looming, Dana was allowed supervised visits. Though the reunion wasn't what she'd hoped for.

Meredith had taken one look at Dana and turned the other way. Every subsequent visit was the same. But Dana refused to give up. She showed up daily with flowers, finding it odd that they were never there the next day. When she asked the nurses, they told her Meredith requested they be thrown away.

Annoyed at Meredith's stubbornness, Dana went down to the gift shop and bought a pack of stationary. The paper was white with tiny yellow daffodils across the bottom. The flowers made her think of funerals, but she ignored the morbid thought and started writing.

Her message was short and to the point. *I will not give up on you.*

Instead of signing it, Dana drew their tattoo. A heart with the first letter of each of their names inside. She folded up the letter, slipped it inside an envelope and marched back into Meredith's hospital room.

"I'm not giving up, Mere. Just give me a sign that you won't either."

Dana set the note down and fished in her pocket for the tiny ladybug charm she carried with her since the fire. She placed it on top of the envelope and left.

That was two weeks ago. So far, the charm hadn't been thrown away. She'd specifically asked the nurses to keep an eye out for it. Yesterday, Dana swore she saw Meredith rolling the charm between her fingers before she walked into the room. Of course, Meredith shoved her hand under her pillow and pretended to be asleep as soon as Dana showed her face.

Still, it felt like progress.

One thing that bothered Dana even more than Meredith's stubbornness was the way her family treated her. Meredith had been less than a two-hour drive from them for months, and they hadn't been to visit her once. Dana tried to speak to them about it, but Elizabeth refused to let her in the house.

From what Dana could discern, Archer continued to bury himself in his work, Elizabeth became a self-medicating recluse and Abby moved in with her boyfriend. Dana didn't know the status of Abby's pregnancy, but she hoped some space from her controlling family would give her the freedom to make her own decisions.

Dana knew the importance of space when making important decisions. Jake's question popped into her head again as she rode the elevator up to Meredith's floor. *What about us?* She stuffed the question back down. Dana only had a few days left to get through to Meredith before her transfer. She couldn't afford to be distracted.

The elevator dinged, and Dana walked briskly onto the familiar hospital floor. She planned to stop by the viewing window first to see if she could catch Meredith off guard. Jake had once told Dana that it was easiest to see a person's true nature when they thought no one was watching.

Today, it was Dana who was caught off guard.

When she saw the empty hospital bed in Meredith's room, she froze. No agent on guard. No name or meds scribbled on the white board outside the door. She rushed forward gripping the door frame for strength as she searched the sterile room. "No, no, no, no."

There had to be some kind of mistake. Dana had been here every day. Meredith was making a full recovery. What happened? A stroke? An aneurysm? Or did the Bonesmen come for her?

"Dr. Gray." She whirled around at the sound of her name. One of Meredith's nurses hurried toward her. "I tried to catch you before you arrived. Didn't want you seeing an empty bed and thinking the worst."

Too late. "What happened?"

"Her transfer came through early."

"Transfer? But I thought that wasn't until Friday?"

"So did I. I guess St. Elizabeth's had a bed." She shrugged. "Do you need the address?"

"No." Hope replaced the plummeting despair coursing through Dana. "I know where it is." St. Elizabeth's was in D.C. Dana squeezed the nurse's hand. "Thank you."

She turned to leave, but the nurse called her back. "Wait. Miss Kincaid left something for you." She fished an envelope from the pocket of her pink scrubs and handed it to Dana. "Good luck, sweetie. To you both."

Dana waited until she was in her car to open the envelope. She took a deep breath and tore open the flap. A single item fell out. Dana caught it in her palm. She stared at the tiny ladybug charm, then back into the empty envelope as the last kernel of hope inside her flickered, then went out.

UNWRAPPING another piece of cinnamon gum, Jake pressed play. He'd watched the videos they'd recovered from Senator Scott's drive dozens of times searching for something new. It was the definition of insanity, but he couldn't seem to stop.

The brutal sacrifices had been burned into his brain. He couldn't stop seeing the terrified women, including the one they found in the Basin. Her name was Helen Latke. Her murder haunted Jake the most.

He pressed fast-forward, skipping to the part where Terrance Vega pulled Helen's hood off. Senator Scott and Meredith walked into the room. Meredith smiled, the knife gleaming in her hand. He knew what came next. He didn't need to see it again.

He hit stop and minimized the video screen, pulling up the report he was supposed to be working on. The cursor taunted him, each blink mocking the empty spaces he'd yet to fill in. He'd been staring at the report all day, but sheer willpower wasn't going to fill in the blanks. He needed to stop wasting his time and close the case already. Terrance

Vega was in the wind and there wasn't anything he could do about it —*for now*.

His time would be better served going through the stack of cases that had been piling up while he'd been chasing ghosts.

Jake minimized the report and opened his email. As usual, there were too many. Rubbing his temples, he started to scroll through them. A message from Jenkins stood out. Jake opened it, hoping she'd found something new. Instead it was a guilt trip.

You owe your uncle a phone call.

Jake exhaled and shoved back from his desk. He stood and paced to his window, stretching his neck until it popped. He and Wade had left things on good terms, but Jake hadn't exactly been holding up his end of the bargain to stay in touch. He'd told Wade he'd come visit when they wrapped up the case. Technically, the case wasn't closed, just tabled, but Jake knew he wasn't ready to make a trip home yet.

Truthfully, he didn't know where home was anymore. For a minute there, he'd thought he found somewhere he belonged, but that remained to be seen.

The sound of his door jerking open drew his attention. He turned around to see the very person he'd been thinking of standing in his office as if she'd been conjured from his thoughts.

Dana marched over and placed a small ladybug charm on his desk, her eyes burning with fury. "She gave it back. I spent almost six months killing myself trying to get through to her, and what do I get? A slap in the face!" She shook her head. "Go ahead. Say, 'I told you so.'" Lifting her gaze from the charm, she pinned him with the hurt in those big brown eyes. "I can't believe she gave it back."

The angry wave she'd rode in on broke, leaving Dana swiping at her eyes. "Shit. I'm sorry. I don't know why I came here." She was moving toward the door as quickly as she'd barged in.

Jake moved faster. He cut her off, blocking the door with his back. "Stay. Tell me what happened."

"It doesn't matter."

"Maybe it does." Coaxing her back to his desk, he offered her a chair and pulled a flask from his drawer. Dragging his chair around, he took a seat across from her. He unscrewed the flask cap and took a sip, letting the smooth heat warm him before passing the flask to Dana. She took a sip, then two more before passing it back.

Jake nudged her knee with his. "Start from the beginning."

The flask was empty by the time Dana caught him up on her last few months with Meredith. He'd spoken to Dana during that time, but she hadn't revealed how truly difficult things had been. He knew it couldn't have been easy to see her friend that way, but he had no idea how much the hospital visits were eating her up inside. And now this business with the transfer and the charm ... He wished he hadn't ignored his instincts and given her space. He should've pushed harder for her to let him in, but he'd been trying to give her the time she'd asked for.

Dana exhaled. "I don't know what to do. St. Elizabeth's is in D.C. but Mere clearly doesn't want to see me."

"I don't know. It all depends on how you look at it."

"Jake, I gave her a life raft. She threw it back in my face."

"Not everything is as it appears. You taught me that."

"Don't patronize me."

"I'm not. I think there could be a lot of reasons why Meredith gave you the charm."

Dana looked down at her feet. "I think her message was pretty clear. She's done with me."

"Or ..." He leaned forward and hooked a finger under her chin, gently lifting it until she met his eyes. "Maybe the message is, don't give up."

Dana blinked at him, the brown in her irises glowing golden in the sunlight filtering in through the windows. "Do you really believe that?"

"I believe some things are worth fighting for."

Dana's lips parted as emotions swirled in her eyes. Jake was done doing things her way. It was time to take his own advice. Done over-thinking, he leaned forward, ready to capture her lips.

"Jake!" She gasped, jerking away before he could taste the delicate skin he'd been fantasizing about. She stood so abruptly her chair fell backwards. Eyes wide, chest heaving, she backed away from him.

He stood too, ready to pull her into his arms, but the fear in her eyes stopped him in his tracks. Jake wanted her so badly it hurt, but not like this. He wanted the moment back, but he could see it was too late. "Dana ... if you still need time."

"No. I don't need time. I've made up my mind."

For half a second hope slid into his veins before Dana's words sliced through him. "I think it's best if we go our separate ways."

"I disagree."

"This isn't a debate, Jake. We don't work."

"Why not?"

"Look what happens when we're together. People we care about end up dead."

"You're looking at it wrong. Together we can make sure death isn't meaningless."

She shook her head. "Death is my work. I can't have it be my life, too."

Her words hit him hard. Did she see death and destruction when she looked at him? It was his biggest fear. He was too broken to be redeemed. "That day at Candlestick Lake, do you wish you'd chosen differently?"

She shook her head. "Not for one second."

"Then give this a chance?" He stalked toward her, grabbing her arms. A flicker of uncertainty danced in her eyes. He pulled her closer, slipping his hands around her waist. She didn't fight him, not even when he leaned in, letting his forehead rest against hers while he breathed her in.

"Jake ..." she whispered his name, the rest of her words startled away by the knock on his office door.

Dana stepped out of his reach. Jake's temper hit a new high when Margot opened the door, peering inside at the overturned chair. "Is everything okay?"

Nothing was okay, and for once Jake didn't try to hide it. He didn't care if he had an audience, he was done living in fear. Ignoring Margot, he closed the distance Dana had put between them. Brushing a wild strand of hair from her cheek, he cupped her face with both hands. "I know what I want, Dana. When you figure out what you want, let me know."

Her throat rolled. "I'm not asking you to wait."

"I'm not telling you I will."

DANA WALKED out of the J. Edgar Hoover Building feeling more confused than when she'd walked in. But she also felt stronger. Stronger than she had since the shooting.

Jake was right about one thing. She needed to figure out what she wanted. That meant she needed to fight her way out of the darkness the Priory of Bones had left her with. But some battles had to be fought alone.

Even if she was only one single flashlight in the void, she knew what she had to do.

Dana drove back toward the Smithsonian, ready to face her demons. And this time, she intended to win.

DID you enjoy reading **Girl on the Hill**? We would love to hear about it! Please consider leaving a review here:

https://www.amazon.com/dp/B098KHCXRT

The story continues in Girl in the Grave. Read on for an excerpt, or order your copy now:

https://www.amazon.com/gp/product/B09DW5MNLR

GIRL IN THE GRAVE: CHAPTER 1

Despite the frigid November air, Dana Gray was glad to be back in D.C.

Five months on the road was grueling, though she still stood by her decision to publish. Sharing the Priory of Bones manuscript was the right thing to do; for her, for her profession, for the world. Knowledge was meant to be shared—something she and her publisher actually agreed on.

One lecture turned into two and before she knew it, a few speaking engagements snowballed into a full-fledged book tour. Thirty-six lectures in ten countries in five months.

She'd never been so happy to return to the comforts of her own home. The orderly quiet of her office three stories below the Smithsonian was calling to her, but oddly it wasn't her first stop.

Dana strode across the icy parking lot toward the J. Edgar Hoover Building. It'd been almost six months since she'd last seen Jake Shepard. They hadn't left things on the best of terms, but he'd been right to tell her to figure out what she wanted.

All her time away had given her ample opportunity to think. The conclusion she'd come to: being alone was overrated. Working with Jake and the FBI had proven it was nice to have backup from time to time. Perhaps there was room in her life to let someone in. The right someone. She couldn't say with absolute certainty Jake was that someone, but it was worth finding out.

Her work would always be important to her. Shining light on the mysteries of the occult was a calling she believed in. The last few months demonstrated how vital her research was. Publishing her findings on the world's most secret society was not only noteworthy, but it would hopefully save others from being manipulated by them. Others like Meredith Kincaid.

That was another stop Dana planned to make now that she was back in D.C.

Meredith was still at St. Elizabeth's. Even with the best attorneys money could buy, she'd spend the rest of her life in a padded cell. That didn't mean Dana would forget about the girl she'd once called her best friend.

Meredith was part of the reason Dana decided to publish. She didn't want the Priory of Bones to steal anyone else's future. Absently, Dana's finger found the ladybug charm on her keychain, rubbing it for luck. She kept it as a reminder of what she was fighting for.

The elevator dinged, and Dana exited onto Jake's floor. Right away her eyes landed on Margot. It seemed the last few months had changed the receptionist's life as well.

"Dr. Gray!" Margot put down her yogurt cup and blinked at Dana in surprise. "Is Jake expecting you?"

The glittering wedding rings on Margot's finger caught Dana's eye, but it was the receptionist's very pregnant stomach that left Dana speechless as she tried to do the math. "How far along are you?"

Margot grinned, resting her bejeweled hand on her swollen belly. "Almost six months. Can you believe it?" She took Dana's stunned silence as an invitation to continue babbling. "It came as a shock to me, too. But it's true what they say; sometimes you find the thing you've been looking for was right under your nose all along."

Dana felt like she'd just done three tequila shots on an empty stomach. She was too late. It'd taken her analytical mind too long to come to the conclusion that she wanted Jake in her life.

This was her fault. He'd told her he wouldn't wait, and she'd practically pushed Jake into Margot's arms before she left. She had no one to blame but herself.

The cell phone on Margot's desk rang, and she answered. "Hey, baby. Can you hang on a sec? Jake's got a guest I need to take care of."

Blood whooshed in Dana's ears, as realization tore through her like a bullet. The baby wasn't Jake's. Margot and Jake weren't together!

Margot pressed the phone to her chest, grinning as she reached for the desk phone to call Jake. Dana caught her hand. "Actually, I think I'll surprise him."

GIRL IN THE GRAVE: CHAPTER 2

"So what do you think?"

Agent Jake Shepard looked across his desk at Jo Walsh. He hadn't been expecting his dumplings to come with a side of bombshell. Jo picked up on that.

"I know it's a big decision, but this is a once in a lifetime opportunity for me. I mean, it's HRT. Not many people get that call."

"I know. But it's on the other side of the country."

"It's Colorado, Jake. Not Siberia. Besides, the FBI has a field office in Denver. They'd be happy to have you."

He put down his water bottle. "You already looked into it?"

Jo's cheeks flushed, betraying the cool demeanor she always exuded. "Look, I know this is new, but we're good together, right?"

He nodded slowly.

"So this just feels like the next step."

In his mind, the next step was letting her leave a toothbrush at his place. Moving to Denver with a woman he'd been seeing for a few months? That was a fucking cliff jump.

"Nothing needs to be decided right away."

He swallowed. "When do you need an answer?"

"HRT knows I'm tied up with this case."

"It could take a while."

"I can be patient." She leaned across his desk, her long blonde ponytail swaying like a pendulum. "But Jake, I know what I want, and I'm ready to go after it. You need to take a look in the mirror and ask yourself the same question." Her fingers caressed his jawline, nails scraping across his scruff. "And maybe invest in a better razor," she teased, her thumb tracing his lower lip before she kissed him.

She wasn't playing fair. That mouth of hers could get her anything she wanted, and she knew it. She grabbed his collar, deepening the kiss. Her tongue swept his, erasing all his objections to her plan.

The sound of his door opening pulled them apart. Seeing who was standing there was like plunging into an ice bath.

"Dana?" Jake stood abruptly, tie askew, heart pounding. Even though she was the one who'd shown up unannounced she seemed as shocked as he was to be standing face-to-face. Walking in on him groping another FBI agent probably hadn't helped.

"No way!" Jo was standing, too. "You're Dr. Dana Gray."

Dana finally broke their staring contest and turned to look at Jo. "You know who I am?"

"You're sort of a legend around here. Librarian-detective who took down a serial killer and a secret society." Jo walked toward Dana, hand outstretched. "I'm Agent Joanna Walsh, but everyone calls me Jo. I really enjoyed your book, by the way."

Dana blinked. "You read it?"

"Figured it'd help me get some insight on my new partner here." Jo thumbed at Jake over her shoulder. "Speaking of, if you could not mention you walked in on us sharing more than lunch, that'd be great. The FBI hasn't joined the twenty-first century when it comes to workplace romance."

Dana's eyes were on Jake again. He felt like he'd just been caught cheating. He reminded himself he wasn't doing anything wrong. She'd had her chance. "What are you doing here, Dana?"

"I just wanted to let you know I was back and see if ..." she trailed off, looking at Jo again.

Jo's pale green eyes sparked with excitement. "Wait! Did you come to help us with the Card Killer?"

"Jo." Warning laced Jake's voice.

"What? I'm not telling her anything the media hasn't shared. Vultures," Jo muttered.

"Anyway, I would be honored to have you assist, Dr. Gray."

Dana frowned. "I'm not sure Agent Holt would sign off on that."

"Then it's a good thing he doesn't have to." Jo smirked. "Holt retired."

Dana's warm brown eyes filled with questions. "Who took his spot?"

"I did," Jenkins answered, walking into Jake's office. "And I'd love to have you on board considering forensics just identified a significant change in pattern that puts this case in your wheelhouse."

Assistant Director Remi Jenkins held out a folder. Jo grabbed it, flipping it open as Jake joined the three women standing in the middle of his office with trepidation. "What kind of change?"

"The last victim wasn't left with an ordinary playing card stuffed down his throat." Jenkins pointed a manicured finger to a photo inside the folder.

Dana moved in closer, the scent of her perfume taking Jake back to the last time she'd been in his office. He shut down the memory, focusing on the evidence in front of him.

He stared at the photograph of the badly decomposed card. At first glance, it was easy to see it was larger than the others, but that wasn't a major change. "Playing cards come in all different shapes and sizes, Jenks."

"True, but this isn't a playing card."

Jake squinted, angling his neck to try to make out the design. "Then what is it?"

Dana sucked in a breath, her eyes widening. "The Tower." She looked at the group. "It's a tarot card."

Jenkins snapped the folder shut, grinning at Dana. "Exactly. Looks like you came back to D.C. just in time."

Enjoying Girl in the Grave? Download your copy today!:

ALSO BY CJ CROSS

Dana Gray Mysteries

Girl Left Behind

Girl on the Hill

Girl in the Grave

Stay up to date with C.J. Cross's new releases and download her **free** Dana Gray Prequel, *Girl Awakened* by scanning the QR code below:

Find more C.J. Cross books and follow her on Amazon today!

ALSO BY WITHOUT WARRANT

More Thriller Series from Without Warrant Authors

Dana Gray Mysteries by C.J. Cross

Girl Left Behind

Girl on the Hill

Girl in the Grave

The Kenzie Gilmore Series by Biba Pearce

Afterburn

Dead Heat

Heatwave

Burnout

Deep Heat

Fever Pitch

Storm Surge (Coming Soon)

Willow Grace FBI Thrillers by Anya Mora

Shadow of Grace

Condition of Grace (Coming Soon)

ABOUT THE AUTHOR

CJ Cross grew up in a snowy little Northeast town, cutting her teeth on true crime novels to stave her love of all things mysterious. The writing bug bit her early and she found her way into the publishing world, writing 50+ books under various top secret pen names over the years.

Now relocated to a place where she can safely trade in her snowshoes for flip flops, she's found a reason to dust off her old Criminal Justice degree and she's turned an old passion into a new flame, writing compelling thrillers novels.

When she's not writing you can usually find her drinking bourbon with fellow authors or spoiling her rescue pup.

Sign up for C.J.'s newsletter and download her free **Dana Gray Prequel, *Girl Awakened*:**

https://liquidmind.media/cj-cross-sign-up-1-prequel-download

Made in United States
North Haven, CT
03 June 2023

37329918R00209